Celtic Sunset

Roy Edwards

Acknowledgments

Celtic Sunset is for Julie who believes, and whose help, patience, love and understanding makes everything worthwhile. Together we have found our True Fidelity of Being.

I would also like to thank Norah Edwards, Ruth Scales, Brian Gray, Steven Edwards and Margaret Baxter for their help and support with this enterprise.

There is no such thing as a primitive race, language, religion, ideas, way of life, ad infinitum. The very concept and complexities inherent within primitivism state otherwise. It has to do with measurement of view point inherent within the nature of the observer, which states the observers reality will be in direct proportion to the observers ability to expand - broaden viewpoints to encompass, what would otherwise be, an alienism of non-confrontational reality.

R. Edwards 1996

CELTIC SUNSET

(The Culann Scrolls)

Roy Edwards

CONTENTS

The pattern weaves as the Maker wills
Culann - Circa 10 BC

Introduction

Discovery

Autumn 1987.
The Black Hills,
South Dakota USA.

Thin autumn sunlight washed the hills in pale gold and burnished rose. Cool fingers of air brushed against his face. Above the hills the sky had a scrubbed shiny look about it, as though the recent heavy rains had washed it clean. Empty it was and incredibly blue.

He breathed deep of the moist air as he hiked along, his back pack a comfortable weight tugging at his shoulders. He walked the Black Hills, revelling in the unquiet mystery of the land. He followed trails that began somewhere and seemed to lead nowhere, ending abruptly in the middle of some insignificant patch of barren ground.

Roy Edwards

Long ago the trails had meaning, even the ones that ended at the foot of some blank rock face. Now it seemed no one could remember, or cared to say, what the *Ancient Ones*, the *Ones Who Came Before*, had used them for. *Spirit* trails, some do call them, not that it mattered. His joy was gleaned from the walking of their sinewy length, and the quiet hauntingness that seemed to thicken and surround him, the deeper he hiked into the hills.

The hills he walked had been sacred to the Sioux for enough centuries to stretch back into thousands of years. Few believed that, but he did. The hills still remained sacred to *The People* and he had no doubt that he was probably trespassing as usual, and as usual, no one bothered him. He had been coming here for more than fifteen years. Most everyone on the nearby reservation knew of him, at least by name if not by sight.

The elders had agreed that he walked the ancient trails in peace and harmony with the land and the spirits. He would, they said, have already heard their voices on the moving airs. All he had to do was be at peace and listen.

So it was, that he was left alone to walk in peace, completely unaware of the unspoken courtesy gifted to him by the Sioux.

It was not a thing he gave much thought to. Like so many westerners he was unaware of the gifting, that to the Sioux had no need of vocalisation to make it none the less real, silence is a courtesy, a sign of good manners.

The trail he followed was faint, and growing fainter. He wondered how far it would take him before disappearing completely or ending abruptly, as so many of these ancient trails had a habit of doing. When that happened, which it often did, he would think of it as 'that Indian thing'. He used the phrase to cover anything and everything to do with

4

Indians that couldn't be explained, or otherwise recognised as having a logical reason for being. Like the ghost trails he loved so much to follow, he would gaze around in baffled surprise when the trail ran arrow straight towards some featureless hillside too steep to climb, or to a jumble of rocks too carefully positioned to be natures work. He loved the hot dusty mystery of it all and the occasional thrill of fear, when he felt he was being watched by unseen eyes.

He could remember when he first started using the phrase 'that Indian thing'. About thirty years ago it was, during a trip to Arizona. He was on vacation and to his disgust he was alone. All his friends, both male and female were away working on digs in various obscure locations scattered around the world. Usually when he had time off, be it a few days or even weeks, he always knew of someone from his circle that he could spend time with, but not that year.

It was late summer 1957. When he realised that none of his friends would be around until after his leave had finished, he made a spur of the moment decision. Throwing camping gear, food and water into the back of his ex-army jeep he headed out for Arizona. A few hours after crossing the state line he spotted a desert trail meandering away from the highway. He swung onto it and followed the trail for three days. It led him deep into the desert. A timeless land of heat and silence. At night, rolled up in his sleeping bag, his last sight before sleep claimed him, was of a night sky thickly encrusted with stars that seemed incredibly near and yet impossibly high and far away.

During his second night in the desert he awoke with a start. Inky blackness lay thick around him. The stars were faint dim lights casting little or no illumination of their own. Unsure of what had woken him, he fumbled around for his torch. As his questing fingers touched the cool metal case he suddenly had an eerie feeling of being watched, as though somewhere out there in the darkness unseen eyes watched his every move. A small fitful breeze blew across his face. Somewhere, a stone rolled and clicked against another. The sound of it small and far away. The desert night was, he realised, full of sounds if you listened hard enough. For a few moments the wind gained in strength sighing its way across the land in a whisper of secret voices. It faded away as quickly as it had come. Leaving behind it a deep well of silence, and an achy empty feeling inside him of something lost.

He settled back into sleep. The eerie feeling of unseen eyes watching him, fading away into a small dream of sunrise, spilling red-gold light over an empty land. In his dream, a face cracked and seamed with age, smiled down at him from out of a pure, deep blue sky. The face was framed as though it peered through a window. When he awoke, the dream stayed with him like some fond autumn memory of childhood.

He drove hard through the following day, knowing he must soon turn back before he ran out of gas, food and water. He wasn't quite sure why he continued, he simply felt that he must. Three days in. Three days out. Six days alone in the desert wasn't quite what he had in mind in the way of a vacation. He cursed himself for continuing, and yet at the same time he felt compelled to drive — just a little further. By late afternoon of the third day the trail had completely disappeared. Vanishing, or so it seemed, into a maze of jumbled rocks and clumps of sere desert grass.

Satisfied that he had reached the trail's end he turned around, prepared to start his long drive back there and then. Hot thick sunlight poured through his windscreen, momentarily blinding him. He cursed softly, his eyes ached, feeling sore and gritty from the days drive. He didn't relish driving into the sun for the next hour or so, besides, he hadn't realised the day was so far advanced, what was left of it that is. Cursing, he decided to make an early camp, and away with the dawn, he thought tiredly, as he dragged himself out from behind the wheel.

Later, after eating, and feeling somewhat more energised he decided to explore the mound. A jumble of rocks they were, but they looked like a mound, a burial mound. A dim trail led to the base of a small boulder with a smooth flat top. 'Like an altar,' he mused out loud. In the lurid glow of sunset, the flat smooth surface of the rock caught the sun's dying rays, thick red light pooled on it's surface, shimmering like molten copper. As he walked slowly towards the mound he felt a faint dampness on the air. The hot desert air was cooling rapidly, its remaining heat insufficient to evaporate the moisture rising from somewhere within the mound. Intrigued, he began to poke around. Wary of snakes, he used a stick to move small rocks aside as he searched.

He found it a few paces from where he began. On the opposite side of the flat topped rock, a small spring bubbled up into a cup sized depression. He knelt down, cupped his hands and drank. The water tasted cool and sweet.

Deep shadows crept over the silent desert in fingers and pools of night. He crawled into his sleeping bag and swiftly fell into a dreamless sleep.

He awoke suddenly, his heart thudding against the wall of his chest. Stars, aloof and cold shed a faint glimmer of light. Ghostly it was — and silent. The night held its breath. Something had disturbed him, reaching down into his sleep and pulling him up. His heart raced, his mouth felt dry, butterflies danced in his stomach. He climbed out of his sleeping bag and slowly looked around — nothing. The night was empty and silent. No breath of wind stirred the air, and then he heard it. His flesh rose in goose bumps, his guts contracted with atavistic fear.

Chanting, soft and melodious, a gentle rise and fall of voices chanting in unison, faint with distance. Like a radio signal fading in and out, the sound of chanting rose and fell, reminding him of a calm blue sea, foaming over an ancient sandy shore, strewn with bits and pieces of pink and white sea shell. Somewhere a bird began to sing, its song trembling upon the air like a promise.

He turned a full circle, slowly, eyes questing, quartering the dark terrain around him. Nothing, just an empty desert night. For a few moments the chanting seemed to be all around him, as though he stood in the middle of a procession making its way towards the mound. Mouth dry, he turned, facing directly toward the mound, his heart raced. The chanting seemed to emanate from above the flat topped rock, as though the sound of it drifted through a slightly open door. Surprisingly he no longer felt afraid, his heartbeat had resumed its normal rhythmic thud, his mouth no longer dry. He felt, with a sense of wonder, like a guest, unexpected but none the less welcome. The sound of chanting began to fade away, and then it was gone. Only silence remained and a faint pearly glimmer of dawn. He stood alone in a vast desert and knew he had encountered a mystery he could not even begin to explain. 'It's an Indian thing' he thought to himself, and spoke of it to no one, at all.

He'd just about followed the trail as far as he was prepared to go. Removing his back pack with a sigh of relief, he sat down to rest aching joints. He wasn't, he admitted to himself, as spry as he used to be. He shivered in the cool afternoon sunlight.

Celtic Sunset

George Pemberton was fifty eight years old, of medium height and weight with a scholars thin aesthetic face. He wore his hair long and was considered to be slightly eccentric by his small circle of friends. His life and position as senior lecturer at a small midwestern university specialising in archaeological studies, anthropology, epigraphy and sundry other related subjects, was unexcitingly comfortable. His salary, whilst not large was adequate. A rent free cottage, situated in a quiet corner of the campus, more than compensated for his meagre bank balance. He was, in his own way, content. At least that is what he repeatedly told himself.

Twenty eight years ago he had graduated with honours in the field of archaeology, from the very university where he now worked. After graduation he had fully intended to pursue a field career. His sudden, and unexpected application for the vacant position of lecturer, with emphasis on Indian Studies of the plains tribes, came as a complete surprise to everyone who knew him. The university's board of directors granted the position to him with alacrity. They were only too pleased to have such a bright young man on their staff.

He gave no reason for his sudden change of direction and in the following years more than fulfilled the boards expectations of him. His solitary hikes into the wilderness occasioned no undue comment and, if the board of directors were aware of his sometimes on, sometimes off, affair with one particular member of staff, they gave no sign of it.

Margaret Wilder was a small, slim woman on the wrong side of fifty. Her habits, like her dress sense, were neat and precise, and like George she was unmarried. George found everything about her sexually attractive, from slim legs to flat stomach and small, firm breasts. She had cool grey eyes, generous lips and a thick mane of dark brown hair shot through with silver. Occasionally she and George went out for dinner, occasionally they enjoyed great sex together. Neither one nor the other suggested a more permanent relationship. And like George, Margaret had her own area of expertise. A skilled epigrapher, ranked amongst the world's top six, she was fluent in ancient and medieval Latin, Greek, Cuneiform and a smattering of Celtic. Well known in her field, and often published, she was considered to be one of the university's most valuable assets.

Celtic Sunset

Black Hills. Autumn 1987.

He sat with his back toward a scattering of rocks, face upturned towards the meagre warmth of the autumn sun. Directly in front of him, a small hill sloped gently upwards toward a washed out sky of pale blue. The sun's thin amber light coloured the hillside in varying shades of dusty yellow and brown. Squinting against the glare, he could see, where over the years, the action of sun, rain and wind had worn the thin soil away, exposing rocks and stones that had eventually rolled down the slope obliterating the trail. As his eyes adjusted to the brightness, he noticed a dark patch high up near the summit of the hill. The hillside was reasonably smooth, there wasn't, as far as he could see, any rocky projections or eroded shelves to cast a shadow. The longer he looked, the more convinced he became that the dark patch was in fact an irregular shaped opening — a cave. His stomach fluttered at the thought. Still sitting, he looked again at the rubble piled up at the base of the hill. 'Yes', he thought, 'it could have broken away from the summit causing a small rock slide and exposing the — what — hole — cave or what ever it is.'

Suddenly his mind took a flight of fancy. What if it was an entrance to a cave that had sometime in the past been deliberately sealed and hidden by caving in part of the summit, and if so why? 'I'm here,' he thought slowly, 'I might as well take a look before I head back. Besides,' he grinned, 'if I don't satisfy my curiosity it'll only come back to haunt me.'

Sticking a torch into the pocket of his desert jacket, he began to scramble up the slope. The hillside was soft and loose from recent heavy rainstorms. Panting for breath, he scrambled closer to the hole and saw to his surprise that it appeared to go back quite a ways, a jagged open mouthed wound driving deep into the hill. With trembling hands, he began to enlarge the opening, rolling away small rocks and boulders.

Once inside Pemberton straightened up and waited for his eyes to adjust to the gloom. He could have used his torch but enough sunlight came through the opening to illuminate all but the more remote recesses of the cave. Once his eyes grew accustomed to the dim light, he looked around. A soft oooh, of astonishment woofed out of him. He hadn't consciously been expecting to find anything other than an empty hole in the side of a hill. He wasn't sure yet, but he thought he might just have stumbled onto something quite incredible. He wished he'd thought to pack a camera. Tremors of nervous excitement ran through his body as he slowly walked deeper into the cave.

His first thoughts were that he had discovered an ancient Comanche burial chamber. The Comanche had often buried their dead in upright positions facing towards the rising sun. It was, he had sometimes thought, very Celtic, and then the absurdity of it all came crashing in. These were the sacred hills of the Sioux. A Comanche had about as much chance of being buried here as Custer or Kit Carson. Nervous laughter slid up his throat. He breathed deep of the musty air, once, twice and managed to suppress the impulse. 'Christ' he thought irreverently, 'this is it, this is bloody well it. I've found the impossible.' He danced a little jig, dust puffing up from beneath his feet, catching at the back of his throat, he coughed and told himself to calm down.

Examine, check, verify, he intoned softly. He walked forward hesitantly, as though suddenly afraid to verify what his eyes perceived. He began to sweat. An eerie feeling, of having been drawn to the cave, flooded through him. He shrugged the feeling away impatiently, eyes glittered bright and hard. He had found what no one believed was there to be found. He would be famous now, he exulted, famous forever. He, like so many of his kind, didn't realise that such fame was no more than a kind of second hand immortality. Discovery is one thing, understanding what you have discovered, is something else entirely.

The corpse had been placed in an upright position facing towards the east, towards the rising sun. Its flesh had long since rotted away exposing bones yellow with age. The length of the skeleton and the thickness of bone told him that in life the corpse had been tall, and heavy with muscle. The skeleton was a rare find in itself but it was the dusty outline of a long sword laying at the feet of the corpse that excited him.

Breaking all the acknowledged rules of discovery, he reached down a trembling hand towards the sword hilt. How came it here? What was a tall man, with a long sword doing in the Black Hills? Who had sealed the corpse away in a hillside tomb and why, why here? The cave, he reasoned, had only recently been exposed. The condition of the sword indicated that the cave had been dry and its temperature relatively even for eons, else the sword would have dissolved into rust centuries ago.

He sat down in the dust, and regarded his find with awe. Whilst he sat lost in thought, the sun moved down the sky. Winter pale rays edged deeper into the cave, lightening the gloom, deepening shadows. He stood, intending to search the cave and saw to his amazement six cylinders of baked clay, standing upright against the far wall, as though they had but recently been placed there. Placing the sword carefully on the floor of the cavern, he shuffle footed over and hesitantly examined the cylinders. They were about three feet long by twelve inches or so round and the mouth, he realised, of each cylinder had been sealed with some kind of substance resembling bees wax. With difficulty he restrained himself from prising open the cylinders there and then.

He would take them. He would leave the sword and the skeleton and take the cylinders. Why, he wasn't sure and by doing so, was for the time being committing himself to silence with regards his find. He could question his motives later, for the moment he was working on instinct, and his instinct like a small voice at the back of his head told him to take the cylinders, leave the rest and reseal the cave.

One by one he carefully carried the cylinders down the hill and stowed them away in his back pack, wrapping spare clothing around them to prevent any chance of breakage on the long hike back to the land cruiser. His last act was to scramble back up to the top of the hill. Locating a slight overhang of compacted soil and rocks above the cave's entrance, he smashed it away with his boot heels. It was enough to cause a small rock slide. It tumbled down the hill in a shower of soil and loose stones. Sealing the mystery deep within the silent darkness of the tomb. Unknown to Pemberton, a secret cavity within the tomb contained a legendary scroll of power writ by a Druid's hand, perhaps it was that ancient power emanating from the hidden scroll that had pushed his attention away, perhaps it was not.

Who can say with certainty what the ancients of long ago knew that is now lost, or at best, surviving as a weak, parody of its former self, that few, if any, give credence to. We lose much when we dismiss what we fail to understand. However it may be, the tomb of the unknown warrior retained its secret. The scroll, unlike any other in existence. One day it will be found and revealed, but not by George Pemberton. He was not the one it waited for. He did not possess spirit strength, or courage enough to carry its burden and its unblemished light out into the hungry maw of the Twentieth Century. But then, he did not believe there were such things as words of power either. He was simply a pawn to be moved down the long road of prophesy.

His study reeked of chemicals, with infinite care he applied a final coat of preservative to the last of the scrolls. Magnificent, he breathed softly, bloody magnificent. He surveyed the last scroll fondly. He had time now, a breathing space, time in which he could decide what exactly he was going to do with them. He knew, at least he thought he knew, but somehow he kept shying away from the confrontation of his own decision. He would not allow the scrolls to dissolve into dust. Long before that should happen he would, if necessary, ensure the scrolls were placed in the conditions necessary to ensure their survival.

A month ago he had unsealed each cylinder and carefully withdrawn what had been concealed within. Each cylinder had contained tight rolls of what looked to be a primitive form of papyrus, or something closely resembling papyrus. He wasn't sure, and without access to the facilities of a fully equipped laboratory, he could for the moment, only guess as to what materials had been used to form, what was obviously intended as a format upon which to write. The clay cylinders had obviously been made for the specific purpose of housing the scrolls. Both the inner and outer surfaces had been carefully coated with a substance that rendered the cylinders not only waterproof but also air tight, once the seal was in place. George had quickly realised that someone, a long, long time ago, had possessed both knowledge and skill. The one who lay in the cave, was he warrior or scribe or potter, perhaps all three, thought George, and what was he doing sealed in a cave in an area that had been sacred to the Sioux for generations.

When he finally unrolled the scrolls the mystery deepened. The study of ancient writings, epigraphy, was not his forté. Even so he knew enough to recognise, if not translate, a variety of ancient symbols and glyphs and possessed the rudimentary ability to at least recognise some of the more well known types of ancient alphabets.

When he unrolled the first scroll he looked away, paused, then looked back unbelievingly. He then sat motionless for what seemed like endless minutes as the enormity of the discovery slowly sank deep into his bones. It couldn't possibly be true, but it was. The evidence of what had long been considered an impossibility, lay before him. It was all an elaborate hoax. He knew it was not, it might be many things but never that. He poured himself a drink with trembling hands.

The scrolls were written in both ancient Greek and Latin, from somewhere around the First or Second century BC. It could be earlier or later he wasn't sure. His gut feeling was that it was from the time of Caesar, the infamous Julius Caesar, who had destroyed the Celts and in his turn been destroyed. His next problem was that he couldn't read the scrolls. He recognised the writing for what it was but he couldn't read it, at least not fluently enough to detect all the inherent nuances. Although he didn't want to involve her in what was now essentially an illegal act, he knew he had no choice but to try and enlist the aid of Margaret Wilder, his sometime lover and friend.

The next day, Friday, he caught up with her in the staff room. Over coffee he told her in a soft voice, that on his last

trek into the Black Hills he had found something that would
be of interest to her, and could she come round to his place
the following day, 'early', he added and he'd be obliged if in
the meantime she didn't mention to anyone that he had found
anything. To his surprise, she agreed without question and
assured him she would be at his place in time for breakfast.

Late afternoon sunlight poured through the study window.
He paced, and made endless cups of coffee whilst Margaret
read. Indigo shadows of evening had begun to gather when
suddenly, she looked up and spoke into a pool of silence.

'His name is Culann,' she said, 'Culann of the Arverni, at
least,' she added, 'that is one of his names. Culann wrote the
scrolls, he is, or was, Celtic.'

George was stunned. Margaret, overriding his silence said,
'It will take time George, a full translation, I mean. Maybe I'd
better move in with you for awhile,' she said with a smile
hovering around her lips.

George looked at her in confused amazement. He said,
'What the hell is a Celt doing in a hill tomb in Dakota, of all
places. It's crazy for Christ's sake.'

Margaret, ignoring his outburst, said, 'The scrolls are
written in the form of a narration by Culann. He speaks of
his flight from the Roman invasion of Gaul, of his journey
here, and his life. He was also a Druid.'

George stared at her in stunned disbelief. 'Was he alone,'
he whispered hoarsely.

'No,' replied Margaret, 'he mentions the Veneti, a Celtic
seafaring race, and others of the Arverni tribe.'

Forestalling any more questions she said softly, 'George,
have you decided what you are going to do with all this?'

'No,' he said sharply, 'why do you ask?'

'Well,' she said, 'you'd better make up your mind by the time I finish the translation.'

His face had a hunted look about it. Walking over to him she kissed him and said carefully, 'You never did care over much for fame, did you George?'

He began to caress her breasts. 'No,' he growled throatily, as he hiked her skirt up around her waist. They made love on the floor of his study, and for a few precious moments banished all thought of *The Culann Scrolls* from their minds.

The scrolls had the potential to blow the academic world apart. Vindicating some whilst destroying others. Men of renown and high social and academic standing would bribe, cheat, lie, steal and condone murder to prevent publication of what George now thought of as *The Culann Scrolls*.

Fourteen months later George read the last page of Margaret's translation. They were sitting at his kitchen table, cups of coffee at their elbows. Wind driven rain beat against the windows, falling from out of a leaden grey sky. The story had moved them both. Culann it seemed had a way with words. Being Celtic how could he not. It was, she realised, all up to George now. His find, his decision.

George shuffled the stack of papers in front of him, looked up at Margaret, took a deep breath and said.....

Ψ

Celtic Sunset

Monday. June 1989

George sat alone, a pile of unmarked exam papers in front of him. His office was small, cluttered and comfortable. He gazed up at the ceiling, and then, decision made, picked up his desk phone, and punched a set of numbers. His hand was steady, voice calm as he spoke quietly and succinctly. His face wore a slight smile of satisfaction. A meeting had been arranged. It would take place at a certain location the following Monday, at precisely 8 pm.

The house was a long low rambling affair, screened from the road by a thick stand of trees, the front porch lit by a single light in the shape of an old fashioned carriage lamp. At precisely 8 pm, George, grasping a large carry case in one hand, knocked on the door.

It was opened immediately by a silent, well dressed man, who motioned him in, and ushered him through a doorway into a spacious room, dominated at one end by a large, highly polished table. An elderly distinguished looking man sat at the table flanked on his right by a younger man dressed in a grey three piece suit.

George sat down placing the case on the table, no names were asked or given. The elderly man pushed the case towards his companion, who picked it up and left the room.

The elderly man looked at George and said, 'You may as well make yourself comfortable, this could take quite awhile.'

George said, 'Authentication.'

'Yes,' replied the old man. He pointed towards a well stocked bookshelf that covered the entire inner wall. 'Read if you wish, but please, no more conversation.'

19

Time passed slowly as George nervously flipped through book after book. The old man ignored him, conveying the distinct impression that he was totally unaware of any other presence within the room.

George longed for a cigarette. The room was devoid of ash trays, he decided to wait. Hours melted down into hours. 'How long was the bloody man going to be', he thought irritably.

Around midnight, the young man returned, handed the old man a piece of paper and silently left the room. The old man read the paper in silence, then folded it neatly and placed it in his jacket pocket. He picked up a pen and a nearby note pad, wrote some figures on the top sheet and pushed it across to George.

George read the figure and broke out in a cold sweat. He pushed the notepad back towards the old man and nodded his head in acceptance of the offer.

The old man said, 'Country and currency?'

George replied, 'Greece, US Dollars.'

The old man nodded and rose, indicating the transaction was now complete. As George left the room, the old man called after him, 'A bank account will be set up, you will receive confirmation within seven days.

Ψ

Celtic Sunset

July 1989

A few minutes before boarding their flight to Greece George Pemberton and Margaret Wilder posted their resignations.

Three weeks later they purchased, for cash, a comfortable villa situated on a small, but well populated Greek island. The villa overlooked a bustling picturesque harbour and Homer's legendary wine dark sea. Here, midst sunlight and herb scented winds, they both sought to forget, or at least block out, the riddling words of power contained in the last scroll Margaret Wilder had translated.

The words had filled her heart and head with dark foreboding. At first, she thought she had mistranslated. Endless gruelling hours of checking, and cross checking, proved that she had not mistranslated a single word. Even so the sense of it all eluded her, and left George utterly confounded. They both agreed that the scrolls were not complete and that another scroll or scrolls remained hidden somewhere deep within the sealed tomb. George had no intention of returning to the burial site. The mere mention of the scrolls filled him with unease. As though the ancient scrolls exuded a weird kind of power inherent within, not the papyrus, but the words. He was aware of the many stories, legends and myths that purported to deal with words, that once written down, began to emanate a strange kind of radiating power, that could effect the reader for good or ill. Depending upon the assemblage of words, that is, the pattern and weave of the sentence itself.

He had not, until now, thought such a thing even remotely possible. What the missing scroll might contain, he didn't even want to think about. For an archaeologist, George

21

Pemberton was remarkably unadventurous, his imagination, restricted by the confines of his tenure. That he had found the cave at all, was remarkable. That he had stolen and sold most of its contents was almost beyond belief. In fact, there were times when he didn't actually believe he had done so. His mind shied away from the fact that he had felt compelled to do what he had done. Almost as if, having once taken possession of the scrolls he had played his part, and, moved the scrolls on towards some predetermined destination. It was all nonsense of course, but he couldn't help feeling as though he had been used in some way. It was a strange, eerie feeling, like that which came over him sometimes when he walked the Black Hills. Of unseen eyes watching his every move. He knew little of ancient haunts or words of power, nor did he care to learn more. The world itself was a mystery, and he had no intention of seeking others. The maxim of his life, let sleeping dogs lie, seemed particularly appropriate. So it was that he took the money and ran like a thief in the night, and *The Culann Scrolls* moved on.

Neither he nor Margaret, for all their combined vaunted intelligence, had actually understood all they had read of the scrolls. In an odd, illogical sort of way, it all seemed to make a weird kind of sense inside their heads, but they could never quite put that inner sense into meaningful words. If it wasn't so ridiculous it would be scary, 'freaky' George would say in a quiet voice.

They had agreed.

To sell the scrolls but make no mention of a missing scroll, keep the location of the burial chamber secret, take the money — and run as far away from *the Culann Scrolls* as possible.

And yet.

Celtic Sunset

Why then did they both sometimes feel waves of fear sweep through them followed by a sense of dreadful loss? WHY? When the scrolls were no more than a simple narrative of one man's life, Druid though he may be.

Or was it?

What if the narrative had been written on two or more levels and subconsciously they had understood its hidden meaning. The were both familiar with hieroglyphics and were aware that words, like glyphs or pictographs, could be read, and/or, interpreted, translated, defined in more than one way, and often on more than one level. The outer, easily understood words, often had a deeper, far more complex meaning hidden beneath. After all, it was now common knowledge that ancient writers sometimes wrote on two, and sometimes three levels, that required a modicum of arcane knowledge to understand. Which left them both with an unanswered question, ringing inside their heads. What do we know, that we are unaware of knowing? It was both a haunt and a shadow-soft kind of madness.

During the years that followed there self exile to the islands, they never spoke of such an impossible possibility. There was never any need to do so, each would look at the other, through hollow, dark ringed eyes, and know that they shared an equal silent sorrow, too ineffable to articulate.

To voice a deep rooted sorrow requires some understanding, or at the very least, an awareness, no matter how vague it might be, of its cause.

Both George and Margaret, for reasons neither one nor the other could understand, refused to acknowledge even within the private, voiceless regions inside their heads, the possibility of the existence, of the unimaginable arcane knowledge they sensed, if only on a subliminal level, *The*

Culann Scrolls might represent. It shivered them through, and brought them together during the nights darkest hours in a breathless frenzy of sex, that only partially helped to keep the night shadows at bay.

Lost they were, and silent howling for the 'Mother,' of all wounds to heal them. Well it was that they had chosen to live amongst the isles of the once — younger Gods. Sometimes they listen, often they do not. However it may be, Greece is their only domain — forever.

On that once upon a far away day, George had left the long sword of blue metal lying in its dusty bed. Symbolic perhaps of his future non-involvement. He had taken the clay cylinders with no thought given to their being more. In fact he didn't really search the hill tomb at all. As soon as he had carried the cylinders away, his mind had shut down in an odd, can hardly think straight, sort of way. The only thought that had begun to pound through his head was one of flight and concealment. He had resealed the tomb with unseemly feverish haste, returned to his four wheel drive, and drove away without a backward glance. He had felt pursued and watched by something unseen until he had driven far and away from the Black Hills. By the time he reached home a bit and piece of sanity had returned to him, along with a feather touch of shadow-soft madness.

Months later, when Margaret had completed the translation, he had thrilled to Culann's narration, and graphic descriptions of events that had destroyed a world so completely, today, few people were aware that it had actually existed. The Druid's arrival in America and what he found there so long ago, had literally taken his breath away, and then he rejected Culann's words, and like Pilate the Roman, washed his hands in symbolic rejection of what he didn't want to understand, or even acknowledge, if only in part, as being true. It was all too much, it rocked the boat of his staid, academic life and set him on the road to ridicule and possible loss of tenure. The resulting pain-guilt of it all began to fester deep down below the bedrock of his suppressed soul. George Pemberton did understand and that was his splintered cross, his keen of sorrow, his anguished wail of terrible loss.

He simply did not want to know. It involved decisions and a measure of personal sacrifice he wasn't prepared to make, and so he cowered inside his head and let revenant mendacity rule.

Margaret, who was far more pragmatic and wide of eye than George, simply did not relish the storm of controversy she knew would rage around them both, once the contents of the scrolls were revealed.

That the scrolls proved once and for all, the existence of early Celtic settlers in America, was in itself a minor detail, compared to what the scrolls ultimately revealed. Culann, Druid trained and Indian named and what else, she had thought, what is he trying to tell us, what have we missed.

Dear God in heaven, she thought helplessly, what have we done. So it was that Margaret, like George, blocked out any necessity of knowing and its attendant responsibilities. Margaret urged and condoned the theft and private sale of what she ultimately didn't want to understand.

Now it is that they walk through days of endless summer, along the white sand shores of a wine dark sea, carrying deep within the innermost core of their being, an ineffable sense of aching loss. A compound of gloom and light that both had failed to carry.

Years of extensive and intensive study coupled with decades of experience within and outside the scope of their chosen fields, wasted. They had failed to recognise the one path that could have led them out with no loss of position, no diminished reputation.

Steeped in the traditions of ancient cultures as they were, the riddling sense of the scrolls should have been easy to identify, isolate and understand. They chose to ignore the pattern and its weave. Instead of shouting hallelujah, they both cut and ran, accepting money, ignoring the grand mystery prize dangling before them. Now they shiver awake in the deep of night with eyes wide and staring and wet with tears, their guts all knotted up with an ache of loss so bitter, it fills their mouths with dust and ashes and a lingering scald of bile.

Even so, some divine providence watched over them, for it is true that their remaining years were free of travail and mortal strife. Perhaps providence considered their unceasing haunt of loss, punishment enough. They were, after all, exiled upon an isle that once was home to younger Gods, who punished transgressions it is true, but were never considered to be cruel, or uncaring of those who dwell upon an isle of their rule, capricious perhaps, but never cruel. Or so it is the ancients teach, and who are we to say they are wrong, when so many continue to worship a younger God and the thrice blessed aspects of power. Only the names have changed, but the soul-hunger remains the same. Gratification of crass enunciations cannot change what is inherent within words of power. Only now, the words are hidden beneath dross and brass, whilst the pontification of small words, hide the face of the God we created in our image.

The hidden scroll remains hidden.

Collusion and avarice have sealed it away.

The one who bought *The Culann Scrolls* received little joy from the possession of them, nor did he own them for long.

After four fruitless years of study, he was unable to grasp the full import of the hidden meaning, or find any clue as to the location of the hidden scroll, but then, he had no knowledge of ancient words of power either.

When he could riddle the scrolls no more, he died. Suddenly, shockingly of a heart attack.

After his death the scrolls passed into other hands, and the world moved on, unaware of the existence of *The Culann Scrolls*.

Philip Hainvar it was who took possession of the scrolls, and if he had his way, the scrolls would remain hidden — forever, but then, Philip Hainvar was an educated buffoon, who considered x-factors to be no more than whimsical fabrications, postulated by mathematicians, to symbolise what they were otherwise unable to define, within the scope of their computations.

*T*he *Culann Scrolls* were written with purpose and intent, by a mage-man we call Druid. It is assumed that the hidden scroll will remain hidden for as long as it takes the world to understand the full import of *The Culann Scrolls*, but then, nothing is certain, and nothing remains hidden for long once determined men set out to find it.

Roy Edwards

Winter 1994 - Midwest USA.

The elderly distinguished gentleman had never suffered from a days illness in his life. Ten years previously he had sold his lucrative brokerage business for thirty three million dollars. Freed from the pressures and stress of handling other peoples money and there crazy whims, he looked forward to a long and happy retirement.

He had two passions in life, his wife and his private collection of old and rare books, manuscripts, odd pieces of art, artefacts and antiques in general. His collection was by no means large but it was very, very selective. So much so, that apart from his wife and an odd friend or two, no others were aware of its existence. His passion for collecting was not shared by his wife, however she held within her breast a deep and abiding love for him and so did not begrudge his one small eccentricity. It was, after all, harmless and gave him a great deal of obvious pleasure. She loved him, she cared for him, he was her life.

He died suddenly, unexpectedly from a massive heart attack. His widow was devastated. Childless, she mourned him alone. It was too much, too much to bear within the echoing confines of a huge old home. The house was an old rambling structure filled with rooms that now held only memories. She decided to travel and to continue travelling in luxury until the hour of her death.

She sold the house, and on an unprecedented burst of generosity, donated her late husband's private collection, of what she called, 'his antiques', to a moderately well known museum she had heard her late husband praise for its excellent pre-Columbian exhibits.

Celtic Sunset

Winter 1994

Winter was traditionally a slack time for the museum. Staff were allowed to take their annual leave on a rotating basis. New exhibits were planned and prepared for the spring/summer tourist months ahead. Inventories were made and the all important acquisition fund reviewed with regards purchase and/or hire of exhibition items. When the Curator was informed of the donation to the museum of a private collection of rare and valuable artefacts with no strings attached he was overjoyed. So much so that he postponed taking his traditional winter holiday until after he had personally itemised the entire collection.

Philip Hainvar was small, stout, middle aged and balding. He was also the Director/Curator of the museum. He was a self opinionated, bombastic, little man who ran his dusty, rusty world of ancient dreams with strict, if pompous efficiency. He expected his entire staff to perform a variety of duties, irrespective of their positions.

His staff did not like him, a fact of which he was totally unaware.

Many of his contemporaries considered him to be an odious little man full of self righteous misconceptions. He was if nothing else, incredibly vociferous in his oft times repeated denials, of their ever having been the slightest possibility of any Celtic exploration of America. He was for unknown reasons almost paranoid on the subject. That there was some evidence to support the Celtic exploration theory was totally immaterial. 'Besides', he would argue, 'the evidence is purely circumstantial, no single piece of irrefutable evidence has yet been found and,' he would add, 'it never will, because it doesn't exist.'

His contemporaries gave him a wide berth, his staff could ill afford such luxury. However Philip Hainvar possessed a single saving grace. Beneath his vociferous bombastic exterior, beat a heart full of a genuine love for old and ancient things. Antiquities were his passion, his driving force, his reason for walking this earth of constant travail.

Philip Hainvar employed a staff of eight, of which Gerald Strathmore was the most recent addition. Having joined, 'The Team', as Hainvar put it on a full time basis during the summer of '94. He was twenty four years old. His main function was to escort groups around the museum. However, he often found himself sweeping floors, answering phones or otherwise relegated to the storeroom. The storeroom, like museums the world over, lay directly beneath the museum and was, in many cases a larger underground structure than the museum above. 'Things,' were hidden in dark corners, manuscripts, items, objects, artefacts that didn't fit the accepted historical scheme of things and/or otherwise couldn't be explained. No museum in the world willingly displayed incredibly old objects that they had no information and/or explanation for. The unwritten rule was that 'You can only fool some of the public some of the time, never the whole of the public all of the time.' There were too many astute people out there who had the annoying habit of asking embarrassing questions, Curators and staff alike would rather not have to try to answer. Hence the maxim 'Bury the item,' which simply means put it in some dark dusty corner of the storeroom and hopefully in time it will be forgotten.

Gerald Strathmore sometimes indulged in incredible fantasies woven around finding such a hidden treasure.

Celtic Sunset

Hainvar had almost finished his inventory of the donated collection. Much of it, he realised, had been bought illicitly. However, nothing was actually on the monthly updated stolen list, so he would have no qualms regarding display. He pulled the final item towards him, and wished the storeroom had brighter lighting.

The museum was closed, his staff already on their way home, apart from a night security guard prowling around the upper floors, he was alone. The storeroom was long and wide with additional rooms leading off from both sides of the main floor area. A series of huge support columns ran down the central aisle giving the storeroom a medieval look. Hainvar would be glad when he was finished. There were times, he thought, when this section of the museum complex gave him the creeps, but then, he was a righteous man with no fear in him of ghosts or beasties that might haunt dark places.

The box top was hinged, secured by a simple hook and eye arrangement, he opened it. He could see in the dim light that it contained clay cylinders packed in straw. A thick stack of loose papers lay on top. He picked the papers up, shuffled them together, and began to read Margaret Wilder's translation of *The Culann Scrolls*.

He stared unseeingly into the gloom. A thin sheen of perspiration slicked his face.

'Jesus Christ Almighty' he breathed raggedly into the silence. He was appalled, shocked to the inner most core of his being. 'This can't be true. It simply cannot be true,' he moaned.

But he knew that is was.

His head felt tight and achy, eyes sore and gritty, his heart hammered, and there was an empty feeling way down in the pit of his stomach. He licked lips suddenly gone dry.

It was a nightmare, his worst fears come true. He fought down a rising wave of panic. When this became known he would be humiliated, a clown amongst his peers. He would never again dare show his face or raise his voice in dissent.

'Jesus, sweet Jesus,' he whispered, 'this is awful, I'll be ruined, my reputation torn apart by a pack of bloody mouthed sharks. I will have to resign my position.' The thought made his blood run cold. The museum was his life, without it he would be nothing, less than a voiceless whimper crying in the wilderness. 'Unless. No! no!' the thought was too terrible to contemplate. He was, after all, a righteous man, incapable of base perfidy.

But —

He looked around, peering into the gloom of the silent storeroom, assuring himself that he was indeed alone. He would destroy everything, the clay cylinders, the scrolls, the translation, and erase any mention of them from his lists. 'Yes,' he thought wildly, destroy them, 'now, immediately.'

He couldn't do it. His breathing was ragged, his heart pounding. His love for old and ancient things held him back. Wild eyed, panting for breath, his hands trembled, as he almost but not quite began to tear the translation into pieces, almost but not quite.

He couldn't do it.

He tried, his eyes grew moist with tears of frustration, but he couldn't. He couldn't destroy something that had survived intact for almost three thousand years.

With a sigh of resigned defeat, he placed the translation back in the box and sat down, staring at it with blank, moist eyes. For years he had denied the existence of any kind of

Celtic Sunset

Celtic link with America's history, and now, ironically, irrefutable evidence of such a link lay before him. 'Why me?' he groaned aloud, his face mirrored despair. And then it came to him, a bright, white hot idea.

He couldn't destroy the evidence, but he could make it disappear. He grinned, his belly sagging in relief. Not forever to be sure, but with luck it would remain hidden, until long after he had retired with grace. 'In fact' he thought blithely, 'he would probably be dead by the time it came to light. Oh yes' he breathed softly, 'I will bury you so deep no one will ever find you, no one at all', he chuckled, pleased with his solution to the problem.

At least that was his intention. Philip Hainvar was a righteous man, and being a righteous man had its drawbacks. Knowing how, and where to hide things from prying eyes was one of them. He was a fool. An educated man, but a fool none the less. In fact he was the worst kind. An educated, academic buffoon, who absorbed data and retained it like a leaking sieve. Unable, incapable, or unwilling to acknowledge truths, or any kind of evidence that did not in some way support his incredibly shallow, narrow view points of what he, revelling in blissful ignorance, considered to be the way of the world and its nations of the dim and distant past. Like others of his ilk he was prepared to go to extreme lengths to protect pride of position and his vociferous opinions based upon scholastic, academic, call them what you will, vagaries.

Devious but not criminal is perhaps an argument based upon semantics, depending entirely upon the outcome of the act itself, which was based upon Philip Hainvar's vanity, and arrogance stemming from continual claims of negation that were based upon nothing more than his own superior attitude of what he considered aspects of the past to be. The majority of his contemporaries at least possessed enough foresight and wit to cover themselves against future discoveries by admitting that whilst they considered a particular historic incident to be this or that, there was always the chance that new discoveries may prove them wrong, or at least partially right, as the case may be.

Hainvar, being a righteous man, considered such mumblings to be nothing short of prevarication and refused to moderate his fixed ideas and opinions with even a modicum of wit. The revelations contained within *The Culann Scrolls* had hit him with all the force of an enthusiastic swinging sledge hammer, smashing reason, if only for the moment, into a grey fog of mental dust. Within moments of reaching his decision, he had, within his head, already justified the rightness of his action. 'It isn't as though I'm going to destroy them.' He convinced himself that he was doing the academic world a favour by hiding what could only be regarded as controversial documents, of dubious origins and authenticity. His mind burned with the zeal of a religious fanatic. He called it goodwill towards all men. 'After all,' he mused, as he closed the box, 'why add more clutter to an already overcrowded field of research.'

Carrying the box carefully in both hands, he began to wander around the storeroom, searching for the one perfect hiding place, within minutes he found it. At the extreme end of the vaulted storeroom, behind a clutter of empty packing crates and thick cardboard boxes, he located a small recess cut into the wall. It was partially hidden from sight by a support column that blocked out most of the light emitting from a nearby low wattage bulb. The area behind the column was dim and gloomy. The mouth of the recess hidden by dark shadows. It was he thought, the perfect hiding place. At least that is what Philip Hainvar believed. His idea of a hiding place would probably fool a determined child for about ten minutes, but then Philip Hainvar was not by nature a devious, cunning man.

His thought process was made up of narrow streets with an occasional intersection. He had never heard of conceptual thought, or straight line logic, and would have dismissed them both as rubbish if he had. Unlike other historians, academics, archaeologists he had yet to embrace disciplines other than his own, to aid in the unravelling of Earth's most ancient and mysterious secrets. Hainvar would have been better off taking the box home and burying it in a deep, deep hole in his garden.

He failed to heed a simple axiom accepted by professionals the world over, which is 'All the plans of mice and men contain an unknown x-factor.' It is an immutable law of the universe in which we live. Failure to be cognisant of its existence practically guarantees failure.

The unlooked for, the unexpected, the unknowable x-factor. Inherent within Philip Hainvar's life was one, Gerald Strathmore. A young, likeable man, possessed of a pleasant disposition and an insatiable curiosity to explore dim and dusty corners of museum vaults, in the hope eternal of unearthing a forgotten treasure, whilst seeking his own entrance to the valley of the grail. Lovers of antiquity are often found to be possessed of a spiritual or philosophical nature. Gerald Strathmore was no exception.

Fortunately, in his haste, Hainvar had neglected to read the entirety of Margaret Wilder's translation. If he had done so, he would probably have driven home and killed himself in a messy, amateurish sort of way.

Perhaps the latent power inherent within the scrolls prevented this. No one will ever know. Beyond the argument that the attracting force, or power of any mystery is dependant upon the structure of the mystery, be it secular, religious or otherwise, the power source of any mystery is — the mystery.

Philip Hainvar would forever regret his hasty omission. If he had read the translation in its entirety, he would have destroyed it there and then, despite his love of antiquities, and then, in all probability he would have shot himself.

Hainvar's announcement that he was taking his annual leave as planned, was greeted with smiles and quiet sighs of relief by his staff, Gerald Strathmore included. His duties were light during the winter months with only the occasional group of visitors to escort round the museum. No one bothered him with additional duties whilst Hainvar was absent. If he was needed, everyone knew he could always be found poking around somewhere, within the depths of the storeroom vaults.

Fate lay gentle hands upon him and led him unerringly towards the dusty clutter that had accumulated over the years in a dim and gloomy corner of the storeroom.

Moving around behind a support column, he didn't see in the dim murky light, an empty box directly in front of him, he stumbled over it. As he fell forward, he automatically stretched his arms out to help break his fall, his left hand slapped against the wall, his right hand disappeared into what he thought was a hole, and hit against what felt like wood. Thrown off balance, he fell to his knees with a startled oath, as pain ripped through his kneecaps.

Celtic Sunset

Sitting on an upturned box in the gloom, he massaged his bruised knees until the pain eased. Standing, he flexed his legs, and curious about the hole in the wall, thrust his hand inside and slowly withdrew an oblong box with a hinged lid.

It was the second day of Hainvar's leave.

Gerald carried the box towards a nearby table. He placed the box carefully on top, pulled up a nearby chair and sat down to examine his find.

Fate watched over him with tender care, ensuring no one entered the storeroom whilst he examined his find.

His long sought *treasure* his grail

Roy Edwards

Spangles of pale rose-gold sunlight faded swiftly into the gloom of an early, shivering winter's night. Frost covered the sidewalks, crunching and crackling beneath booted feet of rugged up pedestrians, hurrying home to warmth and light. Street lamps winked on, one by one, shining like warmless candles above the petty considerations of scurrying human kind.

Breathe in and out, hide behind the coiling vapour of your own breath Gerald thought, already half drunk on rough red wine. The sound of soft, reggae rhythms filled his small three roomed apartment, as he moodily surveyed his almost empty glass. He didn't want to admit it, even to himself, but he was worried, and just a little bit frightened by what he had done. The rich, lilting Jamaican harmonies of *Claude Buffer and the Mighty Zones*, singing of their eventual return to Zion, did nothing to alleviate his dour frame of mind.

It wasn't the theft of the Culann translation that bothered him. He didn't actually consider he had stolen it. All he had done, was photocopy the pages and then replaced it in its hiding place, knowing, he thought savagely, Mr pig and spit Hainvar, would be none the wiser. Unless the translation was published, and then of course, the shit would hit the fan and someone might, just might, happen to remark that he, Gerald, had spent a lot of time photocopying something whilst Hainvar was on his annual vacation. That wasn't so bad really, he could always come up with some plausible excuse to explain it away but, and isn't there always a but, the incident might, just might, make Hainvar suspicious, and well, there you go boy, out of a job. Hainvar, the vindictive slob would put the word out and he had enough clout to ensure he was, unofficially of course, black listed, and that was only part of the problem, he thought sourly.

After reading the translation, Gerald realised there was another, very different story buried beneath the obvious. He hadn't actually found it, at least not yet, but he sensed it. He had glimpsed it now and again as though it strove to break through and grab his attention. Only, when he thought he might be able to grasp it, it slipped away.

The narration itself filled him with unease. He didn't doubt the truth of what he had read. It was just that there was something odd about it, but he couldn't quite figure out what it was.

He had already dismissed, as job suicide, or worse, his original intention of revealing the manuscript to the world. Now he was stuck with it. He couldn't destroy it, the thought itself was almost unthinkable, but what to do? He couldn't throw his copy away or otherwise pretend it didn't exist. 'There has to be a way out of this,' he mused, as he refilled his glass. 'All I have to do is think of a way to ensure its published with no kick back on me.'

He drank cool rough red and switched his CD player to repeat mode, sat down and stared at the one and only winter dark window, and completely missed the obvious.

Gerald Strathmore was considered to be a bright young man by his fellow workers, destined to go places they said. He was indeed a bright young man, but that did not imply that he possessed an over abundance of intelligence. The world is full of dumb-bright young men, who are unable to think beyond the boundaries of education. Such people limp through life like mental cripples, often completely unaware of their own self imposed limitations.

An education is, after all, easy to acquire. The hard part is thinking through it, or adding to what you know so that you can realise what you don't know. The final premise being of course, a realisation of how little you do actually know. We are, in many ways, students for the entirety of our lives. Only arrogant educated fools, articulate the sublime stupidity that they are in possession of knowledge that encompasses the whole of any one discipline, let alone several.

The scrolls were written in Latin and Greek, knowledge of which should have made a single translation immediately suspect. Single definitions of modern words are a rarity. Something written in a dead language using words, whose definition, varies by sound, tone and inflection coupled with another ancient language should have alerted Gerald to the possibility that the writer was trying to hide something from the casual reader, whilst alerting those with knowledge, to the fact that more was to be found, but you would have to search for it.

The writer of the scrolls was a Druid, a Warrior, Bard, that was the first, most obvious clue, everyone had missed. Also no one actually knows how to pronounce (common - vulgar) Latin, we can only assume that this or that pronunciation or definition is correct. It is, after all a dead language, and not to be confused with medieval or church Latin.

Gerald knew all this, it was part of his education. He knew it as well as he knew that Egyptian hieroglyphics can be read in two and sometimes three different ways, commoner (vulgar), Lord (middle) and Priest (high) to whom, the same words (glyphs) mean different things. All three, reading the same passage receive a different message. Gerald failed, and so the scrolls (The translation) moved on.

Celtic Sunset

He had a nice buzz going, the music shoop-shooped along in lazy relaxing rhythms. *The Mighty Zones* laying sweet harmonies over the music like drifting smoke. He'd drunk just enough wine to retain his faculties without actually causing a short circuit inside his head. He was mellow and feeling okay. His room was mellow and his grubby, faded curtains looked, well, mellow. His fear was still there, coiled in his stomach like a snake, but his awareness of it had dulled along with his innate sense of oddness about the translation.

Blood red wine slipped down his throat in a long cool swallow. A smell of happy weed permeated the room. He rose unsteadily to his feet intending to open his one and only window, as he moved towards the window, it came to him, the answer to all his problems. He began to laugh, a hint of weed induced hysteria in its sound. 'It's so obvious,' he crowed aloud, 'I don't know why I didn't think of it before. Amen.'

Lurching towards the phone, he made a call.

His friend arrived about forty minutes later. The evening was still young, though dark and cold. Whilst Gerald talked, his friend made coffee, lots of strong, sweet, black coffee. He also dumped the remains of Gerald's happy weed in the trash can.

Gerald talked, drank coffee and gradually sobered up. Eventually he handed his copy of the Culann translation to his friend. His friend sat down and began to read.

Gerald lay down on the floor and promptly fell asleep. He felt as though a great weight had slipped from his shoulders. The translation was now in other hands.

41

During the early hours of the following morning, Gerald woke up to find his friend staring at him. 'We have to talk,' he said in a flat emotionless voice.

'Yes,' said Gerald through a yawn, 'we'd better.'

Gerald's friend was a writer. An author with a few published books to his credit, but no best seller. In fact his books hadn't sold well at all. Barely generating enough income to pay his rent. He lived frugally, balanced on the knife edge of starvation. The author presented a lean, intense face to the world, viewed through quiet eyes that sometimes flared with an intense inner passion, whenever he could be reluctantly persuaded to talk about his work. Like many writers he read books by the dozen and spent long hours in solitary thought. His publisher continued to publish his novels, despite poor sales figures, because he wrote a good book. His publisher was convinced that he would, in the near future, write that one book that would sell the magic million. Gerald's friend rarely gave much thought to selling a million. He wrote because he loved to write, and he wrote what he wanted to write, not what other money hungry individuals considered he should write.

Here's the way it is,' he said to Gerald.

Outside, darkness had begun to pearl with light as a new day forced its way through clinging winter shadows.

'It reads like God's own truth,' Gerald's friend said, 'mind you, I don't really care if it's true or not. There are a few words I can't even pronounce let alone recognise, so we'll have to sort that lot out first.' He looked at Gerald intently, 'Now, you've explained how you got this little lot, so we're all right on that, but I'll have to change a bit and add a bit to make it my own. What I mean is Gerald. I'll rewrite it in my own style but I won't leave anything out, so if there is a message in there somewhere it won't he lost and if the right ones, whoever they may be, happen to read it, well, that's it really isn't it.'

'Yes,' Gerald said happily, a big smile on his face. 'If it's published as historical fiction or just as a fantasy novel, it doesn't really matter, so long as it's published.'

His friend said, 'have you ever noticed that a lot of people seem to recognise a story as being true, even when it's published as fiction, maybe the public are beginning to realise that that's the way a lot of writers get something published when it's too unbelievable to publish any other way.'

'What the hell,' said Gerald smiling broadly, 'fantasy, who gives a shit. So long as nobody's claiming it's the gospel according to Judas, who cares.'

With a vampirish smile suffusing his features, Gerald's friend left the apartment, clutching the translation to his chest like some metamorphic pot of gold, or, at the very least, gilded brass.

With the passing of the scrolls (translation) into other hands, Gerald felt as though a great weight of responsibility had been taken from him. Lingering traces of fear, regret and hope sighed out of his mouth. The memory of them fading from his mind, like some dream of gossamer winged summer during the dark chill silence of winter's night.

Once he held the translation, now he did not, and a bittersweet sense of regret and hope faded from his consciousness. He had not, after all, compromised the integrity of the existence of *The Culann Scrolls*. He had simply acted as an intermediary, helping to facilitate their acceptance into a different age. An age of doubt, political calumny and legalistic obscenities. An age of feral, self destructive complacency, bereft of Sir Altruism and his Knights of Compassion.

'Welcome to the nightmare.'

'Welcome to the Twentieth Century,' whispered night haunts into the silence of an iron hard frost bound winter's night.

Ψ

Celtic Sunset

Spring 1996

Almost two years later a book published under the title of *Celtic Sunset* with a subheading (*The Culann Scrolls - Vol I*) went on sale.

Within three months the book had entered the New York Times best seller lists, eventually making it to the number one spot, where it stayed for an unprecedented length of time. Published as fiction, it was none the less surprising, how many people came to regard it as a factual account based upon extant scrolls.

The following Spring saw the release of a companion volume titled *Indian Dawn*. The book included an author's postscript, whereby the author claimed the existence of more scrolls hidden within a lost tomb somewhere deep within the hills of south Dakota.

Across the world, on a small, sun drenched isle set like some exotic jewel, midst Homer's legendary wine dark sea, an elderly man and his lady walked hand in hand along the white sands of the sighing sea. Unspoken thoughts jumped, wailed and jived through their heads. Each knew that the other no longer woke in the dark of night, eyes wet with tears, bowels clenched in dread of some nameless dream haunt. Each knew, without vocalisation of thought, that the rusting, saw toothed blade that by increments slashed an unhealing wound deep into the essence of their being, had begun to heal. Slowly it is true, but with the passing of moon bright nights, the sense of complete loss and utter despair that had filled their lives grew less. Perhaps the younger God of the exotic isle deemed their suffering enough. To expiate guilt of collusion and avarice, born of their attempt to hide what had now been thrown into humanity's sea, causing an expanding ripple that would in the fullness of time break upon dim and distant shores. The final scroll, found and loose upon the world of human kind might change it forever. Though it is true, the scroll has yet to be found.

The writing of *Celtic Sunset* and *Indian Dawn* by Gerald's friend, was actually accomplished within an astonishingly short period of time. It wasn't so much that the author was inspired, how could he be, when his work was all but done for him. It was simply that, as he copied from the scrolls, lines seemed to flare with a silver like radiance inside his head. He knew instinctively what words to use, to fill the story out without actually altering it. At times, he felt it was all a little spooky, however he was so caught up in what he was doing, he didn't really give much attention to his feeling of spookiness, at least, not until he altered a portion of Culann's narration dealing with the first way of Druid. He decided to smooth that particular section out. Whereas before he had only added a sort of filling between sentences, a padding out without actually altering or deleting a single one of Culann's words. Now he began to change the actual narration, adding words to round out and end off what he assumed were incomplete sentences. He altered words where a sentence read as though written backwards. He shuffled words around so that a line might read better. Not realising of course that through doing this he had destroyed, or altered, any hidden meaning inherent within the written lines. Here and there he deleted words, replacing them with his own.

When he had finished, he read over his altered version of Culann's narrative feeling smugly satisfied with himself. 'Yes,' he thought in satisfaction, 'that's better, much better

46

and eminently more readable.' At that point, he decided to call it a day. He showered, ate, read for awhile and then went to bed.

He couldn't sleep.

He felt as though unseen eyes watched him inside his head. Whenever he began to doze off, he would suddenly snap wide awake, mouth dry, heart pounding, eyes staring into the darkness of his room. Something flickered at the corner of his vision, at least he thought it did. Eventually he got up, made a pot of tea and spent the remainder of the night drinking tea and smoking hand rolled cigarettes.

He didn't write at all the next day, or even bother to read through the next section of the scrolls he was due to start work on. He moped around smoking endless cigarettes and drinking cups of hot strong sweet tea. He felt ill, something kept moving at the corner of his vision, but whenever he turned towards it, there was nothing there. He began to feel edgy and uptight, his head ached.

Even though it was broad daylight, his sense of unseen eyes watching him remained. His thinking seemed slow and blurred, as though his mind was constrained by some invisible viscosity that never quite let go. His eyes felt sore and gritty, he put it down to lack of sleep from the night before. His body felt heavy and lethargic as though he had been on a two day eating binge. He hadn't yet realised the nature of what the scrolls actually were, perhaps he never would.

The second night was a duplicate of the one before.

The following morning found him sitting in his study, head between his hands moaning softly. He knuckled his eyes and gave a sigh of defeat, allowing thoughts to drift away on a turgid river of weariness and thick headachy pains. His guts roiled. He couldn't write, he couldn't read. He felt constrained, but why, why? Everything was fine until..., his head reared up and back as a sudden wash of realisation flooded through him. Thought blossomed inside his skull like a flower opening its petals, reaching out towards the sun. He realised he had been doing fine, until he had altered the last section he had been working on, to fit his own idea of how it should have been written.

With feverish haste he reached out and pulled his working manuscript towards him. Crossing out his alteration of Culann's narration, he began to copy out exactly what was written, adding only a few lines of his own to smooth its way into the following section.

That night he slept soundly.

During the days and weeks that followed until his work was finished, he at times, felt as though a presence stood behind him, looking over his shoulder with a sort of detached curiosity, suffused with a sort of friendly willingness to guide. Words flowed from his pen, turning Culann's narrations into a rich, wild, story without actually altering the original sense of it all. The blend was done with such expertise, that when the manuscript was finally released as a published work, few, if any, could tell where Culann's narration left off and the author's began, and yet the author failed to recognise what Culann's narration actually was.

Others did not, The *Brotherhood of the Book* included.

The *Brotherhood of the Book*, the oldest secret society upon the face of the Earth, who's origins predate the pyramids of Egypt by thousands of years. Sumerian and Babylonian texts make mention of them some 7,000 to 8,000 years ago. They called them Protectors of Knowledge, Guardians of BK (Book).

Celtic Sunset

Who they are, no one knows. Militant or benign, who can say. Legend has it that they have been rescuing written knowledge and gems of literature, from certain destruction for about 12,000 years or more.

Rumour has it, that just prior to the Chinese invasion of Tibet this century, many Lamaseries, monasteries gave into the hands of an unknown group their most precious books, many of them more than 2,500 years old, for storing and safe keeping in the 'Great Library.'

Culann mentions (briefly) the Brotherhood and his swearing of 'the oath' prior to joining their ranks. That the Brotherhood included warriors is attested to. Perhaps it was this same Brotherhood, who were responsible for the removal of scores of ancient books from Alexander's (Alexander the Great) library prior to its destruction, and also from that mysterious and now legendary Library of the Desert, thought to have been destroyed by invaders some 12,000 years ago. If it existed at all, The Library of the Desert would be Earth's oldest library.

There is an ancient way of writing that has long been lost to the world. The way of its reading is known only to a few, and is at best, only guessed at, by others who claim the scholarship of its knowledge. Some have come close, but that is all they have done, come close. However, the way of it all, is slowly being rediscovered by various forward thinkers.

The *Brotherhood of the Book* retain full knowledge of its use. Within the depths of their secret archives they hold original copies of such writings dating back thousands of years. In all probability back to the beginnings of the great Library of the Desert itself. The Brotherhood were probably aware of the existence of *The Culann Scrolls*. They may in fact have been searching for them, obviously without success. The Brotherhood possessed the arcane skills necessary to read *Celtic Sunset*, in the way it was intended to be read, that is, based upon the Celtic, three fold, way of body, mind, spirit. This, in conjunction with Egyptian and Semitic methods, enabled the Brotherhood to recognise the true story inherent within Culann's words even though they were, to all intents and purposes encapsulated, that is, surrounded by and hidden, within a protective shield of modernistic words, that in themselves neither added to nor detracted from, Culann's.

Margaret Wilder's translation of *The Culann Scrolls* was a work of inspired genius, though it is doubtful that Wilder was aware of her somewhat unique achievement. Providence conspired, or so it may seem, to create a unique melding of a time, place, event, framework within the confines of Wilder's willingness to accept and express past and present realities, based upon her own instinctive and scholarly knowledge of both. Moved she was, like a diamond shard glittering upon the chess board of the pattern's weave.

So it was that only a handful of adepts independent of the Brotherhood, riddled the truth within the dragon's snare of *Celtic Sunset* and the bittersweet birth song of an *Indian Dawn*.

$$\Psi$$

PART ONE

CELTIC SUNSET

Roy Edwards

THE DRUID CURSE STONE

A stone tablet from about 50BC, found in Bordeaux, France. To date it remains the only known example of a curse, carved in stone, surviving from the time of Caesar. Caesar's name is inscribed on the curse stone — there can be no mistake. Literally translated as follows

Julius Caesar, Commander of the Legions of Rome
He who walks in the shadow of 'The Gaunt Man'
Crom Cruach — Bowed One of the Mound
This is our promise to you
We hate you forever
We will oppose you forever
Until the sky doth fall and crush our bones
Until the Earth cracks open beneath out feet
Until fire consumes our flesh
Until the air chokes our throats
Until the sea doth rise and drown us
Until iron poisons our bowels
Until the Spiral of Immortality is broken
We bind thee in hate - forever (or)
Until thy house (of flesh) lays reeking, and torn upon the stones.
Bereft of all life even unto the darkening of the light of Atomism
We make this promise unto thee in the prescribed manner of the Seven Fold Malediction of Arum

Celtic Sunset

ARUM   A Celtic word, literally, Priest of the Oaks (Druidae -Druid)

ATOMISM From the Greek - Atoma. Circa 500 BC
Postulated by the early Greek, Founding Fathers of Philosophy, (from which all western philosophies derive) as being, sentient energy with no location in space or time. Creating mind as a means of communication, through which sentient energy can manifest, thoughts, ideas, concepts, ad in finitum, through individual perception of the reality of the physical world. Eventually sublimated to denote 'The Spirit,' 'Soul, 'Self-being,' 'I.' That which exists despite its existence being ultimately unprovable. Also known as an 'Act-of-Faith.' To the ancient Celts it was an every day reality of existence. They knew they were tenants of flesh, and that the spirit survived its death and moved into a new forming house within the womb.

ORDER OF ARUM
(Priests of the Oaks - Druidae - Druids)

There are seven orders, or ranks. Each order containing more than one discipline. Each discipline is taught on three levels, physical, mental, spiritual. Each level is considered to be a separate discipline, whilst at the same time remaining dependant upon the remaining two disciplines for its existence. The Celtic Trinity Triangle. Its roots can be traced back to ancient Babylon and beyond. Disciplines are taught over a period of three times seven years. Of the three levels (physical, mental, spiritual) emphasis is placed upon reaching, or attaining to, a fourth and final untaught level. Few Druids aspired to the fourth level, or 'Way'. Of those who did some did not survive. The *fourth way* is known and yet remains unknown. Its attainment personal to those few who survive its walking. It was considered to be the ultimate in spiritual revelation and is known as — *Skan Taku Skanskan* (Something in movement). Spiritual vitality.

FIRST ORDER

BARD OLLAMH - Master of all disciplines. Second in rank only to a king.

BARD COLLOQUY - Master of Form. (Rules and laws governing, verse, poetry, song and speech) without form only common or vulgar expression remains. Bard speech is sometimes known as 'The Language of Kings.'

HARPER - Composition of satires, music and verse. Able to recite without error five times two hundred heroic verses.

SECOND ORDER

PHILOSOPHER - POET - PRIEST - Poet considered to be a lore master and historian. Philosophy based upon natural (of the earth) and creative thinking.

THIRD ORDER

PHYSICIAN - HERB MASTER - Spiritual healing. Dream Interpreter. Sciences.

FOURTH ORDER

JUDGE - ADVISER - HERALD - Law, both man made and natural. Truce makers.

OBSERVERS - The penalty for utterance of a false observation or malicious comment was death or, more commonly, expulsion from the order.

FIFTH ORDER
LANGUAGE MASTER - Celtic, Ogham, Runes, Greek, Roman, Persian, (both written and oral).

SIXTH ORDER
WEAPONS MASTER - All weapons, unarmed combat (wrestling), Tactics, Strategy.

SEVENTH ORDER
NEWS SHOUTERS -Trained in straight memory recall and some aspects of observers. (For a News Shouter to knowingly broadcast a lie, the penalty is death.

Ψ

The Culann Scrolls

Roy Edwards

~~~~~~~~~~~~

To the one who holds the scrolls
Greetings
I, Culann of the Arverni, greet you as a free
person of 'The People' (the Celts) who are now
no more than a suggestion of memory in the
minds of barbaric arrogance
And yet
Like the great standing stones of Danann we
remain unriddled
Riddle then, the scrolls and the melding of
'The Way' with the sacred circle of the cross of
The People of the Plains
Hanto Yo (clear the way)

Culann

~~~~~~~~~~~~

CELTIC SUNSET

Chapter One

Mother
And if I touch the earth
Will thou cleanse me?
When the midnight comes
spiritually refresh and anoint me?
Mother
And if I touch the earth
Will thou unfurl thy greening hands?
Will thou heal me?
Mother
And if I touch the earth
When the midnight comes
will thou - - - - - - -

from - The Book of Insights

It began for me upon the first day of Lugnasadh (August)
I remember it well
It was my seventh summer

Druid voice sang the song of welcome to the rising sun, his face upturned towards the paling sky. Arms open wide, in the traditional gesture of his acceptance of light and life, not for himself alone, but for all *The People*. I remember thinking, how pure the sound of his voice was, as it rose up from the hush of earth like some sweet singing bird, winged and eager to greet the molten eye of the *Maker*. Each day we give thanks for our gift of life, be it at *Dawn Song*, or in some other more personalised way. The way is not so important, it is the acknowledgment of recognition of life and the spiral, that really counts, or so it is that the Druids teach.

For myself I can only say, that dawn has ever been like a door to me, that sometimes I might find open, and step through into a world beyond, and why should this not be. To a boy seven summers young anything is possible, all magic is attainable. Whilst we dream we live, and walk the *Makers* Spiral of Immortality.

After *Dawn Song*, *The People* dispersed and I stood alone, my head wrapped all about with something I had not the words to define.

All about me glimmered a soft haze of thick, butter yellow light and moist leaf, all a shimmer with dew. Cool it was, though warming as the sun rose above distant, tree thick hills and filled our valley with soft heat and light.

Our town was the principle town of the 'Arverni.' It lay in a pleasant valley protected on either side by a series of low wooded hills that bore the brunt of winter's ravening winds. To the south of the town the hills and woodlands gradually gave way to a thick forest of dim green light, faint trails and misty airs. A wide shallow river wound its way through the valley, flowing in from the north in a lazy, meandering sort of way. Eventually losing itself in a haze of distance, as it flowed on, towards the sea like some giant glistening serpent, full of coils and loops of sun spangled skin.

Free I was, with no hand restraining me when sometimes I walked the hills alone, or sat high upon a rocky shoulder overlooking the town in its valley's cradle. I would lose myself then, in a beauty of sunlight upon moving water, or follow with detached eye the upcurling feathers of blue smoke, drifting like mist upon windless airs from the town's cooking fires.

Young though I was I had at times, or so it is I like to think, a poet's eye for the beauty of the pattern and the *Makers* casual tangle of weaves. Young I was, I saw only the beauty of our land and gave no thought at all to the blood cost of its keeping. But then, I was barely seven summers old and the ancient king of dreams, had I think, taken up permanent residency inside my head. Of Roman cruels and hates, I knew nothing at all.

Even so, my childhood was short. Ending abruptly upon as fine a day as ever the *Maker* has gifted. Short it was, more so than other boys of my age, who had not yet riddled their calling.

Amongst *The People*, childhood ends when a boy unriddles whatever it is he is to become and do in this life. Be it warrior, or a recognition of skill to bake fine bread, or seed the soil. It is this way for females too, who are of course our equals in all things. After all, it is a truth sealed beneath the *Makers* eye, that we all know what it is we want from one life to the next. It's just that sometimes it can take a chain of seasons to recognise what it is. Some there are, who never find the truth of their life and die unknowing. At least so I have heard, though I can scarce believe it true, it would be so wasteful and an ultimately, joyless existence. Like carrying around an unopened gift. You deny yourself the pleasure of inspecting its contents for the whole of a single life, and who is to say you will fare better the next time. True it is you can only come to incipient awareness through love and approval of self. That is, of course, the unopened gift upon which an expanding self awareness resides. It is the first of all barriers to be overcome as we tread the Spiral of Immorality. So it is that Druid teach.

The morning of my last day of childhood, was a fine amber coloured morn, with a soft feel of warmth about it. A small breeze carried a pungent smell of crushed heather and fresh baked bread, causing my stomach to growl as I stamped and whirled, slaying my imaginary enemies with consummate ease.

My father, a high born warrior of renown, who always wore a torc of hammered gold around his neck, and arm bands of silver, gold and enamelled bronze, had made a long sword of wood for me. Being uncommonly tall and strong for my age, I think it was his hope that I would choose to follow his footsteps along the warrior's glory road.

The pattern weaved otherwise, but of course he didn't know that, nor for that matter did I.

I once heard him say to his friend Streng, who was himself a superb warrior, that if *The People*, did not soon change their method of warfare it would be used against them to the utter ruin of all. Streng laughed, incapable, or so it seemed, of being able to envision defeat, or *The People* as a broken subjugated race. Of course no one at all took the slightest bit of notice of my father's words, concerning our method of warfare. He never mentioned such a radical idea ever again and became the grimmer for it.

In the years to come I would rue the folly of my people's unbreakable, honour bound traditions, whilst at the same time, loving them for their uncompromising adherence to, the *Way*.

I had yet to learn of Roman Loathes, Cruels and Hates. Those small, supremely arrogant men with devouring eyes, who are, or so I believe, ruled by the Gaunt Man — Crom Cruach, Bowed One of the Mound.

The heavy wooden sword felt good in my hand, like a true weight of steel as I shuffled and danced the *steps of courage*, midst swirling clouds of sun sparked dust cast up by my stamping feet. I had not yet mastered the true swordsman's lightness of tread, but then, I was still a child whose inner visionary feats far out matched mere physical limitations.

As always, the sword hilt felt familiar, and for the space of three heartbeats a vision filled my head. It sometimes came to me during weapons practice, though I have yet to unriddle the reason why. The Druid Dream-Seeker, could I am sure, explain it to me, but I had not the courage to ask, thinking in my foolishness that he would not be wanting to be pestered by a child, over a single recurring vision. I know now of course that it wasn't a vision at all, but only a reminder of a far memory resulting from the familiar feel of a sword hilt in my hand.

I was tall and dark of skin with long flowing hair, black as a raven's wing. My mouth was open in a soundless scream of defiance as I faced a charging mob of armed men. Behind me a huge door of bronze closed with a hollow thud of finality. The long sword in my hand gleamed, its blued steel blade catching and reflecting the sun in drips and bobs of light, as I held it before me. I had a targe, a small round shield of metal strapped to my left arm, its surface polished mirror bright, the round edge of it honed to sword blade sharpness. To one, trained in its use, a targe is a deadly weapon as well as a shield. I used it well in defence of the great Library of the Desert, of which I was its principle guardian. I sensed there were others fighting beside me, but inside my head I saw only myself and those I fought. My name was Tabath, and the outcome of the battle I cannot recall. Perhaps I died, perhaps I did not. It is, I think, of little importance, being only one memory, amongst countless memories of previous lives we are able to recall. We are after all, tenants of houses of flesh again and again as the pattern wills, and the only truth that remains when flesh grows cold is *the way*. The Spiral of Immortality and the way of its walking.

Beneath a clear, deep blue sky full of sunlight and small lost winds, I stamped and whirled, lunged and parried, delivering a series of sweeping blows that made my wooden blade sing as it cut through the air.

Tranced inside my head, I imagined myself to be Lugh-of-the-Long-Spear, an ancient Champion of the Arverni, who it is said, defended the Hall-of-Heroes alone against invaders. He challenged them all to single combat, laying geasa (a taboo or promise) on them to ensure they could not refuse and still retain their honour. He killed and defeated twenty one of the invaders before they decided that the hall and its treasures really wasn't worth the taking. Lugh, it is said, rescinded his bond of geasa and allowed the survivors to depart with honour.

My father says it wasn't an invasion at all, but only a cattle raid that had somehow gotten a little out of hand. Probably, he said, through bad planning and lack of information, because nobody in his right mind would want to go anywhere near whatever it was that Lugh-of-the-Spear was guarding. However that may be, he was a hero, bold and shining and I liked the story, and the deeds the Harper's attribute to him in songs and epics set to harp music.

So it was that I lunged and danced, defeating all my imaginary foes with what I thought of as my swordmaster's skills. After all if you cannot win in your own contrived dreaming, where can you win.

Today my childhood came to an end.

I was seven summers old by our measurement of time, which is the same as the Greeks but different from that of the Roman barbarians, who, having slaughtered the Etruscans and taken their lands, model their ways upon the very ones they defeated, an oddness, no doubt due to their lack of spiritual awareness. Growth is, after all, a compound of many nuances. Foolish are they who judge nations only and solely upon the height and thickness of their walls.

I think me that Romans are not comfortable in the living flesh of their house. So it is that they strike out like frustrated children, and in their spirit blindness seek to destroy nations who offer them no harm, beyond a refusal to trade or bow down to gods, other than their own.

Being seven summers old I was of course already familiar with and at ease within my own growing house, and remembered with an easy clarity, my tenancy of a previous house of flesh, but then, excluding Roman Cruels, who cannot.

We of the Arverni are, I think, more fortunate than most, in that we are, more often than not rebirthed within our own tribe. It is I like to think, because our Druids take especial care to instruct us in this wondrous mystery of the pattern.

Druids of other tribes such as the Helvetii and the Nervii focus on transition with little thought given to location. Though I dare say it all turns out as the *Maker* wills. *The People* are constant and one tribe is probably just as good as another, even though we, in our pride, do not like to think so. The pattern weaves irrespective of men and their foolishness. Having lived as a Celt, a free person, who would wish to choose otherwise.

The Greeks have lost their way and no longer recognise the pattern, or the Spiral of Immortality, at least that is what Cumall the Druid says. Whilst the Romans are nothing but Cruels and Hates, literate barbarians, Cumall calls them, who at their best are little more than educated savages. Spirit children in adult bodies, who one day will despoil the world and give credence to false greatness.

The People love and revere children, after all they probably knew them in a previous life, that is why there are no orphans amongst us. Left parentless, for whatever reason, children are immediately cared for by the whole tribe, and if over the age of five, it is their right to choose, if so they wish, with whom they will live. Romans kill children, enslave and use them in strange perversions we of *The People* cannot comprehend. It is I think a measure of their spiritual sickness. Indeed, as I grew within the Nemeds, the sacred groves, I came to understand that any nation condoning the enslavement and slaughter of hundreds of thousands of men, women and children within the walled confines of the arena and, looking upon such horror as casual entertainment, is sick within itself and sows the seeds of its own destruction.

Still and all I could have wished my childhood longer. The pattern it seems wove otherwise.

Celtic Sunset

Fire bloomed inside my head as I struggled against my imaginary foe. Steel sparked against steel in a raspy sort of ring. Dust, and sour, fear induced sweat, mingled with the hot brassy smell of blood, filling my nostrils, coating my mouth and tongue with a foul coppery taste. It was death and joy upon a wild winged flight of heroes, alight with sunglow and the jewelled eyes of heaven. It was real, I lived it inside my head. A compound of memory and boyhood dreaming. Dark green leaves enamelled orange-gold beneath a hot summer's sun. Sultry air, thick with reeking flesh and the honour wounds of a Champion, standing alone against the invading hordes. Ah, it is good to be a child amongst a people able and willing to let a child be a child, with no pretensions otherwise.

Celtic I am, and I will always be a free person of *The People*, at least so it is I used to think before the rude world of adults and reality forced its way inside my dreaming head.

Ψ

Immersed in my game, it wasn't until a shadow blocked out the climbing sun, that I realised, in a dim far off sort of way, that someone stood before me. Inside my head feathery whisperings died away as my vision refocussed upon the real world of human kind. I could feel the hard, sun baked earth beneath my booted feet.

Tall he was, silent, with a grim look about him, as he stood there, outlined against the sun and a backdrop of sky, blue as a robin's egg. His long, thick white hair lay loose about his shoulders, blazing like white fire beneath the sun. He wore a white robe and a fine green leather Belt-of-Calling about his waist, with a buckle of enamelled bronze, blue it was with the spiral of Immortality outlined in gold.

Suddenly, inexplicably, my heart lurched and my guts knotted with tension. I recognised him now, though before this moment I had only seen him from afar, an aloof, commanding figure who walked in the company of Kings.

Cumall, he was, Chief Druid of the Arverni.

'Why was he here?' I thought wildly, standing in front of a seven year old boy. I felt the skin of my face tighten. 'What have I done that is so terrible it warrants the attention of the Chief Druid.' Panic welled up inside me, as I desperately tried to think of what it could be, of how, in my ignorance, I might have given offence. Suddenly, seemingly out of nowhere, recognition flared inside my head, if not for my far dreaming, I would have recognised it before.

The Druid was wearing his robe and Belt-of-Calling. Druids only wore Belts-of-Calling when they intended to claim the right of (spiritual) recognition. A rare honour indeed. Though of course the one claimed has the right to refuse Nemed training. We are after all a free people, and the Nemeds, sacred groves, are a world unto their own. But who, I thought, has he come to claim? Certainly not my father, he was too old and warrior bound. My mother, well no, I didn't think so. She was quite happy being who she was. I had no brothers or sisters, so that leaves — only me. My mouth went dry, my wooden sword suddenly felt heavy in my hand as I slowly raised my head and looked up into the Druid's eyes. His gaze speared my soul.

His eyes had a look of stones beneath water about them, winter grey and chill, and though I strained mightily, I could not break away from his eye lock. Sweat stood out on my brow, heat suffused my face, my head began to ache. My feet felt like stone, deep sunk in earth. A picture formed inside my head, suddenly I was distant memory walking, a time when I was tenant of another house of flesh. How incredibly real it is, I thought in wonder, but then, it was nothing I had not done before.

Tabath, standing alone, his back toward a pair of closed bronze doors, a long sword of blued steel held in a two handed grip. Blood trickled down his body from a score of open wounds. His voice rose, above a sound of stamping feet, in a mighty roar of rage. His unbound hair flowed down his back, challenge to any man who thought he could take it.

Of all the defenders of the great library, he was the last. Honour bound to defend his trust with his life, he grinned like a jinn at the advancing warriors, and stepped forward to meet them.

Tabath's 'thousand' lay dead, or dying amongst untidy heaps and kicking mounds of the enemy. The carnage was unbelievable. The smell of blood and ripped out guts, mind numbing. Vultures wheeled high and above, patiently waiting to start their grisly feast. Tabath was well content.

His 'thousand' had cut down over six times their own number, since first the rays of morning sunlight had brushed the huge, sandstone walls of the library with rosy gold fingers.

Tabath could not betray his trust, he didn't know how. The very idea itself was alien in concept to his thinking. His only regret, was that he would die beneath the blades of a crazed army of stinking desert shepherds. No matter that they styled themselves Shepherd Kings, they were, he knew, honourless. A rag-tag army of sheep herders, intent upon destroying all forms of knowledge that was not in sympathy with their own. The great Library of the Desert was the last bastion, it was also empty, or nearly so. The *Brotherhood of the Book* had already spirited away its contents, stripping the halls and endless alleys of books with incredible speed and efficiency.

No one knew where the books were taken, no one bothered to ask. It was enough to know that they were safe, stored — somewhere.

Tabath, and his 'thousand', had chosen to remain and fight a holding action only. Buying time for the fleeing scholars to cross the desert to the safety of the river cities. Even so, the sheer size of the Shepherd Kings army, swept Tabath's breath away. He would be lucky indeed, to delay the advancing army for the passing of a single hour of the sun's moving shadow.

Delay them he did. From dawn, all through the day and long into the breathless hush of a blood eyed sunset.

Tabath and his 'thousand' preformed a stupendous feat of arms that gave birth to a legend. And like the *Brotherhood of the Book* and, the Great Library of the Desert, legend fell down the centuries into myth, until the many denied that the few had ever existed at all.

Celtic Sunset

They crashed into the charging Shepherd Kings with a sound like rolling thunder, as a thousand shields smashed against thousands of shields. Tabath and his 'thousand' swiftly formed a defensive square, with a flying column of ten at its centre, to plug any breach. They fought like heroes against overwhelming odds and stopped the advancing army in its tracks.

Above the din of battle, a single voice cried out again and again, urging the Shepherd Kings on, exhorting them to destroy utterly, the unbelievers, who dared to oppose them in their righteous destruction of all false knowledge. The voice urged the howling shepherds on, in the name of God and all his prophets. The words themselves were a blasphemy of violence, that shrieked up towards a silent sky devoid of approval.

As the hours bled by in vociferous fury, the shepherds sheer weight of numbers ground Tabath and his 'thousand' down into hacked and bloody lumps of twitching meat. Slowly they pulled back, falling in ones and twos, until Tabath stood alone with his back to the great bronze doors of the library. His huge body covered in sticky gore from head to foot. His sword a gleaming slick of red in the lurid glow of a sullen setting sun. Tabath made his stand bathed in the sun's angry fire, eerie it was, and frightening.

The Shepherd Kings had thought to roll over Tabath and his 'thousand,' squashing them like ants beneath booted feet. It was only now, as the longest of all days neared its end, that they realised they were broken. More than half of the shepherds soldiers lay face down in the desert sands, or stared unseeing, up into a darkening sky. A wailing cry of shock, fear, and horror spread through decimated ranks. The shepherds looked at each other in disbelief. How could this be? How was it possible for a 'thousand' to destroy six times their own number? They were unable to comprehend the magnitude of their defeat. Born as it was, out of an unthinking foolishness, that claimed their God of the desert was supreme, and all other Gods false. They had assumed, with arrogant ignorance, that they were invincible.

Tabath and his 'thousand,' bound in honour and a steady belief, that all men have the right to pursue knowledge, and the right to freedom of worship, forced the Desert Kings to think otherwise. Realisation shocked them to their core.

A terrible weight of silence fell over the survivors of the Shepherd Kings' army. Hot sultry air tainted with the reek of blood and vomit, stung crying eyes.

Horror gripped stuttering hearts in awful hands. Sanity began to replace righteous insanity. Somewhere behind the silent soldiers, a gaunt shadow slipped away noiselessly, merging into the desert's gathering gloom.

Tabath charged, his war cry shattering the silence, long black hair streaming out behind him like some unadorned banner of defiance. Men moved out of his way, unwilling to meet his whirling sword.

Stained they were, doomed for the sin of pretence, enforced with violent intent upon others, who offered no harm, no opposition to their right to believe in and follow their own chosen God. Theirs was the price to pay. There is always a price to everything, even unto the smallest of beliefs.

Tabath hewed down unresisting flesh. His stomach heaved as he danced, and whirled, 'fight' he screamed, 'fight desert turds, fight.'

A cold voice, loud and clear, rang out. 'Kill me this unbeliever.'

No one moved or spoke.

Celtic Sunset

Tabath's sword hissed through the air and — stopped in mid stroke. He looked about him. His dark face shone like a devils mask, in the ghastly glow of a red flaring sun, sinking slowly below the horizon.

The cold voice spoke again. 'Kill me this dog of an unbeliever — NOW.'

Tabath grinned and advanced soft footed towards the speaker.

His blade hummed as it arced through the air, slicing cleanly through the fanatic's neck. His head leapt into the air, and then falling, hit the sand with a dull wet thump, rolling to a stop against a fallen shepherd warrior. Using his hands, Tabath scooped out a shallow hole in the sand, kicking the lifeless head into the hole, he said softly, 'You used man's fear of the unknown against them.' He spat three times, once into each staring eye and once into the mouth of the bloodless head.

'Let this days weight of death be upon you,' Tabath spoke in a harsh ringing voice that cleaved through the heavy silence like a flame. 'For you and others like you, redemption is a kindness you may never find, and I am not saint enough to forgive you, not ever.' With a casual flick of his foot, he kicked sand into the open sightless eyes of the severed head.

A great sigh escaped from those around him as though they awoke from some strange dark dreaming. Tabath turned on his heel and walked away into the desert and the feathered arms of a hushed and gathering night.

The Library of the Desert is legend now, but the spirit of Tabath remains.

Eyes, grey as winter stones bored into my skull, and then, with a slight smile playing about his lips, he released me. I

73

felt strange, remote and warm and sure. My calling, my recognition of self.

Soft voiced, the Druid said 'Your boyhood ends this day, Culann of the Arverni.'

He strode off then, towards our house, calling out in a loud voice for my father to stand forth. I followed behind him, my heart thumping away inside my chest, with a sound like a great hollow drum. Fear and excitement coursed through me, and a bit and piece of wonder for the coming unknown.

My father heard only the loud and commanding tone of the Druid's voice. Thinking himself challenged, he rushed out of the house, a battle cry upon his lips, long sword swinging in a two handed grip, his dark unbound hair streaming out behind him. My heart leapt into my mouth, I truly thought he was going to attack the Druid, so fierce and swift, did he come.

Recognition flared in his eyes, 'Oh! it's you Cumall.' He sounded disappointed, but then, he was a warrior, a professional fighter, proud of his skill. Lowering his sword, my father stuck it point down into the dirt, and extended both arms in an open gesture towards the Druid, hands open, to show that he held no weapon and stood unarmed in the presence of a guest-friend.

My father smiled then and said, 'Cumall, my friend, next time you come a calling, moderate your voice. You sound like a young bull in heat.'

The Druid's eyes twinkled, 'Ah,' he said, 'if only I was, but I fear me the fires burn low with age,' his laughter filled the air.

'Talk so to others, but not to me, Cumall. I know you too well,' my father said with a smile. 'You'll live forever Druid, and you know it.'

Celtic Sunset

My father was a handsome man, tall and broad of shoulder, with a deep chest and the thick muscled arms of a warrior in peak physical condition. 'Prime, he is,' so it is I have heard others say. During arms practice and in combat, he moves with the easy grace of a dancer, all fluid motion and deadly skill. He was a Champion, and proud. He was also a Celt, a free person of *The People* flamboyant, boastful and loud, wearing a fortune in precious metals about his neck and arms. His hair unbound and flowing, a challenge to any who thought they had strength and skill enough to take it. He no longer used war paint or tied feathers in his hair. It had of late, become unfashionable. Like all *The People* he was possessed of incredibly good manners and politeness where guests were concerned. Recognition and banter complete, my father welcomed the Druid into our home.

'My house is yours,' he said formally, 'your enemies are my enemies whilst so ever you sit beneath my roof.' He then lay geasa upon himself not to break or dishonour, guest-law, whilst so ever his guest remained. 'May the earth open and swallow me, the sea rise up and drown me, the air poison me, the sky fall down and crush me, if so I do not honour my given word.' Formalities complete, my father stood quietly, politely waiting for the Druid to enter our home, or otherwise speak of the reason for his unannounced visit. The Druid was, after all, second in rank only to the king and was not, Culann's father knew, in the habit of wandering around town paying surprise visits without a reason.

Cumall said, with a small smile playing about his mouth, 'Rest easy friend, not this day will I drink your house dry. Now is not the time, and besides, there is good reason for my being here.'

The Druid stood tall and straight. He possessed a degree of presence, denied to lesser men, power rippled the air around him. To my young eyes he was awesome, exuding a kind of majesty denied to Kings. You could almost feel his presence.

In the years to come, I too, would master the secret of concentrating the whole of 'being' into a single location in time and space. Some men do it through anger, Druids learn *the way* of it, at will. It aids the bodies healing amongst other things, and can sharpen the mind to hitherto unknown levels of clarity. Cumall spoke in the formal, bardic way, that carries and yet seems not over loud. His words changed the entirety of my life.

'I am here to claim Culann, your son, by right of Druid recognition.'

My father's mouth dropped open in stunned astonishment. Of all the reasons he could think of for the Druid's unexpected visit, this was not one of them. To have a Druid claim spiritual recognition of a son or daughter was a great honour not to be lightly tossed aside or otherwise dismissed. It was not unheard of amongst the tribes for a Druid to claim recognition of a son or daughter, but it was rare, very rare indeed, and usually only happened when the one recognised was needed for a specific purpose, relative to *The People*. Not even a king could command a Druid to reveal that purpose. Awareness of its existence was deemed, enough, for anyone to know, outside the Druids circle.

My father's chest swelled with pride. It was an unlooked for honour, that would reflect upon his clan for generations to come. The tribe of the Arverni was in need, and flesh of his flesh had been chosen to fulfil that need.

My father breathed in deeply, swelling his already powerful muscles. He drew himself up to his full height, squared his shoulders, looked the Druid straight in the eye, and said in a loud ringing voice, 'Druid right or no, you cannot take the boy if he is unwilling to go.'

Celtic Sunset

Knowing what it must have cost my father to say that, my heart came nigh to bursting with love of him, and pride for his thought of putting me before the honour. There are some amongst us who would not have done this. Fortunate am I, to have his caring.

I could see that Cumall was well pleased by my father's answer and he played his part accordingly, much to the pleasure of the crowd who had by now gathered around us. Important it might be, it was also an entertainment, something that would be spoken of again and again in the years to come. No one amongst the silent crowd wanted to miss a single word, smile or gesture. The News Shouters, would carry the news from tribe to tribe giving faithful re-enactment of the whole of it all down to the last word spoken.

The Druid Cumall gave his familiar half smile and said in a less imperious tone, 'Why don't you ask him?'

The Druid and my father turned towards me. Cumall smiled knowingly. My father hesitated, his eyes seemingly all aglow in the rich morning light. The silence of the gathered crowd deepened as they waited expectantly for me to answer what had not yet been asked.

The summer sun poured down its heat and haze of gold, striking the hard packed earth in bouncing points of light, like arrows and lances of the small fey folk of dreams and deep forest hauntings. Small thoughts rattled around inside my head like stones in a metalled drinking cup.

'My life will end this day,' I thought wildly, 'and a new life will begin. Dare I face the challenge of it all? Am I strong enough? Are my wits keen enough? And the unknown purpose that I must make my own, do I have the courage to run it to its end? Am I worthy?' Fear piled upon uncertain fear inside me, my guts churned. I felt like a spear about to be cast, poised and quivering, into a melee of confusion and incredibly clear light.

I could see Etain, my mother, hovering in the doorway of our house, all a drip with flooding sunlight. Biting her bottom lip she was, her fine steady eyes moisture bright with unshed tears. She looked fine and proud, her long, thick red hair tumbling over her shoulders like living flame from out the core of sunsets. Tall she was and full of a majestic grace. A worthy wife of a Champion.

My mother was also a Rune-singer, a daughter of earth in service to the Goddess whose vaginal blood refreshes the fields and the world upon which we live. She is not the *Maker*, she does not weave the pattern, and yet without her, the *Maker*, cannot dance creation or weave the 'People' a fecund pattern. She is the apple of wisdom, that tempers the oak of immortality. She is the stone within the forest that grows.

Strange it was that I noticed small things and gathered small thoughts whilst all around me 'the moment,' gathered.

The drum beat of my heart was more a fluttering now, like some humming bird captive within my chest.

I would go with the Druid. I would face whatever destiny awaits me and hopefully wrestle it to the ground. I knew I would go when first his eyes speared me. Something had clicked inside my head. As though I had been waiting for that one glance of instant recognition, to know who and what I was or might become. Tabath was a memory flaring white behind my eyes.

I had no doubts as to the road I must follow, none at all.

If I had known then, what I know now, in the final breathing of my body, I think I would have fled screaming into the forest.

Celtic Sunset

When I said yes, in a small quavering voice, a great sigh of relief escaped from *The People*. Suddenly everyone was laughing and shouting and slapping my father on the back. Mead and ale appeared as if by magic, and though it was only midmorning, a small celebratory feast was gotten under way.

The Druid came and stood by me, he said, 'Say farewell to your mother and father boy, your old life is no more. From this moment on you begin a new life, and this I say to you Culann of the Arverni. I have seen your destiny. It is uncertain to be sure, though I'm thinking one day it may take you away from *The People* forever, but nothing is certain Culann. That is one constant we can be sure of, nothing is certain in this life. The pattern weaves as the *Maker* wills'. In a softer more friendly voice, he said, 'Your instruction within the sacred groves will not be the same as others you will meet there, but this I can promise you, you will receive the best of specialised instruction. You will not fail, else your destiny fails with you, and a single druidical hope of remembrance for *The People* will not come to be.' His voice trailed off then and he said no more.

I stood within the noise of a happy boisterous crowd, uncertain, fearful and with a taste of sadness within my mouth, for all that I would leave and the love of a family I would no longer share. I didn't understand a single word the Druid had said.

After saying goodbye to my parents and receiving the well wishes of friends, the Druid led me away. I walked in his shadow until he curtly told me to walk by his side.

People waved and shouted greetings to me as we made our way through the town. I couldn't help puffing my chest out just a little bit. Afeard I might be, but I was still child enough to want to strut for awhile.

So it was that I came to the Nemeds, the sacred groves, during the summer of my seventh year. It was the first day of Lugnasadh (August). Start of the midsummer festivities.

That night, as I lay upon my pallet, in the Druid's round house, I wondered if my training would take the customary twenty one years to complete

Ψ

CELTIC SUNSET

Chapter Two

You do not need religion.
What you need is its reminder of 'The Way',
to progress along the Spiral of Immortality.
Whilst this is not the province of religion,
it is intrinsic to its nature,
independent of dogmatic ideologies.

Culann
(From his dissertation on The Fourfold Way)

We lived alone, Cumall and I, in a round house at the edge of the forest that borders our town. Behind the round house, footpaths led every which way towards the sacred groves.

Every morning at sunrise, a young Druidess in training would appear. She prepared our meals, washed and repaired our clothing, cleaned the house and in general did whatever Cumall told her to do.

There were other trainees in the groves, some from distant tribes I had not heard of before. They lived altogether in a single lodge, and thought it strange that I should live in the round house of the Chief Druid. They made no fuss about this, as it was generally known, that I was receiving special instruction for a purpose unknown, but none the less having something to do with *The People*, apart from an odd hand fight or two, I was left alone.

At first I missed the companionship of other boys my age, and then I did not. Content with the Druid's company and the sometimes meetings with others in the Nemeds.

Cumall became my mentor, guide and teacher in most things, except for some of the lesser, more basic disciplines, that he deemed others competent enough, to teach me.

He was a hard man was Cumall, with no give in him at all. Impatient with fools and unthinking men. He none the less, seemed possessed of an endless store of patience when dealing with me. He said it had to do with my 'purpose'. of which I of course knew nothing. I asked him about it once. It was one of the few times when he gave me no answer at all. Simply stood there and looked at me he did, through those queer coloured eyes of his. Once he said to me, 'With training there is a chance, without it, you have no chance at all. You will fail and die beneath a Roman sword.'

I didn't think I would, die beneath a Roman sword, I mean, but I didn't tell him that. Me being a boy and all and not yet come to my strength. Besides, who but a sense fled fool would dare to disagree with the Chief of all Druids. Even so, I found his words discomforting to say the least.

My first few seasons in the Nemeds were mostly taken up with weapons training. 'First,' Cumall said, 'we forge your body until it sings and thrums like some fine tempered blade, and then we hone your mind. I'll be rasping away at it until you can bend and weave and unriddle the way of all I set you to do. And then young Culann, when I'm thinking your ready, we'll start you along the third path, the *Treas Fillim Slighe*.' (Three Fold Way). 'I gave promise,' he said, 'laid geasa upon myself to see you through. You'll not be failing lad, not ever,' he said with a hot edge to his voice. 'Besides,' he added softly, 'It was I who recognised you at birth and then waited the customary seven years before claiming you.' He paused for a heartbeat and then said softly, 'I know who you are. Your line is long and ancient, older than *The People* even. You'll not be failing, you don't know how.' He gave me that half smile of his and that was an end to it, my introduction to training, I'm meaning.

Seven of days fell down the long sky and became thirty, and the thirty became seasons that bled into years. It is hard for me now, to realise just how swiftly those first few years fled by. Like stallions they were, racing the wind across an open sun drenched plain.

I remember with a smile now, my surprise, that first cool, dew wet morning of my weapons training. I had envisioned the Druid Weapons Master to be a tall lithe warrior like my father. At first I thought I had lost my way and entered the wrong training grove. A slim woman of middle height and pleasing form stood in the centre of the grove. Early morning sunlight making of her dark hair a bright and shining wing, laying as it did across one shoulder, the plait of it all bound around with green and white strips of cloth. She wore a short red fighting kilt that ended well above her knee. Young as I was, I could not help but admire her long, shapely, honey coloured legs. A thin piece of woven cloth bound her breasts. She stood before me, legs apart, hands on hips and a mocking smile on her face. Her teeth were small, white and even. Her eyes pale blue with a distant look about them.

Roy Edwards

Cold they were, and shining, like broken chips of ice beneath a warmless winter sun, she was beautiful, in a high cheek boned foreign sort of way. Full lipped she was, smooth skinned and glowing.

I stammered out an apology for my untimely intrusion and turned to leave, trees towered dark and thick all around me, my heart was a jumping spider inside my chest, I was smitten with love for this guardian of the grove. Surely a Goddess she must be, I thought wildly. My love lasted no more that a hands breadth of the suns rising. I failed to notice the weapons laid out on the flattened grass behind her.

Her voice had a sound of a sharp whip crack about it. 'And where are you running off to, little man?'

'Oh no,' I breathed a silent prayer, and turned around to face her, feeling my face flush with embarrassment. We of *The People* come early to gifted moments, whilst I had not yet lain with a woman even in play, I was not unaware of the feelings women arouse in men, having seen couples at their play during the Beltain (May) festivities, that follow the *Deasgnath Earrach* (Rites of Spring). Besides, it had been impolite of me to stare at her for so long before speaking.

'Well,' she asked. 'Do you not know who I am?'

'No,' I replied softly.

She strode towards me halting a few paces away. Her cool appraising eyes looking me up and down as though I were a horse she was thinking of buying, but was unsure as to its soundness of limb and wind.

'Well,' she said again, and then said, 'I might be able to do something with you, if you be Culann that is.'

Before I could reply she continued, 'You've the strong look about you,' then she bent forward and down, looked me straight in the eye and said in a scathing tone 'for a boy, that is.'

Celtic Sunset

I managed to return her intimidating stare without flinching, but only just, my guts roiled. Gathering together what little remained of my courage I said, 'Who are you? It's a Weapons Master I'm to be meeting.'

Her laugh peeled out, filling the grove with its merry sound. 'So little man, it's a Weapons Master your looking for, is it?'

I wished she'd stop calling me little man.

'Well *little man* you have found one.'

My jaw dropped open in astonishment. Of course women fight, but I had never heard of a woman becoming a Weapons Master, of a Nemed. With a cold start, I suddenly realised this was not a game any more and that, as of now, my recent boyish games must be cast aside forever. A part of me died then. Its death, giving birth to something new inside me, something dimly remembered that I just couldn't quite grasp. It was to do with Tabath I think, then the moment was past.

The Druidess said, 'You will call me Bridgit, not Druidess or lady and I will call you Culann.' She smiled, 'Now that you have cast away your boyish fancy,' she added, 'I will no longer call you little man.'

'Was she,' I wondered, 'able to divine my very thoughts, gods, let it not be so,' I thought worriedly.

Bridgit, Druidess and Weapons Master was neither young nor old, and had, I was to learn later, trained my father. In the years to come she would grant me a single gifted moment, a single night of passion, devoid of love, on both sides.

Her skill with weapons was uncanny and smacked of the *Otherworld*, filling most men with superstitious awe and more that a little bit and piece of dread.

She was a killer, whose love of killing had been tempered through Druid training and a mastery of the lower disciplines. Beautiful, cold and distant she was, with ever a trace of cruelty simmering, just below the surface of her mind. She was a battle hag, a war crow, whose killing lust had been leashed. Skills harnessed, and directed towards the teaching of her deadly skill to others, a chosen few, of which I it seemed, was one. She taught me well, I bear the scars to prove it. As one's skill improved, she demanded full contact from her pupils, with no holding back. Death was rare, wounding was not.

Battles, that is, a general melee, demands different moves from those used only in single combat. Bridgit devised a method combining the two, to the utter consternation of our enemies. At least, that is how it was before the invaders came. The world has moved on since then, and I have grown old in a strange far away land. Even so, old though I may be, my body still retains knowledge of the sword dance, though I doubt I have strength enough left to dance it.

I spent my life, at least that is how it felt at the time, acquiring warrior skills I did not think I would ever have need of, and waited for the day Cumall considered me ready to hone my mind, as he put it. The day never came and so — I continued.

She walked like a cat, lithe and predatory, seeming to flow over the ground towards me. The blade of her long sword pointing down towards my feet. Her eyes had a feral glow about them, mouth pulled back from her teeth in a silent snarl. I began to sweat, gripping the hilt of my sword the tighter.

Cumall had laid geasa on her when first she had agreed to come to the groves, never to kill without Druidic sanction.

Celtic Sunset

The thought brought me little comfort as I faced her advance.
I was in my seventh year of training and had long since come
to recognise her moods. This one was the worst of them all,
she would play me, the way some sleek swift cat plays with
a mouse, driving me to the very brink of fighting madness.
When it was over, I would stagger back to the round house,
covered in blood from a multitude of small cuts that she
seemed able to inflict at will, with a casual flick of her sword
point. Cumall always greeted my return from such
encounters with silence. He would look at me, give his odd
half smile, and then return to what ever it was he was doing.

Hazy sunlight poured down upon my head, not this time, I
vowed silently to myself. Today I win, at least that was my
intent. For almost seven years Bridgit-of-the-Sword had
trained me without mercy. Season through endless season,
through the heavy heat of summer and the cold of winter and
on into the green season of growing. For seven years she lay
upon my back like some gripping war hound of death, until I
scarce could tell one year from the next.

Nor would she allow me to leave Nemed seclusion to
attend seasonal rites or take part in the festivals of *The
People*. I missed Imbolc (February), a time of marriage and
feasting and the Rites-of-Prognostication. Not that it
mattered, as I was allowed no free time to celebrate Beltain
(May) and the ritual washing of hands in the fire, burning
within the sacred circle. Nor was I able to take part in the
midsummer games of Lugnasadh (August) in honour of the
Sun God Lugh-Long-Hand, who is called Apollo by the
Greeks. Samhain (November), I did not miss at all, what
with its slaughter of cattle for winters salting, and its nights
of freedom for spirit weirds and haunts. Feast for the Dead
we call it. We celebrate its end on the fifth night (5th
November) with much drinking and feasting around a huge

bonfire, though I dare say it is known by others not of *The People*.

Bridgit was almost upon me.

The day was cool and still, with a thin veil of sunlight hazing the air, softening the outline of tree and leaf. The sun was all melting gold, against a pale milky blue sky. I drew in great lungs full of moist, earth tangy air, as Bridgit came stalking me like death on two legs. Beautiful she was, with silent sunlight all around her. Her blade gleamed as she moved it in small mesmerising circles, the point of it flashing now and then, as it caught bits and pieces of light pouring out from the sun, in rivulets and runs of melting, butter coloured light. Beautiful she was, a cold and deadly killer without remorse. Mistress of the ultimate dance, her eyes glittered like ice shards beneath a winter's moon. I gripped my sword, my feet sliding into familiar steps without conscious thought. I began a pattern that would bring me close to the outside of her sword arm, she countered it with contemptuous ease. Sparks flew as our blades crossed, filling the air with a ring and rasp of steel sliding along steel. I broke away and launched a clumsy, round house swing. As she ducked under my blade I suddenly flicked the point down, its tip nicked the lobe of her ear. She gave a spitting snarl of rage and turned on me with a vengeance. For the first time in seven years I had drawn her blood, a scratch only, but it was her blood not mine, that dripped like ruby droplets upon the smooth, honey coloured skin of her shoulder. And then it was all stamping feet and the clash and ring of steel. I held her off, much to her surprise and mine. I began slowly, to shift the pattern of our moves, and then it came to me, as though it had been waiting for such a time as this, for me to reach a certain level of sword skill, and the skill of it all acting like some mystic key that unlocked knowledge already gained, long and long ago in some ancient, distant smeared life.

I moved with an easy grace into a new and completely different pattern, not of Bridgit's teaching, whilst at the same time keeping her blade away from my flesh. We fought as if in slow motion, and yet, our blades flashed like the quicksilver of Greek magicians. Parry and thrust, feint and lunge, blow against counter blow, and all the while memory without vision flooding through me.

Bridgit's face contorted with rage, her eyes disbelieving the art of my defence. Now it was I, who held her back, as she tried again and again to break through my defence. And all the while, ancient memories of arcane sword dance sank deep into my muscles, guiding without thought, hands and feet and swaying body. I knew without knowing how, that in moments I would switch to the attack. Blood sang a hot wild song in my veins. I began, what I would later come to know, as the *nine hand step*, the like of which *The People* had never seen before.

I gulped air, my strength easy in me now, and the once heavy sword, light in my hand. Not yet come to my full height and strength, I none the less looked down upon Bridgit. I, who once looked up into her cold, hauntingly beautiful eyes. I have always been tall for my age, with a good breadth of shoulder about me. Seven years of continual training had put a weight of muscle upon my back, deepening my chest and thickening my arms. I stood nine hands high (6'), and would in the fullness of time stand nine and one half hands (6'4").

Bridgit wore a look of desperation about her face, though I was pleased to see the killing glaze had gone from her eyes. She be something the world rarely sees, I'm thinking. It was not my intention to kill her, therefore, I held back from the ninth step and contented myself with sending her blade spinning from her hand.

She looked shocked her face ashen, she said, in a low voice, 'Never in my life has another disarmed me.' And then to my relief she laughed and came forward to embrace me, saying, 'Culann of the Arverni, you are your father's equal, I'm thinking. You may even be better than he in time. Perhaps,' she mused, 'you already are.' She looked up at me with an impish smile. 'Would you be accepting a gifted moment from me now?'

I stared at her in startled wonder and delight, my loins tightening at the thought of her naked flesh.

'Here, *now'* she said, 'upon this field of weapons, midst blood and sweat and the sweet smell of it all. Lay thee down Culann,' she husked softly as she slipped out of her battle skirt.

And so I did.

Bridgit is legend now, she died a terrible heroes death. Those of *The People* who yet remain, hold a feast day once each year upon the day of her death. In this way they honour her memory and carry it down through the ages. In a distant time yet unborn, a new faith will rise and yet retain remnants of the old. They too will honour the memory of Bridgit, though they change her name for another, the way of her life and death, yet remains — unchanged.

Whilst the memory of her burns like some bright flame inside my head, I will speak of her, though it be untimely I feel she is close. Waiting no doubt, for me to vacate my worn out house of flesh.

Celtic Sunset

When the barbarians, the Roman Cruels, invaded our lands, Cumall removed the geasa that bound her, to fight and instruct only within the Nemed of her rule. He turned her face toward the invaders and unleashed her, saying 'Take what weapons you need and any warriors who might follow you and go.'

'Go' he commanded, 'and kill'

She smiled then, and all that once was leashed, sprang free, like some slavering war hound.

Bridgit led a small tight band of young warriors, who cared not at all for the honour of single combat. They swore blood oath and bound themselves with geasa never to betray or abandon their small group. I think they in their fancy, thought Bridgit 'Goddess' upon Earth so clearly did they worship her.

Upon my behest they agreed to spend a few days within a weapons training Nemed, before setting out. There it was that I spoke to them and showed them methods of fighting that lay outside 'The Peoples' traditionally accepted mode of combat. Too few of *The People* were willing to change their methods of fighting, even though it was brutally obvious that such methods failed to halt the invader. *The People's* unwillingness to accept new modes of warfare would be the death of us all.

Many of Bridgit's young men died during their first encounters with the enemy, those who survived became battle hardened veterans, professional killers. Bridgit was more than a simple war leader, well versed in strategy and tactics she used her skills well. Even so, she was the death of any who faced her.

Under her cool leadership, they attacked supply columns and small remote outposts, held by bored and weary legionnaires. They left no one alive behind them, cutting the heads off cooling corpses, they would impale them on long stakes, setting the stakes up here and there along forest trails and roads. The heads would rot swiftly into things of horror. Frightening, so it was hoped, any Roman who might come upon them. Sometimes her band would take only the hair of the fallen enemy. It was a gesture of contempt, though I'm not at all sure the Romans regarded it as such. Scalping, they came to call it.

Bridgit and her group called themselves *An Fiain Oans* (the wild ones) and *Gailiana* (elite warriors). They began to wear war paint on their faces and braid their hair. A few tied feathers of many colours into their braids. The steel of Roman swords was of a temper and hardness superior to our own, except for those made by Boltain of the Nervii tribe, who were later destroyed by the Romans. Indeed, the legions wiped them from the face of the earth, so that no trace at all remained, even unto the death of new born children. Do you not wonder then, why it is we of *The People* named them Cruels, Hates and Loathes, and Caesar be worst of all. So it was that the *Gailiana* eventually discarded their own long swords in favour of the Roman gladius or short sword as it became known.

Bridgit and the *Gailiana* struck terror into the hearts of the invaders, who never knew where they might strike next.

Traditionally, *The People* scorned the use of bow and arrow in combat, deeming it dishonourable to kill from a distance. Honour could only be gained in face to face combat. Indeed, it was not unknown for warriors of *The People* to refuse combat on the grounds that their opponent possessed weapons inferior to their own. Often, in such cases, the warrior of *The People* would re-equip his foe with weapons comparable to his own before fighting and invariably killing him. The bow, therefore, was looked upon as a dishonourable weapon and its use confined to hunting.

The *Gailiana* laughed at tradition and what they considered to be, old fashioned notions of honour. They practiced with bow and arrow in secret glades, hidden deep within the sprawling forest of Gaul (France).

The *Gailiana* attacked desperately, often, against seemingly insurmountable odds, as news of the plight of *The People* filtered through to them. Where once they only attacked small groups of legionnaires, roughly equal in number to their own, they now began to attack and ambush larger groups. Even going so far as to harry the flanks of an entire Cohort (500) on their way to join a legion. The *Gailiana* used the bow to devastating effect. Standing off, and hidden amongst trees and thick shrubs, they shot volley after volley high into the air, creating a deadly hail of steel rain. When the legionnaires moved towards them they broke and fled through the forests, leaving many a Roman corpse rotting behind.

It couldn't last, she was too shiningly bright and eager to kill. Lesser Gods grew jealous and began to grind her bones.

Barbaric savages they might be, but no one, least of all I, could accuse Roman commanders of outright stupidity, especially not those serving under the command of 'The Evil One,' Julius Caesar. He who walks in the shadow of the Gaunt Man — Crom Cruach, Bowed One of the Mound.

Roy Edwards

The Tenth Legion, under the command of Legatus (officer commanding) Titus Labienus, personal heart friend to Julius Caesar, was tired. If he had had his wits about him the incident might not have occurred, and the war against *The People* might not have become a war of total extermination. But then, lesser Gods are jealous Gods and, they had already begun to crack the bones of Bridgit and suck out her marrow.

Bridgit Bright Face, the *Gailiana* called her. An aspect of the Goddess personified upon Earth. They loved her, I think, with the kind of love that soars above physical need. For her they would die. She named then her *Mo'dilieas-cu*, my faithful hounds, which was as close as Bridgit would ever come to expressing her affection.

Titus Labienus, had never known such tiredness, it swamped him like some murky river mist, fogging his mind, drowning his war sense beneath an all enveloping desire for sleep. He was a handsome young man in his mid twenties, above average height, slim, with a mop of unruly blonde hair framing fine autocratic features. His fine boned hands and fingers, were long and sensitive, though his palms were hard and thick with calluses, silent testimony to their familiarity with sword hilt. His eyes were pale blue in colour and failed to recognise anyone of rank below that of Tribune. Imperious he was, with a sort of casual arrogance born out of the belief that anyone who was not Roman, was either a slave or a human animal, whose importance, was about equal to that of beasts in the field. In this he was not unusual, his attitude merely reflecting that of his class.

Titus Labienus made a silly mistake. Though still in what was regarded, as enemy territory, he assumed it was safe.

Celtic Sunset

The main fort that was home to the Tenth Legion, was still a good six hours march away and already dusk was falling. Returning scouts reported the road ahead clear and the area free of any roving Celtic bands. Titus decided to make camp for the night. Holding back a Century, he sent the remainder of the Tenth on ahead, towards the fort.

His Century quickly threw up an earthen rampart. Dug a shallow encircling ditch and lined it with sharp pointed stakes. More stakes were set around the outer perimeter. A single opening in the earthen wall was the only means of entry. Two wooden posts were sunk into the ground and a transportable gate of hardwood quickly erected. The legions were nothing if not efficient. Sentries were posted, cooking fires built, off duty soldiers relaxed. Wine appeared and a pair of dice. To the legions, home was wherever they camped for the night.

The Century of Titus Labienus was under the command of Centurion Jugurtha Sejanus, a cruel and brutal man who had followed the Eagles for almost twenty years. Titus Labienus, heart friend to Caesar, lay down upon a hardwood pallet and fell into a deep, dreamless sleep.

Morning dawned misty, hushed and cloud pale. Smoke from cooking fires curled lazily up into the still damp air.

The legionaries camp lay in a shallow depression on the edge of a small stony plain bordering thick woodlands. To the north, beyond the plain, a range of mountains, small and blue with distance, reared up like broken teeth towards empty sky. To the east, south and west thick forest stretched for as far as the eye could see, green and shiny with moisture it was, quiet, lovely and peaceful. The early morning sun flared, throwing out spears and thick columns of orange-red light before disappearing behind a thick bank of cloud cover.

If there was a sun for the rest of that day, none saw it, as soft veils of fine silver rain began to drift down through the cool tranquil air. Soldiers sat around, cleaning weapons, or breaking their fast, unaware of the eyes that watched from the concealment of the forest. Moisture dripped down from leaf to earth, nothing moved or stirred the forest's breathless hush of violent promise.

Legatus Titus Labienus, was in no great hurry to break camp and move out, he had all day to cover a mere six hours march. 'Be ready to move out by midmorning,' he advised his Centurion.

Jugurtha Sejanus, a cruel, brutal veteran of twenty years, whose cruelty would inadvertently change the course of a war already six years long. Sejanus ruled his Century with a fist of iron, and a reputation for gratuitous brutality unequalled throughout the Tenth. When any of his Century fell in battle, he replaced them with the kind of legionnaire other legions were glad to be rid of, putting them through his own personal induction. 'To find out,' he would say, if they have the stomach to be one of Jugurtha's Century. 'It's hard cases I'm wanting. Not any of yer parade ground boys posturing like tarted up soldiers.' He'd grin then, showing yellow, broken teeth. In an army of tough, competent soldiers, his Century was looked upon with awe. And no one, no one at all, ever stepped forward to disclaim his boast of leading the toughest Century in the whole damned army. The Tenth had a name for them, *Urceus Lupinus* - Jug's Wolves.

Bridgit could not have found a more formidable Century to fight if she had tried. Lesser Gods may move slowly, but the grinding of bones is inevitable.

Celtic Sunset

Come midmorning the legionnaires moved out, grumbling as they did at the fine, misty rain, that slowly, but surely, soaked through everything. Rusting blades in sheaths, and Gods protect any legionnaire Jugurtha found with an unoiled rust spotted blade. Hidden eyes followed their every move.

Of Bridgit's original band, a mere sixty remained. She gave no thought at all to numbers. Six years of fighting perfidious Romans guilty of insensate cruelty towards *The People*, had burnt away her wits.

When she judged the Cruels had marched far and away from their earthen walled camp, she split her small force up into two groups, sending one group flitting through the trees. They would attack the roman Cruels from the rear, whilst at the same time, placing themselves between the Romans and their abandoned camp, in an attempt to deny them the comparative safety of its walls should they attempt a retreat. It may have worked if the Century they faced had been any other than Jug's Wolves.

Bridgit waited until the first group were in position before launching her attack. She gave birth to a legend that day, the world still rings to the sound of her name, different though it may be.

Bridgit attacked, leading her *Gailiana* in a silent rush towards the advancing column. They flowed over the stony ground like wolves closing in for the kill.

Titus Labienus rode a steel-dust gelding, maintaining the standard three lengths distance at the head of the column of marching men. Centurion Jugurtha Sejanus marched two standard lengths behind his commanding officer, leading a

97

Century of legionnaires who marched in step, one standard length behind their Centurion.

His mount gave him an advantage of height, even so, the *Gailiana* were almost upon him, before he saw them slipping through the veiling rain like silent painted ghosts, feathered braids streaming out behind as they ran. His eyes bulged in disbelief, and then, gathering scattered wits, he bellowed out a warning, booting his horse forward, intending to use the horse's bulk to break the *Gailiana* charge. They flowed around his horse in the way that water flows around a stone. As they passed by, one of the *Gailiana* gave a casual back handed flick of his sword, deftly hamstringing the gelding.

Titus Labienus barely had time to jump clear as the horse fell heavily, breaking its neck. White with fury, he drew his short sword and chased after the running *Gailiana*. Sejanus fared better, he was, if nothing else, a thorough going professional who had survived countless encounters from one end of the Empire to the other.

Titus' shout had alerted him to the blurred figures of painted tribesmen coming at him through the rainy mist. A veteran he was, with a veteran's agile mind. He saw his officer go down, and having no idea at all of the numbers he faced, reacted instantly. Bellowing out commands, he pulled his sword free, as the column, moving like some well oiled machine, did an abrupt about face. Sejanus sprinted forward, to its head .

By the time the first of Bridgit's *Gailiana* made contact, Sejanus and his Century were double marching back towards their abandoned overnight compound and the relative protection of its earthen walls. Sejanus hadn't as yet seen the silent braided warriors who stood between him and the camp. Suddenly, three *Gailiana* went down and as many legionnaires. The rest of the *Gailiana* flowed into the gap left by the fallen soldiers, hacking and stabbing. The *Gailiana* wrought havoc amongst the rear of the column. Bridgit was grinning death, her short sword of Spanish steel, honed to razor sharpness, sliced across unprotected throats. Unable to manoeuvre, shocked by the sudden savagery of the attack, the legionnaires fell in bloody heaps, severed limbs twitching like landed fish. Then it was, that Lesser Gods clenched their fists and began to grind bones down into a powdery dust.

Recovering swiftly from the surprise attack the legionnaires at the rear of the fleeing column came to a halt, closed ranks and formed an outward facing square, trapping a few *Gailiana*. The *Gailiana* trapped within were quickly hacked to death. Those outside the square, led by Bridgit, attacked again and again, stabbing over and under shields at Roman groins. Legionnaires fell to be replaced by others, silent cold eyed men who neither asked for, nor gave quarter. The *Gailiana*, too few in number, were quickly cut down, until only Bridgit remained. Titus Labienus coming from behind, knocked her unconscious with the flat of his sword.

Sejanus, unmindful of what was happening behind him, suddenly saw figures looming up out of the misty rain. His feet didn't miss a step, he carried on as though there was no one at all in front of him. He barked out a command, behind him, his men formed a flying wedge as they ran with Sejanus at its apex. He had courage, which is all that can be said of him. His flying wedge, armoured and running, smashed through the unarmoured, lightly armed ranks of the *Gailiana* with horrifying ease. The *Gailiana* rallied, and looking around, were dismayed to find they were alone. Bridgit and her force were down and dying. They were alone, and only the thirty of them there were, it was the end. On Sejanus' command, the flying wedge reformed with unbelievable speed, surrounding the surviving *Gailiana*.

A terrible weight of silence fell over the battle field, as Roman eyed Celt and Celt stared back unafraid and defiant, gaudy and fierce. They were the *Gailiana*, they would die as they had lived, sword in hand, geasa unbroken. War cries fractured the silence, as they leapt at their enemies. Sejanus and his Century were broken that day, and because of what came after, Caesar had the few remaining survivors put to death.

Bridgit awoke to find herself spread eagled and naked upon a hard packed dirt floor. Her wrists and ankles bound to four stakes driven deep into the earth, she lay within a leather tent. Her head throbbed from the blow she had taken, it felt curiously light, her mouth tasted foul and bitter. She moved, testing the strength of her bonds. As she moved, her eyes caught sight of a thick clump of shiny black hair tied to the shaft of a pilum, a light throwing spear, that had been driven, point down into the dirt. The ribbon that bound it all around, looked familiar. Her violated flesh felt cold and clammy, her guts knotted in greasy coils.

Suddenly her eyes grew moist, it was her hair. She growled then in savage fury, the Cruels had cut off her hair, only stubble remained. White fire blazed inside her head, she was alone, nor could she move, bound as she was and naked. She went cold and still. 'NO,' she thought wildly, 'this cannot be, Goddess save me,' she screamed silently. She was bound in a position for rape.

Celtic Sunset

Late that night, coarse, brutal men with bloody hands and the rank stink of death about them, used her the whole night through. Venting their lust and anger upon her bound flesh. She went away somewhere deep inside her head, where only the silent weeping of the grove could be heard.

It is said that Titus Labienus condoned what was done that night, but did not take part. Like Caesar, he viewed cruelty from afar, and considered himself above an acknowledgment of another's pain. Such cowardly men are the cruellest of all.

The night was nearing its end when the legionnaires had done with her. Bridgit had not struggled or screamed at all, which was, they considered a disappointment. The shrieking wail of helpless victims was considered good sport by such men.

Cruel and angry men they were, twelve only had survived the *Gailiana* attack. Questions would be asked. Answers demanded, and if the answers did not please, they would be put to the torture and asked again. Cruel, angry and frightened they were. So it was that they gave vent to their emotions, upon the bound and helpless body of the captured Druidess, whilst Titus Labienus skulked within his tent, shaking and alone, red of eye and sore of heart. His vaunted pride and courage dribbling out between the cheeks of his arse.

We of *The People* consider such to be 'things' not men. Dark of spirit and howling are they. May the moon set upon their bones.

Unmoving she lay, cold and still, no breath of life could be discerned within her. Thick, woman's blood welled out from her secret place, dark, staining her inner thighs and the earth beneath. Torn she was, and bleeding. Within her broken house, a spark remained, like a summer butterfly it was, hovering within the hollow bone of her skull. Thinking the Druidess to be dead, rough hands unbound her and threw the cooling body into a dark corner of the tent, like some bound up sack of old rags. As death she lay — WAITING — the spark within her prayed to the Goddess for life. Life enough to seek death, offering herself as sacrifice. Bridgit's prayer received answer. Lesser Gods moved away, content to have ground their bones of jealous cause. Mother Goddess wept, and placed her breath within Bridgit's skull.

Four legionnaires slept within the tent, snoring and snuffling like pigs in the forest. An oil lamp flickered, its wick almost burnt through, filling the tent with dancing shadows and an eerie curdled yellow light.

She sensed beyond doubt that the pig legionnaires were asleep. Stifling a moan of pain, Bridgit groped with questing hand. Something had torn deep inside her whilst the animals were at their rutting, her hand came away wet with blood. First she must bind herself, ere she bleed to death, and be left owing a Goddess. Questing fingers found the ruin of her war skirt. Slowly, silently Bridgit rolled it into a single thick length, and pulled it up tight between her thighs, staunching the blood flow. Pain it was, fire and ice and enervating. She wound the two free ends around her waist and pulled them tight, tying the ends together in a single knot. She searched for, and found, her breast binding. A glint of reflected light caught her eye, a silent cry of joy belled inside her head. It was her own blade, half hidden beneath a soldiers discarded cloak. Bridgit's hand closed about its hilt like a fulfilment of ultimate promise. A growl of hate laden fury began to build deep down in her throat. She stood in a half crouch, eyes gleaming in the flickering uncertain light, blade extended, dark panther she was. Aspect of the 'unnamed one' on earth new come, seeking vengeance. Warm life blood trickled down her legs, staining bruised flesh. Death she was and herself dying.

For long moments the Druidess crouched unmoving in the flickering gloom, gathering her will, not to live, but to die in a final outpouring of released energy. 'In death do I find my seeking,' she breathed silently. Fear did not touch her, it had no place within her broken house, as all the staining of life fell away. Within her head, spirit soared across 'Freedoms Field,' and became one with 'The Opalescents.' She could see the 'Lord of Perfect Knowledge' standing before an open door of gold. With one hand he beckoned her to come to him, with the other he pointed towards the 'Weaver' who held a single broken thread. Tears of joy spilled down her radiant, ravaged face, 'I be coming,' she intoned silently, 'I be coming lovely one, be you waiting to take my hand.' Tears glistened like pearls on her hollow cheeks.

Bridgit moved in complete silence, and had slit the throat of the fourth legionnaire before the first realised the fountain of blood spraying up into the air was his own. They died, all drumming heels and wet, wheezing breath. The air within the tent grew fetid and foul with a sick sweet smell of warm blood cooling and voiding bowels.

Bridgit paused at the tent's entrance, she felt giddy and weak from loss of blood. Her torn insides were fire and hot forge iron, she bit her lips to quell an involuntary cry of pain as she moved, looking out into a night, dim lit with falling starlight. The camp was quiet, even so she knew there would be sentries posted. As she looked around, Bridgit smiled at the smallness of the camp. She had not known only twelve of the Cruels Century had survived the *Gailiana* attack, and now they were eight.

She heard it then, a distant calling of voice to voice. Bridgit slipped out of the tent and sped away into the night on silent feet. Death reached out with a finger of steel and of all that Century, only six remained.

Titus Labienus sat alone within his tent, hollow eyed and haggard. His clothing foul and reeking of vomit and excrement. Pretty boy lost he was, and deserving of his fate. A minor skirmish had turned into a disaster. This one, he knew, he could not walk away from, or hide it behind his heart friend's power. The loss of a Century was nothing, Caesar expended men in their thousands, and would think the loss of a Century no more than a temporary annoyance.

'No', Labienus thought tiredly, 'it wasn't the number of soldiers killed that would condemn him before the Senate, when he was recalled,' as inevitably he must be, 'it was, what the Senate and Caesar would want to know,' that he had no acceptable answer for. They would ask and demand to know, 'How it was possible for sixty unarmoured tribesmen, armed only with swords, to destroy a fully armed and armoured Century? A Century, they would say that in the opinion of most legion commanders, contained some of the finest professional fighters to be found within the legions of Rome.'

He knew he would be unable to answer such questions, because he simply didn't know the answer. It shouldn't have been possible. The Century should have chopped the Celts into bloody pieces. He looked up, as a draft of cool air touched his face. A shadow slipped by, he turned towards it, and felt a searing tongue of fire run across his throat. His vision darkened, he tried to speak through a gout of blood, it filled his mouth splashing up into his eyes. And then something pushed his head down, exposing the back of the neck. He felt a fleeting instant of incredible pressure and then — his head fell away and rolled across the dirt floor. His last thought was, 'No need for an answer now.' Foolish man, did he think their was to be no reckoning taken in the beyond.

Bridgit swayed on her feet, as the blood stained sword slipped from her hand. A great rush and roar of sound beat around her ears, she felt faint, distant seeming and weak. Blood no longer dribbled down between bruised thighs, it gushed in a red steaming torrent of thick dark blood. I am dying, she thought in a kind of detached wonder. She sat down with a thump on the hard packed earth, her body soaked in blood from the waist down, a spreading pool of it all around her. 'Crimson is the colour of sunset,' she cried out softly, smiling as she watched her life blood drain out and away. 'The pattern weaves as the *Maker* wills,' she husked softly in a broken voice. Her torn, ruptured body spasmed.

As though it came from a great distance, she heard a loud cry of rage beyond the leather walls of the tent, and knew someone had at last found the bodies of the sentries. Centurion Jugurtha Sejanus it was. The unnatural quiet of the camp had aroused his suspicions, dragging him out from his tent in a fury of disturbed sleep. Steel rasped, as he drew his sword. 'Front and centre,' His bellow, shattered the silent night. 'You drunken whoresons,' almost inarticulate with rage he screamed, 'Ah'l 'ave yer, ah'l 'ave yer guts for this.' Four bleary eyed soldiers stumbled through the darkness towards the sound of his voice.

Sejanus felt a cold hand of fear clamp around his heart. 'Gods,' he breathed softly 'Do we be all?' He turned and ran towards the tent of Labienus, fear scalded his mouth with bile. A faint glimmer of grey began to lighten the darkness, as false dawn pushed against night. Sejanus rattled the closed tent flap. 'Sir' he called out urgently. 'Suuur,' he moaned, 'wake up, gods blast yer bloody eyes, WAKE UP yer ferkin idiot, WAKE UP.' If his commanding officer had been killed during the night, Sejanus knew he was a dead man walking. Suddenly a blade lanced through the tent flap narrowly missing his face. He jumped back, knowing instinctively that his worst fear was realised. In the strengthening light he ordered the four remaining legionnaires to gather brushwood and stack it against the tent. Positioning men around the tent, he ordered them to kill anyone trying to break out, and set the brushwood on fire.

Bridgit, her last blow spent, was already dead before the flames engulfed her body. Free and soaring she was, far and away from an empty, broken house of flesh.

Later, after a brief inquiry, Caesar put the four remaining survivors to the torture, to ensure the truth of their words. Then he had them strangled and the bodies dumped in a forest bog. His grief at the loss of his heart friend, turned into implacable rage towards *The People*, the Celts. Returning to Rome, he partitioned the Senate for more Legions. Returning to Gaul, Caesar Cruelheart began to systematically destroy *The People*. Wiping out entire tribes even unto their name. Under his command, and at his express orders, the Legions committed wholesale acts of inhuman cruelty, that have become legendary amongst the histories of the world.

Celtic Sunset

There is much I have not told you concerning Bridgit. Of what she became after her death, in the minds of men. The purpose of her life. The reason behind her lusting passion to kill. Riddle it as you may — for I'll not be doing it for you.

For me it was a day of rejoicing, I had at last bested Bridgit. Sending her sword spinning through the air in a shiny spin-wheel arc. Dumbfounded she was, but I think, a little pleased too. It was then, that she offered me a gifted moment, upon trampled grass, amongst a disarray of weapons. An act of passion, devoid of love. Later, straightening our clothing we were, when Cumall came a puffing and a panting into the grove. How he knew I had at last bested Bridgit, I cannot say. He came into the Nemed all a steam with delight. The face of him shining like a great harvest moon. Though he frowned somewhat when he realised what we had just been doing. He looked away politely, hummed and aarred and then turned to Bridgit and said, 'A chosen one comes to you at dawn's light woman.'

To me, he said with half a smile on his face, 'Tomorrow we shall begin to work upon that weak mind of yours, lad. Come away now, there is nothing for you in this Nemed any more.'

As we walked away, Bridgit called out. 'His name Cumall, what do I call this new pupil of mine?'

'Call him *Vercingetorix*,' Cumall said. 'It means World Ruler or World King, I forget which,' he added absent mindedly.

And that was odd. If there was one thing I knew, it was that the Druid Cumall never forgot anything. He only said he did, more for a convenience than an actual truth.

Roy Edwards

So it was, that my first seven of years came to an end. Nor will I ever forget the Nemed, the Sacred Grove of Bridgit, Weapons Master, killer and something else. Something undefinable, something for which I have no words to express. A thing it is, of the pattern and its weave, I'm thinking.

Ψ

CELTIC SUNSET

Chapter Three

We came out from Darkness
Not as supplicants to the rain
But as joyous spirits
Eagerly seeking harmonious accord
Beneath the eye of the sun
From this came knowledge

OF THE ONE IRREFUTABLE PERMANENCY
INHERENT IN THE UNIVERSE
'THE CONSTANT FIDELITY OF BEING'
IT IS FROM THIS SINGULARITY
THAT ALL KNOWLEDGE IS ULTIMATELY DERIVED

Culann - Circa 12 BC
From the First Law of Druid

Forest, cool and dim. All around me tall, ancient trees reached up towards a serene sky of perfect blue. A thick spread of branch and leaf grew one into the other, blocking out the sun's golden-apple glow. Beneath the trees, filtered light had a look of pale green-stone about it.

Hushed it was, eerie and still.

And I alone within the quiet green heart of it all.

I followed a dim trail that wound its way through the forest to who knows where. So faint and overgrown it was, that if you did not know it was there, I doubt you'd be finding it, or even recognising it for what it was, a path. A path of the old ones who we call *Aonioira Romhainn - The Ones Who Came Before.*

The People do not come here, lest it be an accident of strange circumstance. Afeard of wood-haunts and sprites, they are.

Cumall once told me, that only Druids walk the green-heart. And of those, Druid though they be, some there are who have never returned.

Sometimes, I'm thinking that Cumall enjoys laying fear upon the bones of men. I be not one of them, though he tries, he surely does. Him and his half smiling ways. Friend I am to him now, though it has not always been that way.

Ours is an ancient land, and we an ancient people, who have now lived upon this land for a thousand years and more. Our harpers have songs that tell of an even earlier time, when *The People* lived in a hot and steamy land that is to be found upon the other side of the world. Lived there for over a thousand years so the songs do tell, until the freedom of our ways were threatened by invaders whose skin was not pale like ours, but dark like the skin of trees. Small in stature were they, and as many in number as there are grains of sand. Where they came from we do not know. They spoke not the language of *The People* and we had not the time to learn theirs, ere we be engulfed or utterly destroyed. Strange priests they had, with painted faces of blue, and collars of white metal about their throats. It is said they were able to call down fire from out of a clear sky, causing it to fall like rain upon the armies of *The People.*

Against such magic *The People* could not stand, and so they agreed to leave behind all that they loved, and go out upon the broad face of the world.

And so they did.

Expending long centuries, sometimes here and sometimes there. Ancient Kings of Egypt knew them. Sumerians feared them, for they would not be contained. And decadent 'UR' envied them their secrets of freedom, that not all their armies could compromise, or their wise men divine.

So it was, that as the long centuries wound all about the spiral, we came into this very land of Gaul. Here it was that our wise men, Druids all, advised *The People*, to stay. They said it was *An Naofa Na Fearann,* The Sacred Land of Birth.

Even so, others had come before us. A tall, graceful race, pale of skin, with eyes the colour of grey morning mist and hair the colour of sunset shades and moonlight. *The People* had never seen their like before. They were, so it is told in song and rhyme, the first born of all human kind upon Earth. A mysterious, secretive people. More ancient than dust, who claimed mystic union with this broad, fair land of sheltered valleys, greening trees and clear tumbling waters.

In our legends and songs of distant memory, they are called *Aonioira Romhainn,* The Ones Who Came Before.

They, so we believe, are the ones who raised up the great standing stones to mark their passing, and to identify and contain, doorways of power, within the great circles of stone.

This power, waning though it is, can still be sensed by those of Druid, though we be ignorant of its use. The old ones knew secrets and possessed a wisdom that we do not. They knew of doors and windows in the air, whereby they might pass from one world to another, or so it is that we believe.

When *The People* first came into the land with sharp metal and spear points gleaming, they did not defeat that strange, enigmatic race, who held claim to all the lands around. The did not defeat them in battle, or otherwise displace the grey eyed ones.

They were there — and then they were not.

And through all the years that have bled slowly by, since then and now, no trace of the grey eyed ones has ever been found. No glimpse, not even a breathing sigh, only songs remain, legends and tales of occasional unlooked for help. Stories of strange paths of stone deep within the forest, that seemingly lead no where, and begin where so ever you may find them. Stories of paths with circles cut into the surface of the stones. Stories of paths, amongst whose stones, only one bears a carved surface and that not a circle alone, but a cross enclosed within a circle. Why one path be carved with circles, and another with a cross within a circle no one knows.

I'm thinking Cumall might know. Once, long ago, soon after I began my second of seven years, I asked him one evening, when we were talking of nothing in particular, if he had ever found one of the paths that the Harpers sing of. The only answer he gave me, was that half smile of his and a long quiet talk on Druid symbology, of which the cross within the circle was part.

Long shadows gathered about the smoke hole as he spoke, breathing down the melting wax of a dancing shadow flame. The night drew in and gathered in a hush of darkness all about the round house.

Trees whispered, somewhere a night bird called. Cumall's voice filled my head. The *Otherworld* drew close around us, drawn it was by the weirding wonder that he weaved upon the air.

'Four,' he said, 'is a sacred number. The People of the Sea used it (four cardinal points of the compass) to find their way across the Bitter Sea (Atlantic) long before the Egyptian Thoth (the traveller) taught it to Greek seafarers, who in their turn carried it to the shores of Asia. Hermes, the Greeks called him. It is said that, 'Men who came before dawn,' first had knowledge of it, though they could not count they knew it as that which governed their lives. Earth, air, fire and water from which did come a great and lasting religion. Though it is true, few there are, who now remember its wisdom and the benign rule of the *One King*. The four great paths, or directions (N.S.E.W.) became known as the 'Across.' Knowledge of it helped travellers to find there way 'a-cross' land and sea. Men revered the sign of it. Sacred, it became symbol of *The Four Fold Way* from which our own *Three Fold Way* is derived. The fourth way, the hidden way, remains forever unknown, and no man has memory of its beginning.

It is the final path the *An Bhfolach Slighe*, the Hidden Way, or *Slighe Na Spiorad,* Way of the Spirit, recognised only by the *Walker*. It is a personal thing and different for who so ever shall walk it. It remains therefore, for ever unknown. Some there are, who say it will lead you to the *Maker*. Others say it enables you as spirit to become ONE-WITH-ALL. Warriors call it *Val Na hal,* Hall of Kings or *Tir-na-og,* land of eternal youth, feasting and fighting. It is *Ha-van* (Heaven) and *An Halla Na Foire Feasa,* the Hall of Perfect Knowledge. All are right and all are wrong, it is what ever you consider it to be. Roman Cruels call it *Perfectus,* which is about all you could expect from such barbarians.

I tell you Culann, no one knows. Since the dawn of life, few have walked the way of it. And of those few none will speak. Why should they? Who would understand it if they did? Sense fled, or 'stone rattling in the head,' people would be thinking them. Mad they be, god touched and forever unknown.'

'I do not think,' Cumall said, 'that those who walk the fourth way to its end, remain for long upon this world of men. They rise above the need to inhabit houses of flesh. Unless, that is, they choose to become less than what they have attained to be, so that they might remain amongst men, not shining from within, and strive to teach others of the three lesser paths. Some become prophets or teachers of the *Right Way*. Others claim a gift of sight or a weight of dreams, and strive, if they are able, to steer men away from paths of darkness with unriddling words. Though it be they must contend with Gaunt Man — Crom Cruach, Bowed One of the Mound, for in truth they trespass upon his domain.'

'Of course,' Cumall said with a quirky smile, 'I cannot say if this is true of false.' His quiet, steady eyes never left their regard of me. He said, 'Your study of *The Three Fold Way*, prepares you for your journey along the fourth, though I'm thinking, few progress much beyond the second path. Indeed, my young friend, I have found to my sorrow, that few possess, spirit courage enough, to face the probable cause and sometime effect of their actions throughout their many and varied lives.

Spirit, like body, needs time in which to grow, to learn and mature. It is a thing not easily accepted by many or even considered to *be*. We teach *The People* an acceptance of this as part of their lives. Others, outside *The People*, want only what they can obtain now, thinking they only have one life, they want all and everything today, and end with little or nothing of lasting value, beyond stone or precious metals. Lands they crave, and slaves, and they, all unaware that they be the slaves, living as they do in the shadow of Crom Cruach.

Roman Cruels and Spites gave us the lie when they heard that it takes twenty of years to train a single Harper, and twenty five of years to reach full Druid. They cannot imaging such learning, it is incomprehensible to them, so caught up are they in the here and now of a single house of flesh. They do not believe that a Harper must know, word perfect, three hundred of songs and thirty of three hundred containing two hundred and twenty verses. Barbarians they are, enamoured of stone and war, blood and the ownership of flesh. We are as alien to Roman as they are to us. And I fear me, that one day they will be the death of *The People*.

Cumall's eyes had an empty, far away look about them as he stared into the candle's dancing flame. I wondered if the *sight* was upon him, for in truth his words lay a chill upon my heart, though I be scarce understanding much of what he said. The *sight* is sometimes clear, though more often, vague and shadowy, quick glimpses of things, as though seen through water, pre-visions of what might be seen through a weaving mist of shadows. You are born with the gift of *sight* or you are not. I have it a little and would be rid of it if I were able. Having no liking for unwanted visions, or unlooked for glimpses of this and that.

In the years to come, the *sight* would grow stronger within me, and all the teachings of the second and third path only served to make my inner visions clearer. But that was yet to come.

Cumall broke his gaze away from the candle flame. I mentioned that I was hungry. He grinned at that and said 'A few words more Culann, and I am done for this night. It wouldn't do for me to end without mention of the circle or send you to your sleep wondering about it.'

'How,' I thought, 'did he know that? Can he divine thoughts the way I once assumed Bridgit could. Ah well, no matter, I'll have the way of it myself one day.'

Cumall's voice filled the air about my head like rich dark peat, all loamy and earthy fresh.

'Without landmarks or knowledge of stars to guide them, men move upon the great oceans and land in circles. Lost and wandering, they often return to their point of origin. The land from which they came.'

'Chaldean wise men took note of this and thought upon it. In time they declared the circle to be sacred. It was, they said, a circle of life, of man's birth, life and death in endless repetition. They called the circle *Imor* (immortal, without end) and said that man without knowledge, was doomed to wander in circles for all eternity. Only through knowledge could he harvest truth, break free of the circle, and continue his journey towards unbound freedoms, independent of the shackles of flesh.'

'So it was that the circle came to symbolise a somewhat unclear immortality. A confused mix of physical and spiritual needs, without any clear guide towards one or the other. In time, Priestly knowledge was thought to be the all of the *Way*. When in fact, it was only a single part of a far greater whole.'

'In this, I think, we have progressed beyond the ancients of Chald, in that our knowledge of the existence of the Spiral of Immortality, recognises an ability inherent within all, to change and progress either up or down as a spiritual entity. We became, within limits, masters of our own destiny. From such humble beginnings did we forge the *Way* of *The People*. Whilst others became moribund, seemingly bound without end to an endlessly familiar, repetitive cycle, of life, decay and eventual death within a single house of flesh.'

'To such as they, the circle became a constant wheel of purely physical motion. Lost all knowledge of its sacredness they did, and the spiritual aspect of its cycle. Empirical they became, in the way that Rome is empirical and the Greeks of today.'

Cumall paused, as though lost in thought. His face a mask of shadowed stone. Hard he looked, his face bitter, etched in the fitful candle light. He said, 'Sad it is that so few now live, who can recognise *An Treas Slighe Na Spiorad*, the Third Way of the Spirit, or even acknowledge that it exists at all. Surely,' he mused softly, 'men cannot be so blind to the obvious. But then,' he said in a louder voice, 'we comprehend so little of what we really are. Taking on trust a belief we would readily die for, unlike the ancient Kings of Rome and now it's Senate, who strive mightily, or so it seems, to lambast their people into stupidity and an unbelief in the journey of the immortal *Sprid* (soul or spirit).'

'Know they not that upon this earth, the whole of human kind are incomplete, without at least some knowledge of *An Treas Slighe Na Spiorad*, the Third Way of the Spirit. If'n it be only a vague acceptance of its existence, it is something. A beginning at least, a graspable reality, upon which an Opalescent might work. Be it ever so small, be it dim beyond all sight, it is at least something, which is better than nothing at all. In its absence do we find basic cause for all misery and suffering, and man's continual inhumanity towards man.'

'So it is we teach within the Nemeds, the Sacred Groves of learning, attainment towards light. And we will fight bloody wars to protect our chosen way of life.'

'I tell you Culann, Roman Cruels and Spites denigrate all wisdoms not born of Rome. A contemptuous race they are and a sorrow upon the land, that I'm thinking will not soon be forgotten, and those who come after, down the long years of tomorrow, will see it not at all, and laud achievements born out of an ocean of blood. They will come Culann. I have seen it. Casually dismissing the cruel and bloody deaths of countless thousands in justification of monuments. Culann, I tell you in truth, sometimes the *sight* is a burden, I bear not with ease.'

He gave a half smile, and said in a light bantering tone. 'Pity it is that the Etruscans had not more soldiers to field. They were the better fighters, 'twas only numbers they lacked. Had they defeated the invading Romans, well, I'm thinking they would have remained crushed for ever and the world the better for it. So effective were the Etruscans, in battle, that Rome copied them. The legions of Rome were born of this knowledge, drills, formations, tactics, weapons and armour, all Etruscan. Rome itself is a model, though larger, of an Etruscan city. They even copied Etruscan modes of dress, but then, it is ever the way of conquerors to take on, at least in part, the identities of the conquered. Without Etruscan knowledge, Rome's defeat of Greece might never have happened. Six years it was before the legions stood supreme. The Greeks too few, the Romans too many.

Of all the Greek states, Macedonia was the only one with a standing army. Rome did not face the massed might of a united Greece, they faced only a small standing army of a single state. An army composed of descendants of men who once fought for the Great Alexander, son of Philip of Macedonia. Warriors they were, everyone of them a hero. They held the entire might of Rome's legions at bay for six years. Defeating legion after legion, and those they did not defeat, they fought to a standstill. Rome's leaders had not thought to face such opposition. The legions march in and there's an end to it. And so it was. City states surrendered. Not a one of them opposed the invaders. The vaunted courage and fighting skills of the Greeks seemed not to exist at all. Lysander of Sparta, Alcibiades, Theseus, Pericles, Ulysses, Achilles, ancient heroes, whose spirit seemed not to live at all in the land they once walked. And then', Cumall smiled, 'the legions entered Macedonia and encountered bitter defeat. The war lasted for six years. During which the Macedonians received no help at all from the whole of Greece. No fighting men from other Greek states came to aid them, no men, no weapons, no provisions - nothing. The end of it all was terrible, and marked the Romans for what they are, barbaric, savage and cruel. When, what was left of the Macedonian army lay down their weapons in surrender. The legions put them to the sword. No terms to a gallant enemy did they give. Only death in return for defending their homeland like the heroes they were. Some were crucified, most were simply butchered, until not a one remained alive. Then it was that the legions turned away from what was left of Macedonia and fell upon the city states, who had so meekly surrendered six years before.'

'For the first time in all of Rome's history, the legions were loosed without restraint, and allowed to do what so ever they willed. It was an act of spiteful vengeance, condoned by a Senate of ridiculous men.'

'No one knows how long it was before the legions were brought under control. It is known only that at the end of it, Greece was all but a ruin. Civilians slaughtered in their thousands, children impaled upon spears, women raped. In the year that followed the end of it all, a great many children were born. Swarthy skinned were they, with dark curling hair. Through rape, the invaders destroyed for ever the Hellenic image of tall, fair haired, blue eyed Greeks.

Anyway lad, enough of all this,' Cumall said. 'Get yourself a bite to eat and then off to your bed.'

Here in this new land, it is easy for me to write from a distance of years. Indeed, the more I write the more vivid my memories become. I sit here amongst friends, and feel the warmth of the sun upon my flesh. I am well supplied with food and drink, and in fact, want for nothing at all. I am long lived and known throughout the tribes. When my work is done, two of my friends will take my empty house of flesh to a secret place already prepared.

And the Scrolls.

They too shall rest within my tomb.

Soon, but not yet, there is still much that I would say. True it is, that I fulfilled the destiny foretold by Cumall so long ago. Now the riddling of it lays hidden in the way of Druid.

Ψ

CELTIC SUNSET

Chapter Four

- - - - - belittled and defamed by Caesar,
and the Greek Orestophon
- - - - - we rose above petty jealousies of
spirit-small men, and their idealisation
of Roman Perfectus.

— Culann

Tired I was, when Cumall finished his talking, and me with the young years on my bones. Even so, sleep continued to elude me as I lay upon my back staring up into darkness.

Warm nights we still had. Though in truth Samhain (autumn - November) was not so far away. Outside, I could hear wandering night winds whispering the leaves and sighing softly all about the walls of the round house.

Sleep did not steal easy upon me that night. My thoughts were uncertain, rattling around inside my head. Cumall's words, instructive though they be, filled me with foreboding. I sensed that for all his talk of Roman Cruels, there was much he had left unsaid. Somehow, though as yet I knew not

121

how, my mysterious, unspoken destiny was all a'ravel. Bound up it was, with *The People*, Romans and something else, something beyond Druid, that Cumall spoke of not at all, and I only sensed in a dim, unsettling sort of way. He said I would know it when it came, until then be content and learn, he said.

During my years in the Nemed of Bridgit, I had come slowly to my strength, like a reluctant child called in from play. Cumall had said, when he came for me, that my strength of arm was fine, it was my mind that was weak.

'But not to worry lad. We've the years ahead to strengthen it, and I'd not be sending you off into the green heart, if'n I wasn't thinking you'd be ready.' He said then that I would not learn much of *An Treas Slighe* the Third Way, until I had walked the green heart — and returned. For some do not, he said, though we know not the reason why. Search for them we do, and not a whisper or trace do we find. It happens rarely Culann, but it does happen. So fill yourself with all that we would teach you, let knowledge be both your armour and your sword.

He insisted I learn Latin, that most barbarous of tongues, 'Speak it, read it, write it, he said. The better to know and understand those who one day may become your enemy,' he said. So it was that my studies of Latin, Greek, Ogham and Runes began.

Cumall tutored me without mercy. Again I became uneasy, thinking that I might not have the years he spoke of, and he preparing me as best he could, to face the wolf of my unknown destiny. It lurked ahead of me, an unknown thing waiting to pounce. Romans drew near, and I knew it not, secluded as I was, within Nemed and now round house. I didn't know what it was that I must know. So it was that I sat like a thirsty man drinking all that I could gulp. Be it from Cumall, or any Druid I chanced to encounter.

I studied the works of Thucydides, Dionysius, and Polybius, until Cumall deemed me reasonably proficient in the ways and language of Greece. He set me then to reading 'Livy', Nepos, Sallust and sundry other writings of Romans. Then it was all Ogham and Runes, until I felt that my head was a whirl and I could scarce remember in what tongue to speak.

That night as I lay staring up into darkness, listening to small night sounds and thinking, Rome has not yet invaded our land. I'm thinking they will. The thought of it chilled me. One day soon, they will send in their legions, to the utter consternation of us all. The thought of it lay an icy band around my heart. It was a sending I think. A piece of un-visioned *sight*. I knew, as I lay there, in the warm darkness, that they would come, and the way of *The People* would be no more. I had read their writings, it was inevitable. Such as they, could not allow *The People* to breath free.

A sound of hollow whisperings leaked inside my head, rustling like brown falling leaves against the bone of my skull. Fear, bitter and coiling, wrapped greasy fingers around my guts.

I slipped away then, into the embrace of sleep, and saw within my head, lamps of groaning light illuminating a dark stone altar, buried deep beneath a mound of reeking flesh. Stained it was, wet and running with blood. I cried out within the silence of my skull and slipped down into a dark deep sleep.

Memory of that sending, haunted me for days. I buried it beneath a weight of study and spoke of it not at all. Young I was, and there was much for me to learn. I drank deep and demanded more. Discovering, to my delight, an unquenchable thirst for knowledge within me. Unaware I was, of the stark and terrible years to come.

Can it be that my second of seven years are almost done. Is it truly I, Culann, who stands here with the warmth of summer about my head.

How swiftly the seasons have flown. Cumall says it is my time. That I must walk the green heart. I feel not ready, but then, is anyone ever truly ready for such a testing. And when I return I begin *An Treas Slighe*, the Third Way, *An Slighe Na Spiorad,* way of the spirit.

And I walk the town. They call me Druid.

And I fail to return there's an end to it all.

'Five of days,' Cumall said. 'If you have not returned to the round house by sunset of the final day we shall come and search for you. Though we'll not be finding anything,' he said, giving me his quirky smile.

These have been the best of years. Gaining knowledge, tracking it down, like a hunter out in the forest. Endless discussions within the Nemeds of learning, all bright with sunlight and through Samhain (Winter), hard with crackling frost. Come Beltain (Spring) and leaves reach out like questing minds, unmindful of Imbolc's (February) sting, and its threshing hail of rain.

I think it is in me to say that I will be a student of knowledge all the years of my life. I will take it with me when I leave my house of flesh, else it be a waste otherwise. Cumall teaches that it is not enough to simply recall previous houses of flesh and your tenancy of them. Most anyone can do that without any training in the disciplines at all. It is the knowledge gained through occupying that flesh, that is needful of recall, and the way of knowing if what you have done is right or wrong, and you being able to accept the dark or the light of it as you walk the way of spiral. Being a free person of *The People* the choice of course is left up to you.

I think Cumall has in some small way, come to regard me as a friend. Living as we do in his round house, we have come to know each other quite well. There is of course a silent part of him I can never know. It comes I think, from his having walked the Fourth Path. Which is something I don't think I will have the courage to do, even if I were able. Cumall is a strange man, sometimes dour, sometimes smiling. He is old, very old, and yet the power is strong within him. An old man with stone under water eyes. Not as tall as I, few of *The People* are, there is that about him that sets him apart from other men. He has what we of *The People* call presence, spiritual vitality. Where so ever he would go, you know he is there. He is a man, and honoured I am, to know him. He is also Druid, Master of The Mysteries, teacher of the *Way*, the Four Fold path of life, Guardian of the Spiral of Immortality.

Through the passing of seasons, no matter how foolish my questions or unthinking my words, he always listens and gives me good answers. All the while regarding me through his quiet, steady, strange coloured eyes. Tomorrow I walk the green-heart. Will I return, and if I do, will I be forever changed? There is a mystery there, that I must find, and in its finding become its master. Those who do not, are the ones who do not return. The mystery takes them.

Cumall says I must have faith in who and what I am, and in all that I have been, and will become. 'You have ever served the way of light and will be called to do so again,' he said to me. Is that my destiny? Is that what he's saying, that soon or late in this life I will do what I have always done? As

Roy Edwards

Tabath, as Ra'man, or as Culann of the Arverni. Druid of *The People*, a free person, a Celt.

The sky was a high and fragile dome of purest blue. The forest below, cool and dim. Shafts of green-stone light wove delicate tracery between the trees. A smell of moist, rich earth pervaded the air.

Cool was the forest, quiet, and the way of its breathing incredibly hushed.

I had left the round house behind me. Dusty blue smoke curled lazily upon the air, as wives and daughters rekindled morning fires. A fragrant smell of bread, hot and fresh from the ovens reached me, as I walked away towards the waiting green, leaving Druid round house and the town of Arverni far behind.

I carried no sleeping blanket, no food, no water. Weaponless I was, save for an old hunting spear I used as a walking staff. Wolves roamed the forest and wild boars, whose wicked tusks could gut a man with the speed of a striking snake. Bears there were, huge, shaggy, bad tempered brutes, it was best to avoid. Deer a plenty, wild cattle and small, hardy forest ponies. Most all the big cats (European Lion) had been hunted out long ago, though now and again some traveller would tell of an occasional sighting.

And of them all, animals and men, none entered the green-heart.

Sometimes Germans raid deep into our lands, attacking small, isolated towns and villages, carrying off young girls and whatever bits of gold and enamelled bronze they can find. Metal work of *The People* is highly prized by others. Jewel-Ry they call it.

We kill all such raiders when we can. They are of a particularly savage, brutish race, who delight in torturing

126

their captives. Honourless are they in combat. Groups of them will attack a lone warrior, and with no finesse at all, hack him to death, piece by piece, and then, place his remains upon a stone, in offering to their equally brutish and blood thirsty god. Even so they are strong fighters, much to be feared. The have no Druids to guide or advise them, only unwashed priests, who's crude clothing is often stiff and hard with dried blood.

The Germans are tall like we of the Celts, though often much thicker in the chest and arms. They scorn the *pattern*, spit upon the *Maker*, and ridicule the Spiral of Immortality. They be indifferent horsemen. We of *The People* can often best a mounted attack. Though if it be on foot, we are hard pressed to hold them, rarely achieving victory, unless a Champion be amongst us. We strive mainly to hold our ground and prevent them from entering our towns. Content to have turned them back, only occasionally do we pursue them. German tribe wages constant war upon German tribe, which is fortunate for *The People*. Should the Germans ever unite under a single war leader, I think they would sweep us away, or drain all our resources in constant war. Unlike *The People*, the Germans will eat anything, be it cooked or raw. It is said, if greatly hungered during the season of greatest cold, they will eat the flesh of men. They sleep anywhere, with or without shelter and seem to care little if it be raining, freezing or not.

Perhaps we Celts have become too soft, our way of life too easy. Though I'm thinking it be not quite that way.

The pattern weaves as the *Maker* wills. To visit cruel pain and torment upon the helpless, simply for the joy of it, has never been the way of *The People*, or even part of the warriors pattern. Indeed, we are taught the opposite, to protect the weak and helpless, if so we are whole ourselves.

Roy Edwards

We hold no slaves and cannot imagine such an institution,
even though we are aware its practice is common amongst
other nations. To enslave a free person, to buy and sell, and
use them like pigs. This is, I think the very stuff and fabric of
nightmare. Work of Gaunt Man — Crom Cruach, Bowed
One of the Mound. If not, how else to explain such horror.
Surely no nation upon all the earth, no matter their
achievements, no matter their accomplished writing and
rantings of being noble, articulated men, possessed of
learning or high education, can think they are even remotely
civilised, when all that the nation 'IS' — is built upon, and
dependant on the destruction and enslavement of free people.
To we of *The People* it is a horror beyond horror, and the
work of a spirit-sick society, guilty of ineffable crime.

If captives we take, they are placed in a guesthouse, fed
and cared for, and allowed to roam the limits of the town.
After a period of seven days they are called forth one by one,
and asked if they choose to remain amongst us. If they do not
wish to remain, they are free to go. Most often, captives
taken in raids, choose to stay, thereby adding new blood to
our tribe, and sometimes new skills. It is the way and the
pattern of *The People*.

The trail I followed was barely discernible to the naked
eye, faint it was, and growing fainter. Whose ancient feet
walked here, passing to and fro with such frequency they
wore a path down into the earth of the forest floor? Where
did they go, and why? Who placed the standing stones? Why
is there no trace, no trace at all of town or village? And yet,
the land was occupied before we came. Who were they,
those shining opalescent ones?

Might this be the mystery of the green-heart, revelation of
the past. Or is it, could it be something else. I hungered to

find out, to explore, to know, to learn and perhaps to meet, who knows what.

Before I left the round house Cumall said that the *Rath*, the fort of white stone, was more ancient than the memory of Harpers. And not all of Druid who came to walk the green-heart found it. Perhaps, he said, it was the *Rath* who found the seeker.

Sometimes Cumall's odd sense of humour has a way of chilling a man's blood.

A fresh and lovely morning it was, full of cool sunlight, and thick, early morning shadows that shyly lay beneath bush and branch. Breathing deep of the liquid amber air, I strode out into the morning towards a mystery I would fondly embrace.

My stride was long, free and easy. Full with a young man's vigour I was, the strength of me resting easy on my bones. I was not afeard, indeed, I was more curious that afraid. Full of a shivering excitement that stems from my love of the mystery of old and secret things. A flaw in my nature perhaps, who can say?

True it is, none of us are born so perfect as to be free of all flaw. It is in my mind to think that not even the *Maker* claims flawlessness. But then who am I to say, me being flawed and all.

I am Culann, something of a Druid to *The People*, with an unknown destiny before me, and a terrible sense of premonition. Of *sight* and sending, of irrevocable disaster sweeping inexorably towards the Arverni, and ultimately the whole of the tribes of *The People* (the Celts).

Roy Edwards

Green and still it was. The air about me full and heavy with an unnatural quiet, a sort of breathless, hushed expectancy. The feel of it likened unto that of earth and tree when, for a few moments, they cease to breath, whilst gathering strength to withstand the onslaught of sudden winds and storm.

Even so, I felt no threat, no trace of any ancient malingering evil. It was, or so it seemed to me, as though I pushed against some unseen, weirding barrier, and all I had to do was continue until I broke through.

It crossed my mind then, that if I were unwanted, unlooked for, the barrier, if such it be, could just as easily repel as admit. It was a disquieting thought that did me no good to dwell upon.

I sought a mystery, I would have it, I would not be denied. Twice times seven of years training had led me to this moment. I would not be here otherwise. It was then that I realised I had somehow gotten turned around. The trail had been heading in a westerly direction. I had almost walked the sun down, what I could see of it that is, through the tight weave of branch leaf. Even so, I judged the hour to be late. Any brightness of the setting sun should have been in front of me, a little to the right maybe.

It was not. The only bright glow, diffused though it might be, by the thick canopy of branch and leaf, was above and slightly behind me. Somehow I had walked in a circle. I couldn't believe that I had done so. Woodcraft was a lesser discipline I excelled in, my sense of direction, faithful as any hound's. Or had all this something to do with the mystery. If so — what?

There are tales of men, seen walking across ancient rings of power, only they never reach the other side. Disappear they do. Only their voices can be heard for a time, sounding faint as though with distance. Calling for help, though not in a voice of fear, sounding more surprised than afraid, or so it is the old tales tell. Did they, I wonder, all unknowing, step through an open door into another world, a door, not for men, but for beings we know not of, and yet, it is possible to step through. Why is it none return? Perhaps they do. There are stories amongst *The People* — of now and again — sometime strangers, who have been found wandering the land, sense fled, and rambling of clansmen dead these hundred years and they their brothers, who had gotten lost in the forest for a few days, and when they eventually found their way home, one hundred years had passed. Cumall once said, that time and season as we have come to measure it, is peculiar to this land and that on other worlds it would be different again. True or false I cannot say, me not having set foot upon any other world but this.

We Druids do not deal in magic. And yet there is much that we are capable of doing, that is looked upon as magic by others, who lack the knowledge to understand how certain things are accomplished. Doors and windows in the air could, for all we know, be the natural order of something we lack the knowledge to understand.

Who can say it is not so? Are we so sure of our knowledge that we think we know the WHOLE of it? I think not, though I am sure there are those who think otherwise, and some there are who will kill you, should your knowledge equal or contradict theirs. Cumall says he has met such men amongst the Romans and the Greeks. Shadow tainted they are, and think themselves only slightly less than gods. The are like physicians who betray their trust and oath given unto *Leigheasaim* God of Healing. It is to him they give promise and bond of geasa, to heal. Now it is that there are some physicians who claim high reward before they heal, and if their treatment fails, they do not return what so ever they were paid. It is this way, or so I have heard, amongst the Romans and Greeks. Should a Druid of Healing do such a thing, he would be shamed, and cast out from the circle and *the People*, as punishment for betraying his trust and breaking geasa with *Leigheasaim*. To heal is to hold a kind of power, a special power dispensed by the *Maker*. To deny another his right to claim healing simply because he cannot pay an exorbitant fee diminishes the healer, though he be too blind and spirit-small to see. You deny the sick a right to a continuance of life. Only the *Maker* can claim such right of denial.

To we of *The People*, physician/healers are not god, nor are they godlike. They be men and only men. Brief tenants of a house of flesh, who make less their spirit of beingness through avarice and false pride of position.

Amongst *The People*, there dwell no such Cruels and Spites who, in blindness walk in the tainting shadow of Gaunt Man — Crom Cruach, Bowed One of the Mound, the Romans and Greeks have them all.

I had not walked in a circle.

It was to the edge of a mystery I had come. The faint track I had been following had petered out far behind me. There were many such trails to be found round and about, and within the forest lands. They always began — somewhere, and came to an end — nowhere at all.

I had yet to unriddle such trails. That they had once been well travelled was obvious, and yet, they were made seemingly without reason or clarity of destination. They led to no altar, deep within the forest, to no standing stone upon plain or meadow, to no Nemed. Unless it be, that the small shield size clearing or circle sometimes found at the end of an occasional trail, was an ancient sacred circle of a one time dominant power. Was the circle a sometime window through which a Shining One, an Opalescent might look or even speak, or perhaps a door that once led elsewhere? I cannot say. For true it is I do not know. Maybe the answers are to be found on *An Treas Slighe*, the Third Way, *An Slighe Na Spiorad*, Way of the Spirit, *The Three Fold Way*. If it is, Cumall isn't saying. I have asked enough times, but on this he remains silent. He likes keeping secrets I think.

Something had changed, the air had a moist greeny smell to it. And the unsettling sensation of walking through something unseen, had vanished, nor could I sense the weight of it against my body any more.

The storm had passed me by. What ever it was, I had passed through it. I stood beneath a spread of trees the like of which I had not seen before. Huge they were, thrusting up towards the sun until surely their tops pierced the sky.

I leaned on my spear and slowly looked around. The sun was still above and behind me. Suddenly a faint gleam of light caught my eye. A stray shaft of sunlight had managed to find its way through a hole in the foliage above. Its light reflecting from something on the ground, almost hidden it was, beneath a growth of wild grass and ferns. I stood for a moment, allowing my senses time to adjust to the surroundings. Faint sounds slowly made themselves known. Somewhere ahead, a stream wound its way through the undergrowth, I could hear the sound of its rustling sigh and feel moist coolness about the air. Somewhere a bird called out, the first I had heard this whole, strange day through.

I thrust my spear deep into the soft earth and walked forward, heart pounding in my chest.

Standing in the shaft of sunlight, I looked down, and saw a smooth white stone embedded in the earth, a circle carved into its surface. My breath caught in my throat. 'There be truth in some stories,' I thought, as I let my gaze run on.

Fourteen stones there were. Each one fitting neatly into the next. The thought came to me that it was like a shield wall. Neat and precise with a mystery about it that I had yet to unriddle.

I walked beside the path without actually touching it. Cautious I was, and maybe just a little afeard. A path deep within a forest, that began no where in particular and led, as far as I could see, nowhere at all. Who built it? Why? And why here? What is there about this place that makes it special and what, if any, was the purpose of the path? Was it a symbol of some kind left by the Old Ones? Or does it serve a purpose I know not of? 'Cumall,' I thought wearily, 'sometimes you just don't tell me enough at all.'

I was here for a purpose, I knew that. But what purpose? What am I supposed to learn, or witness? Was that it? There is something here I must see. 'Look,' I told myself. 'Use your eyes and Druid sense.' Then it was that I noticed every other stone had a circle carved into it. I made my way back to what I thought of as its beginning.

'Walk it,' something whispered inside my head. 'If Druid you be — walk it.'

The forest around me was quiet and still. A vagrant breath of air brushed my face, welcome it was and cooling. I sensed there was no threat here in the green-heart, at least not to me. Others had failed to return, I would not. I looked up and behind, the sun's bright ball seemed not to have moved at all, though I dare say that was only my fancy.

'Walk the stones,' something whispered inside my head, with a breathy sigh.

I hesitated, and then, lifting my right foot I placed it carefully upon the flat surface of the first stone.

Celtic Sunset

Nothing. Shrugging my shoulders, I stepped forward and walked the stones. A wave of giddiness swept through me, as though I had drunk too much wine too quickly beneath the heat of the midday sun. It passed as I strode across the last stone. What had caused it, I couldn't say. Had I passed through some unseen barrier? I looked around, nothing had changed. I was still within a forest glade, or was it a Nemed of the Ancient Ones? It was cool and dim with a green water look about it.

DIM! I looked up. The sun seemed not so bright as it had been a few moments before, or was it? I could not be sure. Suddenly I was no longer certain of anything. Who had spoken to me and why? Where had the voice come from? I was alone, or was I? Something warm and rich flooded through me, rising up from my gut into my head. A silver toned voice of incomparable wonder chimed softly behind my eyes, reminding me of our beginnings in that far away land of myth and legend. Where, it is said, wind chimes hung in the trees, creating music born of the sounds of earth.

Words played upon the harp string of thoughts saying, 'Walk the second path that lays before you.'

I had always thought myself to be an observant man, and yet, when I stepped from the last stone of the first path I had seen no other before me, only the clutter and crumble of a forest floor, with a sound of flowing water hidden somewhere about, and yet, there it was, but a few paces in front of me. A second path of fourteen stones. Was the first one a test of some kind, and if you failed, you saw not the second path? Where did they go? How did they go? A fine sheen of perspiration began to bead my brow.

'Walk the second path,' the silver toned voice inside my head prompted. Politely insistent it was, like a concerned mother urging her child to eat.

I spoke out loud into the still air. 'Well now,' I said bravely, 'the first path was nothing at all, can the second be so different?' The giant trees around the circle shook in silent mirth. Leaves rustled, and yet I detected no breeze. The air before me had a faint bluish cast to it, or had it? I shook my head, suddenly unsure of my own certainty. After all, what did I know of my world? What did anyone know? Beyond books and the rise and fall of nations, lay our meagre searchings for knowledge and a truth that at times became as convoluted as a raggedy, searching wind. What lay behind the stars? Who walked these lands before the coming of *The People*? Why do Romans claim right of all life other than Roman, and Greeks definitive reasoning? Why do men make slaves of other men? Why should they want to? Why is knowledge owned by some and yet denied to others? I have read what Greek and Roman have written. Lengthy specious words of that and this, that serve to hide how little the writer knows, how little we all know. Is that why invaders always seek to destroy the great libraries of the world? Knowing little, they intend that others should know less and thereby become dependent upon those who claim, sole ownership of knowledge, and thereby create an elite, a special class of Aristokratia, best born, as the Greeks do call them.

Amongst we of *The People*, you make your own way. You are what you become, what you intend to be. You are not born an 'Elite', you must earn that right, irrespective of class or conditions. To make a king you must also have the right to unmake a king, else you be no free people, and become the playthings of fools, and those who covet only wealth, with no thought given at all to the Spiral of Immortality, or the pattern of the *Makers* weave.

Celtic Sunset

Cumall has told me of Romans and others who have declared themselves to be divine, and then wailed like new born babes at the approach of death.

Mad are they who walk in the shadow of Gaunt Man, Crom Cruach, Lord of the Mound, short lived are they and doomed to weep forever, deep within the well spring of souls.

As I stepped upon the first stone of the second path that lay before me, I heard a sigh amongst the trees. I looked up, and saw only a faint blue light, like a reflection of a pale blue sky upon still water.

I looked down, and could see a cross contained within a circle carved into the stone. I looked ahead and could see that each of the fourteen stones had a cross within a circle carved deep into its surface.

The stones had a look of incredible age about them, as though they had lain there since the dawn of beginnings. The passage of countless feet had worn them smooth and shiny. Whose feet? What men other than Druid had walked here? Were they men? Might not they have been something else, something old and forgotten that walked like men.

I moved on, slowly, carefully, expecting I knew not what. As I stepped onto the seventh stone, a flood of memory filled my head. I felt safe and yet unbalanced, as though I might fall and plunge down from a great height. The feeling passed and, memory was my vision.

It was the whole of my vision within and without. There was for me no glade, no trees, no rustling sounds of running water, no brightness of sun above and behind me. I was not at that moment Culann the Druid, with an unknown destiny before him. I was, and had become both spectator and part of a dim long forgotten memory. I knew now, why it was I had been sent here. Why Cumall had tirelessly trained me in arcane disciplines.

Ψ

Celtic Sunset

The age that first gave birth to *The People*, the Celts, had almost reached its end.

A new age was about to rise.

The age of *An Iolar Grian*, The Eagle Sun. Beneath whose rule there was no place at all for *The People*, the Celts. Indeed there would be no place at all for any nation possessing high spiritual values, in the new age.

The Eagles of Rome were about to fly.

Envisioned by Cumall, who had seen, *An Tiarna Na Dorchacht*, The Lord of Darkness, commanding and his captain, Gaunt Man — Crom Cruach, Bowed One of the Mound, leading.

The Eagles of Rome were the harbingers of a Dark Age, that would spread where so ever Rome claimed rule. A dark age that would, to the joy of the dark thing, last for centuries. It would be looked upon by those who come after as an age of reasoned enlightenment. Such be the power of Dark to twist and deceive, that few would live, in those as yet unborn years, who had memory or wit enough to find out what had gone before the birth of the Eagle Sun the *Iolar Grian*.

Ruled and controlled by a *Tiarna Na Dorchacht*, a Lord of Darkness, Rome would use its legions to seek out and destroy utterly, any nation aspiring towards spiritual enlightenment and the banishment of shadows.

Under the Aegis of Darkness, Rome would invent, and create its own gods, fashioned in their own dark and bloody likeness.

Memory roiled and surged inside my head like a restless sea pounding upon an ancient and distant shore.

I was Tabath and Raman the Egyptian and more, much more. The sum, it seemed, of the total reason for my being.

Roy Edwards

It came upon me then, and for a span of heart beats consumed me utterly. Envisioned, dream seeing, far memory walking. I stood upon the seventh stone and felt the warmth of an earlier age seep through me.

I, Culann of the Arverni, Druid, free person of *The People*, walked the meadow lands of *The Peoples* beginning.

We journeyed down from the Mountains of the Sky (Himalayas) pursued by a nameless *Haunt*. The same *Haunt* it was, that had driven us out of our green valleys, hidden deep within the vast and empty range of the Mountains of the Sky. We, so it is our Harpers sing, who once knew the *An Sciathanfear*, the Winged Men, left our hidden valleys in fear of the dark, gaunt thing that had come amongst us. A stained, unwholesome thing it was, the like of which our Holy-Men, had no knowledge of. A young race we were, upward climbing the Spiral of Immortality. Innocents, our language contained no word for evil, we had yet to taste that most bitter of fruits.

We are a hardy people, colourful and loud, given much to boasting and the making of riddles. We fight in a playful way with sword and shield, spear and axe. The bow we use only for hunting.

When the dark thing came, it filled our hearts and minds with fear. Shadow haunting our days, filling our night dreaming with whispered commands of obedience to its unwholesome desires. So it was that our Holy-Men advised us to flee, whilst they sought out ways to contain it.

We fled then, down long stony ways, through narrow windy valleys, until we came to the mountains edge. Strong we were, but afeard of the unknown. The feel of it remains with us still

Celtic Sunset

The *Haunt* stayed in the mountains and thankful we were that it did so. Our Holy-Men said it had not yet the power to pursue us beyond the mountains. Not yet, they said, but one day it too would leave the mountain fastness and go out amongst the nations of men. We shall think upon it, they said, and learn how we might combat its wounding influence. In time, our Holy-Men became known as *Draoi's,* Druids, and they healed our spirits full well. We became aware of the *Maker* and the pattern of his weave. We studied the paths of upward rising spirits and called it The Way of the Spiral of Immortality, *The Four Fold Way.*

So it was that we came down from the mountains wearing sunlight about our shoulders, and crossed the sacred river (Ganges). Spreading out upon the plain of *Edena* (Ganges delta, East Pakistan), the plain of beginnings, we laid the first stones, the like of which had not been lain before. As the many columned city rose tier upon tier, we gave thanks and praise, joyful in the eyes of the *Maker*.

We were the first of all *The People.*

Centuries passed by in a wonder of discovery, of life and metals, of enamelled bronze, and spiralled torcs of gold. We defeated all who, envious of our gains, came as invaders into our lands. We were *The People, An Ceilteach*, the Celts.

And darkness stalked us like some final doom.

Twenty centuries slipped by in the way that centuries do, sliding down alleys of time and far sunset dreaming. *The People* had become what they would always remain, until the last of all days was swept away upon a sea of blood, and incredibly destructive spirit-pain.

Roy Edwards

Tall we are, pale skinned with tawny hair and eyes of deep summer blue. Boastful and loud, we are in love with a love of life. Free people we are and will so remain.

We met the small, dark skinned invaders along the borders of our land, driving them back with a casual contemptuous ease. We were tall and strong, our blades long and sharp and they were but few.

They came again and again, each time greater in number. We won each battle, but never a final victory. The invaders sheer weight of numbers began to grind us down. Eventually our battles became no more than an endless series of holding actions.

We fought with our backs pressed against the stones of the city and then we fought them atop our walls.

Druids advised us to sue for peace and maybe a portion of land. It was not to be.

The pattern weaves as the *Maker* wills and the invader wanted the whole of all we laid claim to. We were the better fighters but too few in number and, too many of our finest warriors had been slain.

We fled under cover of night towards a distant land we knew not of. Behind us, we fired the city and fields of golden grain. Racing the flames towards an unknown promise of safety.

We became nomadic, aggressive and warlike. Our numbers increased as we moved slowly through many strange and oft times beautiful lands. Many battles we fought, contesting our right to move through already settled lands. Eventually, few nations dared to send their armies against us.

Celtic Sunset

Harpers and bards of *The People*, made song of our wanderings and our once upon a city life. Adding it to the song of our remote mountain home, it comprised a history of *The People*, more accurate than many that were inscribed upon stone, or the little baked clay tablets that the Babylonians do so love.

Slowly the memory of it all began to fade, as I, without consciously intending to do so, stepped forward upon the white stone path. I had almost reached its end when again I froze upon a single stone. The twelfth stone it was and the last to bear the mark of the cross within a circle. I sensed that the sun was still above and slightly behind, as it paled away like the trees and greenery around me, far memory filled all the inside of my head. I lived that memory, I could feel and taste it as Culann of the Arverni, Druid to *The People* faded away beneath a pain I had thought long forgotten.

I am, and always have been, a guardian of knowledge. It is what I do, my reason for being. In the long ago years that are now no more than dust upon the earth, I gave promise to the *One* and bound myself for all eternity to its cause. Sometimes I could remember who and what I was, or had been during times before this life, sometimes I could not, unless there came reason for me to do so.

Throughout thousands upon thousands of years I have kept my faith, my promise, my reason for being.

Except once, when belief in self and my chosen path, bled away, and I began to doubt that I had any reason to exist at all.

A white fire sun, pouring down molten heat from out a hard, brittle blue sky. Desert sands soaked up the heat, its

143

grains refracting light in snarls and snags of eye searing glare. Hot it was, as hot as I had ever known it to be.

I stood alone at the head of a shallow valley looking out across the harsh desert lands. Behind me, almost lost in the suns glare, a small group of buildings dozed through the worst heat of the day.

The main building was a depository. A place where written knowledge could be stored, It was called a library, and I am its guardian, commander of ten.

The library, though small, housed rare and diverse writings. Brought here from the far corners of the world by men who called themselves, the *Brotherhood of the Book*. From time to time, men from far away lands came to study, and debate amongst themselves, or with any of the scholars, wise men or priests who often came a visiting.

I held guardianship of the library, and the desert strip road that led to Kish, a half days march away. Kish was a small, prosperous town of merchant traders, who maintained a small, but efficient fighting force. To the north east of Kish flows the two rivers. The Euphrates and the Tigris, any one of which will take you to mighty Babylon or Nineveh. Nimrod the Assyrian it was who built Nineveh. It is said that he ruled with a closed fist that could smite his enemies mightily. Though I'm thinking it cannot have been so mighty, the Babylonians threw him out with spectacular ease.

Now it is that Nebuchadnezzar rules all of Babylonia. War like he is, and ever eager to extend the boundary of his rule. The walls of Babylon are high (60') and thick (25'). Built of sun baked mud brick, encased in white plaster. It was, I am told, a monumental task, but then, he has slaves enough to do it. What with the capture of Jerusalem and all, and his enslavement of the Hebrews.

Celtic Sunset

Sometimes, the People of the Sea, the Phelishtim (Philistines) sail up the two rivers to Babylon. They came for trade and the selling of war booty. Fierce they are, tribal and contemptuous. Legend has it that they are the remnants of a once mighty, sea going race who lived on an island that sank beneath the sea.

As for me, I am of no land and all lands. Of no faith and all faiths. I care not who rules or disrules. Nor do I interest myself in the affairs of Kings. I am Hammer (Ha'i'mar), a guardian, it is my reason for being. It has always been my reason for being, since that first day I gave promise and bound myself for all eternity to the guarding of the *Way*. A faint *trace of blue* it was and that is all that I am willing to speak of. I go where I am called and that is all that I know. I dance the sword dance and the wide sands travelling, and revere the written word. Sometimes I study, in my endless search for knowledge, of a *trace of blue*. Always I am guardian.

Word had reached me that day, as I stared out across the sands, of a marauding band of desert nomads said to be moving in this direction. I was uneasy, without knowing why. Something felt wrong, I shrugged the feeling away and thought about tomorrow. A small, hot, dry wind blew by me, whipping the sand into swirls and eddies of golden dust. Heat waves shimmered, distorting vision and distance. Sweat trickled down my face. The sky had turned a strange milky white, a sign of great heat and more to come. 'If any one was out there, they would need a blind man's luck to find this place,' I thought idly.

The *Brotherhood of the Book*, built their libraries far and away from walled cities. Cities fall and rise, and then fall again as invaders come and go, and always it is the libraries that are destroyed first. Here in the desert, if they are attacked and destroyed perhaps the destruction will not be total and always, always there are secret places, to hide scrolls, papyrus and texts inscribed upon thin rolled sheets of unperishable silver, gold and poor mans copper.

Tomorrow, at first light I would lead my ten out into the desert. I trained them in secret, for I would not have others know the level of our skill. Now and again marauders came, thinking we be no more than ill trained desert guards, bored with duty and heavy with wine. Few survived to rue such thoughts. Even so, I was a known man, a Weapons Master. Few there were, amongst the desert nomads who would dare challenge our swords. In that, I was guilty of complacent pride. And in all things there is a price to be payed. Be it soon or late there will be due payment made.

I left only Karnak, the Nubian behind, when I led my small force out in the cool pre-dawn light of the next day.

A thin column of dense, greasy black smoke rose up like an accusing finger into the still and silent air. Staining the perfect blue of heavens dome like some spittle laden curse.

We came in from the desert with the sun behind us. Swords whispered free as we padded towards a smoking mound, heaped up against the rubble of fallen walls. Scraps of torn and part burned scrolls littered the central courtyard, around which the library and out buildings were grouped.

The library had been reduced to a pile of broken bricks. The smoking mound heaped up around its base. Out buildings had been fired but otherwise left standing. The library had been the objective, nothing else. And they, the canny ones to attack whilst I was gone. Well hidden they had been, of that I had no doubt.

146

Celtic Sunset

I slipped through the courtyard like a desert haunt, as I came closer to the smouldering mound, I recognised it for what it was. My eyes widened in horror.

The scholars had been slain, and there bodies thrown one on top of the other in a reeking heap. Scrolls had then been piled on top and around them, soaked in oil and set on fire.

I deal in death, it is, after all, my one consummate skill, but not like this. Never against mild, defenceless men whose only wish is to be left alone to their studies. Bile rose in my throat as an errant flow of air wafted the charnel stench of smouldering human flesh towards me.

My nine gathered around in a silent group. 'Find the Nubian,' I barked at them harshly. They fanned out, searching, whilst I stood there staring at my guilt. A soft 'hoy' drew my attention.

Karnak the Nubian, had made his stand against the barracks wall. It faced inwards towards the courtyard. He had been inside resting, when the marauders came like ghost dogs, overrunning the library before he was even aware of their presence. Screams and cries of pain had alerted him. He had barely reached the courtyard when they came at him in a rush, pushing him back against the mud brick wall.

Karnak stood alone, fighting desperately for his life. He cut down eight before taking a spear through his chest. Thinking him dead the raiders left him where he fell.

He told me this, whilst I cradled his head on my lap, and watched the bright life of him drain out upon the stones.

He looked up at me, his eyes like wounds and said, 'You are guardian, where were you?' He coughed, red stained his mouth. He laughed weakly, 'You came guardian, too late.' Lung blood flecked his mouth and lips, breath rattled in his broken throat as dark eyes dimmed and the heart of him stopped beating. His dying words speared my soul.

I knelt upon the stones cradling the lifeless body, blind with tears and knew that something terrible had happened. Something beyond death and mindless destruction.

Betrayal.

I had betrayed my trust. I felt my body begin to tremble and I think something broke inside my head. I knelt, with my head bowed in shame. The burning desert sun hammered against my exposed neck, head whirled, vision blurred, and the heart of me tried to smash its way through my chest.

With trembling hands, I laid Karnak's body down, and rose slowly to my feet. 'What have I done?' I screamed silently. 'How was it that I could have let this horror happen? Why did I ignore my unease of yesterday? Never before had I ignored my senses where my guardianship was concerned. Why now? Why did I do it? Why, why, why? Where now lay the anvil to expiate my guilt?' I moaned softly, lost in a drowning weight of despair. My body felt weak and hollow my thinking muddy and shallow. 'Why am I alive, when all about me lays death,' I thought brokenly.

A low murmur of voices invaded my bruised senses. My 'Ten', stood grouped a few paces away, looking towards me with cold unfeeling eyes.

Karnak was dead. The library destroyed and all its scholar-librarians slain, and it was all my fault. I could see it writ upon their faces, and they be right. It was my fault. My guts were churning ice. I felt faint and distant as though all this horror was just some dreaming fantasy. Would that it was.

I swallowed, my throat suddenly gone dry. Cruel are the realities of life, and heavy, sometimes, the burdens we bear.

Celtic Sunset

How was it possible for me to betray my trust? I do not know — but I had done so.

My fractured mind, like my head, whirled, I trembled and shivered inside. Me, Hammer, who has never walked in fear of man, beast or haunt, filled with a scalding bitterness, as I began to sink beneath waves of self contempt.

'Hear me Lord' I cried out silently, 'I hath betrayed all thy trust in me. Release me, I beg of thee, release me from my vow, scatter my unburied bones across the sands. I hath proved unworthy and cannot face what I have become.' The *Lord* gave me no answer, disdaining my offer of self sacrifice.

I felt the weight of my sword, heavy against my hip, and I thought its weight would drag me down upon my knees. There was something wrong, deep inside my head. I am no coward to drown in a deluge of self pity. Even so, I betrayed my trust. Words boomed around the hollow, inside my skull. All unknowing I became something else.

Mazar, one of my 'Ten,' stepped forward, placing himself directly in front of me, his lean body outlined by the sun against the hard blue of the sky. Foul eddies of smoke swirled around us. The sun's heat blasted down upon unprotected heads with stunning force. Unsteady I was and trembling.

Mazar said 'You should have known. You should have known, or sensed something was wrong,' he said accusingly. 'You are the guardian. You command us. You should have known,' he ended gruffly.

I looked into his face, his dark implacable eyes boring into mine. 'I was uneasy but thought nothing of it.' I said in a broken voice. 'I denied my own knowingness and I have betrayed you all. Its not fit I am. No guardian am I.'

'Tell it to them, not me,' Mazar said harshly, pointing an accusing finger towards the still smouldering mound of dead. 'Tell it to them, tell it to the Nubian, tell it to your master who ever he is.' He spat upon the stones at my feet. 'We'll follow you no more.' With a dismissive, contemptuous snarl, Mazar turned away. He led my troop out into the desert. I never saw them again.

I stood alone amongst the bloody carnage and the rubble of a once upon a time building. The smell of scorched human flesh heavy in my nostrils. Desert vultures circled high above me, gliding upon unseen airs. They are always the first to sense death, winged garbage eaters they be, the desert cleaners.

I felt wrong inside and I didn't know why. It wasn't a testing, there be no such thing, though some there are who would have you believe otherwise. My heart ached with a strange kind of pain I had no memory of. My guts were ice and fire, sloshing about inside me like some accursed desert jinn, drinking a dead man's blood.

Spirit sick I was, and weaving. Something had changed inside my head, I had become other than what I was. The spirit of me cowered all unknowing, in some deep and dark guilt stricken place of no tomorrows, only an endless today. Tears spilled down my face.

Dying sunlight flared in my eyes as I stumbled away. Away from the silent testimony of all I had betrayed. I couldn't think straight. I tried, but lucid thoughts kept slipping away into something I could not name. A grey, nowhere kind of light sat behind my eyes, as I shuffled away into swift falling darkness.

Sometime during that awful night of cold starlight, I stripped my sword from me and buried it beneath the sands. Throwing my head back, I screamed and howled at the unfeeling sky. Crying out in awful pain, I called upon the *One* to bear witness. 'Here I am,' I cried, voice cracked and raw. 'Here' my voice fled across the empty desert. 'Can you not see me. I gave promise unto thee. Where art thou now in my time of bitterest need.' Roiling emotions stretched me out upon a bed of sharp pointed flints. I sobbed then, gulping air, chest heaving. Pounding my fists into the sand, I screamed my dry throat raw.

I remember, in a dim sort of way, standing up midst a haze of madness, shaking my fists at the stars of heaven's gate and crying out in a terrible voice, 'Bear witness, I bury my sword and will fight no more whilst so ever I live.' I fell down then, into a deep dark well of nothing.

Burning lances of heat, probed and prodded reluctant flesh into wakefulness. I remembered little of the previous night. A voice shouting and crying out, sounding terribly alone, no more than that.

Hungry and thirsty, I staggered to my feet, heading north, towards the desert road, and the town of Kish. I stumbled and shuffled across the desert. How I survived I do not know, I know only that I did. I fell often, wanting only to lay there upon the sand, full of a strange kind of weakness I had never known before. Mad I was and raving. Each time I fell I clawed my way back up onto my feet. Sometimes I crawled on hands and knees, a spark hidden deep inside, driving me on.

Sun hardened, my exposed skin didn't blister, except for the places where repeated falling and crawling through sand had rubbed the skin raw. I wore only a battle kilt and sandals, studded with iron. Tall I was, and desert lean with a hawk like face and long unbound hair the colour of a raven's wing.

There was something wrong inside my head. I could feel it and it shivered me through. A darkness of some kind, a darkness of another's making. How I knew that, I cannot say, I simply knew, or at least sensed as much with what little of wit was left to me.

I stumbled down a long stark road of agony, roasting slowly beneath a funnelled furnace of heat. The sun was molten copper and brass, in a sky of enamelled bronze. The night sucked away the heat of the day, leaving me shivering with cold, midst an awful blistered silence. I licked my wounds for the blood salt, whilst cold starlight wove a net of white fire around the silver coin of the moon.

I staggered into Kish upon my own two feet, more dead than alive I was.

Under Nebuchadnezzar's rule, Kish became a wealthy town, second only to the city of Babylon, in its accumulation of riches.

Kish, an unwalled town of merchants and traders. Kish, a clearing house for desert caravans, carrying Egyptian cotton, rolls of papyrus, inks, rare and costly paints of red, purple and royal blue. Kish, whose streets and market squares teemed with a colourful, jostling, shouting throng of humanity, beneath the hot white glare of an ageless desert sun.

To the east lay the two rivers, the Tigris and the Euphrates, whose waters were the very life blood of the land. Babylon was a slow three day caravan journey north. South and west were desert lands. Indeed the whole of the river lands were surrounded by deserts.

Along a single 3,000 mile stretch, whole civilisations rose and fell, and then rose again. Each time bearing a different name.

Celtic Sunset

Kish was home to Moabites who once fought and conquered the Shebites, only to fall in their turn beneath Assyrian swords. Amorites walked amongst Canaanites, Hittites and small unsmiling groups of Philistines, those legendary people of the sea, of whom it is said, once lived upon an island that sank beneath the captured sea (Mediterranean).

Nubians rubbed shoulders with Chaldeans and haughty Egyptians, whose civilisation was already old before ever a desert king was born, or the first mud walled city rose above the sand.

Here and there, Iramites could be seen, a strange, enigmatic people, tall they were, supple and slim, with pale, honey coloured skin, and eyes of weirding colours. Unlike the city people of the two rivers, the Iramites did not pay tribute to the King, Nebuchadnezzar of Babylon, nor did they, in any way, acknowledge his rule. They were a proud, fierce people, who came, it is said, from the far off fabled land of Ind (India). They built a magnificent city in the desert, the like of which not even Babylon with all its tiered gardens could rival. Iram, the many pillared, the city of columns, built of rare rose coloured stone, amongst pillars of plaster, coloured white, pale gold and blue. Its streets all paved with interlocking stones of painted amber, and burnt orange. Men still live, who once walked its streets, and they say it was a marvel, a magnificence, too rich for simple words to express. Its beauty touched the spirit, they said, and forever laid claim to any who walked its way, so it is the Iramites would have you believe, if you can prevail upon them to speak to you at all. Proud they are, those who still yet live, with eyes full of wounded sadness for what was once, but is now no more.

The ancient builders of the Lost City of Iram made a mistake, they built the city upon what they thought was bed rock. It was not. It was but a plate of rock and thin at that. As the city grew in its magnificence of coloured stone, so did the weight of it all. It began to sink beneath the desert sands, and not all the ingenuity of man could halt or stay it otherwise. Eventually, the people of Iram had no choice, they abandoned their beautiful city and left it to its fate. In time, the whole of the city sank beneath the sands. It sleeps now, waiting, waiting for those who will come in a distant time and dig it free, uncovering the marvel of it all for all the world to see.

Once more the Iramites took up their ancient nomadic life, and wandered away from all the length and fertile breadth of the two rivers. A few remained behind working as traders, merchants and now and again as paid soldiers of Babylon, but they are few, and will soon be gone, and all that will remain to mark their passing will be a legend of a lost city of many pillars, somewhere out there beneath the sands. Of all those who inhabit Kish, they are the sad ones. The others know and accept that they are the surviving remnants of once great cultures. Now it is that the King of Babylon rules all.

A thousand different smells perfume the hot, still air about Kish. A mix of all the goods bought and sold, and displayed from one end of the town to the other. Kish doth stand beneath a rainless sky of unfeeling blue, whilst a fiery orange-gold ball pours down heat and light.

Ten thousand different voices hawk their wares and spit upon hands sealed in bargain. Soldiers are everywhere, squads of ten and five ceaselessly patrol their sectors, keeping the peace with a hard eyed ruthlessness, amongst a melting pot of cultures, who not so long ago fought against each other. Driven by an all consuming passion made up of greed and avarice and a taste for blood.

Hot waves of hard brilliant light, sucked up smells and mixed them all together in a vast aromatic cloud peculiar to Kish. A keen nose might separate the smell of fragrant amber (frankincense), from cooking spices and beeswax, aromatic oils and vials of sweet scented body perfumes, mixed all about with the smell of rare woods, cedar, ebony and camphor. Beside stalls piled high with exotic fruits, metal workers sold ingots of silver and gold, copper, bronze and costly tin. Merchants sit in small, shady booths, trading pearls, rubies and emeralds, for coats of ring mail and bales of dyed and undyed wool, robes of summer blue cotton and lengths of hand woven cloth of gold, edged all about in silver and tassels of green and crimson. The foul stench of slave pens and human waste mixed in with the aroma of fresh baked pastries, filled with a mixture of sesame seeds, crushed almonds and honey. Chewy confections there was, of Nougat and sweet crushed dates baked in cinnamon pastry and then soaked in melting honey.

Here and there, soldiers new come from the Hebrew wars, dragged chained and weeping captives to the slave blocks, there to be auctioned off to the highest bidder. Hebrews they were, and much unloved, by some.

Kish, a melting pot, overflowing with the rag and taggle end of broken cultures, whose glory was no more than a desert memory of fallen crumbling walls and dusty banners above blunt and rusting swords.

I staggered into Kish upon my own two feet, and then fell to my knees in the dust, when a loud, commanding voice shouted, 'Halt.'

A face, burnt brown by the desert sun, looked down upon me. It seemed to slip in and out of my sight. I mouthed words, but only a faint croak came out of my broken, sun dried throat. Raving I was, but only inside my head. There was a darkness there, strange and alien and not of my making. Where it came from I didn't know, the memory of it slipping away, whenever I tried to grasp it. I think my madness began at a place of books, somewhere out in the desert, but I couldn't be sure. I held a sword once, at least I think I did, I don't have one now. I betrayed something, a trust, vague it is and dreamlike. Did the dark thing crawl inside my head then? I don't know, perhaps it did.

I felt strong hands grip and lift me, as I slid down into a dark cool well, where nothing in all this world could reach me.

I awoke in the house of Azar, the Chaldean, errant son of the city of Ur. Small he was, like an Egyptian, but stockier, with well muscled arms and shoulders and a thick broad chest. He carried himself well and looked what he was, a professional soldier, a mercenary, paid by the lunar month. Captain he was, of a small garrison of elite soldiers, whose task it was to guard and police the town of Kish. An unsmiling, well mannered Chaldean, who would not, I am sure, have been out of place in the court of nobles.

Azar fed and clothed me and allowed me the freedom of his house. He remained politely silent, when I said I had little memory of what had happened at the Place of the Book, as he called it.

He said he knew of my reputation as a fighting man and commander of Ten. I smiled at that, and said he must be mistaken. 'I lead no men nor do I own a sword,' I said, 'You mistake me for another, my friend.'

Celtic Sunset

'I do not think so,' He looked puzzled, 'but as you say,' he said politely, 'I could be mistaken. You are a guest in my house and have eaten of my bread and salt, it ill behoves me to say that you are wrong. Perhaps,' continued Azar, 'when you have regained your strength, you may wish to continue your journey.'

His words were coldly polite. It was, I knew, a polite way of informing a guest that his stay has been overlong and that he can leave sooner than later.

'Two days my friend,' I said to him, 'give me two more days.'

'Agreed,' replied Azar.

He relaxed a little then and spoke to me of his city of Ur, that he had not seen these twelve years past. 'Ur is,' Azar said, 'as surely all men must know, a city of great and enduring beauty. Its walls, are in part, sheathed in burnished copper, beneath the midday sun they glow like flames of sunset,' he said. 'Groves of fruit trees and flowering shrubs had been planted all about the inner city so that their perfume might sweeten the air. But I,' said Azar with a sigh, was born with a wandering heart. Soldiering came easy to me, so it is that I travelled here and there, hiring out my sword, when I was in need of a bit and piece of food and such. I came here some years ago, midst a busy time of trading, offering my services in place of a previous Captain, who had gotten himself killed in some minor skirmish with a group of Nubians, who were just passing through.' He grinned like a desert lion, 'He must surely have been a fool. Nobody in their right mind willingly fights Nubians.'

'But you would?' I asked him.

He looked at me then, all cool and distant. 'When I fight it is because I choose to do so. Be it with Nubians or any other who breaks the peace, or otherwise ignores the laws of Kish.

157

Babylon is distant,' he said, 'Kish is here. Besides, 'he added softly, 'I am paid well to do what has to be done, irrespective of any personal feeling I may have in the matter. One day,' he said with a far away look in his eyes, 'I will return to Ur if,' he said with a smile, 'its walls are still standing.' He eyed me speculatively.

I told him again, that I could not in truth remember what had happened, prior to my emergence from the desert.

Azar said he had heard of such things happening to men who had been dealt terrific blows to the head.

I shook my head in denial. 'No,' I said, 'its something else, something dark, I think. For in truth I am not myself. My head feels strange, as though some unseen weight has crawled in and sits upon my thoughts. Is it possible,' I asked him in wonder, 'to be a captive inside your own head?'

He looked at me oddly and said, 'Seek a priest or a dream speaker, I know less than nothing of such things.' He rose from his couch, buckling his sword about his waist, 'I must be about my duties,' he said quickly.

Azar left the small house, pushing his way out into a milling, bustling throng. He paused for a moment and looked up at the sky. 'I believe you, Hammer of Ten,' he said softly, 'may Baal bring light to the darkness inside your head.' He walked on then, knowing somehow that when he returned, Hammer would be gone.

The sun had begun its descent, streaming out a spreading stain of crimson and apricot coloured fire. Behind it a small thread of clouds, edged in burnished silver, had snagged against the sky's deep blue vault. Unmoving they were, reflecting the sunsets polished glow, spreading its final, fiery moments with a careless hand, staining the deepening blue dome of the sky in a magnificent array of colours, no human artist could ever hope to paint.

I left then, walking out of Azar's house into a blazing glory of colour and a fast descending night. I had neither coin nor food, and the only clothes I owned were on my back. Of weapons I did not even think.

Darkness had truly fallen by the time I reached the cities edge. Without hesitation I walked out into a darkness, sprinkled all about with bits and pieces of starlight. I had no clear idea of what I was doing, or why. Without food or water, I could not hope to survive the desert wastes for long. Something inside me registered that, something else made it seem unimportant and distant. 'Am I mad?' I wondered to myself, 'Yes, I think so,' I murmured.

A cool wandering night breeze touched my face. Above me the sky was a deep pure black, thickly encrusted with a breath taking brilliance of countless points of winking light. My sandalled feet rasped over sand, the sound of it loud in the night's breathless hush. How small I am beneath all this, the immensity of it all threatened to engulf me. I felt as though I stood upon the open hand of God. Where am I going? What is it I have done? Why cannot I remember? Who am I? What have I become? The silent night, holy and unstained answered me not at all, and remained what it was — a dark and silent night.

Behind me lay Kish, before me, the unknown. I walked upon a desert road going nowhere.

Suddenly, waves of tiredness swept through me, spinning my head. I stumbled off the road and lay down upon the cold sands, hitching my desert robe close about. I pillowed my head upon my arms, closing my eyes, I slept the stars out of the sky and a sliver of moon down into its bed.

Roy Edwards

That night as I slept alone in the desert, a strange and terrible dream came to me. Was it a dream? Or was it not? When I awoke I couldn't be sure, even though the memory of it stayed with me. Unlike most dreams, that upon awakening, swiftly fade and are soon forgotten, or only remembered in a vague bit and piece sort of way.

As I lay sleeping *He* came for me.

A tall, skinny man with coins of shadow and shields of darkness around him. *He* came pounding across cloud dim sands, thin, skeletal arms open wide to embrace me. Grinning he was, thick blubbery lips all wet and shining with spit, teeth broken and yellow like splinters of chewed bone. The eyes of him blazed like burning suns, smoky yellow and hot. There was a charnel house smell about him, a sick, sweet smell of old dried blood that seemed to envelop his reeking flesh and reach out towards me in a vomit inducing cloud. Fear clutched at my heart with an icy hand. Sharp, unclean talons hooked my guts. I screamed inside my head, as the dark thing pounded across the sands, drawing closer and closer towards me. I screamed again, full of rage and fear, or was it something else that screamed for me? I sensed it then, brief though it was, I sensed it. Something behind the pounding man, something unseen, immense and implacable, in its hatred and evil design. Something unnameable, an ancient, immovable evil whose minions had stalked the lands since the dawn of time. And then it was gone, as if it thought that by remaining hidden it could not be known. The gaunt thing was almost upon me and I had neither wit nor will to defend myself. The spirit of me bound and unmoving, beneath a greater darkness that somehow had crawled inside my head.

Celtic Sunset

Raving I was, inside a dream.

He came for me. *He* would embrace and devour me, and I would become and remain *His* thing. What trust? What have I done that was so terrible? I am abandoned alone and weeping in darkness, without even knowledge of who I am. Of what crime am I guilty? No defence am I given. Lorn and bereft is the withering of my soul.

The unclean thing reached out, heat from dirty yellow eyes seared my flesh. A moaning cry of anguish echoed around and around inside my head. I began to shake and shiver with a passion of unreason and then, my dream, if dream it was, faded into a warm shimmering sea of tranquil blue.

I awoke with a start, gulping air down into my lungs. The heart of me hammering against my chest. I was sense-fled, of that I was sure. Something had saved me from death's final dreaming, or worse. The colour of it reminded me of something, but I couldn't quite grasp the remembrance of what it was. It kept slipping away like some elusive humming bird, like a spangle of sunlight dancing on water.

As the sun rose above the horizon, its warmth chased the chill from my flesh. Standing, I turned back towards Kish. Full of a childlike wonder, at the certainty of what it was I knew I had to do. I did not then think of evil or the shadow that lurked within my head. I did not then know, that light can sometimes cause darkness.

The great arch of entry stood silent sentinel in the early morning light. A wash of apricot colour fell down the arch into pooling shadows and a quiet stillness born of the desert.

As you stand beneath the great arch of Kish looking outward towards the horizon, a flat featureless landscape of lion coloured sand meets the eye. Fierce it is, sere and lonely. Above, the vault of heaven looks down through an unbroken eye of blue. Small winds dance and sing, in dry dusty voices, building pillars of sand and then blowing them down again. There are mysteries out there that no man has ever seen. Lost cities and the bones of marching men. Treasures found and then lost again, buried beneath a whispering golden sea. Restless it is and moving, beautiful and deadly, like the cobra, to those who care not to learn of its ways.

Harsh are the religions born of the desert. Of fire and bones are they made and the blood of sacrifice, with no thought given to changing ways or the insensate cities of men. We bind ourselves all about with chains and kill those who come to free us. We move upon the land in a momentary spasm of time and then, in the blink of an eye we are gone. Whilst the world moves serenely on, oblivious to the squalling cries of men who discover too late the lie they have lived.

Dawn's light it was, and beautiful. I stood before the great arch. The sands had yet to shimmer with heat.

Soon.

Between one heartbeat and the next, the sun's heat would pour down, pounding the earth with a molten hammer, until the whole of the desert lands became a gigantic metal smith's furnace, a forge for the shaping of the world to come. I loved the desert, the vast and empty silence of it all.

They would think me some sun crazed prophet, new come from out the stony wastes. In a land that had spawned prophets since the dawn of time, what price one more.

I stood outside the great arch of entry. Unwalled though the town of Kish was, its single arch of entry was the only entrance way wide enough to allow an ox cart passage through to the market square.

I stood there with a dark flame burning inside my head. I began to speak. I spoke to no one and to everyone. My voice carrying loud and clear above the rising hubbub of noise from the town's market squares.

Two soldiers flanked the entrance arch. I could feel their cold, stony eyes on me as I continued to speak. No one bothered to listen that first day, or the next. I had no food, no water and nothing with which to trade, for either one commodity or the other.

When darkness fell I slept on the desert floor. I had no dreams or weird sendings, and yet I knew, in a vague sort of drifty way that something was wrong, inside my head. I should not be standing here preaching, I should be....

I didn't know what it was I was supposed to do. I didn't really know anything at all. And so I stood before the great arch and spoke of this and that and hoped someone would listen, before I died of thirst and hunger.

Unknown to me, Azar had been informed of what I was doing. He, in his turn informed the ruling council of Kish and awaited orders. Others, round and about the market places heard my words from a distance and repeated them. Others became curious and wanted to know more. It was not, after all, a common practice then for a prophet to speak of the *One,* a single all powerful creator God, to those who, like all Kishites and Babylonians worshipped many Gods and Goddesses.

'Is there,' I asked rhetorically, 'a single God worthy of worship amongst all that grinning pantheon of Gods you serve?'

I argued against the necessity of throwing living children into an open furnace in the forlorn hope that some witless, idiot God, named Baal, would look with favour upon those who had willingly thrown their own children into the sacred flames. Such words would earn for me impalement upon an iron stake, but then, was I not already crazed and dying with a crouching shadow inside my head.

And still the soldiers did not come.

Towards the end of the second day, faint through I was from hunger and thirst, I spoke of The Way of the Four fold Path, the pattern and the *Maker*. The Spiral of Immortality and the never ending struggle of spirit to spiral upwards. I spoke of those possessed of a small dark spirit, willingly descending the spiral, spreading hurt and grave wounding where so ever they did go. I hung words upon the air and set them free. I spoke of one faith, one people and how it is that the pattern weaves as the *Maker* wills. My cup of madness was full, and I drank deep.

On the morning of the third day everything changed.

Weak now I was, scarce able to stand for the trembling in my legs, and the voice of me no more than a vulture's croak.

And still the soldiers of Azar had not come.

I stood, in my now accustomed place, before the great arch, hanging words upon the air, for those who travelled to and from the town to catch as they may.

Some listened and then hurried on by, horror writ clear upon their faces. Others wore frowns of puzzlement, as though my voice be foreign and my words not easily understood.

An early blush of dawn crowned me with its light whilst I spoke of the fourth way of spirit, that remains forever unknown. Bands of dusty desert travellers passed by without a glance, whilst the two soldiers flanking the great arch of entry, stared at me, as though I be something unclean. In their eyes perhaps I was. The desert began to shimmer with heat waves. High and above, a lone desert eagle screamed out, its wings all gold and fire from the glow of the sun. Stark the scene was, yet noisy and rich with a thousand mixed aromas.

Empty of food and water, the guts of me boiled with pain, sharp enough to moisten eyes.

Today would be the last. Without sustenance I could no longer endure, and I had not the will left to find it.

A cold voice of sharpened silver laughed inside my head, brittle sounding it was, and cruel, my sanity balanced upon the edge of a knife.

I stood midst the heat and dust, a starveling, speaking of things best left unsaid, and knew not why I spoke. I, who am a somewhat silent man was now verbose to the point of lunacy. I ordered my mouth to close, and ignored my own command as though it were not I who was in charge of my flesh. Something dark and coiling had wrapped itself all about the inside of my skull, strangling the sweet breath of reason. I know that now, I could not know of it then, else I'd not have become its creature.

It is easy to speak of evil from behind the safety of hallowed walls and, an unshakeable faith in the power of good. To be possessed by evil and remain all unknowing. To obey, thinking you serve the light, whilst your eyes wear dark mirrors. What then the price of awakening. To speak of evil and the purity of its form, first you must face it.

The struggle for my soul was not yet over. *He* was out there somewhere, pounding across the burning desert sands arms open wide to embrace me. I had betrayed a sacred trust that was both my strength and my weakness. I who once gave promise to a faint *trace of blue*. Blue, as all men know, is the true colour of God, the *Maker,* and I had nothing but worms dancing inside my head. Soon they would fill me and crawl out my ears or fill my throat with rotting slime.

I stood in between today and tomorrow without any remembrance of yesterday, and yet I struggled, in my own silent, stubborn way I struggled. Beneath the conscious level of knowing I refused defeat, I refused its acceptance. I denied its existence, therefore, within the core of my being, it did not exist. As the armies of Babylon found out to their cost, it is not enough to chain and enslave a people and call them defeated, when they do not consider that they have fought a battle and lost.

The dark thing stalked me, and pounced.

In my pride I had not thought it possible to ever betray my trust. The mere thought itself was unclean. That I had done so, left me shocked and hollow and — vulnerable.

Darkness struck with the swift, venomed violence of the desert cobra. I, who could out dance its speed was bit, venom invaded the sacred precinct of my house, tainting the spirit of me with poison, feeding it hopelessness, anguish, and the stark desolation of utter despair. Unable to remember, to reason, to understand and correct failure, my betrayal of trust.

Whilst all unknowing I struggled to break free, to return and seek forgiveness. To return and embrace a faint *trace of blue*.

As the sun's light grew in strength and intensity my vision wavered and then cleared somewhat. My throat ached, my head spun. It seemed as though I gazed down upon the throng before me from a great height. Silent they were. Whilst I had battled the spinning of my head, a crowd had gathered. I could hear a voice babbling on about the fourth way of the spirit. To my astonishment, they listened in complete and utter silence. Unnerving it was, and then some few came forward, and lay food and drink at my feet. And then they were gone.

I sat where once I had stood, slaking my thirst, eating greedily of fruit and bread with trembling hands.

And still the soldiers had not come.

When darkness fell I had not the will to move. I simply lay there on the sand and slept like some gorged ox.

Later, I came awake with a start, head empty, my belly nearly so. The sky was a pale wash of indefinite colour, deepening even as I watched. I stood and turned towards Kish. Its dun coloured arch loomed massive against a cloudless backdrop of sky. Light glimmered and gleamed upon the arms and burnished armour of the guards.

The scene had a stark unreal look about it. I sensed that something terrible was about to happen and that I was helpless to prevent it. I tried to fasten onto a piece of memory, that suddenly slipped through my head. It fell away from me like some tattered wind blown cloud. A sense of small hands, groping, fumbling splintered the back of my head with sudden pain, and then it was gone. I was here and yet not here, and wished I was some place else.

A large crowd had gathered, trooping silently through the arch towards me. I watched them come, staring through empty hollow eyes. The crowd swelled, those close by looked at me expectantly. All ages they were, men, women and children. Robed for travelling I noticed, and each one of them carrying a bundle of food and a skin of water. And still they came. WHY? Something cold lurched in my belly when an old man stepped forward and said, in a soft hesitant voice, 'Lead us, show us the way. Four hundred we be and are agreed. Teach us of what you know, in return we shall care for thee, feed and clothe thee and if it be your desire, there are women amongst us who will willingly lay with thee. Come, lead us.' A murmur of agreement rose up from the crowd like some winged bird seeking the sun.

I stared at him appalled. 'What have I done,' I thought wildly, and then, like memory, thought slipped away from me. Before I could answer the old man, the sound of marching feet drew near.

A squad of soldiers, armed and armoured marched through the great arch, led by Azar the Chaldean. Pushing the crowd aside they came to a halt in front of me. No parade ground soldiers these, menacing they were, and ominous. Battle hardened veterans every one, exuding a cold, quiet efficiency.

Azar stepped forward, halting no more than four paces in front of me. His face looked like some graven image, so cold and still it was. He stared at me through bleak eyes devoid of any hint of friendliness. He was, as he had warned me, a professional. His shield was at rest, his right hand resting lightly on the hilt of his sword. His unsmiling eyes failed to acknowledge me as anything, other than an obstacle in need of removing.

I should have been afraid. I should have known what was to follow, but then, I didn't know who or what I was. I had no memory of my own weapon skills, or what I was doing, or why I was standing there in front of him. Soul bound I was and weeping.

Azar spoke, his voice devoid of all emotion. 'I have argued with the Council to spare your life. They have agreed on condition that you move on — NOW —' he added with force.

I turned away from him and walked into the desert.

Celtic Sunset

I counted five hundred paces and then stopped and turned. Behind me followed the four hundred, silent as death.

'Go,' shouted Azar, pointing towards the open desert, 'Go, else I be forced to kill thee.'

Again, I turned and walked towards the sun. The crowd followed me.

'Go back,' I shouted at them, 'go back, leave me.'

The old man said, 'Never! You are the mouth of God. Where so ever you lead, we shall follow.'

I looked for Azar and his soldiers, but they had returned to Kish.

I could not lead four hundred men, women and children out into the desert, nor could I stay. With a sigh, I sat down on the sand to await the outcome of it all. I felt tired inside my head. Azar would return, of that I was certain. His return to Kish was no more than a return for new orders. I was the one ordered to go, and if not, kill. He had no orders regarding the four hundred who followed me.

The sun had begun its descent, when Azar returned at the head of a full Century. Red streaks of late sunlight gleamed along spear heads of bronze and burnished armour. They marched towards us with deadly precision.

A terrible sense of foreboding filled me. Uncertain of there intent, I walked slowly forward across the sand. Metal chinked against metal as the Century came to a crashing halt.

'Seize him,' commanded Azar pointing towards me.

Soldiers leapt forward to obey, binding my arms, whilst another lay his sword across my throat.

'Do not move,' warned Azar, his face grim and bleak, 'do not even think of moving, or you are dead, and my orders are that you should live.' He spat at my feet. 'You are a fool,' he hissed at me. 'A fool with an empty head. Why,' he asked, 'did you not just walk away? You are no prophet. I know who you are. At least,' he added, 'what you once were. Now look at you,' he kicked out at my shins viciously. 'Because of you,' he hissed 'I have now a distasteful duty to perform.' His voice throbbed with anger. 'I would kill you,' he screamed at me. 'Why? Of all people, why you? What is it inside your head that made you stand before the great arch, foretelling the coming of a new god? ARE YOU BLIND?' Azar bellowed, 'can you not see we have gods enough, what use,' he shouted 'be one more? Moloch aid me,' he muttered angrily. 'Well, speak man, speak, tell me why, God curse you?'

My head felt curiously empty, even the feel of scrabbling little hands was no longer there. Was I buried so deep I could never rise? I did not know.

'Why?' Azar demanded.

I looked him full in the face and said 'I don't know.'

'God's weep,' he exclaimed, 'you don't know!' His voice rose, full of frustrated anger. 'You poor, sore arsed son of a she goat, — of course you know — HOW CAN YOU NOT?'

He spun away from me, and then suddenly turned back. In a quiet chill voice he said, 'What I do this day, will stain me forever, and all you can say is, I don't know.'

People stood around us, huddling together in small frightened groups. I think they knew what Azar had been ordered to do, and not a one of them tried to escape. Mothers pulled children closer to them. Husbands looked around with vacant eyes. And no one uttered a single word.

Azar gave a quiet order. With amazing speed his Century fanned out, enclosing the four hundred within a ring of armoured bronze. He spoke again. Swords hissed from their scabbards, the rattling hiss of metal drawn against metal filling the air. And then, with a deliberate measured tread the soldiers began to tighten their ring about the four hundred.

Celtic Sunset

'NO,' I screamed and began to struggle. Someone hit me over the head, driving me to my knees. Bound and weak I could do nothing, not even weep.

Swords rose and fell, flashing in the light of a baleful sun. Screams of pain filled the air, and the moans of the dying. Ruthlessly efficient, it didn't take long for the soldiers to hack and stab four hundred people to death.

I moaned, my head pressed down upon the sand.

Azar grabbed my hair, jerking my head back with a vicious pull, twisting it so I faced the hacked and bloody ruin, that lay strewn about the desert floor.

'Look, dog turd,' he growled, 'look at what you have done.' He spat in my face, 'Know you this,' he said, 'by order of the council of Kish, your life is spared,' he grinned like some demented baboon. 'Your life,' he hissed, 'is your punishment. Now you must live, knowing words from out your own mouth caused the death of four hundred. I would kill you gladly, Moloch stay my hand,' breathed Azar, 'but you be not worth it, you be nothing at all. Now go.' He pulled me to my feet and pushed me roughly forwards, cutting through my bonds as he did so. 'Go,' he shouted, pointing towards the desert, 'go and find your death, it is all that is left to you now.'

I stumbled away from the reeking dead, picking up a water skin here, a bundle of food there. I gathered up all I could carry as I walked down a long alley of darkness out into the desert. I walked and stumbled the stars out of the sky.

Come morning, I found myself close to an outcropping of worn, sun weathered rocks. Searching I found a small wind hollowed cave and some evidence of it having been enlarged by human hands. The cave was no more than twenty paces deep, the roof of it brushing the top of my head, cool it was and dim. Dropping my bundles with a sigh of relief, I looked around. As I settled down on the cave floor, I knew that I would go no further into the desert. Here I would stay, until I wrestled free of what ever it was that bound me, or die in the trying. I shut away memory of the previous day's horror, and fought to regain my sanity. I had water enough for ten days and food for ten more, it was enough. I lay down then, whilst the morning sun filled the desert with heat. Within the cave the air was cool and dim, with a faint look of blue about it.

I felt safe here, though I cannot say why. As safe as any man can be, alone in the desert, that is. 'Why is that?' I thought sleepily, 'Is there something here that recognises me? Is it a sacred place I am in, left over from a time before?' I knew not, and then I was falling, spinning down into a deep dark well of sleep, healing it was and dreamless.

Something left me then, slipping away in quiet confusion. It slipped out of my head and away. Away from an ancient hand cut cave, that once knew light. A light that still lingered, its essence having seeped deep into the rocks. It had waited through endless eons, knowing one day, someone would return, and, if only for a brief span of time, worship again within the sacred cave of blue light.

The small ones had left long ago. Driven away by tall, long haired strangers, carrying weapons of metal against which, the flint folk could not stand. Now, another stranger had come, with shadows inside his head. The light brushed them away and was content. Others would come in a time not yet born. It was content to wait, knowing light was still of use in this new world. Those who had yet to come would recognise the cave for what it was, and dig beneath its floor, uncovering an ancient secret. The cave would become a shrine, a holy place of men. The light was content to remain.

Celtic Sunset

I came up through a deep well of sleep, like a drowning man striving for air, and then, awake I was. The whole of me refreshed in *The Three Fold Way*, of body, mind and spirit. I lay there for a moment, exploring a bright sense of wonder, alive inside my head. My body, weak though it was from lack of food and exercise, felt fine. It was whole with no draining wound upon it, and the spirit of me, that too was whole with no taint of darkness about it.

I was able to think clearly, to reason and — to remember. A chill hand clutched my guts, as I recalled all that had happened since I left the place of the book. Guilt drained out of me, as though some friendly hand lanced a desert sore, drawing forth its thick creamy poison, leaving me weak, but relieved that the poison was gone.

Somehow, in my blind wandering, I had stumbled across a cave, feeling safe, I slept. Whilst sleeping, I had been healed. I looked up at the smooth rock above me. Here and there I could see marks, as though someone had chiselled away bits and pieces of protruding rock, leaving the surface smooth and shiny.

Was it the cave, I mused, was there some mystical healing quality about it? Limestone it was, with a look of incredible age about it. The light, I noticed, within the cave had an almost bluish tint to it, or was that only my idle fancy.

I sat up, stretching arms, shoulders and legs, working out cricks and creaks. I gloried in a wonderful rush and return of sensation. I would think on my guilt and betrayal later, here did not seem the place for it. There was something here, I was sure of it. I came here with a leach of darkness attached to my soul, sucking out the spirit of me it was. Now it was gone. How, I didn't know. It was enough for me to know I was again myself. The why of it all I would reason through later, when ready. First I must regain strength, and then retrieval of a blade buried so carelessly beneath the sand.

I drank some water and ate a bit of food. The bundles I had carried here contained slabs of pressed dates, goats cheese, and hard round cakes of unleavened bread. Simple nourishing fare it was, enough and more for my needs.

As I ate, I felt the floor beneath me with my left hand. I expected to find rock beneath a thin covering of sand, blown in by the desert winds. I was no more than curious to see if the floor had been chiselled smooth like the roof and walls. To my surprise, I could feel only sand. Impelled more by my own curious nature than anything else, I finished my food and began scooping out sand with both hands. I uncovered three flint arrow heads, beautifully shaped and still incredibly sharp. A little further down I found a rare and ancient treasure, a flint knife. The length of it half again as long as my hand. It was, I knew, a masterpiece of the art of flaking, chipping a piece here a piece there until a flake of flint broke away in exactly the right spot. Skilled work it was, like the cutting of a jewel stone, where a single wrong blow can shatter it into worthless fragments. The knife handle was about the width of my palm, its rough outer surface having been lovingly smoothed. The blade was thick, sharp and tapered down to a deadly needle point. The whole thing, lovingly crafted, though it was fragile compared to metal, even so, in the hands of one who knew how to use it, it would be a deadly weapon indeed. Laying it to one side, I continued to dig. Outside the cave the light had grown bright and heavy with heat.

I found it then, my questing fingers brushing against its hard smooth surface. Caught up in the thrill of discovery, I quickly cleared away more sand, exposing a round, wide mouthed clay pot. I pulled it free. How long it had lain there, buried beneath the sand, I didn't know. I knew only that it was old, incredibly old. It wasn't so large, one hand held it easily. Of baked clay it was, the kind that will last forever if left undisturbed. Its outer surface had been painted with alternating bands of red and black, and then fire glazed to seal and protect the whole of it. Beautiful it was, and old.

But why, I wondered, bury a clay pot with flint weapons? Was there a connection? Was someone from the past trying to say, or at least indicate something? A melding of cultures perhaps, or an indication of trade with others, skilled in ways the flint folk were not. I tipped sand out of the jar, something glinted, catching the light as it fell. Placing the empty jar carefully to one side, I scrabbled in the sand and pulled free an astonishing piece of metal work. An ornament, to be worn about the neck. I held it up.

Suspended on a thin chain of silver was an incredibly beautiful piece of workmanship. A small thin disc of polished silver about the size of a copper coin. On one side two circles, one alongside the other, lay next to five stars. What they might represent, I couldn't think. And then I had it, the two circles were the moon and the sun, and the five stars represented the five moving planets that we can see with our eyes. The names of the five planets I couldn't recall. The mystery of it all deepened. Flint weapons, a glazed clay pot of ancient design, and a silver neck ornament with a design of stars on it. I turned the medallion over. To my utter confusion it bore the design of the cross within a circle, man's oldest and most sacred of symbols. There was something here I didn't understand, and I'm not at all sure I wanted to.

I sat for awhile, simply looking at the ornament suspended from its chain. There was something odd about it. Still a little mind weary, I didn't at first realise what the oddness was. Having handled much gold and silver over the years I was familiar with the feel of it and its look. Polished silver had a way of reflecting light, that was different from this that I held in my hand.

Silver shone with a rich glow. The chain and its medallion sparkled with shards and glittering slivers of light, that comes from a harder, more polished surface than soft, malleable silver. My breath caught in my throat, surely it couldn't be, I thought wonderingly. I tried to scratch the surface of the medallion with my nails. I couldn't even mark it, though not yet returned to my full strength, I none the less remained a strong man, certainly more than the equal of most men. I tried to bend the medallion. If silver it be, it would bend, if it was what I thought it was, it would not, or at least very little. It bent hardly at all. Silver, I could have bent and straightened causing it to break in half. The mystery deepened.

I looked at it in a kind of astonished wonder. The coin or medallion whatever it might represent, was made of white gold (platinum). And that was, as I knew full well, having known more than one or two metal smiths, an ore smelting secret known only to a few. The kind of heat needed to extract and smelt white gold, produced only small amounts. Turned into ornamental jewellery each piece sold for a fabulous sum. And, it was only during Nebuchadnezzar's rule that such advanced technology had been discovered or, so it would now appear — rediscovered.

White gold, a clay pot and flint weapons. Again I wondered, had there been three different cultures, existing side by side in harmonious accord with each other? Each culture on a different level to the other. Was it possible? Would not the flint folk desire clay pots or metals? I couldn't reason it out. Why weapons of flint, and jewellery of metal.

Celtic Sunset

The culture that made chains of white gold must surely have been capable of smelting iron.

There was a mystery here I had not the time to fathom. Carefully, I replaced the chain back in the pot and reburied it along with the flint weapons. Whatever the mystery might be, I felt that the items belonged here. Perhaps they, like the cave of blue light, were waiting to be found by the right person, and certainly I was not he. 'Now why,' I wondered aloud 'did I think that?'

During the days that followed my discovery and reburial of the old things, I ran. I ran and began to lift rocks to increase my strength. At night, beneath the cold white light of the moon, I danced the spear dance, and the way of the empty hand. I danced the nine fold step of the sword until I could once again execute its steps with all my former speed and grace. And I ran, always I ran. During the cool of early dawn, I skimmed the desert floor upon winged feet, until sweat flew from my body like sea spray from the bow of a ship.

On the morning of my seventh day in the desert I ran down a gazelle. Coming upon it unexpectedly, it stood for a moment in shock, at my sudden, silent approach, and then it was off, bounding across the wasteland in huge springy leaps. 'Meat,' I thought, 'this day I dine on meat.' I laughed out loud from the pure pleasure of it all. The chase, beneath a spreading blush of pink along the horizon's rim, the wondrous feel of muscles powering me along. It all combined to fill me with an exultant sense of freedom.

I ran the gazelle down into exhaustion, leapt upon its back, grasped its horns in my hands, and then, with a sudden, sideways wrenching twist, broke its neck.

That night, after dining on cooked brains, heart and liver, I sat for awhile, gazing up at the stars.

I was ready now, to leave this place, I had regained all that I had lost, and more I was thinking. My understanding of my reason for being, had grown. My reaffirmation of promise made. The slaughter of the four hundred was something I had yet to think on, I would do so by and by. If so there was reason to find, I would find it. They would have died beneath the sword irrespective of my being named as the reason for their deaths. They had, I knew, come too easy to me. Azar and the Council of Kish, had, I was sure, already marked them down for death. Malcontents, trouble makers, denial of Babylon's blood thirsty Gods, whatever the reason, they were doomed. Perhaps my sudden appearance as a sun crazed prophet, with no memory, was simply part of an inevitable cycle of execution. I like to think it was so.

Being a guardian of houses of knowledge, I paid scant attention to the posturing of men. They be a bloody lot, ever wishful of slaughtering each other like cattle. The Hebrews be slaves, in a land where once, they too had put every man, woman and child to the sword in the name of their God, sparing only virgins for their own use. Now it seems it is their turn to be slaves.

And I.

I have known the foul touch of darkness. It found a weakness within me and used me like some night soil pot, but for a *trace of blue* it might have me still.

I sat there, before the mouth of that strange, mysterious desert cave, and thought upon how little I had gleaned of the way of men.

Is it not, I mused, a measure of a man to suffer adversity and grow the stronger for it, in mind and spirit? We ask not for such testings and yet they come, falling upon us when least expected.

Is not the measure of a man to be found in the way he faces adversity? Some do despair and go far and away into a dark place hidden deep within, whilst others curse their ill fortune, using it like some blame for the whole ruin of their lives. Woe is me, I have heard men moan. Unloved am I, my God hath turned his face away. Woe, woe is me, I am undone. Such men grovel in the richness of their own misfortunes with never a thought given to its cause, or the striving to rise above such grim despair. Gloomy are they, and remain so, living out the balance of their lives midst shadows and grey mind walking. With never an eye cast toward the beauty of heaven's light and its warming glow of an apple-cheeked sun.

I have seen such men burn precious books and disclaim the sound of vibrant strings of music as an affront to the silent sanctity of Baal's temple, whilst throwing living children into the furnace of his mouth. Ruins of spirit are they, Spites and Hates upon the land. And then there are others, whose spirits are forged the stronger upon adversities anvil. Plunged down, they ever struggle and fight to crawl up, towards the light. Standing, they reach out towards the sun, voicing praise and thanks to the *One*, for his precious gift of life. Such as they, might stand upon a feather weighted scale of truth and balance the scales easily.

And I, staring upward into a vast, star encrusted night sky, felt a dust of blue-white starlight drift down inside my head. A small moaning wind skittered across the desert. Behind me a rustling sigh, as wind blown sand trickled down the face of the limestone hill. Suddenly, unexpectedly, I stood outside my body. A fat, golden moon cleared the distant horizon, I sensed the rich weight of its borrowed light, like a melon it was, all huge and glowing, swollen and amber skinned. I returned within like some jinn to its wax sealed jar.

All unknowing, I had been used by a shadow of *The Lurking One*, the Prince of Flies, whose master broods in sullen, solitary anger, far and out beyond the stars. Darkness, thinking I be slaved and broken from the faith of my trust, bent me to its will, with no thought given to spirit's striving towards a trace of distant blue.

How foolish.

But then, evil ever has an unthinking idiot's way about it.

I writhed within a cauldron of scald, guilt wrapped all about my head like cerements, and shadow haunts. I had ignored a feeling of unease, a sensing of approaching danger. Never before had I ignored my inner sense. Always I responded, in one way or another to my intuition. It is, as all men know, the sixth sense of any true warrior. So it was that I walked blind, and a score of gentle scholars bled out their lives upon unfeeling stone.

I spoke of secrets I should not have shared, at least not in this land, where many gods rule. Not in Babylon, where jealous priests hold sway, and yet, I knew, if only in a small way, that I had not command over my own tongue, when I spoke of the *Maker,* and the pattern of his weave, thereby causing the brutal death of many. Used was I. Even so, I reasoned, because of me vultures gorged upon human flesh until they be too waddling and heavy to fly. Am I then to blame, yes, I think in part I am, no matter the dark shadow over me.

I sat beneath a night sky full of a rare and wondrous beauty with a heavy weight of guilt about my shoulder. Pierced I was with sharp needles of remorse, pummelled by stones of self castigation. I had been used like night waste linen scraps.

Celtic Sunset

So be it.

I cannot undo what has been done. I cannot give back life, or rebuild broken stones. I cannot raise the Nubian, or erase the contempt of the soldiers who fled from me. I can only go forth from this moment on, secure in who and what I am. A promise I gave, long ago, before the dawn of men midst the light of a faint *trace of blue*. It is my trust, and my reason for being until the last day of days, or an upward climb about the spiral that will take me I know not where. Here and now, beneath this desert sky I am Hammer, sword dancer, master of the nine hand step, guardian of knowledge — and my spirit is good. I am all that I want to be. I am all that I strive to be. Imperfect though I am, I approve of myself and the way of my walking. Approval of self is the first of all the secrets of the *Way*. I drove it from me and a shadow climbed in. Now it is gone. I am Hammer. I choose the way of blue and not its brother — darkness.

One day it will come for me. It will seek me out and find me waiting. So be it. Let others cavil its presence. I do not. I am awake now. It knows me for its enemy. I, who am a protector of the *Way*, will fight. I will fight — forever.

I had thought to return to Kish and kill Azar and his soldiers, and then I thought not. What use revenge, perhaps he too acted whilst shadow haunted.

I retrieved my sword from beneath the sands, near the ruins of the place of the book, it was.

It came to me then, in the way that it always came, like a wandering thought. A sense of certainty, of knowing where I must go, and what I must do.

Roy Edwards

I walked out from the desert with a glow of sunset behind me. Dark red it was, like the embers of a cooling fire.

He stood there, where the desert sands merged with scrub and small broken stones, the last of the suns ruddy light bathing his skin in crimson and gold-orange fire. Small he was, and dark with a scholars dreamy look about his face. His eyes were a faded, washed out blue, set in a wrinkled, brown face that looked like a pickled walnut. He wore a loose, pale green robe, and sandals of rough leather. As I drew near he gave me greeting and said, 'I am Menacratus of the house of learning.'

'I am Hammer,' I replied.

He said, 'You are the one?'

'Yes,' I answered quietly, 'I am the one.'

'Then come,' he said briskly, 'and be about your duties.'

He turned on his heel and walked away towards a low, dun coloured, fort like building, squatting against the base of a small, flat topped hill.

I followed. Warmed by the blood red rays of a fiery setting sun.

Ψ

Celtic Sunset

Where go the years?
How bright they are.
How swiftly they fly.
My hair turned grey and then white, and that was the only sign of change the years lay upon me.

My fifty were superb warriors. An army of such men could easily conquer the world.

Sometimes we fought armed raiders, sweeping in from out the desert wastelands in search of loot, women and grain. Undisciplined they were and over confident of their own warrior skills. My fifty could defeat two hundred such warriors with ease. Once, we turned aside a force of three hundred, for a loss of only twelve of our own.

Vigilante I was, off duty, only when I slept.

Sometimes, I wandered through the great hall and its many rooms filled with books. From time to time I read a little, or studied ancient texts of medicine and science, astrology and strange philosophies of races who no longer exist. Scrolls there were, found amongst ruined temples, by men who said they were of a brotherhood who seek out such things. No one knows who built the temples, or who worshipped there. Such scrolls that were found, often contained ancient wisdoms, or spoke of dark things that have ever haunted the lives of men.

And always we trained.

When ever one of my fifty fell in battle, another would come out of the desert to take his place. Sometimes more than one. Who called them I cannot say. Perhaps like me, they simply knew where they should be.

When the end came, it came swiftly, like a plunging stallion in heat.

Roy Edwards

I awoke one morning full of restless unease.

Buckling a blade about my waist, I strode beyond the walls and stared out across the desert. Nothing.

I turned then, and made my way up towards the flattened summit of the hill that towered above and behind the long hall. From its height, I slowly scanned the desert from horizon to horizon. Nothing moved, nothing stirred at all in the rising heat of all that empty desolate waste. My guts felt empty and tight. Something was wrong, I could almost taste the wrongness pervading the air I breathed. Suddenly, shockingly, a memory of a burnt ruin and the tumbled smouldering bodies of slain scholars filled my head. 'MOVE,' a voice screamed inside my head, 'MOVE — NOW.'

Venting a roar of rage, I leapt over the edge of the hill, bounding down the shaly shifting slope in great lunging leaps. Desperate I was, and shouting as I raced towards the hall. My fifty boiled out through its huge single bronze door. Alerted by my shout, they quickly formed a fighting square as I pounded towards them.

'Something,' I roared, 'something comes.'

Panting, I skidded to a halt and said breathlessly, 'I can see nothing.' I lay a hand on my chest. 'I feel it here, something dark is moving towards us. *I am not mistaken*,' I added softly. 'Now,' I ordered, 'form up in groups of ten, spread out, be alert. At the first sign of danger or anything, anything at all, rally to me here, outside the door. Now move — MOVE,' I bellowed.

This would be no skirmish, no casual raid, I could feel it in my bones.

I ran swiftly through into the inner court yard and across into the great hall, shouting for the scholars to assemble immediately. They came, all of them and gathered before me in a silent group. I said only that we stood in danger of immediate attack, from what might very well be a large fighting force. 'This be no casual raid of wandering desert marauders, I know it, I can feel it,' I told them. Swiftly, urgently, I advised the scholars to hide their most precious writings in the many prepared secret places, cut out of bedrock and hollows beneath slabs of stone deep within the library.

Later, the scholars, all sixty two of them, reassembled and advised me that they had agreed amongst themselves to remain and fight if they must. I smiled grimly at that, but I could not force them to leave, nor did I have men enough to spare, to guide and protect them, if they did.

Their's was the right to protect that which they love, if so it was they desired to do. They were, I realised, realists enough to understand that, if your life and the way of its living be threatened, then so must you be prepared to fight to protect your way of life, and its future continuance. Always, there are those who would take it from you, or seek to destroy it simply for the joy of destroying what others have so painstakingly created. It is a form of denial. I don't want it, but you can't have it, therefore, I will destroy.

There is no such thing as a perfect, peaceful society. There can only be at best, an uneasy truce whilst ever man contends with man.

Words are of little use when faced by an armed and dangerous invader, be it your home or your land, he will simply take what he wants and then kill you. It is as casual as that. Understand it or die. Civilisation is a word, a concept used by thin skinned men who feign a pretence to being civilised. Civilised men make war, uncivilised men do not, they fight small battles.

Long ago there was a civilised city, built by civilised men, deep within the desert. What is Nargal now, but a ruin of bones and crumbling brick lying beneath a windy sun. Where fled the wise men, the poets? Who now is the magician? What price wisdom without the means of its protection?

Scholars there were, wise men, farmers and poets, musicians, artists and magicians, men of science, medicine, and high learning came together and said, 'We shall build a city and rule it with sweet reason and compassion for all men.

Long did they labour, and long again until a great and beautiful city towered above the sands. Nargal did they name it, for its light and colour, its open airy walks and broad paved avenues.

Men came from the lands of the two rivers and beyond. Entering the city of Nargal they preyed upon its people, like wolves upon lambs, committing murder, rape and robbery. Caught by city wardens they were brought before the Council, who as all men knew, ruled with sweet reason and a compassionate understanding of those who had fallen down into evil ways. In white wisdom's blindness they were unable to comprehend or even begin to understand that there are some of human kind who are evil by choice and determined intent. They like to rob and kill. They enjoy inflicting pain and suffering upon others, they do it knowingly and willingly, that is the evil. Sweet reason cannot and never will understand a willingness by some, to embrace and be a knowing cause of evil, such is the flaw of reason. It made them feel good, just and pious when they set murderers free to kill again, with no thought at all given to the horror they smilingly unleashed. Victims were forgotten. The saving of murderers, rapists and child killers became all. Fed they were and clothed and taught to mouth insouciant words of

'I'm sorry - I regret.' For this they received rewards and were set free.

The Nargalite fathers soothed such men with honeyed wine and sweet reason. Building an open prison of many pillared beauty, it was, to the Nargalites, a fulfilment of reasonable compassion. So good did the Nargalites become they erred on the side of evil and became a good and pious evil in their turn, with no thought at all given to the concept that evil, by its very definition must be contained else the whole of society becomes its victim.

So it was that civilised men of reason through their own compassionate acts condoned murder, and made of it a fine and glorious thing. Such civility, such manners, tumbled down and became a kind of loose insanity.

Nargal is no more.

Freed murderers burnt it to the ground and slaughtered its reasoned population in a frenzy of lusting hate, so it is the story is told.

'Something is coming,' I said softly, 'something soon.'

They came like whispers of wind across the sands with the early morning sun burning behind their backs. Desert men they were, lean and hard with a cruel, cold look about them.

They stood in silent ranks, a spears throw from our walls. There sheer weight of numbers dismayed me. 'And why,' I wondered, 'do they allow us time to form our defence? Are they so confident of victory? Do they think my fifty are to be so easily brushed aside?' I smiled grimly at the thought. Did they, like others before them, assume the great hall housed treasures of gold and silver. Few it seems have the wit to understand that wealth means different things to different people. 'Well now,' I thought bleakly, 'I would use their cool arrogant indifference against them.'

Barking out a single command, my fifty formed a fighting square in front of the great bronze door in less than six heart beats. There was something odd about the silent raiders, it worried me. They made no move towards us. No threats, no jeers, no demands for our surrender, nothing. The sun climbed towards its zenith. Swiftly now, I organised our defence. I counted over a thousand raiders and we but fifty and sixty two scholars. We would not easy come through this, I'm thinking.

Swiftly, quietly I gathered the scholars about me in the courtyard before the hall. The sky above shone brittle blue, the air still and heavy with heat. I explained to the scholars what it was I wanted them to do. They scurried away and returned puffing under heavy loads. War shields are weighty, clumsy things to anyone not trained in their use. The scholars would not be able to bear the weight of one for more than a few heart beats let alone use it. I had other plans.

Leading the scholars out through the great bronze door, I formed them up behind my fifty and said, 'Dig a trench to the depth of half the height of a shield, place the shields in the trench and overlap one against the other in as straight a line as you can manage, back fill the trench and stand behind the shield wall.'

They scurried to obey. As they began to scoop sand out with their hands I said, 'Flimsy though the barrier might be, it will slow the raiders down and afford your legs some measure of protection.'

'At least,' I added silently, 'I hoped it would.' The scholars puffing and panting at the unaccustomed work I asked of them, sank a line of overlapping shields into the sand. The length of it when finished was about as long as a fighting square of fifty, is wide. Whilst some scholars filled in the trench, others fetched stabbing knives from the armoury.

The raiders had not yet made a move. It was odd, very odd. 'Are they,' I thought, 'waiting for some one? A war captain perhaps.' There delay was my gain and I used the moments full well. Quickly demonstrating the use of a stabbing knife to the scholars as they stood around, holding the unfamiliar weapons in awkward hands.

'The name of the weapon explained its use. No finesse or real skill was needed,' I told them. 'You stab towards the groin or stomach, or for that matter,' I added, 'any where you are able. The blade of a stabbing knife is long and slender, tapering down to a sharp wicked looking needle like point. The blade is double edged and incredibly sharp. It was designed for close quarter fighting when there was no room to swing or use a sword. Thin and sharp, it could, with enough force behind it, pierce through armour or ringmail. Stab,' I explained, 'then twist the blade and pull it out. If it won't come, sometimes muscles spasm holding the blade fast, leave it and use another blade. We have plenty,' I added softly with a feral grin.

None of the scholars would last long against a determined warrior, but as a group they might just make a difference, no matter how small.

Wearing a tight, grim look I walked away and entered the courtyard. With a clang of bronze on stone, I closed and barred the huge bronze door from within. Alone, I looked towards the empty silent hall of my trust. Silently I reaffirmed my promise. Suddenly, I spun and jumped, my outstretched fingers scrabbling for a hold on the outer wall. I hung there for a moment and then slowly pulled myself up until I sat astride the wall surveying the scene below.

The raiders stood in silent ranks facing my own equally silent ranks. Behind my fifty, the scholars shuffled nervously, there backs to the now closed door, long blades gleaming in their hands. In front of the scholars, the half buried war shields of polished bronze seemed to glow with a sullen red coppery light, as they caught and reflected the rays of the climbing sun. There was a feel of menace in the air and something else, something taintingly evil.

I dropped down from the wall, landing lightly on the balls of my feet. The scholars in their green robes looked strangely out of place in all that grim tableau.

There was nothing more I could do. I made my way across the sand and stood in front of my fifty, easy and relaxed as the sun's warmth loosened tight muscles, it felt good. I stood shieldless. When the attack came, sword skill would be all but useless. I intended to use my strength and height to the full. A shield would be an encumbrance.

'Come then,' I thought silently, 'I am ready.'

As if some silent command had been given, they came with a rush. Like desert haunts they were, whisper drifting across the sands as my blade hissed free of its scabbard.

'Come then,' I growled, 'take my hair if you can.'

We hacked, stabbed, cut and died.

In ones and twos, we died as we fought the sun down from the sky.

Now the raiders yelled, now they screamed. No man remains voiceless when iron slices through his flesh, unless that is, he be tongueless. The raiders were not, they came in yelling, leaping waves. Each time we beat them back, our numbers were fewer.

Celtic Sunset

And then we were ten and stared death in the face.

Covered in blood and sweat we fought like demon jinns. Of the raiders thousand, I judged a bare three hundred remained alive. Broken bodies lay in mounds, six deep, so great a slaughter had we wrought. The wild beating heart of me gloried in their ruin. Strong I was and free. Blood pounded inside my head, a wild recklessness filled me, 'Come then,' I screamed, 'see, my hair is unbound, take it if you can, bastardai, take it if you can.' Yelling, I swept my sword round in a great sweeping arc, cutting through flesh with ease, the strength of me driving the blade through, splintering bones. It went on, mindless, endless repetitive slaughter. I spat, howled and screamed. Each time I cut a man down another was there to take his place. Was there no end to their numbers, I thought wildly. This was, I had realised, no ordinary raid. The raiders seemed intent only upon our destruction irrespective of their own losses. They had come to destroy the hall and all it contained. White hot fury raged through me, driving me into a frenzy of blood lust. My sword whirled a hewing song.

The scholars defence lasted less than a heartbeat. They were swept away like grains of sand before a howling wind, staining the great door with gouting blood. The air throbbed with screams as I was driven back, by a sudden rush and cut of crimson stained swords.

I stand alone now, with the salt taste of blood in my mouth. Ropes of spittle hang from my chin, like a war hound I am, cornered and salivating. My warriors, broken in death, lay sightless upon a field of hot desolate sand. I can feel the hot sun on my reeking flesh, the sting of sweat in my eyes. Air labours in my lungs, and a fierce wild joy burns in my heart.

191

Roy Edwards

This day I will die midst a howling horde of my enemies, sword in hand, defiant. A warriors death, and a fine day it is to be dying.

'Come then,' I whispered, 'take my hair if you can.'

Something wild and hot flowed through me.

Something of Tabath and Thomas and Raman the Egyptian.

Wild, savage growls tore at my throat. Raising my sword above my head, I charged, knocking down warriors to the right and left of me, my sword a whirling, flashing arc of sharp cold fire, as I strode down the final heartbeats of my life.

I spun. A whirling dervish dance midst my enemies, hewing men down as though I were chopping wood. Even so, my strength was ebbing, draining out of me from a score of vicious wounds. Ruby droplets spun through the air, as I raced towards the final measure of my heartbeat.

Death rode my blade. Hot was the sun. Full was the air with the roar and cry of desperate men.

Alone I was, screaming out a long forgotten war cry, upon the fallen edge of all that brutal day.

My God came to me, burning inside my head like some blue-white flame of vengeful sorrow.

And then, suddenly, shockingly, I stood alone midst an island of silence. My enemies, drew back, their eyes full of awe, wide and staring.

Fury consumed me like an edge of God's anger.

'Come,' I screamed at them, my throat ragged and hoarse. 'Come,' whirling my long sword above my head I yelled. 'I be Hammer, a warrior, and today is a good day to die. It is,' I cried out, 'my chosen day.' I laughed, my voice croaking and dreadful, 'Any day is a good day to die, but this,' I yelled, 'be the best of all days, Come,' I shouted, 'come whore sons,

Bastardai, take my hair. It be white, and I be old and the death of you all.' Boasting I was, and why not, soon I would boast no more.

The raiders shuffled nervously. They would kill me, of that there was no doubt. Now they were afraid and uncertain, knowing some few of them had yet to die in the taking of my head.

Thankful for the respite, however brief, I sought to delay them longer whilst I gathered the last of my strength. I stuck my sword in the sand, resting the tired weight of me on its hilt. My body cracked and aching, the life of me draining out with my blood.

'Look about you,' I said softly, 'look at the ruin my fifty have made of your ranks.' I smiled then, a ghastly grimace, 'We have destroyed you,' I said, of all your tribe only women and children and a few old men are left, even your name will soon be forgotten.

A wailing moan filled the air as the surviving invaders looked around, realising too late, that the heaps and mounds of slain, scattered about the sands, were all their own. We had numbered but fifty and they a thousand or more.

I almost felt sorry for them then. They stood there beneath a darkening sky of blue, its horizon all smeared with the crimson edged gold of a sinking, flaring sun.

Stunned they were, mouths open in shocked disbelief. They had not thought it possible for fifty to destroy them utterly between the rising and the setting of the sun.

Some cried out in horror and threw down their weapons. Others wailed a broken song of grieving as they looked upon mounds and scattered piles of their dead. Of the thousand or more raiders less than three hundred stood alive upon the sands.

They could not allow me to live.

When news of their defeat reached other tribes of the desert, as surely it would, and it became known they had been defeated by a mere fifty of men, those who survived would be forever shamed and devoid of honour. Should I live, then the greater there shame would be.

I could almost see it all going on inside their heads. Moans turned to growls of anger.

It was dying time.

The setting sun had begun to flare out, sending up great columns and pillars of silver gold light. The sky was indigo with scarlet streaks. Here and there I could see glimmers and gleams of stars and the faint ghostly outline of a silver crescent moon. Beautiful it was, and I thanked the *One* silently for granting me a last sight of it all. My enemies edged closer, a dark shifting mass of hate and steel and silent weeping, feet whispering upon sand, the sound of it all I could hear. I felt a small breath of wind caress my face like a blessing — and then it was gone.

The light of the glory road filled my eyes, beckoning it was, somewhere westering the sun. My God waits. 'I come,' I mouthed softly, 'Patience Lord, I'll not be long.'

In the last of the sun's flaring pillared light, I screamed out a challenge and lunged forward, swinging my sword in a savage sweeping arc. I danced the sword dance with them, hacking and hewing, tearing out throats, shearing through limbs. The savage power of my blows shearing through bone.

And then I was down on my knees, sword blades slashing open my back. With a terrible cry on my lips I surged up, swinging wildly. My body was fire and pain and burning, I felt my strength slip away. My vision blurred and there was a sound of voices singing inside my head, and then I was

194

down. A thrown spear through my chest, the blade of it sticking out my back. Something crashed against my head with stunning force. Blows rained down, turning me into a butchers thing of hacked meat and flowing blood.

My strength slipped away. Shock and pain spasmed muscles as a flicker of life dimmed inside my head. Swordless I groped blindly for the hilt of my stabbing knife, my left hand gripped the spear shaft sticking out my chest. I felt the knife cool in my hand.

With a final mighty heave I lunged up and forwards, stabbing blindly. I felt the blade sink in flesh — and then I heard it, that faint melodic whistling sound, of a tempered steel blade slicing through the air. My head jumped free and rolled across the sand. My final flicker of thought was — 'They have taken my hair.'

Back in the forest glade, I staggered away from the stones, my head pounding, as though someone had cracked my skull with a hot forge hammer. Sick I was and reeling, the image of Hammer's death fresh inside my head. The feel of a blade slicing through my neck all too real, like a sharp stinging burn it was.

I sat down on the forest floor gulping air. 'I am Culann of the Arverni,' I whispered softly, 'a free person, Druid to *The People*.

The pain around my neck eased, the pounding in my skull faded away. I had walked the third path and survived. I thought then, that my trial of testing was over.

I was wrong.

Above me, the sun seemed scarce to have moved, and yet, I felt as though I had been walking the stones forever.

Roy Edwards

The forest lay cool and dim around me. I found the small hidden stream and drank deep, it tasted earthy and fresh with a tang of something about it I couldn't identify, cool it was. I stood up then and looked around. The forest was quiet, no leaf stirred or rustled. The air had an expectant feel about it, as though it had suddenly paused between one breath and another. I had lived through memories I had yet to think upon and unriddle. The memories were mine, though parts of them I had not recalled before.

It all had something to do with my unknown destiny and that of *The People*, though what, I did not yet know. There was experience to be found in my memories, knowledge I stood in need of. A sudden chill of premonition swept through me, Romans. My life, my training, my destiny and *The People*, it all had to do with Romans.

There was something I had to do. A year from now, two years from now, I didn't know. What I did know, was that my life and that of *The People* would become bound up in some way with that of Rome. Cumall, I mused, what is it you have not told me? What secrets do you hide?

There is a reason for far memory recall. It is one of the first secrets of learning Druidry. Without it, little in the way of advance can be made along the first, second or third path. The third, being the way of the spirit, remains closed to those who are unable to recall at all. It is, when all is said and done, simply the spirit's way of learning or remembering.

So it is we are taught within the Nemeds circle. Cumall once said, 'The difference between memories and dreams is that dreams are a confused melange, a tacky confection of real and imagined images. A mix of spirit and that other dark side of memory, left over from an age when men were not human kind, but reptiles prowling a new forming world.'

196

Celtic Sunset

'There are wide plains of memory,' Cumall said 'that we only glimpse from time to time and then strive to forget. Memories,' he said, 'though confused, vague and uncertain to any who are not trained in the way of Druid, are a mix of this life and times before. We, who are trained in the secret way, can differentiate one from the other with consummate ease, and recognise what is relevant and what is not. We know,' he emphasised, 'what memories are of this life and what are of a life before, We are aware of what we have done, and of what has been done to us. The pattern weaves, Culann, the pattern weaves. We must confront our own demons. We have all, in one life or another, been both villain and hero, wise man and fool. Thus we face the bones of yesterday and what we are today is what we have made of ourselves. Yesterday is of little significance if no lesson be gained from the memory of it. True it is, much that is past, is not worth the effort of recall. It is the events,' he said, 'the experiences of both past and present coupled with an ever widening accumulation of knowledge, that help to shape us. It is a fine thing to remember how good, wise and noble you once were. Think you then, that you have never walked in darkness, like some self deluded fool, doing unto others what you hope will never be done unto you. Our world is indifferent, it is humankind who are good or evil with shadings in between. The choice is yours, it is always yours. The pattern weaves to the *Maker's* will, to the steps of your own dancing. Remember how dark you once were, if only to balance the light of the way you now walk. If you do not, how then can you climb the spiral. We are both light and shadow. You seek to rise above, or banish forever the shadow within you as you journey towards the light, until you become more light than dark, eventually attaining to a state of being, where the white spirit of you is supreme, and the shadow stains you not at all. With knowledge,' Cumall said, 'awareness, Culann, and only with knowledge can you attain that brightening state. Know you this Culann and think on it, knowledge is in part, made up of an accumulation of experiences, mistakes made and corrected, words studied and pondered upon, and more, a great deal more.'

'This is what we know, against which a true measure of spirit's advancement along the way, and a beings worth, can be reckoned.'

'Be your words and deeds evil, be you of dark intent, then recognise what you are and strive to rise above your shadows. Blame not others for what you have done. As you rise, as surely you will, do not regress, though the temptation be great. To be evil, to continue evil ways from one life to the next, is to walk the downward spiral of spirit's ruin. To sin, to err, to recognise and correct, to strive towards light from one life to the next, is to climb the Spiral of Immortality. Thereby is judged the true worth of being. We of Druid teach that memories are an integral part of the journey. True memories can reveal the errors and the joys of times before, revealing experience upon which wisdom stands. Knowledge,' Cumall said, 'does not imply wisdom. It is what we do with our knowledge that determines, or may lead to wisdom. A learned man without the wit, will or experience to use his knowledge, is a vain seeking useless sort of creature. Such men are incredibly protective and jealous of their positions. They live in fear of others realising how empty they are, nor can they tolerate anyone who might equal or surpass their level of learning, forever putting obstacles in their way hindering or utterly destroying their will to continue. Such be mean and small in spirit, like Caesar and his barbaric friends. We of *The People*, we all be walkers of the path, Culann. In one way or another, Druid or otherwise, we all be walkers. Though it be not true of all human kind. Some do walk backwards with deliberate intent. Some do walk and fall, then rise again, always striving towards the light. Others move in circles without ever attaining a given end. And many there are, though it saddens me to say it, who move not at all along the way. Disdainful are they of its very existence, with no memory at all of what has gone before, they deny the very breath of their spirit within its house of flesh.' So it is that Cumall says, perhaps he is right, perhaps he is not. Memory of all is fine, but right now I have a more immediate concern.

I found myself standing beneath a spreading canopy of trees. Cool it was, and moist, with a fresh turned earthy smell to the air. I stood beside a stream as it chuckled and laughed its way through fern and bracken. Small, star shaped flowers of white, red and pale yellow grew in clumps scattered all about the glade. Bright they were, and startling against the rich green and brown of the forest. Strange, that I had not seen them before. Above me, the sun seemed not to have moved at all. Was this a magic place then, a rath, an enchanted grove, of the *sidhe* (shee), the *Shining Ones* who had gone before.

I looked about as I walked towards the centre where the two white stone paths lay, it was then I noticed slender growths of silver birch trees growing alongside huge forest giants. I hadn't noticed them when I first entered the grove of the green heart, and that too was a strangeness as I am a reasonably observant man. Were they symbolic of something, I wondered, and if so, of what? Had the *Keepers* of this sacred place planted them? Why? And who were the *Keepers*? Cumall had told me that sometimes Druids did not return from this place and that no trace of them was ever found. What mystery lived here? What secrets lay all about me that I could not see?

I walked on the path, the one that had a cross within a circle carved into its stones. Nothing, no sudden far memory came clanging into my head. I felt easier then and wished myself gone from this place. I do not believe in magic. It is, I think, no more than a word used to describe something we as yet do not understand. We gave the iron rimmed wheel and the plough to the Romans, who looked upon them as wonders until wonder was replaced by understanding and a knowledge of how such things are made and used. So it was when we gave them soap, and flour ground by our rotary mills, nor had they seen the like of our rotary grain reapers, handsaws or files. Even now they consider our metallurgical crafts to be the result of at least a partial magic. Small in body be Romans and not overly endowed with wit. Is that why they be such a cruel and avaricious race I wonder? Overflowing they are, or so it seems to me, with jealousy and petty hates.

It came to me then, though I asked not for its sending. A vision of Rome's legions marching into our lands, led by a scrawny little man with thin cruel lips and mean hooded eyes. He would have our wealth, and the death of us all in its taking. Visions of fire and smoke and sounds of screaming filled my head, wild ragged shouts and the ring of sword on shield, and then it was gone. Leaving me shaking, afeard and alone, in a strange green place that is, so we believe, the secret, sacred heart of all *The People*.

Much given are we to romantic stories of valour, sorrow and love, yet we be a hearty, boisterous people in love with life, and there is that within us that will not allow us to live as slaves or as kick-balls to some conquering tyrants whim. Was it for this I had been chosen and trained, to fight against

Celtic Sunset

Rome? The stones of memory gave me reminder of ancient promise, sworn so long ago, when the Earth was young and ungroaning. I know what I have been,. I know what I have done. I know what promise I gave whilst spirit young. I do not seek to say it is otherwise, and yet, I cannot accept that my destiny is to be a war leader, that had not a feel of truth about it. My destiny must lay elsewhere. That it has to do with *The People* I know full well, but what, what have you not told me Culann? What is it you are holding back? I'll have the truth of it out of him when I return, I assured myself, at least, I thought I would. The prying loose of it all might not be so easy. Cumall can be, at times, an infuriatingly, silent and stubborn man when so it is he does not wish to speak, or reveal some bit of this or that, he thinks you don't need to know. I love the mystery of it all, perhaps that is why I be Druid.

I spoke softly to the air and the trees of the glade. 'I am Culann, a free person, Druid to *The People*, and never have I betrayed my trust. As Hammer I did not betray, though I fled into the desert sick in spirit with the weight of many deaths upon me, betrayal of trust was not my guilt. I have never failed in my trust, though it has at times led me to embrace an untimely death, I remained true. Now it is that I have grown in spirit, and knowledge of both truth and darkness. Druid hath taught me well. The Gaunt thing — Crom Cruach, Bowed One of the Mound, Baal, prince of flies, I know thee now.'

As if in acknowledgment to my soft voiced words, a slow warm wind stirred the leaves and set the ferns and grasses to nodding. The sun's light brightened, as though a thick layer of cloud cover had moved away. The glade filled with its warmth and light. How sweet the taste of air, how bright the green of leaf, the colour of flowers, how soft the earth beneath my feet. Alive I was, and glad to be.

The *Keepers* of the green heart, whoever, or whatever they might be, understood and approved. I could sense it in the movement of air, the stir of leaf and grass. I could feel it in the bone of my skull, and the heart of me was lighter for the knowing of it all and, the reminder of memories long hidden.

'Now,' I said to myself, 'all I have to do is find my way back into the real world of Culann of the Arverni.'

Ψ

CELTIC SUNSET

Chapter Five

VAE VINCERUS
(Woe unto the vanquished)

Caesar of the Cruels

- - - - we cannot live as slaves.
Therefore, we cannot live at all.

Culann - Circa 40BC

Geimhreadh — Winter 57-50BC

Snow dusted the trees.

Cold it was, cold and the earth hard, like beaten iron beneath my feet.

I stood about the crest of a small tree crowned hill, watching a Roman cohort, of about five hundred legionnaires settle in for the night. A chill, bitter wind moaned about the hill and through the shallow valley that lay before me.

Hidden I was, amongst trees, dead ferns, and the sere, brittle stalks of last summer's bracken. To the west, cold sunset flamed the peaks of mist enshrouded mountains and the sky above, with bits and pieces of rose-gold bog fire.

Beautiful it was, and warmless.

Below the mountains, a wide plain of winter grass stretched out, narrowing down as it crept towards the north, forming a shallow valley.

Arverni lay to the south, a good five days march away. Of horses I had none.

I have heard it said, that the legions of Rome, boast of their ability to march a full twenty of miles in a single day and fight a battle at its end. Warriors of *The People* can run a full thirty of miles and give good account of themselves at the end of it.

Bitter winds moaned and sobbed, brushing exposed skin with dull gripping fingers as I crouched hidden behind trees and thin bare bushes.

The feast of Samhain (November) had come and gone, leaving behind, ice and snow and biting blasts of feral winds. The warmth of Beltain (May - spring) was a far distant memory of might have been. Breath fled from out my mouth like steam from a stewing kettle. Cold it was, and growing colder, my teeth and bones ached from its touch. What price a warm fire, a full belly, and a cup of hot spiced wine now I'm thinking. I pushed the thought of it away. I had come here from our own lands, not to fight, but to observe, and return undetected if that was possible.

News Shouters, had come to Arverni bearing words of invasion, and deeds so foul that for the first time in living memory, we cast shades of doubt upon the veracity of the News Shouter's words. We did not shame them by saying so, it was later, after they had gone, running swiftly towards the lands of the coastal Veneti tribes, that many amongst *The People*, came forward with doubts concerning the truthfulness of what they had heard. Cumall settled all arguments by sending me towards the lands of the Nervii, and on towards the town of Bourges where he thought I might find Vercingetorix who the News Shouters said, was trying to unite tribes against Caesars invasion.

Should all the tribes join together, forming one huge army, there is no force of men upon all the earth who could hope to defeat them. Disunited, Caesar's legions will wipe them out, tribe by tribe, this I have always known. My father spoke of it when I was but a child, before the Druid Cumall claimed me. Since then, Cumall and I have spoken of it often. Unless the tribes put aside their rivalries and notions of honour and unite, defeat is inevitable. We of Druid knew this, *The People* did not. In this one thing only, did they fail to heed the words and advice of Druid. Now they will die. We have not fought as a united people for centuries, we no longer know how.

Our history tells us that even the Greek who is called Alexander the Great was given pause to consider, when his conquering army came in contact with a migrating tribe of *The People*. Alexander's mighty army had crushed the Persians, killing Darius their king upon the field of battle. The Persians numbered hundreds of thousands. Alexander led an army of thousands, hardened veterans all, who, under Alexander's leadership had not suffered a single defeat.

Our ancestors came out of the far eastern lands, travelling towards the west they were, towards sunset's fires and a promise of dreaming spires. They travelled down the long fertile corridor of the two rivers, making camp beneath the fallen walls of Babylon, and wondered not at all about who might have once lived there.

Somewhere ahead lay the land of Persia and beyond Persia the lands of Greece, that is all they knew or cared to know. It was in fact, a matter of supreme indifference to the migrating Celts with regards whose, or what lands they passed through, their hot blue eyes looked beyond the mountains of Greece towards a promised land of wide, fertile plains, bound all about with thick forests and rivers flowing through broad meadows of sweet grass. Rain there would be, warm sunlight and cooling winds. Their's was a holy journey, divined by seers and prophets long before the armies of Alexander gathered along the way.

Alexander's army had made camp, resting, celebrating their victory over the supposedly invincible Persians, when outriders rode in, yelling and pointing over their shoulders towards an advancing dust cloud. Herald of an approaching host.

Alarmed, but not overly concerned, Alexander's commanders had trumpeters sound a general alert. The sun was hot, the air dry and dusty, waves of heat shimmered over the plain, bleak it was, forbidding and cruel.

Soldiers groaned as they groped around for discarded weapons and bits and pieces of armour, arming themselves with weary sighs of resignation.

They stood then, in silent orderly ranks facing towards the east. Confident in their own abilities and the leadership of seasoned Centurions, they viewed the approaching battle horde, if so it proved to be, as little more than a military exercise in extermination. They were, after all, an army who had never known defeat, and who had but recently, completely destroyed a supposedly invincible army, whose numbers were many times greater than their own. Confident they were, and just a little bit arrogant.

Celtic Sunset

It was Alexander himself who gave the order to Xenophon, Commander of a Legion, to stand his legion to arms and march them out to a point midway between Alexander's encamped army and the now stationary horde.

Xenophon's legion had born the brunt of the Persian campaign, his once full legion of six thousand was now reduced to five thousand. A formidable force of highly trained and skilled fighting men. No wonder then, that they viewed the distant horde as no more than a nuisance.

Xenophon stood beneath the burning sun and thought of wine, cups of cool watered wine and fresh broiled meat. Three paces behind him, in serried ranks of one hundred, his legion of five thousand stood in stoic silence beneath the sun's blistering heat. They too thought of cups of cooling wine, and the entertainment the captive Persian women, willingly or unwillingly, would provide, when the sky grew dark and the heat of the day had given way to cooling night winds beneath clustering stars.

Alexander ordered four mounted envoys forward, to inquire in his name, of the strangers intent, who were they, where did they come from, where were they going, and why?

The chosen leader of the migrating Celts was Arverni, an intelligent, exceptionally tall, robust man of great physical strength. He had laughing blue eyes and a long thick mane of honey coloured hair. His skill at arms was legendary amongst the people of his tribe. He looked, they often said, like the earth born son of some ancient god come down from heaven's dome.

He was Arverni, the elected leader and king of a tribe of nineteen thousand, of which, twelve thousand were warriors.

The foremost of the envoys, one Hippoclides by name, demanded in an imperious tone to speak with, 'Whoever leads this rabble.'

Arverni stepped forward. He stood, almost equal in height to the mounted Greeks, regarding their small sturdy mounts with amusement. He said, in a cool tone 'Who are you to demand anything of us, and why, when it is obvious, even to ill mannered fools such as yourself, that we are but passing through this land? Arverni glared at the envoy, his blue eyes hot and fierce with independent pride.

Hippoclides, his face scarlet with rage, looked down his nose, sneered and said, 'In the name of the King, Alexander, I demand to know who you are and what you do here.'

Arverni, no longer smiling said, 'king, what king? I know of no Alexander, and you, little man, demand nothing. Now! Be off with you, else you and your companions be crushed beneath our march. I am, he added, Arverni, the elected leader of our tribe and,' he snarled, 'I choose to lead my people forwards. We are Celts, a free people and acknowledge no other king but our own. Tell that to your Alexander, now be gone.'

Hippoclides, stunned into speechlessness, wheeled his mount and raced back towards the Greek lines, his three companions following.

As Hippoclides drew near, Xenophon shouted out, 'What news? Hippoclides shook his head in mute reply as he raced by. Xenophon sighed, 'A fight it is then,' he said softly, and issued a curt command. Ranks separated, metal jingled against metal as five thousand soldiers swiftly reformed into ten cohorts. Each cohort divided into five Centuries, each Century under the command of a veteran Centurion.

Within moments the legion of Xenophon had transformed itself into a formidable, tightly disciplined fighting machine.

Celtic Sunset

In later years Rome would model its legions on that of the Etruscans who modelled theirs upon the legions of Alexander.

Behind Xenophon and his cohorts, the army of Alexander stood to arms, alert and eager to pounce.

Arverni and his people viewed the army arrayed against them with distaste. They had no quarrel with these presumptuous Greeks and no doubt Alexander was a fine king, but he was not king of the Celts to ask this or that, or otherwise hinder their march.

'We will fight on foot,' Arverni told his people, 'until we are settled, our horses be too precious to lose, besides, he added with a grin, these Greeks have not met our like before. They fight for conquest,' his voice rose in a shout, 'we fight for the blood joy of it all,' and laughed.

A wave of sound, like broken thunder, rolled towards the waiting Greeks, as thousands of Celts beat swords against shields, and raised voice to heaven in a great shout of heart stopping eagerness to join battle.

Alexander was heard to say 'Who are these Celts? Never have I heard men so eager for battle. Do they not know who they face, or knowing, don't care? We can only hope there enthusiasm is not a measure of their battle skill.

A thunderous din split the air as a solid mass of charging, leaping Celts smashed against the Greek shield wall.

Xenophon went down, his throat slashed open by a swinging sword. The Greek line held, each cohort merged with the other presenting a solid wall of steel to the howling Celts, and then Arverni waded in, swinging his long sword like a hammer. The force of his blows split shields and the

209

flesh behind. Cleaving through helms, biting deep into the bone beneath. Using their greater height and reach, the Celtic warriors stabbed down behind shields, leaning on their long swords, driving blades through armoured chests. The shield wall began to waver. Celts threw their weight against it, all the while stabbing and slashing with great sweeping strokes. Swords caught the sun, reflecting its light in long gleaming bars of metal.

The Greeks had never faced such savage yelling fighters before. Horrified, the front ranks stepped back, the already weakened shield wall collapsed inwards. Celts leapt high in the air, bounding over the fallen, they hewed their way through the Greeks demoralised ranks, like wood cutters in the forest.

Within a few heartbeats it was finished. Arverni and his people swarmed over the Greeks. Swords rose and fell, until the legion of dead Xenophon ceased to exist.

The army of Alexander stood in mute shock, appalled by the sudden ferocity, and the wild enthusiastic charge of the Celts, who seemed as willing to die, as they were to fight. They had never encountered such people before.

The Celts under Arverni's command, regrouped. Leaning on their swords, they faced the whole might of Alexander's army and laughed, jeering at them, beckoning them forward to fight.

Alexander, reeling from the sudden destruction of an entire legion, stepped forward. He could, using sheer weight of numbers alone defeat the Celts, but the price of such a victory would cost him dear, perhaps as much as half, or more, of his remaining army. Alexander was not a fool, in fact he was a highly intelligent man, superbly educated and well read, a founder of libraries and museums, a builder of cities, patron to art and artists, he did the only sensible thing he could do.

He walked forward unarmed and alone, his men moaned in dismay. Standing before Arverni, Alexander said to him, 'Fight or drink wine with me, the choice is yours.'

Arverni laughed, sheathing his bloody sword he clapped Alexander on the shoulder and said, 'Fighting is thirsty work. We have fought, so now my friend, it is time to drink.'

Night fell about me like an abandoned cloak. Frost crackled beneath my feet, cold it was and growing colder.

The camp below was alive with light and the lip tasting smell of broiling meat. Giving thought to my rising hunger, I slipped away, ghosting down the ridge towards the relative safety of the forest. The air was clear and sharp, though windy and incredibly chill. It was a hard winter we had, the bitterest I have ever known. Cumall, who had knowledge of such things, said that the year to come would be long, dry and hot beneath a blood red sun. Such a year came but rarely and was known as, *Bliain Na Ceilteach Lui*, Year of the Celtic Sun, or simply *Celtic Sunset*.

I spent the night huddled over a small fire, my thick woollen cloak wrapped tight about me, pale green it is, of fine weave and oiled to repel the rain. A fine cloak, a Druids cloak, gifted to me by the king himself. Would that I had brought another, as I sat there, the front of me warm and the back of me chilled through to the bone. Too cold to sleep, not that I felt like sleeping, my head was full of all that I had gleaned over the past few days and I had not yet sorted out the half of it. Terrible it was, I shied away from the thinking of it, like an unbroken horse from an unsteady hand.

The night was dark and bitterly cold and endless, or so it seemed to me. My people were undone, my nation all but destroyed. A cold unfeeling God ruled the night from out his House of Crows.

The tribes, too long a free people, knew not how to unite and they would learn — too late. Romans destroyed them one by one. Vercingetorix, whose very name is a challenge, it means King of the World, sought to unite the few tribes that yet remained free.

Vercingetorix failed.

He wrought a great slaughter amongst the legions, until at last, ringed all about by Caesar's legions, Caesar said to the Celts who yet remained, 'Give me Vercingetorix and I will let you live, refuse and you die, you all die, every man, woman and child. I will destroy you utterly even unto your name.'

Vercingetorix, a true Celt, immediately stepped forward and offered his life in exchange for those who followed him. Alesia was the place of his sacrifice. *The People* barred his way saying, 'We are oath sworn to thee, every man, woman and child has uttered the sacred words and called upon the *Maker* to bear witness, only you can release us from this geasa, and if you do not, then right gladly we shall fight, though there numbers be ten times ten more than our own. Lead Vercingetorix, we shall follow and die here, where our feet rest upon the earth of our fathers. Romans are Cruels, untrustworthy at best and Caesar, as all men know, is tainted by the shadow that rules him. He is a thing of Gaunt Man, Crom Cruach, Bowed One of the Mound. Lead Vercingetorix, lead.'

A great roar went up, the rolling sound of it splitting the air. Though moved to tears, Vercingetorix would have none of it. 'It is better,' he answered, his great voice booming above the din, 'that I release you all from your oath.' He pointed towards Caesar's distant diminutive figure, outlined in the wan glow of a feeble shining sun. 'He will kill you all,' he shouted, and then more softly, 'we have already lost. What care we,' he continued, 'for the reaping of a few more Roman heads, if it cause the death of all. *See*,' he threw his sword down in the dirt, 'I will fight no more.' He drew himself up to his full height and yelled out, 'I will fight no more, whilst ever I live, I will fight no more.' A groan went up from *The People*, then silence.

'It is better that I give myself up to a shadow haunt than be the cause of your deaths. If all had been not lost, fight on I would say,' he said sadly. 'I came too late, and we be too few.' A terrible sadness filled his eyes.

Vercingetorix surrendered. He gave himself into the hands of Caesar in exchange for Caesar's promise to spare the lives of his people.

Oh, thou man, truly art thou a king, thou foolish, brave, honour bound man. Trust not he who walks in shadow, he is a Prince of Lies.

Caesar had Vercingetorix bound in chains and then whipped about his legs until his flesh was blood and ruin. He forced him to watch, whilst grinning, like some demented night haunt, Caesar ordered his legions forward 'Kill everyone,' he ordered, except the women.

When it was done, the captured women were used by soldiers, after which Caesar gave them to his favourites to use, sell or kill.

Vercingetorix wept for the fate of his people and turned his face away from the sun. The air reeked with the smell of blood and burning flesh, the anguished cries of broken women tore at his heart, he wept openly — without shame.

Caesar demanded of Vercingetorix that he go down on his knees in submission to him, and swear fealty to his name. Vercingetorix refused, the clear eyes of him flashing. Incensed by his refusal, Caesar had him whipped again. This time laying the flesh of his back open to the bone. Vercingetorix uttered no sound, no sound at all whilst he was scourged. His silence infuriated Caesar.

The death of Vercingetorix was a long drawn out spectacle much loved by the people of Rome. Caesar, a cruel and vindictive man, sent Vercingetorix back to Rome in chains. Incensed by Vercingetorix's refusal to kneel in submission to him, he had Vercingetorix tortured and starved for a run of three full years. Torturers broke the bones of his legs and left them to heal all crooked and deformed. They broke his arms and cut off his right hand, forcing him to lay on his belly like an animal to drink and eat what little of food and drink they gave him. To humiliate him, they cut off his long hair and tied it round his throat, and shaved his head with a blunt knife. All this was carried out in view of the public, whilst he was chained to a wall. His broken body lay in its own filth.

From time to time they scourged his flesh, until his flesh had been all but flayed from his bones, as he lay upon the stones, passers by poured vinegar upon his wounds. He neither cried out nor moaned and stubbornly refused, no matter what was done to him, to declare his submission to Caesar.

Vercingetorix was tortured in this way for three years. Broken in body, his flesh hanging in bloody strips from his bones, starved and humiliated he still retained his warrior's spirit. Stripped of dignity, of humanness, he wore the brightness of his spirit like unseen armour. And still he was denied the release of death.

Chained like an animal, broiled by the sun, fevered by the cold, starved and tortured, he at last grew so weak and mind wandering he knew not what they did to him.

Caesar, ever cruel, ever cold, looked on with dispassionate eyes. Eventually, after three long years, when even passers by no longer stopped or stared, or tormented, a huddle of bones once named Vercingetorix, King of the World, Caesar ordered his death. Even in this, most final of commands, Caesar's insane malice and cruelty shone through like some monstrous shadow. He ordered Vercingetorix to be strangled by his own hair and that he be strangled slowly over a period of seven days. The shorn hair of Vercingetorix was woven into a noose and placed around his neck. Once each day the noose was slowly tightened until upon the seventh day, chained to a wall in Rome's forum, Vercingetorix breathed his last. As a final indignity Caesar had the body of Vercingetorix thrown into an offal pit where his flesh and bones were eaten and gnawed by dogs. Hail Caesar, a cultured, civilised man.

All through the bitter cold of that long, long night did I slowly put together the bits and pieces rattling around inside my head. News gathered from fleeing survivors, heading towards the dubious safety of coastal tribes. Information, gleaned from farmers unwilling to leave their fields and homes, and all the while, dodging and hiding from roaming patrols of mounted cavalry. Twice I had wormed my way, on my belly, to the outer fringe of a Roman patrol's night camp. Hiding in shadows and behind bushes, just beyond the edge of light cast by their cooking fire, I listened and watched.

Cumall had tutored me well in both Latin and Greek. I could read, write and speak both languages fluently, amongst others. I had no trouble at all in understanding the soldiers camp fire talk of battles and worse, soldiers ever being inclined towards rape, and looting if not held in check by a superior's firm grip. Caesar it seemed, had given his legions a great many unusual freedoms, and why not, I thought sourly, that is what he came here for, to seize the wealth of the Celts. His whole campaign against us is based on nothing more than *Avarus covetous*, extreme greed. Brought about by his inability to repay a debt of some 80,000,000 denari (a coin of pure silver). Now it is he has the wealth of our looted temples, a wealth of coin, silver and gold, precious stones, pearls and thousands of ingots of iron and bronze. He has our grain, our horse herds, cattle, sheep and cloth, bales of dyed wool and metal products that Rome is ever hungry to buy. Only our ships, the huge sailing ships of the Veneti remain, and those he will have too, I'm thinking, if not, then he will burn them and the Veneti shipyards too.

Caesar and his legions have brought a darkness into the whole of our lands (Europe), a darkness that will last for more that a thousand years, a darkness that will one day cross the narrow sea and cover *Bri-tain,* the misty isle of our cousins. I have the *gift,* I have seen a part, a shading of what is to come, it shivers me through and through.

Long the night was, and bitterly cold. The deep forest lonely. Wolves there were, though I saw nothing of them but their tracks. Winds moaned and sobbed about the trees, skittering across the snow in flurries and plumes of wind whipped crystals. A sift of thoughts drifted down inside my head, like chaff of grains winnowed upon the winds. Starlight, brilliant and cold, dimmed as scudding banks of clouds fled across the sky, like stallions running free across the face of a vast uneven plain.

The air had a smell of cold iron and snow about it, though I had not studied the disciplines of weather and wave I knew a little, as all Druids do, who have studied *The Third Way*, walked its path and returned.

Chill, whistling airs filled my head as I sat hunched over my fire, feeding its hungry mouth with bits and pieces of broken wood in a dreamy, absent minded sort of way. Did some unworshipped, lonely god of the forest watch over me this night? Perhaps *Cernunnos* himself walked the darkness, the forest is, after all, his special place of worship.

The night gathered about me, small gusting winds flared my fire, casting huge dancing shadows amongst the trees that stood about the edge of my sight. Leafless boughs clicked and clacked against each other as contrary fingers of wind pushed one against the other. I had no fear of the forest or the night, what is there to fear when the way of its breathing is known. This night, it was my own thoughts that feared me and visions of which I will not speak.

There are those amongst our order who believe that dark thoughts have a way of attracting bits and pieces of a greater darkness to them. Thoughts are alive, they say, and when you loose them, they wing free, flying outward like unseen birds towards other thoughts and fancies of like kind. They are, so it is claimed, little energies that once created cannot be uncreated, only changed, by circumstance and will, into something else that we know not of. I think they had that from the Greeks who make much of sentient energies that I cannot claim to understand. But then it is ever the way of groups, to claim a knowledge no other might possess, or spurn the veracity of any truth similar to their own. There is no single source of wisdom upon all the earth. In heaven perhaps, the starry home of gods, but not on earth though some, outside of Druid say otherwise. It is the supreme arrogance of men, to claim the role of *Maker*, the **One** God, and who, amongst all the nations would dare such arrogance, only fools, madmen, or Romans, I'm thinking. The uneducated at least have the excuse of being uneducated, though it's a poor excuse at best, unlikely to be accepted, when, upon the final day of days, you stand upon the scales of truth and the weight of a single feather finds you all unbalanced and wanting.

Slowly, all through that bitter night, I ordered my thoughts. How else might I speak, upon my return, if I did not. The Arverni would fight and they would die and nothing I might say could change that. I too would fight, what else was there for me to do. Cumall's vision of my destiny, of which he still refuses to speak, was hidden from me. Whatever it might be, it was a faint far off thing I no longer thought of.

The News Shouters had spoken truth. I would repeat the truth of their words and be believed. From that moment on the Arverni would be lost, and the way of Druid would wither away until no one remained who had memory of what a Druid was, keepers of patterns and paths and ways of weave.

All that I had gleaned from running, terrified survivors. All that I had heard from the mouths of Romans I spied upon. All that I had seen and could bear witness to, I reviewed inside my head.

The wind still blew, though most all the clouds had disappeared. A frosted moon had risen, hanging above the trees like some new minted coin of polished silver. Its thin white light poured down through the trees, lending to the snow a sort of magic that is only found in children's night

Celtic Sunset

time stories of might have been. *Fadofado,* a long, long time ago, when the world was young and *a trace of blue* glowed everywhere.

It chilled my spirit and shivered me through.

Roman patrols scoured the countryside in search of Nemeds and Druids. All Druids found were killed instantly, Nemeds cut down or burnt and the sacred soil sown with salt.

Caesar, the Gaunt Man — Crom Cruach, Bowed One of the Mound, had come to walk amongst us. Did the *Maker* tremble in his starry house, whilst his people died beneath a warmless sun?

They came to me then, those ancient words of beginning, words older than the *The People*, words spoken by the *Maker*, so it is we believe. On the first of all days he said, 'I breath upon you — therefore you are.'

Tomorrow, I return to Arverni to unsheathe the sword. Tonight, I sit alone in the forest, Druid of a broken nation. The Nervii are no more. Of 60,000 warriors only 500 survived to be sold into slavery. Of the 600 Nervii elders only three were allowed to live. Of women and children none survive at all. Impaled they were, on spears and sharpened stakes. Of the people of the town of Avaricum (Bourges, France) who's warriors numbered 44,000, only 800 survive, and they are held hostage by Caesar.

The Helvetii advised Caesar they cared not for war and moved out of their lands. 160,000 they were, now they are not. Those who survived the massacre live as a conquered people beneath Roman rule, unwilling to fight, they were forced to it in the end. Caesar would not allow them to leave and take their wealth with them.

His greed is a dark sent thing.

The Helvetii's numbers were too many for them to survive as a migrating people, without gold or silver to trade for their needs whilst they searched out a new land. There warriors were too few to form an army that might, through force of arms, conquer a new territory and take what they need from the Romans. So it was that Caesar turned his legions loose against them. The Helvetii fought and died within sight of their mountain home (Switzerland). Those who surrendered, gave up their wealth to Caesar who allowed them to live, only on condition of their submission to Rome and its authority. They returned to the mountains and lived as slaves, broken, conquered people.

The beautiful city of Alesia, had been destroyed and its people enslaved, for no more that the greed of a tainted man, who dare not return to Rome without wealth enough to pay his debts. We, who trade as equals with Rome, barbarians though they be, and with Greece and the Scandinavian lands, have been destroyed by Caesar who is ruled by the Gaunt Man — Crom Cruach, Bowed One of the Mound. Now he destroys our religion of light, the Spiral of Immortality, and condemns our children and all who come after, to live in a spiritual darkness that will last beyond a thousand years.

My heart grew cold, I groaned into the night and cursed aloud my *gift of seeing.*

How deep the forest, how broad the land of living, how blue and empty a distant sky, how far the purple mountains.

I weep for my people, my nation who, even now, fight to survive. We shall rise again, I vowed silently, you cannot kill us all. When the eagles of Rome no longer fly, we shall rise again, and again, and again.

A grey, dismal light filtered through the trees as I shouldered my small carry sack of supplies and prepared to move out. Out and away towards Arverni, towards warmth and light and hot food, toward Cumall and the gathering of the tribe.

Rome would pay a heavy price for every Celtic life. One day, they too would know servitude, fear and the unremitting agony of total defeat, whilst Rome burnt to the ground about their ears. It will be so, for I have seen it.

A grey and dismal morning it was, of sun there was none. The whole of the sky hidden behind a low ceiling of grey white cloud heavy with a promise of snow to come. It was cold, the wind icy blowing from out of the frozen north. Trees stood tall and dark, branches heavy with snow, pointed down towards the earth like gnarled arms of accusation.

Somewhere behind me a wolf howled, its cry faint and echoey upon the wind. Fear not brother, I said softly, soon they will come, even for you. They will kill you, chain you and feed you to the Arena. They be barbarians grey brother, darkness rides their shoulders like some weirding haunt of curse.

I walked the deep forest where men fear to go, with only a bitter moaning wind for company, it was enough. My thoughts were dark and red and I had need to be alone. Avoiding roads, skirting farms, I whisper-slipped through the forest, with no thought given to resting. Winter days are short and I had far to go. I stumbled through drifts of snow, my feet crunching down through frozen crusts of hard white crystals. Cold, knife edged winds whipped about me. I tugged my green woollen cloak tight, and shivered. My feet were sodden unfeeling lumps. If'n I didn't warm them soon, I'd be losing toes to the cold-rot, I'm thinking.

I travelled south towards Arverni in a wide swinging arc, avoiding the more direct line of travel along the track that cut through the forest from one end to the other. The arc lengthened my journey, but ensured I'd not be running into any wandering army patrols, or squadrons of Roman cavalry.

I wanted the silence. I needed the aloneness of a long trudging journey to order my thoughts before entering Arverni. Cold it was and bitter, my breath streaming away upon the wind. My bones ached, my heart beat, pumping waves and snaking rivers of blood through my veins. I lived, I breathed, and I sorrowed.

I would return and rouse the Arverni to resist the Roman advance. The tenth legion was already on the march, the eighth not far behind. The ninth was still at its bloody work. We would fight and no doubt we would die, but we would die a free people, better by far than to live as slaves.

Fine words indeed, I thought sadly, the truth be less so.

Was that my mysterious destiny, of which Cumall would not speak, to lead our people in a final stand against the enemy? Is that what Cumall has seen for me, ruin and a bloody death?

I trudged on, through snow and wind and trees. My head a cauldron of boiling thoughts. How short the day, how long the night, how bitter the cold winds of defeat.

My depth of feeling, my belongingness to *The People*, is so complete that I feel I have in some mystical way become *The People*. I am the Arverni, a true Celtic creation of *being*. My life, my calling, the very essence of my spirit is all bound up and spiralling around our Celtic heart. Druidry is, I realised long ago within the green-heart, simply something I have come to, in its proper place and time along *the way*. A stepping stone towards a final, far greater fulfilment that awaits me, like some patient god, walking in silence down the highway of a long moonlit road that I have yet to run.

Since the dawn of human kind, I have opposed the *enemy* the *criminal* who is called Gaunt Man — Crom Cruach, Bowed One of the Mound, where so ever he might be found. Sometimes I have prevailed, sometimes I have not. However it may be, who is there who can say he has achieved more, and if so you have, does that make my achievements of less worth than your own? I think not.

We all, in our own chosen way do what we can to maintain a balance that is ever under threat. It is enough that we try, and now and again achieve some small, or large triumph along *the way*.

The People know this. It is a thing of the spirit we call *Skan Taku Skanskan* spiritual vitality, something in movement, it never sleeps, is never at rest. So it is that we of Druid believe.

That God is pure, we doubt. That evil is pure, we doubt. Therefore a balance must be found, an acceptable reality of both. How else can we live, or endure within our house of flesh? How else to explain failure or triumph? How else can we come to knowledge that exists outside the boundaries of logic, and accept it for what it is? A revelation of truths that exist independent of logic, independent of our ability to reason. Logic has limits, boundaries and walls, concepts do not. They are above and exist independent of logic. Without conceptual thought, we are like birds without wings, unable to soar, we fall down the Spiral of Immortality until, all remembrance is lost of what it was like to once fly free. What the Romans are, they would make of us. Everything conforms to the narrow, cruel and unspeakably bloody view of Rome, or is destroyed.

Those who claim logic to be supreme, deny inner exploration of deep thought, and yet it is only from explorations of deep thought that an expansion of logic can be found and built upon. The original concept of logic was based upon the assumption that logic can, and does exist. Thereby did the Greeks tame chaos and in the taming of it glimpsed an unfamiliar order that was the crucible of the creation of chaos.

It was a riddle of epic proportions, that only *The People* have yet unriddled. During my third, seven of years Cumall had me study much of what the Greeks wrote during their *Great Age of Reason*. They gained much and lost only a little, and yet it was the little they lost that eventually destroyed their freedom and bound them to Rome as a conquered people.

The Greeks gained in reason and logic, their enemies did not and remained — their enemies. Like Nargal of old the Greeks used words instead of swords, their enemies did not. A nation cannot rise so high that it abandon all means of its own defence. It is illogical, flawed reasoning born of the Gaunt Man — Crom Cruach, Bowed One of the Mound.

What is, what is not, can be different for each of us. It is a truth we of Druid readily admit and accept. When Cumall gave me permission to read and touch his precious store of writings, that had come to him by way of traders who knew of his interest in such things, he said, 'It is not enough for you to study ancient lore because that is the way it is, nor is it enough for you to read what others have written, with no thought given beyond the reading. You must think about what you have read, what you have studied. Is it right or is it wrong, do you agree or disagree, think Culann. Always you must think. If you do not, then what is the use of it all. You will forever repeat what others have said, and think what they want you to think. If you give no deep thought to what you read, then you do no more that entertain yourself. Think Culann, think and ponder, until the end of all days. It is the only way towards spiritual illumination you will ever find. Don't limit your reading, diversify.'

Under his direct tutelage, I could not help but think, and for me there emerged one truth above all others. It was, I now realise, the truth of Sestoris, Tabath, Thomas, Raman the Egyptian, Hammer and I, Culann of the Arverni, Druid to *The People*, it is the single truth of — the constant Fidelity of Being, the first law of Druid from which all others are derived.

Beneath a clearing sky of blue I came in sight of Arverni. Short the days, cold had been my nights. Bitter my solitude of thought.

A faint lingering warmth in the air had turned the snow into a melting shifting mass of grey slush and mud. It had begun to thaw two days ago and looked set to continue, as I slogged my weary way through it all.

Distant plumes of smoke rose in the air, dark fingers against a pure blue sky. A soft breeze carried a smell of broiling meat to me, I hungered. A pale lemon sun poured down its light to dance and ripple across pools and sheets of ice melt.

Tired I was, and angry.

My head was clear, my thoughts in order. My gut churned and boiled with a deep abiding rage towards Roman Cruels, barbarians of ordered slaughter.

The round house sat as tidily as ever beneath the great spreading oak. Beyond lay the forest. The pale light of winter's end lending it an eerie mystery, as silent and brooding as my own thoughts. Even so, it was a welcome sight and the heart of me beat the lighter for its nearing.

Cold I was, the clothes of me sodden. I had not entered the town after all, avoiding the few who walked abroad., I slipped by the town along a little used path that wound its lazy way in a south westerly direction toward the forests edge.

Fine it was to walk that path, affording me views I'd sorely missed. The valley spread out before me, forest crowding its northern rim. Pale sunlight bathed the valley in a cold half light of running gold and silver, that outlined the valleys rim against a perfect sky of faded blue and small, puff ball clouds, the colour of curdled milk. The river wound through the valley like a silver serpent, carrying winter-melt and debris washed down from distant slopes. The river had broken its banks, as it always did at winter's end, flooding nearby fields, creating a vast lake of shimmering, rippling water that would, all too soon, drain away.

It was all so beautiful, so familiar to my senses, so typically Celtic. War and beauty, beauty and form, song and dance, and riddling words of yesterdays feel.

My heart caught in my throat. Somewhere a bird sang its song of freedom to the sky, the sound of it sweet and achingly pure. A dog barked as I passed by and within the trees I could hear a murmur and occasional shout of children at play. Something moved deep down inside and a strange wetness filled my eyes. We be tears and joy upon this land, I thought sadly. Now — it all ends.

Where now the seasons of my own childhood?

How brief the years.

How vibrant and pulsed with life we are.

Celtic Sunset

Once, I too scoured the forests edge, hunting secrets and small lost pieces of buried treasure. Rambling the hills, standing on top of some rocky outcrop, my face turned up towards the sky, Lugh, the sun an aspect of the *Maker*, warm upon my skin. Fishing along the river's edge. Sitting in some shady spot casting out dreams upon the sun dappled water.

What price now a young boy's dreaming?

We all be sold by the Roman Caesar, for a handful of silver denari and, a loose bound traveller's pocket empty of dreams.

'Well,' Cumall said, 'what now.'

'Raise the tribe,' I answered in a quiet, deadly voice.

We sat within the round house, a good fire burning bright in the hearth. I sat close by, warming my feet. Late afternoon it was and already shadows had begun to gather and dance about the walls and timbers of the roof.

It was the day following my return. The old Druid had welcomed me gladly, his voice gruff with emotion, as he gave me greeting and welcome return. Until now, I hadn't noticed how the years lay upon him, he had always seemed so ageless and indestructible. Sometimes it takes a going and a returning to notice such things.

I had related all I had learned, though I'm thinking he already knew, and had only sent me off to please the tribe and our king, Bardvar, who ever hungered for news, even of the most unimportant kind. Still, he was a good king, given to fairness and not one for standing aloof from the day to day problems of his people.

'Spring will be early,' Cumall said, looking at me with those strange stone under water coloured eyes of his. 'There will be no festivals,' he said, 'no Beltain (May), no Lugnasadh (August), no summer games, no trading fairs.' His voice took on a sombre, ominous tone. 'I tell you Culann we sit midst the end of it all. 'No feast of Samhain (November), no more shall we celebrate Imbolc (February), and its rites of prognostication, or drain the marriage cup beneath warm breathy winds. Your destiny,' he added, 'weaves close about you.'

Suddenly, irrationally, I felt irritated by his reminder of something I knew less than nothing about. I said sharply, 'Destiny, what destiny? Else it be to lay cold and stinking in some misbegotten field of mud. Is that my destiny Cumall?' my voice rose, 'Well, Is it?' I glared at him, willing him to answer me just this once. At that moment my destiny seemed more like some portent of doom, haunting me from just beyond the edge of conscious reach.

I should have known better.

Cumall raised his eyebrows in silent rebuke at my outburst and then gave me that quirky lopsided grin of his, which set me to laughing and an easing of the tension I had caused.

I sighed, shifting my feet closer to the fire as the bright flames of it faded down into glowing embers. Cumall sat off to my right, his hands resting on a small table of dark polished wood. Made of Cedar it was, a rarity in our land. I liked the smell of its polished surface. It always reminded me of something, but I could never remember what it was. Like the inner ache that comes with the singing of the *Dawn Song*, a kind of sad beautiful ache that tugs at your heart, but you have not the words to explain it, weirding it is, and special. A gift from the *Maker* perhaps.

'We will fight'

'Yes,' Cumall answered sadly, 'we will fight.' His eyes had a haunted look about them. 'What else can we do? The Roman Cruel, Caesar, will kill us and sell any survivors into slavery. He is a barbarian, what else can we expect from such as he. We, who have never traded in the misery of human flesh, have little understanding of a nation made up of slave owners. Such nations are doomed, soon or late they will fall.' His old eyes flashed. 'It is an abomination in the eyes of the *Maker*, this trading in flesh. Caesar and all his kind walk in the shadow of Gaunt Man — Crom Cruach, Bowed One of the Mound. The Romans bring a dark age with them,' continued Cumall staring into the fire. 'A dark age unparalleled upon all this earth. An age that will endure for more than a thousand years.'

'So insidious will be the rule of Gaunt Man inside people's heads, they will not know he is there, and those who recognise his presence will be put to death. They who will come to rule, will outlaw books and learning. The arts of reading and writing will be lost. Bathing daily, at dawn and dusk, will be forbidden. Free speech abolished, free worship banned upon pain of suffering a terrible lingering death. *The Four Fold Way* will disappear. Men will live like animals in dark stinking hovels rife with disease. Life will be mean, cruel and short.'

'Culann,' he said fiercely, 'you have studied Druidry for three times seven of years, and you had already lived a full seven of years before I claimed you. I tell you this, in the time to come a full span of a man's life will be reckoned shorter than the years you have spent in study. Even the cleansing rites of medicine will be abolished. Men will operate on other men with unclean hands and filth encrusted instruments, until physicians are looked upon as killers and not healers of flesh and bone. All this I have seen Culann, all this and more, much more. Oh yes,' Cumall said in a distant way, 'we will fight, and we will die, it is better that we do so.'

'One day soon,' Cumall continued, 'his voice heavy and full of fright, 'the way of Druid will fall down into a burning of *Celtic Sunsets* and like *The People*, knowledge of Druidry will become no more than a faint memory of ruined splendour.' Cumall's eyes had a haunted look about them, as though they were windows that looked in on some terrible wounding of spirit.

'The pattern weaves as the *Maker* wills. Do you believe that Culann?' He looked at me sharply, and then, to break the gloom of the moment, he smiled his quirky smile. 'Besides,' he said with a grin, 'there is this small matter concerning your destiny.'

I sat in stunned silence. A log shifted in the fire, sending up a shower of sparks. My mouth felt dry. I am not an obtuse man, even so, what Cumall had revealed to me was, on top of everything else, too much for me to take in all at once. The true reason for my having been chosen, my specialised training, my slow but sure rise amongst *The People*, and now, at last, my destiny was known to me. It was strange, and more weirdly wonderful than anything I could have possibly imagined it to be, it scared me. The thrill of fear, enough to make me cautious, but not enough to spin me into a blind panic. Give me time, I thought silently, give me time to accept it. I shivered, a sort of cold premonition sweeping through me, a compound of fire and ice, hope and fear, and — excitement.

Sometime after I had returned from the green heart, I noticed that some few of *The People* stood away from me. I had not, I hoped, grown aloof from those around me with deliberate intent. Indeed, it seemed to me, during those distant days, that the more I grew in power, the more people stood away from me, as though uncertain of my intent. Cumall said then, that it was ever the way when, one amongst many begins fast progress along *the way*, climbing the Spiral of Immortality far and above the ability of others who, at best, ascend slowly, if at all. During that period of my training the *sight* grew strong within me. It had, I think, something to do with my experience within the green heart. Now it is that I do not cavil sendings, or fight against the muscle loosening fear of horrendous visions. The future is at the best of times an uncertain thing and, only the *Maker* knows the true weaving of its pattern. Now it is that people stand away and even greet me from a distance of paces.

I have, I slowly came to realise, an unlooked for reputation. Standing as I do, second in rank to Cumall, who is second in rank to the king and, often considered by some to be his equal.

I am a quiet, somewhat bookish man with an unlooked for reputation as a Weapons Master. There being no other it seems, who has ever disarmed Bridgit or come close to equalling her skill with weapons. The seasons have seen me grow tall, and lean of face, with a weight of muscle about my chest and shoulders. I wear my long hair unbound, a vanity no one has as yet stepped forward to challenge. I now know, no one will, they fear the Druid I have become more than the hand that grasps the weapon. I sometimes think I do not smile or laugh enough. Since Deidre, of whom I am not yet ready to speak, I seldom laugh or feel the need to smile overmuch. It is this un-Celtic reticence to display my innermost feeling, coupled with my known love of solitude, that earned for me the name and reputation of being *a stern man of the grove.*

I thought of these small things as I lay sleepless upon my pallet. In a vain attempt not to think about Cumall's revelation of what he, with the approval of Bardvar and the Arverni, expected of me. It was an unlooked for destiny and not of my choosing, though I would strive to ensure its fulfilment. If even a part of Druidry was to survive, I could do nothing less. There was no other choice, none at all. Even now, Caesar and his legions had all but erased Druidry from the face of the earth.

There will only, ever be, one book of Druid lore. Though the world believe there is none, and that we, as an order wrote not at all. It is a lie, a Roman lie put about by Caesar, who as all men know is a minion of Gaunt Man — Crom Cruach, Bowed One of the Mound.

The book will be hidden, perhaps for ever, in a far land beyond the great ocean Romans call *Atlanticus* and there it will lay, in an unlooked for place, until *the one* comes to claim it. Future men of learning will laugh at the very suggestion that it might exist and they will ridicule any who propose its finding, except for those who belong to that ancient and most secret of brotherhoods — the *Brotherhood of the Book.*

A few days later.

We are a proud and boastful people, walking the land in a glory of strength and freedom. Bright colours do we wear to show the nature of our being. Long hair unbound, so that enemies might know it is theirs, if so they can take it.'

My voice rose in a hoarse cry, 'We are both challenge and haunt upon the land.' My eyes streamed with tears of emotion as I cried out in a cracked and awful voice. 'WE ARE CELTS. A FREE PEOPLE. WE CANNOT LIVE AS SLAVES THEREFORE,' I shouted 'WE CANNOT LIVE AT ALL. I Culann,

Druid of *The People*, say that this is so, therefore it is.' A great swelling roar of sound greeted my words. Swords and spears rattled against iron bound shields. Women screeched and children yelled. The power of my words sweeping them away upon a tide of emotion.

We numbered 23,000 men, women and children, of which 7,000 were warriors, trained and armed.

Destiny thundered down the sky upon vultures wings, scattering Crows of War from horizon to horizon.

We shall bleed and die, a free people upon the soil of our birth. Who is there amongst you who dare say we die needlessly when you have not faced the utter ruin of all your nation? Who amongst you would choose to live, a branded slave to barbarians? We are Celts, we choose death. Miserable and empty is life when denied the way of its choosing.

Roy Edwards

Two years later.

Our vast horse herds are gone.
Our cattle slaughtered.
Fields lay fallow and weed choked.
The town of Arverni is ash and soot and yellow bones.
Cumall spoke truly when he said we would celebrate no more the sacred rites of beginnings, fruitfulness and endings.
Vercingetorix rots in chains.
Bridgit died singing a warrior's song.
Cumall was taken. Caesar ordered him crucified upside down. On the second day of his crucifixion, wood was stacked around his head and fired, not that it mattered, Cumall had long since abandoned his house of flesh. It is a thing of Druid, a small discipline that is taught along the way of *An Treas Cosan*, the third path.

I think he speaks to me still, if so, it is his voice that I hear, and not just the singing of my own blood.

Our Nemeds of oak, ash, yew and hazel are all destroyed, cut down and burnt, the sacred earth sown with salt. The great stones still stand, the Romans, not recognising them for what they are, have so far left them alone.

Sometimes at night, when I search the silent sky, I wonder what it is about us that frightens the Romans so much, they must destroy us utterly. Our wealth they have, our lands also, and our vast fields of grain.

Caesar is driven I think. The Gaunt Man owns more of him with each passing day. Cumall once said to me, that Caesar will inhabit his house of flesh for only a brief tenure of years. He said, 'Caesar will die at the height of his corrupt and greed filled power, cut down,' said Cumall, 'by his own kind, upon wide steps of white stone. Those who allow the dark one to rule them cannot expect to live a long or productive life. He will die of his own ambition,' said Cumall, 'and destroy us utterly along the way. Without wealth he is nothing and, he owes much to those who otherwise wish him dead. They are a motley lot these highborn Romans, bloodthirsty gullible fools, and we,' Cumall added, 'be blind stubborn fools for not uniting and wiping them from the face of the earth. They sow darkness where so ever their legions tread. A darkness,' said Cumall, 'that will last beyond the counting of a thousand years. Gaunt Man — Crom Cruach, Bowed One of the Mound, has triumphed — for now.' So it is my friend once spoke.

Our valley, where I used to wander and dream away the sunlit days, is a bare and ragged thing now. Unclothed and treeless, where once red deer and boar did run. Its shining river flows dark, the once pure water stinking as it flows around debris, rotting carcasses of horses, cattle and the bloated sightless bodies of men.

The temple that stood upon the crown of the Hill of Heroes is rubble. A thing of blackened timber and fallen stone, plundered of its offerings of precious metals and skilful works of art, to swell the coffers of Caesar, and augment the pay of his men.

Of crops and grain we have none at all.

We met the Tenth legion as they marched across our borders. We fell upon them, full of hate and fire and a wild lust to kill.

A fully trained Celtic warrior is a match for any three or four legionnaires, but he is baffled, when fighting the armed and armoured might of an army that fights as a single whole under the direct orders of a single command. There is no honour in such fighting, no Heroes stand, no battle of competing Champions. What use in fighting, if only to kill.

Our Celtic warriors came to an understanding of Roman ways too late to be of use. There rose only one, Vercingetorix, amongst us and he in truth came to his power of command and rule too late.

Where now the Arverni?

Sleeping cold upon bloody ground.

I fight, and strive toward a destiny that is more strange than anything I can recall throughout the whole of my existence.

Of the Arverni, two thousand live, and they, perhaps not for long.

After my great speech we roared forth like some angry raging torrent.

We did not defeat the Tenth, we slaughtered half their number and then the missing Ninth came charging onto the field. Vastly outnumbered, we fled into the forest with thoughts of fighting another day.

That was two years ago. Since then we have fought and marched and fought again. Few in number, we dare not face a full legion. We lost three thousand that first day of battle. Two thousand more died defending our women and children. The Romans cut our fighting force in half, so great were their numbers one side could not rejoin the other. So it was that the Roman Cruels killed our women and children, sparing only a few to be sold as slaves. Those of us who survived that terrible day fled in anguish and tears.

We lost everything. Now it is that of all the Arverni, a mere two hundred warriors survive. As Bridgit once fought, we do so again, attacking outposts, supply depots, relief columns, and any odd Century we might stumble upon.

Celtic Sunset

The warriors I lead, know I cannot lead them for much longer. The geasa Cumall placed upon me before his death will soon force me towards the coastal holding of the seafaring Veneti, and whatever bit and piece of my destiny I might find there.

Adwin, a man I do not know waits for me. He is a deep sea sailing man, Captain of his own vessel. Caesar hungers for Veneti ships and the knowledge of their building. The Veneti build ships the like of which have never been seen before. Sailing ships they are, powered not at all by oars. Some call them swan ships, so proud and graceful do they sail over waters deep and wide. The Veneti often cross the great salt sea (Atlantic) and trade with the wild people of the Far Land (America), returning with rich cargoes of thick exotic furs, freshwater pearls and strange embroidered slippers of thin, supple leather (Moccasins).

Until my time of going, I fight. We are a thorn in the side of the legions. We whittle away at them, gnawing against their bones like a disease. Caesar offers great reward to anyone who takes him my head. My name is known to him, and that I am Druid, he seemingly cannot tolerate. It is the dark thing inside him that fuels his hate for me. It cannot abide the thought, that one still lives who possesses knowledge of the four ways, the path, the Spiral of Immortality. I am born of light, an adversary of all that is dark. Caesar's recognition of me is no more than that.

I be Culann, Druid no more of the Arverni. I am all that I have ever been and what I shall be is yet to come, in a strange land far and away beyond Roman rule. There is a secret to be found and a waiting mystery. No man there will call me Druid or know what it portends. I be something small that ever serves a faint and humble *trace of blue*. Now I fight, so that I might hold on to my house of flesh the longer.

A faint blush of salmon pink streaked the rim of the eastern sky, giving promise of a fine hot day to come.

My two hundred lay on their bellies, hidden amongst the undergrowth that grew in wild profusion all about the forest's edge. A large, cleared area, ringed all about with trees lay before us. In the middle of the cleared area a small fort had been built on top of a man made mound of rock and hard packed earth. It was, or had been, a small clan holding, home to families who worked the fields around it. They would, I knew, have had a milk cow or two, goats, a few sheep, a few cattle, some pigs for winter meat and whatever produce they grew in the fields. It was enough for those who lived there and, if they had a good year there would be a bit left over to trade for whatever they might need.

Small, isolated clan holdings such as this, did not look for war and therefore expected none. They fought off the occasional raiding party, worked the land and lived out a way of life they had chosen to lead, like any other group of free people.

The eastern sky burst into life, widening streaks and rivers of dark pink and crimson, edged all about in molten gold, splashed its face. The sun arced above the eastern rim, driving away the last lingering shadows of night.

Whatever the clan had once held, they did so no longer.

Two Centuries camped round and about the base of what remained of the north facing outer wall. The rest of the fort lay in a smouldering pile of ruins. Here and there remnants of inner, dry stone walls poked up through a mass of smouldering timbers and rubble, like the shattered edge of a war shield. Whoever had lived here, did so no more.

We had been travelling south, on foot, in the fading amber glow of an early summer's sunset. We had not thought to encounter any Romans this far south, and then our scouts had returned and said two Centuries were camped ahead.

As the last of the light faded from amber to lilac and into the deeper indigo of night, we made our way silently through the forest towards the Roman camp.

Full dark had fallen by the time we reached the edge of the clearing, the air about us reeked of smouldering wood and that other sweetish smell of decaying flesh. We thought the Romans broiled meat, the smell of it was strong upon the air. During the thick of night I sent a scout to investigate what we could see of the ruin. He returned with a sick look on his face and said the smell was from charred human flesh. Inac the scout said, 'There be a mound of dead with burning timbers all around them, how many, I don't know, its too dark and the Romans be camped no more than a few paces beyond the outer wall. What's left of it,' he added gruffly.

We spread out amongst the undergrowth and settled down for what remained of the short summer night. It went without saying that we would attack at first light, or when ever I gave the command. We were a desperate band, who did not expect to live overlong.

They knew I had to reach the coast sooner or later and so we had begun, a few days earlier, to work our way towards the Veneti holdings. Once there, those who survived would stay and fight alongside the Veneti, whilst I went about my Druid's work. Donn, my second in command, had made it plain that he would prefer to go with me, wherever that might be. A few others, Madic, Streng, Ferghus and his inseparable friend Eimher, had also indicated their willingness to follow wheresoever I might lead. It would, I think, be unwise of me to take anyone. Apart from that, I'd given little thought to what might lay ahead. Fighting, and always on the move left little room for anything at all beyond trying to survive for one more day.

That is how we lived now, one day at a time. One battle fought and then one more, and then another, until all battles merged and became one, in an unending succession of weary, tortured days and sleepless, hungry nights. Caesar's offer of reward for my head was a thing we joked about, but I never lost sight of the chance that a frightened, desperate man might betray me.

We hunted for food when we could and never stayed for more than one night in the same place. Should someone betray me to Caesar he'd need a Jinn's own luck to find me, but then, anything is possible is it not, and I be no more under the hand of the *Maker* than anyone else.

Darkness gradually gave way to a soft pearly light, the kind that spreads over the land just before dawn break. I roused my men and cautioned them to remain silent and still, whilst I investigated the ruined fort, and the chances of a fast sweeping attack taking the Romans by surprise. Before I moved out, a picture of Bardvar flashed through my head, a warning perhaps, or was it something else.

What the Romans had done to Cumall came hard to the king, he wept and tore out his hair in handfuls, so great was his grief. That his friend and adviser had been crucified upside down and his still living body burnt, was an act of obscene barbaric savagery, Bardvar the king, could scarce comprehend. The capture and binding in chains of Vercingetorix added to the gloom inside his head and to the dimming of his flame of life. I think it was then, that Bardvar knew, deep down inside the secret beating of his heart, that soon or late, it would end like this, fighting small fights, hiding in the forest, forever hungry and exhausted.

Bardvar, still in his prime chose his own way to die, whilst strength still lay upon him and his eyes blazed clear and unafraid. He was our king, a true warrior of *The People*.

It was after his death, that I began to paint my face in the old way, and braid feathers in my hair. Why I did this I cannot say, except that it satisfied some unworded desire deep within the core of my being. Later, many of the young men copied me and called themselves *An Peint Laochra*, the Painted Warriors.

Bardvar chose to die before the eyes of his people. A cry of defiance on his lips, his long hair unbound and streaming out behind him like some final banner of victory.

He was magnificent, though I doubt the Romans thought him so. Bardvar died *Laoch*, a hero. Harpers who live, sing of it, they call it *An Leimeanna*, the Leap of Bardvar.

We had fought against the Ninth in a small way and then the Seventh legion came marching onto the field of battle. Vastly outnumbered we fled.

The Ninth pursued us with an almost mindless tenacity that allowed us no respite at all, no breathing space to eat or drink. There was really nowhere for us to go, we simply fled south.

Towards the end of our second day of flight, Bardvar suddenly yelled, 'ENOUGH.' He did an about face and started walking back towards our enemies. His pace was leisurely, almost a saunter, as though he had nowhere to go and all day to get there. We all turned as a single whole and watched him. There was not one amongst us all, who did not know what he was about. We call it *An Laoch Siulaim*, the Hero's Walk.

Roy Edwards

The sun came out from behind a cloud and lay its golden light upon his head like a blessing. Magnificent he was. A true king of the *Once People*.

Druid I am, but there is ever a growl of warrior inside me. I have always walked the warriors way, I always will.

The Ninth had come to a halt two spear lengths away, confused I would say, unsure as to our intent, and then a short, high bugle blast shivered the air. The Ninth reacted instantly, forming with unbelievable speed, a fighting rectangle. This narrow, cleared space in the forest was not wide enough for the legionnaires to form their traditional fighting square. It was fine for Celts, but then, any place is a good place for a Celt to fight and die, his long hair unbound, his throat howling a torn out war cry of defiance.

We stood, a silent people beneath the sun.

Tall thick trees edged the clearing about us.

The Romans too were silent and waiting, helmets bright and flaming with reflected sunlight.

Bright was the day.

Clouds, like chariots rode the high blue road of the sky.

Hushed was the air, silent the forest. Rasping and harsh was the breathing of the *Once People*.

Bardvar stood in an empty place between *The People* and the Romans.

He threw down his shield, a fine one it was, with a central boss of worked bronze on iron. He undressed slowly and with care, as befits a king. I knew then that he would make the *Hero's Leap*, but I said nothing. I was moved and filled with pride at the awesome dignity of the man. Bardvar had been known to leap over a tall warrior, striking down and back with his long blade whilst in mid air, land on his feet, turn, and strike again all in one smooth flow of perfect motion. He was our king, it was expected of him. It was also his right as a free person to choose the place and the manner of his death.

Bardvar stood naked beneath the sun, its light shining about his long unbound hair like spun gold.

He stood in beauty, powerful and alive. His skin gleamed white, with a polished look about it like pale veined marble.

We stood in complete and utter silence now, all bated breath and awe.

Tears filled my eyes.

He was the king. The ultimate sacrifice, only a king can know. Coming uncalled to his appointed time and place, to stand before some unseen altar and offer his life in place of his people. Kings of old have done this, but none in living memory.

From this day forth, Bardvar would be immortalised, in song and story, lay and legend. He lived now, like blood upon white cloth.

I could see Roman officers staring at us, shielding their eyes from the sun with upraised hands. They would know that something of importance was taking place. They would, like all Romans, be ignorant of its significance. Who can blame them, or dare castigate them for their ignorance. Theirs is the victory, ours the defeat. All blame upon Caesar for his avarice and greedy gulpings of stolen wealth and blood. He eats of it all like pudding at a feast of Beltain and drinks it down in cups of blood from Samhain, feast for the dead.

Bardvar stood facing toward the legions front rank, the muscles of his thick legs all ropy and bunched, hard knots of tension. He held his sword in a two handed grip, the long blade of it resting across his right shoulder, he turned his head toward *The People* and smiled his farewell.

A beatific smile it was, of sunburst radiance. His square white teeth gleamed in the sun.

A slow murmur of approval rippled through *The People*, swelling, building up into an ear pounding roar of acclaim and love, for this man who had ruled them with strength, justice, and the wisdom of Druid then and now. In a final display of love he offered himself up as sacrifice so that his people might go free. They would not, but then, their fate was in the hands of the *Maker* and he had already woven the pattern of their weave.

Bardvar stood up within his house of flesh and blazed like one of the white gods come down to earth. Courage poured out of his mouth, generosity of spirit leaked from his ears.

Suddenly, Bardvar was running, his long muscular legs a blur of pistoning speed. We could see blood running down his right shoulder, where his blade nicked the skin as he ran.

No one moved or spoke.

The front rank of the Ninth shifted, tightening as Bardvar drew near.

We held our breath, the world about us stood still.

Suddenly, Bardvar screamed out 'I CANNOT LIVE A SLAVE, THEREFORE I CANNOT LIVE AT ALL.' And then with a single mighty bound his feet pushed down against the hard packed ground, his knees bent a little and then he was up and soaring, his long blade flashing in the sun.

His Hero's leap carried him over the heads of the first two ranks. Never had he jumped so well. He struck down with his sword whilst he was still in the air. Two Romans died, their upturned faces cleaved almost in two before Bardvar landed amongst them. With a sullen roar, like an angry sea beating against a cliff, we charged. It was a mad foolish thing to do, but then, we be Celtic, a sometime haunt on the land, boastful and impulsive with ever a surging heart beating within, so we did it anyway.

Bardvar's leap had unnerved the Ninth's front rank, and his deadly work with his long sword, caused panic and confusion amongst the third and fourth ranks.

We raced forward, leaping over the ground like stags in flight. Sword blades flashed red and gold in the sun. Bardvar died as we ran, his unprotected back an easy mark for Roman stabbing swords. He killed ten of his enemies before his spirit fled from its broken house of torn and bleeding flesh.

We crashed into the Ninth and smashed their front ranks down. Leaping over fallen, struggling bodies, we shattered the second rank and then the third. The Romans ranked their legionnaires ten deep. The fourth rank wavered against our fury, held, wavered again and then imploded.

We hacked them back in a ruin of broken limbs, slashed throats and severed heads. The air was full of manic screaming and the gasping grunts of pain shocked men. Blood fountained, misting the air with an obscene rain, the taste of it was hot copper and sweet upon our lips. Panicked officers roared out conflicting orders, confusing the legionnaires who were desperately trying to reform around us. Grizzled Centurions, veterans of countless battles barked orders. Bull voices accustomed to shouting and being heard over the length and breadth of parade grounds the world over, gradually rose above the din of our war screams. Panic amongst the Roman ranks gradually gave way to order. Legionnaires trained to obey their Centurions without question reacted instinctively.

I sensed the change almost before it began, ordering those closest to me to withdraw. I yelled out in a loud, commanding voice, 'Back,' waving my left arm and pointing to the open ground behind us. 'Back,' I screamed at the top of my lungs. 'Back, before our escape is cut off.' Those around me streamed through the hole we had cut deep into the first few ranks of the Ninth. Out they flew, slashing and hewing, preventing the outer ranks from closing in around us.

Our paltry two or three thousand were as nothing compared to the full might of the Ninth legion. Surprise and sheer ferocity had carried us so far, now the shock of it was wearing off and the discipline of the legions would gobble the whole of us up, if we didn't quickly escape. We had fought the Ninth before and slaughtered half the legion, before the Seventh legion appeared and saved their day. They began to remember it now, growling in anger as they closed about those of *The People* unable or unwilling to withdraw.

I stood and watched in helpless dismay as the Ninth closed ranks. Yells and screams came from their midst. Roman stabbing swords rose and fell. Tears coursed down my cheeks. A voice spoke loud in my ear, hands tugged my shoulders as warriors streamed by me, fleeing towards the forest.

'Come,' the voice said, 'there is nothing more you can do here.' The voice belonged to Donn, a spear brother from the days of my youth. Tall he was, though not as tall as I, with thick wide shoulders and powerful arms. His hair was long, a copperish red in colour. He tugged at me again, turning me round.

'You be the Druid,' he said softly into my face. 'The king is dead. Those of us who survive will be looking to you to lead us.' My head cleared instantly. Behind me the noise and din of slaughter continued. The Romans knew to their cost, a fighting Celt does not die easily, he will fight on, where a more reasonable man will lay down and die.

Celtic Sunset

Pushing my sword into the earth to clean it of blood, I pulled it free, sheathing it as I turned to Donn, and with a twisted smile on my face said, 'Run, run my friend, run as you have never run before.'

So it was that we fled the field of our final battle.

We regrouped beyond the forest, in a shallow valley hidden behind a range of low rolling hills. I didn't know it then, but the Ninth did not immediately pursue us. We had given them a savage mauling and they thought our surviving numbers to be far greater than they really were. A bare two hundred of us survived that day. Small groups of survivors straggled into the valley through the waning light. By nightfall I judged that we were all there was going to be. We moved out before dawn break.

They looked to me to lead them and so I did, appointing Donn as my second in command. During the days that followed, I began to paint my face and tie feathers in my hair. My small command copied me. It was a small thing perhaps, a vanity, a craziness. Whatever it was or was not, it was a thing we held in common, peculiar to us alone. It was a thread, a thing of pattern and weave that helped to bind us together. From a company of loose, independent warriors, there emerged under my command and guidance, a tight knit group of warriors willing to obey and follow a single leader. 'It is the only way we can survive,' I told them. We had become I think, reminiscent of Bridgit's *Gailiana*. We were *An Peint Laochra*, the Painted Warriors.

We made our way south, heading towards the coast and, the lands of the Veneti in the violent reds and fiery orange glow of a midsummer *Celtic Sunset*.

Ψ

CELTIC SUNSET

Chapter Six

Where go the years?
Through what valleys do they fly?
How short our mortal span,
Foaming across the earth,
Like a brief and passing wonder.
How fall the years that once,
We so carelessly threw.
And like old tumbling bones
Wish we could throw anew.

Culann

Shadows pooled about the trees. The air was cool and dry. Somewhere a bird tried out its dawn song, the sound of it haunting and sweet.

And then I was moving, shadow whispering across open ground.

I moved swiftly, in a half crouch, crossing the flattened field, between the forest and the ruined fort in the space of a few heartbeats, and then I was up against the tumbled wall.

Celtic Sunset

Motionless, I crouched down behind a mass of fallen timbers for a count of ten breaths and then I lunged up and over the wall. I was inside the ruined fort. Warily, I looked around. A faint murmur of voices from the nearby Roman camp drifted on the air. All else was still and quiet.

A strange brooding silence hung over the blackened ruin. There was something here, I could sense it, a kind of terrible wrongness tainted the air with bitter hum and feel. My skin crawled, something terrible had happened. 'What have the Romans done?' I thought wildly.

Swelling light filled the air, flooding the interior of the fort as the rising sun climbed above the edge of the world. Shadows fled into corners and behind bits and pieces of tumbled stone.

Stealthily, I worked my way in towards what had once been the central hall, living place of all the families. It would be here, at days end when work was done, they would eat together, laugh, drink and plan the next days work. Here they slept, loved, laughed and raised children.

Clambering carefully over a pile of rubble, I entered what was left of the great communal hall. The air shivered with a terrible, silent weight of wrongness, like weeping it was, full of cruel hurt, and yet, so far I had come across not one body. Where were the people? What had the Romans done with them? I drifted through the ruins, my eyes constantly searching. There was something odd in the centre of the ruined hall. I edged away from the wall and made my silent way towards it. My throat dry, my heart pounding against the wall of my chest. I gripped the hilt of my sheathed sword tightly, my knuckles white about its familiar, reassuring feel. Druid I be, and I knew, without knowing how or why, that something horrible had happened in this place. Something unclean and dark. Why else burn a remote, isolated holding that could be used to garrison troops?

In front of me a foul smelling mound dominated the centre of the roofless hall. It was about the height of two tall men. A pile of caved in roof timbers had been piled on top of the mound, some of them smouldering sullenly in the half light of early morning. The air about the mound reeked like a Roman charnel house. Suddenly, I was afraid of what I might find, deathly afraid. The thought of the nearness of my two hundred hiding about the forest's edge gave me some small comfort.

I am both Druid and warrior, familiar with the cruelties of men, and yet there be cruelties I can never accept whilst so ever I live. We name them well, these Roman Cruels who invade our lands.

The outer edge of the mound had a look of charred meat about it. I felt sick inside my guts, bile, hot and acid tasting filled the back of my throat. I stirred the edge of the mound with my booted foot, dislodging a small fire blackened skull. From the size of it I knew it was the skull of a young child who had been perhaps, no more than two or three summers old.

With an unreal sense of mounting horror, I used a long thick piece of broken timber to break open the reeking mound. I worked swiftly, quietly in the grip of an icy unnatural calm. When it was done, the reading of it all was plain. Ten men, fourteen women and twenty two children of varying ages, burnt beyond recognition. It was impossible for me to even guess at their ages. All I could recognise was that from the size of their bones, once they were children. Retching, I turned away, fire boiled behind my eyes.

A dark wind began to rise inside my head, eldritch it was — and howling. Tears coursed down my face. The clan had not been killed cleanly, or swiftly. Only the children's bodies about the outer edges of the mound had been burnt beyond any hope of recognition, the flesh of the bodies I had dragged out of its centre had barely blistered.

The women had been raped and their breasts slashed off, some had been strangled, before or after the mutilations, I could not say. Cords still lay, tight wound around their necks. The men had been used for target practice. Each body pierced many times by the light throwing spears that all legionnaires carry. Pilum they are called, the spear head is designed to break off from the shaft when it pierces a target. Each body had three or more spear points stuck in its flesh. Of what was done to the children I will not speak.

It was horror beyond the concept of horror. The work of dark and evil depraved men — things, minions of Gaunt Man, Crom Cruach, Bowed One of the Mound. Here, midst the ruins, an ineffable evil had taken place. It was this I had sensed when I first came into the tumbled ruins. A cold wind moaned inside my head. I felt tight and full, pushing against the prison of my constraining house of flesh.

I think it was then that I began to lose control, my spirit weave pressed against the inside of my skull. Pain it was and searing, a living flame of blue-white rage that yammered and gibbered to be free.

'Shame, oh shame upon all child slayers. You all be truly — things of darkness,' I screamed silently.

I fell to my knees, midst the carnage, gasping for air. Sobs tore at my throat, my reason slipped away on beating wings, as something savage and incredibly old, uncoiled inside me.

And then my head exploded, light shattered behind my eyes.

I turned my face up towards the empty sky and howled like some mortally wounded animal. Tears streamed down my face, the spirit of me seeped out through the walls of my flesh. The windows of my eyes hazed with a glowing red mist of rage, that was, so all consuming it nigh burst my heart and almost caused it to cease its beating. My body shook and shivered and howled, the whole of my being a tremble with rage. It bit deep into my stomach and ached my eyes. My head felt swollen and yet, strangely empty. I seemed to view the fort within and without from a far and distant place. My chest felt constricted, as though it were bound all about with tightening bands of wild, white fire.

Savage, I was.

As empty of emotion as stone, as cold as frost upon iron hard ground.

Romans — cold, cruel, barbaric Romans.

I lunged to my feet.

And then I was moving, I could no more stop myself than I could embrace the sun.

Ropes of spittle flew from my mouth as I screamed out my hate, pouring it out upon the air like burning oil.

I dragged my sword out of its bronzed rimmed scabbard. Metal screeching against metal.

Eye blind and dreaming, I raged through the ruins towards a running group of legionnaires hurrying to investigate the sound of my screaming. Bursting out of the ruins I raced across the flattened earth to meet them.

Blood filled my throat.

Air heaved and sobbed in my lungs.

I wanted to smash, crush and destroy.

So great was my raging strength that my sword had no more weight to it than a willow wand. And then I was upon them. My first blow cut through the leading legionnaires armour, like a sharp knife through bread. I split him in two from shoulder to crotch.

Celtic Sunset

I danced then, hewing and slashing, cutting down anything that moved. Somewhere a horse screamed in fright mingling with the yells and screams of panicked men. A wave of sound swelled behind me, swamped me and then surged on in a thunder of feet and hoarse, yelling voices. Weapons flashed in the sun. Swords rose and fell and slowly, slowly the noise of it all receded, like an out flowing tide suddenly too far away, too shimmering and bright to reach.

I was spinning alone within a void, weaving a net of steel around me. I killed a great many Romans that day.

I was down on my knees, my whole body shaking and shivering. My hands tacky with blood, I was soaked in gore from head to foot. My sword lay on the earth in front of me. Piece by painful piece my vision slowly cleared, and the sense of me returned to my head. Heaving myself up onto my feet, someone thrust a bowl of water into my hands. Trembling, I drank it down greedily.

Warriors stood around looking at me. There faces mirroring a mixture of awe and fear.

Donn stood close by.

'What happened?' I croaked at him. My throat felt sore and torn. Without waiting for his reply, I staggered towards a barrel of water standing close by a scattered cooking fire. I stripped quickly, and scrubbed myself clean of blood and filth. Silently, Donn handed me a change of clothing.

No one spoke.

I dressed in silence. Found my sword, cleaned it and then, with a ring as I slammed it back into its scabbard, I turned to Donn and said, 'Tell me what happened, all of it,' I commanded. His eyes refused to meet mine. With a sigh I looked around.

The Roman camp was littered with bodies. 'Did we slay them all?' I asked Donn in wonder.

'Yes,' he replied gruffly, still refusing to look me in the eye.

'How many of our own did we lose?'

'Eight,' answered Donn.

'Look you,' I said to them all in a loud voice. 'Gather food and water. We will eat, rest awhile and then be on our way. When news of this gets out, Rome will hunt us forever. Not that it matters,' I added, 'though I'm thinking we should not linger here overlong.'

'Now,' I turned to Donn, 'whilst we eat tell me the whole of it. And you, I pointed to a passing warrior, bring yonder horse over here if it be sound.' It was, I realised, the only horse remaining in camp. What others there might have been had long since fled. 'They will go back to a place they know,' I mused aloud, 'and a patrol of cavalry will be sent out to investigate the cause of horses returning riderless. We have not much time to make good our escape, I'm thinking. Now, tell me what happened Donn. From the moment of my charge. It's all a little hazy,' I added.

Donn spoke slowly and clearly. He seemed uncomfortable in my presence and treated me more like a Druid Elder than a spear brother he had fought alongside these two years past. It was then that I knew my time here was drawing to its end, I must reach the lands of the Veneti as soon as possible. Cumall had told me, when first the Arverni had elected to walk the glory road, that I would know when it was time for me to leave the land — forever.

Donn said that he had begun to worry that I had been gone too long, and then he heard me scream. He recognised the sound of it as a scream of rage, rather than that of a wounded man. They charged then, in the silent way I had taught them.

Celtic Sunset

A silent charge is often more unsettling to the enemy than a noisy one. They cleared the fort just as I charged amongst that first group of legionnaires.

'We had an easy victory,' Donn said, 'not one of the two Centuries escaped.' He looked at me a little oddly then and said in a hushed voice, 'They were stunned, I think, at the sight of you. I can't be sure,' he said, 'it may have been no more than a trick of early morning light, but,' he continued, 'I think the Romans saw it too and the sight of it froze them. By the time some few of then had recovered their senses, it was too late. We cut them down, all of them.' He paused for a moment as if searching for words and then said, 'There was something huge towering over you Culann. I'm sure I saw it. We all saw it,' he added desperately, 'only no one wants to talk about it.'

'What did you see?' I asked, although I already knew what he had seen.

'I saw something that was as thin as air. You could see through it. It seemed to shimmer as it towered over you. It wasn't evil, I could sense that. It was protecting you as you fought. You didn't get so much as a scratch. Anyone who came near you was cut down, dead before they hit the ground. Was it a god?' he asked me softly.

I didn't answer him, instead I asked, 'What colour was it, Donn?'

He shifted uncomfortably, his eyes looking beyond me and said, 'It was, I think it was the palest blue I have ever seen, just a faint *trace of blue* that shimmered a little, like mist,' he added, 'when the sun shines through it.'

Late afternoon sunlight flooded the land in yellow light, thick it was, like churned butter fresh from the vat.

255

Roy Edwards

We built a cairn over our slain and those of the clan. When it was done I placed a child's skull on its top, facing towards the field where we had thrown the Roman dead.

That day gave birth to a sorrow within me. It remains with me still. I think it will remain forever.

Slowly the long, terrible day wound down into the calm of an early, endless summer evening.

An orange-silver sunset edged in blue and gold, smeared the lower sky. Like a tapestry it was, a glory of silent wonder. The light of it softened the outline of the cairn. In time the forest would reclaim its own and the cairn, like the fort would be lost forever within a dark green silence. All that remained of the Roman camp was a circle of raised earth behind a shallow ditch. We did not bury the Roman dead. We piled the bodies up in an untidy heap in the nearest field and left them, food for ravens or whatever could stomach their flesh.

I stood facing the west, the air filled with the sound of warriors bustling around me. Glad I would be to leave this tainted place. Donn, I knew, shared my sentiments. I shivered, though the air was summer warm, a premonition perhaps.

It is easy to lose oneself in contemplation of wondrous sunsets or the rainbow sparkle of a spiders web, all heavy and trembling with a weight of dew. Mankind appreciates beauty, the elusive mystic quality of it all. We stumble through it, our heads full of wonder. Wise men seek to unriddle the mystery of creation, only to discover another ineffable beauty awaiting them. And beyond that beauty lies another, and another like some endless procession of teardrops shining through the edge of the sun. There is no final mystery, this I have come to learn. There are many mysteries, all without end. Some are small some are not.

Sometimes people become stuck, contemplating a single mystery and forget there is an endless supply of others awaiting them. And some there are who claim a single mystery for their own and deny the existence of all others. Such is a foolishness that is often the cause of bloodshed, invasion and, the systematic destruction of ideas, thoughts and the creative spirit of man.

Even I, as Druid, am aware that Druidry is not the ALL of everything or even the ALL of any one thing. There are mysteries and knowledge abounding that we have not yet reached. Perhaps that is why we of Druid acknowledge that spirits are in a constant state of change. You must feed the mind to feed the spirit, so it is we believe. Knowledge must, after all, have a higher use than mere temporal. If not, why then do you bother to acquire it. Foolish are they who use it solely to obtain wealth or position. These are fragmentary, passing things, of little worth when your house of flesh breathes its last. Knowledge of the way of the spirit stays with you from house to house. You build upon its foundations and expand. You climb the Spiral of Immortality. You are *Skan Taku Skanskan* — spiritual vitality — something in movement. That is what we of Druid believe.

Even so, human kind are ever cruel, avaricious and violent, much given to incomprehensible cyclic games. Strange is it not? If the forces of good did not kill to protect, they would soon be wiped out by the forces of darkness and then, only darkness would rule darkness, and drink the blood of its own kind. Why? Is it as Cumall has said, that the reptile within us responds to the Gaunt Man's blandishments and willingly obeys, even his foulest and most obscene of commands.

I cannot say, though I think upon it often and have reasoned it out to my own satisfaction, but then, I am Druid. I walked the green heart and returned.

Sunset's colours slid down my eyes, I was drifting, drifting upon a waveless sea of tranquil blue. Something called my name, an irresistible urge to follow and serve swept through me. I sensed the nearness of higher beings, calling, urging, inviting me to follow, to leave my house of flesh behind and embrace the *Fourth Way*, walk its path. Something unseen whispered inside my head, we are waiting, walk its path.

Suddenly, I was tumbling down inside my head, warriors rushing around me, voices shouting.

My head spun, steadied, my stomach lurched, and was still. 'I am Culann of the Arverni,' I thought in surprise. 'Druid to *The People* — who are no more.'

Away to my right, Donn sitting on a log sharpening his sword, jumped up with an oath, turned and came pounding towards me. I took it all in at a glance. Mordu, who earlier, I had sent out on a scouting mission, was running like the wind across the fields to the north of the fort. He was pointing behind him and yelling — 'Cavalry.'

It came to me then, what it was I had to do. 'Donn,' I shouted as he skidded to a halt in front of me. 'Bring me the horse, quickly now.' I must not, I realised, give any one time to think, only to act.

Donn, puffing a little, returned with the horse. A fine chestnut stallion it was, with the look of one of our own breed about it. I climbed onto its back. Looking down, with a grin on my face, I said to him. 'Into the forest with you. Take all the warriors and run as far and as fast as you can. I will remain.' Before he could protest, I said, 'I have the only horse amongst us, the Roman cavalry will see me, and only me. I will run, they will follow. By the time they realise their mistake you will be far and away, hidden safely within the forest. I will ride on alone to the lands of the Veneti and meet you all there.' Soberly I said, 'Come if you can my friend, if not, then the *Maker* be with you. Now go, GO,' I shouted, 'before the Romans catch sight of you all.' Still he hesitated to leave me. Heeling the horse forward, I began to herd Donn towards the forest. 'GO,' I screamed at him, 'run my friend, run.'

He ran, leading the warriors into the forest and headed south. Within moments the whole of my war band had disappeared, swallowed up by trees and bush.

I was alone in the purple twilight of a dying day.

It was very quiet and still.

I looked to the west, only a faint slice and sliver of sunset remained. It burned behind the trees, its glow barely discernible in the gathering gloom and bloom of a sweet falling night.

I heard it then, a pounding of hooves along an old game trail that wound its way across the fields towards the ruined fort. They swept out of the forest in a tight group, fanning out as they galloped towards me. They had not yet noticed the stallion midst the gloom that gathered about the forts ruined north wall. I kneed him out onto open ground.

Surprised by our sudden appearance, and no doubt suspecting an ambush, they milled around in confusion. Someone barked an order. Romans make poor riders, having no natural affinity for horses they rely solely upon foot soldiers to take care of any serious fighting.

They were an Alae (cavalry) of eight. I drew my sword and waved it about in the air. Through the gathering gloom they could not be certain of my intent. I advanced, making it appear as though I might attack.

Fanning out they charged, how foolish. I was familiar with the forest, they were not, nor could they know if they faced one or one hundred, but then, Romans are not over bright at the best of times, save for an odd few that is.

Sheathing my sword I urged the stallion towards the trees, swinging onto a dim trail heading south.

A fat harvest moon hung low in the sky, like a huge gold skinned melon. Pale, gold-white light poured down through the trees in shafts and pools of ghostly radiance.

Dark reared the trees around me.

Silent it was and still.

The stallion carried me through the night and on into a cool dawn, heavy with dew.

The Roman Alae haunted my back trail, strange that was. I had not thought the taking of a single mounted warrior important enough to warrant such tenacity, unless they had recognised me, or thought they had and hoped to claim reward from Caesar in exchange for my head. Of course, I had seen their faces quite clearly before they charged, why then could they not have seen mine. Paint and feathers alone would be enough to mark me.

I rode across a bleak stretch of moorland.

Roman Cruels followed.

Wide the moors were, wild and empty.

A ceiling of low grey cloud gave promise of rain to come. Wind, chill for the season moaned over gorse bushes, bracken and clumps of yellow and white bog flowers. Somewhere off to my right lay the bitter sea Romans call

Celtic Sunset

Oceanicus Atlanticus. I could not see it, but I knew it was there, I could smell the salt of it on the wind.

Here and there huge standing stones reared up from the moors like unanswered questions. Who erected them? Why? What purpose did they serve? I know the secret of the stones, many do not and if I were to speak of what I know, there would be disbelief, therefore I choose not to speak.

I fled across the moors, past clumps of bog myrtle, splashing through brown peaty streams, galloping by shelves of smoky grey granite and outcrops of weathered limestone.

The Romans came after, following like hounds to the hunt. They rode Taurisci horses bred for stamina and endurance. The stallion I rode was swift and strong, even so, the slower Taurisci horses would eventually run him down. I thought about that as we fled across the moors.

A fine mist of rain began to sift down. I grew cold and damp and angry. 'Would it end,' I thought gloomily, 'would the whole bloody waste of it ever end?'

Three days and still they follow.

Drawing closer with every heartbeat.

The stallion is almost done, his strength leaking away with every rise and fall of the trail. Wind there is, blowing in from the sea. I can see it now, away to my right, blue and gold beneath the sun. Waves foamy and white with an underbelly of green, as they crash and break against rocks, hurling spray high in the air. Droplets shining like frozen jewels as they fall back into the sea. All else is moorland with no hint of a tree, only wild grass bending before the wind, carrying on its breath the high plaintive cry of the curlew which is, as all men know, the loneliest sound in the world. Before me moorland reached out towards forever like some unforgiving hand of doom.

It was my intent to set the stallion free once I was safe in the lands of the Veneti, no doubt he would soon be recaptured but I would give him his chance. Now it seems I must run him to death to escape the Romans. I don't think so, he deserves better than that. A trained war horse, he would fight if I put him to battle. It was something to think on as I rode the day down, into that weird purple hued dusk that often settles over sun warmed moorlands when the last of the quiet day falls down in sleep.

Close they pound — and closer.

They will be upon me soon. I had slowed the stallion, to conserve his strength for one final burst of speed, though what good it would do me I didn't know.

The moors had given way to rolling meadows of wild grass that bent before the wind. The trail was chariot wide here abouts, and showed evidence of recent use. 'They must take me now,' I thought bleakly, 'before we come in sight of some Veneti village or travellers upon the road.'

The grasslands were flat and dry beneath the sun. Meadow larks sang and twittered. Wind set the grass to rustling, it was a pleasing restful sound.

Above me, the summer sky was a rich deep blue. Here and there clouds, the colour of cream, sailed majestically across its face. Windy sunlight filled my mouth and tugged at my long unbound hair. My sword thumped and slapped against my thigh. The stallion snorted as he gamely plodded on.

Taurisci horses or no, they were small and had not the stallion's strength or weight, nor were they trained to war. The stallion would fight.

Suddenly I laughed out loud, a wave of recklessness flooding through me. 'Today,' I shouted out loud, 'is a good day to die.' The words had an all too familiar ring about them. Over the years I have come to learn this about me, I am ever reluctant to fight and for every life taken there is a staining upon the true spirit of me. And yet, when I come to battle, a fierce wild joy enters my heart. I glory in my strength and skill and have at my enemies with a right good will and a fierce exultation for the mad joyful glory of it all. I am no hero, no Champion. I be Celtic, and those who pursue me be my enemies and the cause of the death of *The People*.

Anger flared, deep down inside my gut. 'You hunt me,' I shouted 'now you have found me.' Dropping the reins, I reached up towards the sky, opening my arms in a wide embrace of air. I threw back my head and yelled, 'Today is a fine, beautiful day, a good day to die.'

Dropping my arms I drew my sword. Using my knees to guide the stallion, I wheeled him about. The stallion knew what I intended, he snorted and pawed the earth, as eager as I to give battle to our pursuers. Trained for war, the stallion needed no reins to guide him. We waited. The sun warm about my head and shoulders.

The eight riders drew close. Without hesitation, at sight of me, they drew their swords and attacked. At the same moment I kneed the stallion forward. He charged like a thunderbolt straight into their midst, bowling one horse and rider completely over, smashing two more aside. Yelling, I slashed right and left, my long blade licking out like a tongue of flame. I had the weight, height and reach over the Romans. There swords too short to reach me. I killed two, the stallion another, his great hooves crushing the skull of a fallen rider too slow to move out of his way. And then we were through, wheeling and charging again. I leaned over to my right, my sword cocked across my shoulder. As we charged I swept my sword down in a great sweeping arc, a

Roman head jumped free of its body and bounced over the grass. So great had been my blow the Roman's horse staggered and fell to its knees squealing in fear and pain. Without pause, I swung to my left, slashing through a face and denting the helmet of another. Wild the blood sang in my veins, fierce the cry from my throat, I gloried in my strength, in the feel of tight, hard muscles powering my arms. I yelled and screamed and all the while my sword hummed and whistled through the air.

The remaining riders drew away, shocked by my fierce eagerness to fight. Four of their number lay dead upon the ground. My stallion charged again, rearing back on his hind legs he crashed his hooves down onto the luckless head of a Taurisci horse. The animal crashed to the ground, flipping its rider high in the air, I cut him almost through as he fell. The Taurisci horse struggled to rise, the stallion lashed out, screaming fiercely it smashed in the skull of the smaller horse. Urging him on we attacked the remaining riders, and then I leapt down from his back, standing with legs apart, my blade resting on my shoulder, I dared the Romans to attack me.

'See me,' I shouted in Latin, 'my hair is unbound. I be only one man,' I laughed, goading them on. 'Take my hair if you can, your pig of a Caesar will reward you well. Romans, I shouted, you smell like the arse end of a she goat.' I spat upon the ground and said in a low deadly voice, 'Rome is the whore of the world and you be her sons.'

They came at me then, blind with fury, lusting to kill the foul mouthed thing standing before them. Well, and wasn't that my intent now. As they charged, the stallion pranced nervously off to my left. And then they were on me, leaning over dangerously to strike. I waited until the last heartbeat and then danced aside out of reach of all but one rider. I swung at him as he thundered by, my height almost equal to his, mounted though he be. My long blade cut deep into his spine. He swayed and fell, his mouth open in a soundless scream of pain. Swift as light I was on him driving my blade through his throat. The remaining two riders had turned and came pounding back, their faces ashen and full of fear. Wheeling about I raced toward the stallion and leapt astride his back. He surged forward, the Romans made it easy for me, wielding short swords they must come close to strike. Using my long sword to advantage, I attacked the nearest rider, sweeping him from his horse, his face laid open to the bone. Turning to meet the remaining rider, I opened his unprotected throat with a casual back hand flick of my sword.

Panting, I surveyed the field.

Dead they were, all eight of them.

The pattern weaves as the *Maker* wills.

Roy Edwards

I gave the great red stallion his freedom, a half days march from the coast. The last village was behind me now, the great seaport of the Veneti somewhere ahead.

There is a soft wind blowing in from the sea, fresh it is and cooling to my face. The road I follow is a wide, lazy one, winding through low rolling hills and chequered fields of golden grain and green leaf crops. The sun plays hide and go seek with cloud islands floating lazily across a deep blue sky. How beautiful the day, how throat achingly beautiful.

I am alone now. The way before me unclear. I do not think Cumall told me the *all* of his vision, of what he claims is my destiny. 'It is waiting for you' he said, 'beyond the sea. Waiting like a patient woman for you to come and claim the whole of it.' Perhaps it is true, perhaps it is not. All that is left to me is my promise given, oath sworn, by air and fire, earth and water, metal and spirit, oath sworn and witnessed and now, all the witnesses be dead. Therefore am I released from geasa in the eyes of the law of *The People*. I am Druid and I swore spirit oath. I would be less than all I claim to be if now I break my word. I am not released, and somewhere ahead there is one who is waiting. Spirit brother he be, so it is that I feel.

It is good to walk. To feel the *Maker's* blessing of wind and sun against my flesh. The legs of me stretching out, blood coursing through my veins.

What became of Donn and the others, I do not know, I never saw them again.

After I had killed the Roman Alae, I fell from the stallion. My battle madness leaking away as it always does, leaving me shaking and weak. Legs a tremble. My guts throwing up through my mouth. My head all a spin and ringing like a great flawed bell of imperfect bronze.

266

Celtic Sunset

I do not know why I am this way, it is only in this life that it has happened. Perhaps I am changing. Since walking the Druid's way much has changed. It is a thing of the spirit I think, though of course I cannot be sure, at least not yet. I will know when I reach *An Fada Talamh* (The Far Land, Celtic name for America BC)

We all change, it is the way of life. Though of course there are those who do not recognise change. They wish everything to remain the same — forever. Each day the same as the one before, like those who come to study within Nemeds and when they leave, they seek not to add to their store of knowledge. They eschew reading of any kind and are often intolerant of those who, having read much are able to enter friendly discourse upon a variety of subjects. Are such people truly awake? Do they progress along *the way?* I do not think so. I think they live only partial lives and wake-sleep the rest of it away. The way of Druid teaches that a seeker of knowledge remains a seeker for the whole of his life, and that a true master of any discipline is he who comes to recognise how little he truly knows. A master is someone with specialised knowledge. Overawed by his learning, many do not realise he is often only specialised in a single discipline. That is one of the reasons why Druid training is never less than twenty of years. We are required to learn a great many disciplines, study many different kinds of knowledge. How else can spirit progress along *the way* if not through knowledge. What is obvious to me, what has since childhood always been obvious to me is not, I have over the years come to realise, obvious to others.

There is a foolishness amongst people.

So many assume that if you possess a store of great and varied knowledge, you will speak of it, if you do not, they assume you do not possess any at all.

Credence it seems, is given to those who shout the loudest irrespective of the sense of their words. Knowledge is a quiet personally gained thing, spoken of softly by those who possess it, if they speak of it at all that is, which I doubt.

As Druid I speak rarely amongst men. If asked, I give answer and no more, but then, I am not the same as others, and even as a child was considered most odd. Perhaps it was recognition of my own way of change, that led me to turn my face away from Deidre, those long years ago. There are times when I feel as though I walk down some broken highway all unseeing, for true it is I loved her and did not wish her harm. I tried to tell her, but I have not the gift of words. I must forever search for words and when I find them, it is often too late and the moment has fled. There are some who, like harpers and bards are born with the gift. They wait only for the mouth of the body to grow so that they might then articulate the words inside their head. I have no such ease. Now it is that harpers sing of Deidre. They call her *Deidre Na Brons,* Deidre of the Sorrows.

It happened during my seven of years training within the Nemed of Bridgit the warrior woman.

I thought upon it all then, as I walked the long road toward the coast. I would reach it by sunset, or before. My legs be long and have a way about them of eating up distance. Meanwhile, I thought upon what I had done and the way of its ending, Hag sorrowed I was.

It was during my seventh season within the Nemed of Bridgit. I had by then experienced many gifted moments, the way it was for me I had thought was the way it was for others. I gave little thought to it all, until one day, Bridgit dismissed me early and I chanced upon a small group of warriors in training, sitting together outside the circle of their own Nemed. We spoke of weapons and horses and of trials to come, and then one amongst their number, a young, dark haired warrior with husky shoulders spoke of a woman he had bedded the previous night. Then it was that they all in turn, spoke of gifted moments, whilst I sat in silence and listened. It is not my way to speak of such things. It is a precious gift and not to be made less of by any casual mouthing around. Even so, from what was said, I realised that the way it was for me was not the way it was for others, at least not amongst the young warriors I sat with.

Later, when I was alone, I thought upon it, but I was young and had much to learn. The mystery of it remained unclear, for awhile that is.

The young warriors agreed amongst themselves that after bedding a woman they wanted no more than to sleep, to curl up against warm flesh with the woman smell strong in their nostrils and sleep.

It is not this way with me.

When the gifted moments end I am possessed of a startling clarity of inner vision, of thoughts and colours, as though spirit and mind meld in perfect unison. Whilst the woman breathes in sleep, I lay awake within quiet darkness pondering Druid riddles, contemplating mysteries or something I have read, written by foreign hands. I think upon who I am, or what it is I must do for *The People*, that seemingly cannot be done by someone else. I thought much upon my destiny of which Cumall would not speak.

During those quiet lulled hours, I would often find sense and meaning in hitherto perplexing axioms I had failed to unriddle within Nemeds of learning. It seemed, to my then youthful mind, that the more I lay with women the sharper my senses became and the closer I moved towards something ineffable, that hovered just beyond my conscious reach. Sometimes, after gifted moments, sendings haunt the whole of the inside of my head. Whilst the woman lay beside me all unknowing, my vision would often fill with images of things to come, of deer and wolf, fleeing through seasons yet unrun. From such sendings, I did glimpse an edge of sorrow and irredeemable sufferings laying in wait for *The People*, between the spaces of the dark places that had yet to be spun.

Once only did I speak of this to the Druid of Sacrifice and Dreams. It is, I think, better that I seek my own truth of meaning. He said such sendings and visions and clarity of reasoning were the result of sex magic, and accused me of dabbling in disciplines beyond my ability to reach. Even Druidry has its share of fools and petty minded individuals too obtuse to reason with.

I, like many others amongst the brotherhood, the Order of Druids, am not at all sure what magic has to do with anything at all. Magic is simply a word used to denote something we don't understand. Mankind has a propensity to bury simple, natural things beneath a complexity of words and symbols. He hides it, claims specialised knowledge is needed to understand it and becomes dangerously indignant when exposed. The sad part of it all is, that such men are rarely if ever, exposed. People don't think enough, they are too willing to accept, too willing to be told what is, or is not, without ever once asking why, but then, there is much I have yet to learn, so I dare say I am probably wrong.

Being a society of free people our women have the same freedoms as men. A woman calls upon a man in much the same way as a man calls upon a woman, though of course there are some women who prefer to be courted than to do the courting. It is also that way with some few men.

To be individual you must first be willing to be an individual.

Celtic Sunset

We of the Celts are ever willing to be just that.

That is why every Celt is a free person, unique unto self. Individual expression, we boast, we strut, we adorn ourselves with jewellery and wear bright clothes. We sing and dance, we hunt and drink. We make music, compose songs, create art.

We are life and in affinity with the land.

Amongst other nations conformity is both god and king, even their scholars and thinkers conform, it shows in their dry, dusty writings.

We are Celts and conform only to the *True Fidelity of Being*, and we will fight for our right to remain free.

We wear our hair long and unbound, take it if you can, we are Celts and who can say more.

Ψ

Deidre of the sunset hair, wished to be courted. I did not know that.

When first we met, the sight of her and the sun bright cloud of her hair, was like a dreaming vision revealed. I stood alongside the smithy that fronts onto the main market square, the centre of our town of Arverni. There were shops and market stalls along two sides of the square and a goodly throng about. Bridgit and I broke many a weapon between us. Brann the Smith, repaired them. That day, I was there to pick up a bundle of repaired throwing spears.

A fine day it was, smoke rising from the forge. A soft warm breeze blowing in from across the valley. The sound of voices haggling over this and that. People passing to and fro. A smell of fresh baked bread mingling with wood smoke. A fine yellow sun, set within a curving dome of blue. A warm lazy day I was reluctant to exchange for weapons practice.

And then I saw her, weaving through the throng towards me, sunlight bouncing from her hair, like flame it was. The sun's light accentuating its colour. I never did learn what it was she wanted from Brann the Smith.

I smiled at her, she smiled back exposing small, even white teeth. My heart lurched, my guts twisted into a knot. Sweet gods above, I gulped, my mouth suddenly gone dry.

Tall she was and slim. The noise of the crowd faded away into the distance. I had never seen such eyes, green they were, like river moss. She wore a loose fitting, pale green gown of fine weave. The colour of it accentuating the green of her eyes. A thin soft leather belt pulled it in about her waist, the buckle of it, enamelled bronze. A deep glowing red, the enamel polished and gleaming in the sun. Her skin was smooth and rich, like thick milk that forms atop thin milk left standing overnight in the cool house. Small firm breasts pushed against her gown.

I have read of the Greek Helen and how it was that her beauty sparked a war. I have read the poets description of her beauty, now it is I'm thinking it to be a pale kind of beauty compared to Deidre of the sunset hair.

The smith paused in his work, a knowing look in his quick, bright eyes. He smiled at the two of us and slipped away into the shadows at the rear of his shop. I stood there, heat beating down on my head. Crowds swirling around us, the sound of voices raised in friendly argument, ebbing and surging like a tide. I heard none of it, saw none of it, all I could see was the girl. Words cluttered my head, I tried to speak, but could not force the words past my teeth. I felt big, clumsy and awkward like some unschooled country boy. I who would be Druid stood speechless. The amazing beauty of her silenced me. Mixed emotions roiled my guts. I felt uneasy, unsure of what was happening. I did not think of love, at least not then. Love was something harpers and bards sang about, a bittersweet potion that can render the best of men lack-wit.

She spoke to me, her voice soft and melodious. I admired her mouth, full lips, pink with life. I muttered something in reply, desperately trying to gather my wits. This had never happened to me before, how to deal with it, I didn't know. It went beyond anything I had ever known. I wasn't ready for this, I had far to go and I must travel my way alone.

Is ever man or woman ready for love, I wonder. It strikes without warning and leaves you forever changed. Some there are who welcome it, I could not, I dare not. There was that ahead of me I had yet to face, an unlooked for destiny, a walking of paths. There was no place in my life for love, not yet, not now. Later perhaps, much later. Love, I found out to my cost, has no care of such things, it exists above and beyond the plans or destinies of men. The power of it is frightening, and can be both terror and beauty. It can save or destroy, be wound or healer.

After she had gone, I collected my bundle of repaired weapons from Brann and returned to the Nemed of Bridgit. Over the following days Bridgit almost had my life again and again. My head was full of Deidre, my attention elsewhere and not upon my lessons. Bridgit was a Weapons Master, she was also a killer, bound by geasa (sacred oath) to instruct within her Nemed, but not to kill. She held herself back with rigid self control. My obvious inattention almost drove her over the edge. So much so that she refused to teach me until I regained my senses. She set me to shadow fighting, spear and bow work.

And all I could think of was Deidre.

I saw her from time to time when my duties took me into town. I couldn't understand why she avoided me, or what I might have done to displease her. I admired her from afar with many a sigh and quickened beating of my heart. I had no idea of what to do, or how I might gain her attention. I wished again and again that where women folk were concerned I might be a more courageous man.

The seasons went by, Imbolc followed Samhain and all too soon it seemed *The People* had gathered to celebrate Beltain and we were once again in the season of green leaf.

I had by now recovered my senses and gave good account of myself against Bridgit. I even went so far as to speak to her of Deidre. We were at sword practice when I spoke of Deidre, suddenly Bridgit attacked me with a savage ferocity I was hard pressed to simply hold against. Her eyes were utterly cold and then as suddenly as she had attacked she eased off. What had sparked her anger? Certainly not my mentioning of Deidre. Bridgit, for all the warrior look of her was desired by many. She invariably wore only a short battle skirt and now and again a band of cloth tied about her breast. Her skin was honey coloured from exposure to the sun. And of men, I dare say she could pick and choose. I gave it no more thought.

One day, late afternoon it was, we were resting between bouts, our backs to the trees, legs all asprawl, sunlight warm upon our flesh. Bridgit said, when she desired a man she told him so and he refused her at his peril. I laughed at that, but underneath her smiling banter, I sensed that she was deadly serious and prayed fervently to the *Maker* that she did not turn her eyes on me. She questioned me concerning Deidre and so I told her how it was. She smiled then, much to my relief, and said that Deidre was the kind of young woman who enjoyed soft words and gifts and a modicum of time in which to think about it all and enjoy the attention.

'Go,' she said, 'pursue her or your head will never be free.' She looked at me then with a strange kind of hurt mirrored in her eyes.

I was young and knew little of women, beyond casual gifted moments. Would that I had known you better Bridgit, perhaps I might have eased your inner pain, would that I had known you better. Sometimes I am blind, the hurtful need of you I did not see. When Cumall released you from bonds of geasa and turned you loose upon Roman Cruels, did you kill because you were alone and inside your head spoke only with the dead. We used you Bridgit, like a weapon and now you are legend. Would that I had known you better Bridgit, to my sorrow I did not.

So it was that I gave into the hands of Deidre a gift of new season flowers, rare they were, gathered deep within the forest where few but Druid dare to go. I stood there, towering above her in the late afternoon sun, all a tremble like some new birthed colt, whilst she thanked me in soft voice for my gift and then walked away. Some few of the townsfolk looked on with knowing smiles.

A few days later I gave her a thin silver bracelet set with green stone and small pieces of chalcedony that Greeks call carnelian, and after that a magnificent broach. The large oval kind that you use to fasten a cloak about you. Blue enamel upon bronze it was with a central pattern of green and white. The pattern was a spiral in the shape of an Oak, symbol of wisdom and immortality. She had that from me with a small squeal of delight and then she hurried away, to show it to her friends no doubt. And me feeling the fool for the whole town knowing it.

As chance would have it, at least I think it was by chance and not design, we Celts call it, our luck, not believing that anything happens by chance at all. It might of course, we just don't believe that it does, at least not we of Druid that is. Cumall says you make your own luck and that it comes from — elsewhere — all you have to do is recognise its source.

By chance or whatever, the day following my gift to Deidre of the enamelled bronze broach, found me wandering down by the river. I searched for sweet grass, river herbs and a special cress, water cress we call it. The whole of what I searched for we boil and make a paste of. It is good for soothing and speeding the healing of open wounds and winter sores. Some of the women mix it with oil pressed from olives and rub it into their skin, they claim it refreshes the skin and imparts a youthful look to facial flesh that has begun to sag and line with age.

Deidre found me there, wandering by the banks of the river, my basket already full of this and that. At first we said

Celtic Sunset

little beyond a shy exchange of greetings. She wore a soft blue gown edged in white, the silver bracelet around her right wrist, her long hair was loose cascading down over her shoulders. I thought her face had a faint blush to it but I couldn't be sure. I was trying very hard not to devour her with my eyes, I sometimes unsettle people if I look at them overlong. Cumall says it has to do with my eyes and the spirit within peering through.

She stood there in front of me, the river winding its laughing way behind and off to one side of her. A softness of morning mist not yet burnt away by the heat of the climbing sun, wreathed and coiled all about her long shapely legs. Something caught in my throat, my gut tightened, my tongue began to tie itself in knots. A strand of ropy mist reached out from the river, pink pearl it was in the early morning light. Green leaves, glistened, wet with dew. White-silver fish flashing through breathing waters. Sunlight streaming through trees, dapple painting the earth. And Deidre, sweet god — and Deidre. She moves behind my eyes like starlight upon dancing waters.

The cool morning air had a taste of sharp wine about it. She swayed closer, her thin weave gown clinging about her hips. Her river green eyes sparking with life. She smiled up at me, and I swear before the eyes of the *Maker* that I heard the warbling song of thrush and lark fill the air around me.

Morning sunlight blazed her unbound hair. The green river lure of her eyes swallowed me. I could not speak. My body trembled.

I do not use my Druid sense amongst *The People*. I would not be so ill mannered, even so, it leaked out from me. I could sense the fierce beating of Deidre's heart, and something else. Something profound and unexplainable, love. At that moment I wanted nothing more than to hold her close, to feel the warmth of her flesh against mine. Caress the firm roundness of her breasts and inhale the fragrance of her hair.

We were alone here, by the river. Standing in a small isolated world of our own making. Is this what love is, I thought in wonder? A fine melding of spirit and flesh. Do we celebrate love above the joy of sensation? Is that what poets do? Is that what Harpers sing of? Plato had never such joy, it shows in his writings of platonic love, or is it I, who am the fool and he the master, who rose above the need of a woman's love? A single bell of warning rang deep inside my head, something skitter-shifted in alarm. My hunger for Deidre rode me down like some dark winged haunt of mare, and for all that came after *mea culpa*, my fault.

Wordlessly, I reached out and drew her close. Beneath sunlight splashing down through trees. Beside waters flowing light beneath a pale warm sky of perfect blue.

With a small glad cry, Deidre came willing and eager to my hands, and lips. I embraced her and my heart came nigh to bursting from the feel of her closeness and the warmth of her flesh soaking into mine. Her breasts pushed hard against me, her full lips, warm and moist, crushed against mine. I felt giddy and breathless. My legs weak and trembling. Was there ever such a perfect love as ours. Something clanged shut with a noise like a closing gate, way back inside my skull. I paid it no mind at all.

Her breath had a smell of honey and almonds about it, her lips a taste of wild lemon grass. She closed her eyes with a sigh, her hands pressed firm against my buttocks. She bit my lip in lovers play as we lay down by the river's edge. Dew damp grass and crushed leaves of mint, cool against our heated flesh, as we kissed and with shy, hesitant hands explored each others secret places.

Celtic Sunset

She was joy and wonder, and our gifted moment lingered as though it trembled upon the brink of an endless dawn of creation.

I rode high upon a silver edged cloud of crimson and gold. Bright pearly light washed over me. I seemed to float and bob about like wood on water. I had entered that in between place where those strange bodiless beings, shining ones, opalescents, inhabit spaces different from our own. I had glimpsed them before, but I couldn't quite remember when or where or why.

They regard us with fond amusement, when they deign to regard us at all. They clustered together in a small group, wavering in and out of my vision like midsummer heat waves shimmering above sandy plains. Some few drew close to me, smiling in recognition of my soaring spirit as I looked down upon my heaving body and the closed eyed dreaming wonder of Deidre's face. Her skin was cream and rose and pale dusky gold. The hair of her like a cloud of sunset smeared across green grass. Trees there were, standing in silent majesty about us, the dark of their green leaves reflecting pieces of broken light. A soft haze of pearl beneath a sky so deep a shade of blue it was almost black.

Voices, rainbow coloured voices whispered about me. Is it possible I wondered, for a voice to have colour? Faces, faint and ethereal smiled into my eyes. 'Is that why you are called opalescents?' I asked soundlessly. Voices whisper colouring around me. I fell down towards my body and through the face of my head. Home I was, inside my house of flesh.

I felt the earth beneath me, Deidre by my side, her hand tight clasped in mine. Stunned by the depth and release of our emotions we lay together in silence. Warmth from the sun drying our perspiring bodies.

Roy Edwards

I think Deidre may have slept then, for awhile at least, though I cannot be sure. Bathed in sunlight, I was suddenly seized and in the grip of a *sending*.

Visions I have had. Visions, I thank no one for, and none more terrible than this. It sheared my sight and roared through my skull like some angry, maddened beast intent on my destruction.

Shifting scenes moved behind my eyes. I saw *The People* fighting, falling, running and crying, dying beneath Roman swords. Druids crucified upside down, their flesh peeling away in flames, heads black and smoking. An eagle shrieked in triumph beneath dark clouds, rumbling thunder, spitting lightening. The air grieved and moaned about Roman slave masters as they lashed the heads and shoulders of a snaking column of children bound in chains, sold into slavery. Caesar's face swam into view, cruel smiling he was, his face wreathed all about in shadows. Something dark and awful stood over him. Sacred groves burst into flames. I cried out in pain and anger, dry sobbing inside my throat. Slowly, slowly the images inside my head faded away. I looked up towards the sky through a thick canopy of trees. Pieces of blue floating on a green leaf sea. Beauty all around me, Deidre, trees, water, sun and sky. Beauty, and yet, inside my house of flesh memory of cruel visions lay bleeding down my heart.

Bridgit drove me hard, her eyes fierce and cold. The pink lips of her tight pressed against her teeth. That I had angered her in some way, I knew full well. What I had done to snarl her so, I didn't know. I was young and where love was concerned, I knew nothing, I only thought I did.

Throughout the whole of it, from beginning to ruinous end, Cumall said not one word. During long candle lit evenings, we studied and talked of anything and everything but Deidre or love. I realise now, in that one thing, he could not advise me or even speak of it. I must come to my own realisation of what it is to be Druid and the way of its walking amongst *The People*. It was I think a time of testing, though of course I didn't know that. I would never be the same again, and the haunt of it all would bell forever, within the hollow of my head.

Within the Nemed of Bridgit, I fought well and hard, sometimes driving her back, once, almost disarming her. She would come at me then and end it all with some new trick I had yet to learn, satisfied that she had beaten me once again, she would order me off and away, knowing full well it would be to Deidre that I would run.

Man tall and strong, I was none the less young in years, and like many of my age, oblivious to the hurt my actions caused in another. Would that I had known you better Bridgit. I did not look. So full was I of Deidre, I had not the eyes for any other. Now it is that I think Bridgit did not look for a lover, she sought only a friend, sword friend, forged in the Nemed, heart friend, someone who might listen having first sworn friendship across the blades. Friendship, is ever a jewel so rare, we often fail to recognise the preciousness of so rare and costly a gift.

Thou doth haunt me Bridgit.

To my everlasting sorrow, I failed thee when thou stood in dire need.

Youth blind, was I.

Forgive me Bridgit, how I wish I had been your friend.

I loved Deidre all through the season of bud and leaf and long into Beltain. I loved her beneath the hot sun and on through long lazy days full of yellow sunlight and hazy, purple filled dusks. The games and rites of Lugnasadh gave way to harvest time and a cooling of days. I loved Deidre to the years end, Samhain, and the Feast for the Dead. I stood upon the pinnacle of our love through Imbolc, and the rites of prognostication. I loved her through the last of winter's moaning winds and on into the soft rains of spring. Beltain came again with all its sticky buds of new growth sprouting, and I loved her still.

I was young and only just beginning to understand, the glimmer and gleam of the awful weight of my growing knowledge and, my sometimes *sight* of what might be. I spoke of this to Cumall, in truth I barely understood my sendings and often wished the *Maker's* gift away.

About then it was that Deidre spoke of marriage. The icy shock of her words woke me from my dreaming. Of course she would expect us to marry, and why not, we loved each other. Soft eyed she was and lovely and I the fool for allowing it all to have gone on for so long. No wonder Cumall would not speak of it. He knew what would happen if I remained true to what I am and to the ideal of what I must become. There was a terrible air of inevitability about it all as though I were a piece of wood adrift upon strange uncharted seas. A sudden chill of insight burned behind my eyes.

I loved Deidre but I could not marry her, or any other woman of *The People*. There was something waiting for me, in a far land beyond the great salt ocean, and I must go. Soon or late, I must go, and I must go alone. How I knew this, I cannot say, I just knew and there's an end to it. A river of change flowed through me, and I wailed my loss of a love I should never have nurtured, *mea culpa*, my fault.

Celtic Sunset

What I would become in that far away land was, I realised too late, part of my destiny, and my destiny did not, could not include Deidre. I had some, as yet unknown thing to do, that was of more importance than any emotional alliance of my own. I swallowed then a bitter drink of sorrow, knowing no matter how unintentional it might be, I, and I alone, had caused grievous hurt to one I loved. I tried to tell her but I had not the words. Bound by my oath of Druid, I could not reveal to her what course my future might hold.

I did then, the only thing I could. Not having the gift of words to explain, I drove her from me.

I became cold and aloof, saying only that I was needed within the Nemeds. That my studies demanded the whole of my time. That I was Druid in training and could not be thinking of love until my twenty of years were complete.

My words to her seared my soul with hot forge iron. I grew distant from her, avoiding her whenever my duties brought me into town.

I gave wound unto her heart. She thought me cruel and uncaring in my using of her and the spurning of her love.

Deidre turned away in sorrow and heart pain. Hurt she was and crying inside like some lost and lonely child. She went away from the lands of Arverni and I never saw her again. She went away in gloom and dark despair and I the cause of it all.

During my third seven of years, I learned of her fate.

When she left Arverni she travelled to the coast and sailed to Ierne (Ireland) on a Veneti trading ship. Her beauty was such that the King of Ulster courted her and eventually made her his wife. It was a loveless marriage. He wanting her for a showpiece so that all men might envy him his ownership of beauty. He took her not unto his bed, parading her like a horse before his court, passing her back and forth between visiting dignitaries. Holding out the sweetness of her thighs to sway minor chieftains into swearing fealty to him.

Many had sympathy for her and called her Deidre of the Sorrows.

Ill used by the king, friendless and alone, with no hope of escape Deidre fell down into black despair.

One day she rode out of Ulster alone, 'To taste the wind coming down off the hills,' she said. Once amongst the hills, she found a ravine full of stones and great shattered boulders. Galloping along its edge she threw herself from her horse and smashed her skull against the rocks below.

I am to blame. The stain of it will lay upon me forever.

I walked down the long road with my shadow dancing before me. Behind me an orange-red sun glowed and pulsed with fire as it slowly sank into the west. I wondered if the stallion still remained free, I hoped so. A small wind blew in from the sea, carrying a smell of seaweed, fish and fresh cut timber. The road I followed was wide and paved with stone. I entered the town in the last of the sun's light. The town was big, sprawling and busy. Home to about 65000 Veneti, travellers, traders, and sailors.

The township lay scattered around a half moon bay. To the right of me as I faced the sea, ship building yards hugged the coast, to my left, warehouses stood next to timber yards, metal smiths, and an assortment of eating and drinking houses.

Apart from its location, it was the same as any other seaport to be found the world over. Noisy, hectic and thronged with men from a dozen or more nations.

As I walked through the town towards the docks, I passed Greeks, Egyptians, Carthaginians, Britons, Ibernians and small yellow men from the land of silk. They all eyed me curiously and stepped around me when I drew close. Why I wondered, do I smell so bad? Of course, I suddenly realised, I wore paint on my face, feathers in my long unbound hair. A long sword on my hip and a Roman short sword strapped across my back. My clothes were muddy and stained with blood, my boots of soft leather torn and cracked. I also, towered head and shoulders above everyone. I looked wild, desperate and savage.

Arriving at the water front I stood for awhile, uncertain of my direction in the fading light. The great ocean lay before me, calm, vast and mysterious. Green blue waves lapped gently against wooden docks, their small crests catching fire as the last of the sun's rays tipped them with molten gold and thin watery silver. The sky above the ocean was a deep indigo, dotted here and there with stars that glittered like bits and pieces of broken ice.

There was a smell of cordage, tar and that other indefinable smell that all busy seaports and shipyards seem to possess. The air felt cool and moist against my heated face. My empty stomach growled, reminding me that I had not eaten this day.

I hailed a passer by and asked if he knew where I might find Adwin, a captain of ship. The stranger looked at me curiously, his hand straying towards his sword hilt.

'I stand in peace, my friend,' I said softly, 'I ask only that you direct me, nothing more,' I added with emphasis.

He relaxed and moved his hand away from his weapons. He was medium tall with a shock of dark bound hair hanging down his back, like the tail of a pony. His eyes glittered in the thickening dusk, like chips of shiny black stone. He wore trews patterned with red and green squares and an over tunic of thin soft leather with a sunburst pattern radiating out from the chest. It was a strange symbol, of a kind I had not seen before. I stood no more than a few paces away from him and could see him clearly in spite of the gathering dusk.

There was something odd about this fellow, but I couldn't quite sense what it was. He was not Veneti that much was certain. His skin, what I could see of it, had a coppery look about it, his face put me in mind of a hawk.

His teeth gleamed in a small smile. 'Are you one of the feathered warriors we have been hearing about?' he asked.

'I am the last,' I replied. I added, 'The legions are behind me, they will destroy this town, burn the shipyards and those they do not kill they will sell into slavery.' I wasn't sure why I told him this, they would find out soon enough, except there was something about him, something tantalisingly familiar, and yet I could not for the life of me think what it was. He was a warrior, what else he might be I didn't know, nor was I so ill mannered as to use my Druid sense on him.

There is no true night, at this time of the year and when the moon sheds its light it is often almost as bright as day.

The moon slipped over the horizon whilst I stood there on the docks talking to a total stranger. Its light made of the ocean a cauldron of moving silver. Voices raised in laughter and song floated on the air.

'Who are you?' I asked him.

'A stranger,' he replied, 'and like you a wanderer who has come here from a distant land.'

'Do you know Adwin?' I asked. 'He is a captain of ship.'

'Aye,' he replied with a wary smile, 'I know Adwin and have sailed with him a time or two. What is it you're wanting with him?'

'My name is Culann,' I told him, 'Druid to the Arverni, who are now no more.'

Celtic Sunset

As soon as I mentioned the word Druid a subtle change shifted through him, like mist over water.

'I have heard of you. It is said you once trained with Bridgit, and are the only one ever to disarm her. Did you,' he questioned politely?

'She is dead now,' I said to him, 'she died a cruel and terrible death. Caesar has no mercy for *The People* and seems intent upon wiping the whole of us from the face of the earth to feed his insatiable hunger for gold. He is,' I added quietly, 'a wicked man of shadows.'

The stranger was silent for a moment and then he seemed to make his mind up and said, 'Come, Culann of the Arverni, walk with me and I shall take you to Adwin.'

'And to food,' I breathed silently. He led me away from the wharf, heading in the general direction of the warehouses I had seen earlier. Here and there we passed Veneti ships loading and unloading cargo.

He said, 'The Romans come sooner than you think. The Ninth legion is no more than a two day march away.'

Shocked, I turned towards him. 'How can you know this,' I demanded, 'I have only just crossed the moors leaving a Roman Alae of eight, dead behind me. The Ninth could not possibly get here so fast.'

'Nonetheless he said, they are here, and Caesar rides with them. He intends to destroy the Veneti so completely that no trace of them will remain.'

My blood ran cold. How could the stranger know this? Who was he? I looked at him again, noticing for the first time that his over tunic had beadwork along its shoulders and that the back of it was covered in a gigantic picture of an eagle in flight. Fringe work hung down the arms. The long thin strips of worked leather floating every now and again as small errant night breezes ruffled through them. If he thought me strange, I thought him stranger still.

'You are a warrior?' I asked him.

'Only through necessity,' he replied, 'I travel and seek to learn of wisdoms and there are always those about who would attack and rob a lone traveller, and like you,' he said, 'I am something of a scholar and have mastered some few small disciplines. You my friend have yet to master more. Once, I knew Cumall, your master, his death saddened me.'

Curious I said, 'When did you know Cumall?'

He looked at me slyly, his eyes bright with mirth. 'It was long ago,' he said, 'I had occasion to visit Athens and met Cumall there.'

I knew Cumall had travelled to Athens, but that was in his youth and this stranger had not such a look of age about him. There was a mystery here. My inner voice cautioned me to leave well alone, Druid I might be, fool I am not. I am well aware that for all our knowledge there is much we do not understand, mysteries and secrets no one can explain. Things seen again and again that defy all rational explanation. Powers that can be used even though we lack an understanding of their source, or even why they are there in the first place. The Greek's great Age of Reason claimed to explain everything, only to fall down in dust when it became evident that it explained nothing at all. It is a fine thing for thinkers to say this or that does not exist, simply because it goes beyond our accepted level of reality and understanding. We do not know the whole of anything and are fortunate indeed to know a little of something. The truly wise and learned are aware of how little they know and ever seek to add to their store. Only educated arrogants and uneducated ignorants lay claim to knowing the whole of anything. Each and every day of life is surrounded by mysteries. Our very reason for being, is a mystery.

I am Druid, I have walked the white stones. Twenty years of my life have I given over to study and I will study for twenty more and on unto the last of all days. And this I know, the truly learned ones often say little, whilst ignorance talks much, from out the mouth of others.

This stranger walking by my side all bathed in moonlight is a mystery to me. I am wise enough to leave well alone, and he it seems extends the same well mannered courtesy to me, I accept. He turned to me then and grinned, I smiled back.

Up ahead I could see a ship outlined against the sky. Its rigging looking ghostly in the moonlight. Men swarmed over the yardarm, doing what sailors do. The deck below was a hive of activity. Sailors checked cordage, off loaded cargo, and onloaded stores in a frenzy of controlled activity. The ship, like all Veneti ships had leather sails and was built of Oak, with a high stately bow and an equally high stern. The Veneti built their ships to sail the oceans and seas of the world, through calm and fiercest storm. No other nation built such ships and because of this they would soon be destroyed.

Long had Rome desired Veneti ships. Now Caesar demanded them and the Veneti ship builders secrets of construction. He did not ask or offer fair trade in exchange, he offered no payment, nothing. He demanded the Veneti divulge their secrets, and like the cruel and malicious man he was, he threatened them with extinction if they did not comply. The Veneti refused. As a tribe of *The People*, as free persons it was their right.

They, like all Celts had no idea of the kind of avaricious monster they dealt with. Caesar, willing tool of Gaunt Man, Crom Cruach, Bowed One of the Mound, Baal, Prince of

Flies, devourer of children. Caesar, an arrogant Roman Cruel who served his dark master willingly. May his house of flesh rot and his spirit be sightless. May the earth take him and the air strangle him. May fire consume his bones and water drown his throat. May the beasts of the field piss in his mouth and their excreta fill his nostrils. May ravens pierce his eyes and worms devour his ears. May the sky fall down and crush him and metal pierce his flesh. So it is that all Druids curse him.

It would not help the Veneti, they be shipboard fighters not land trained warriors. Even so, they would fight, they who sailed the world over, trading with any nation or tribe desirous of trade. They sailed once yearly to the Far Land (America) and beyond. Egypt welcomed them and exotic Carthage (Lebanon), worthy descendants of the Phoenicians who once traded with Briton. It was Hanno the Phoenician who first circumnavigated Africus (Africa). Veneti ships sailed the world. It was the Veneti who perfected the shallow keeled deep sea ship, capable of sailing both ocean and river. Swan ships they called them, stately and proud. Caesar destroyed them, he burnt their great shipyards, stole their wealth, killed every Veneti Elder and sold *The People* into slavery. Only a handful escaped to tell their story, the Veneti ceased to exist. Centuries would pass before their ship building skills were rediscovered. I believed the Eagle Warrior, I could feel it in my bones, the legions were near. I thought me then of an old saying, *when evil walks, where now the saviours.*

I stood on the wharf, the dark bulk of a merchant ship towering above me. The moon had reached its height, bathing land and sea in its luminous glow. Silver light filled the whole of the sky from rim to indigo rim. So bright it was, the silver coin of it out shone the stars, and would no doubt ache the heart of anyone who gazed overlong at the white beauty of it all. Perhaps it is true as some do claim, that a remnant of old magic doth infuse moonlight shadows. Certainly, the beauty of it all is awe inspiring.

I stared heavenward, ensnared. The sound of water heaving and sighing beneath the wharf filled my ears with breathy rushing sounds. What lies ahead, I wondered? What strange sights will I see? Will I ever again walk this land? I knew in my heart, I would not. I carried the dreams of *The People* inside me. They must be preserved, else all knowledge of who and what we are will be lost forever.

Romans write of us — from a distance — and say nothing of worth. Greeks pass through our lands and write, claiming knowledge of our ways. How foolish are both Roman and Greek, they have never lived amongst us. How then can they claim to know our ways. And those who come after, will they be as equally foolish and believe them? To my sorrow, I think that they will.

The Eagle Warrior nudged me, 'You had best go aboard,' he said softly, 'the moon will shine as bright in the Far Land.'

I stared at him. How could be know that? Again I was tempted to ask, who are you, from what distant land do you hail, good manners prevented my doing so.

'Where will you go?' I said to him, 'The legions are close, there will be no escape, unless,' I added with a smile, 'you sail with me.'

He shook his head slowly, 'My journey lies elsewhere,' he said, 'there is much I would know and a trail I must follow.'

'What is it you seek?'

'A *trace of blue*,' he replied. Now go my friend, 'go, there is no place for you here any more.' His eyes glittered in the moonlight. 'Go seek the one who waits,' he said softly. 'Follow the river, find the great plains.'

Just then a shout from the ship distracted my attention, an arm waved, beckoning me on board. I turned, words of fare thee well on my lips, he was gone. I looked right and left, but no sign of him could I see, he had simply vanished like mist before the wind. I began to doubt that we had met by chance, he knew too much about me. He knew where I was going, and why, not that it was a secret, it was simply of no interest to anyone outside *The People*. Who was he? From where did he come? I didn't even know his name. What did the eagle and the sunburst symbolise? Again the voice above shouted at me, I waved and climbed aboard.

The deck felt unfamiliar beneath my feet. Sailors bustled around readying the ship for its voyage. I felt tired, bone deep tired, my legs ached and my guts rumbled from hunger. What lay ahead? Who was waiting for me? My head buzzed from lack of sleep. I was about to embark upon as strange a journey of destiny as ever a man could make.

I sorrowed for my land and its people, enslaved beneath the yoke of Rome. Few survived and more had yet to die before the pattern completed its weave. A new life lay before me, I would fare it as best I could. Druid I be, I be also warrior, the final hope of a dying race. I still had no idea of what I was to do in the Far Land.

I was here on board ship.

It was a beginning.

A man of middle height, broad across the shoulders and chest, confronted me. Dawn flushed the sky behind him in pinks and reds and smudgy yellow. A cool wind blew in from the sea, the ship rocked gently beneath my feet. A strange sense of having done this before swept through me, and then it was gone. The sea was not my friend, I had never sailed its face, nor had I studied the lesser disciplines of raising wind and wave. I would be little more than a passenger for the duration of the voyage, and glad to be I thought to my self. My body stood in sore need of rest and a regular intake of food. Cumall once told me that a voyage to the Far Land took many, many days to complete, plenty of time then to rest and eat. I smiled inwardly at my remembrance of Cumall, that wise, old man who had claimed me so long ago and taught me so well, introducing me to mysteries and a fascinating, never ending world of knowledge. I would miss him and his quirky smile, his strange, stone under water coloured eyes and the quiet easy calm of his presence.

The man standing before me had long, streaky, brown hair, its ends bleached almost white by the sun. He wore it bound. His skin was tanned a deep nutty brown from long years of exposure to sun, wind and salty air. A pair of faded blue eyes regarded me curiously. There was a distant look about his eyes, the kind of look that comes from staring into distance or dreaming too many dreams. Even so, they were lively and sparked with intelligence. I warmed to him immediately, he was one of my kind, even though he be not Druid. His feet were bare, he wore a short tunic, with a wicked looking short knife stuck behind his belt.

'I be Adwin,' he said in a deep melodious voice. 'Cumall spoke of your coming before he died.' A flicker of sorrow crossed his eyes, and then he smiled, 'he said you would probably arrive at the last possible moment. Well, he laughed, this be it. We sail with the dawn tide, that means now.' He stepped back from me and wrinkled his nose.

'Phew,' he said, 'you stink like a shit trench. We be a small closed community, my friend, I suggest you bathe as soon as you possibly can.'

I grinned at him and said, 'I've had little chance of doing that these past few days, what with a Roman Alae on my trail and all.'

He looked at me oddly, 'Did you lose them then?' he asked.

'No,' I replied grimly, 'I did not lose them, 'I killed them, eight there were, now there be eight less.'

'Aye,' he said in a soft voice, his eyes boring into my face, 'You be Culann all right. Cumall spoke of your weapons skill and how you once disarmed the Druidess.'

He looked at my filthy blood stained clothes, at my painted face, the feathers in my hair, the sword on my hip and the short Roman sword strapped across my back. Exhaustion sagged the skin of my face, clouded my eyes and buzzed my head. 'If I don't lay down soon,' I thought silently, 'I'll be falling down and that's the truth.'

Adwin led me aft towards a small cabin, talking all the while. A small breeze came in off the sea cooling my heated face. Somewhere close by someone cooked fish, the smell of it made my mouth water and the guts of me rumbled the louder. Sailors eyed me curiously, warily, as I walked by.

The cabin was small, little more that an enclosed sleeping pallet with a roof. It was enough and more than enough, and thankful I was to be having it. I thought to ask Adwin what he knew of the Eagle Warrior, then decided to leave it for another time, there would be plenty of that in the days to come.

Dawn light grew strong around me. Overhead, seagulls squawked and dived for their mornings break of fast. The sky turned misty blue. I knew nothing of ships or the sea or of Adwin. I liked him, but that in itself means nothing when you place your life in another's hands. 'Trust,' I breathed silently — and so I did.

We stood about the door of my small cabin surveying the activity going on about the deck. I remained silent sensing that Adwin had something yet to say, but wasn't at all sure how to say it. I gave him a small spirit nudge, willing him to speak before I collapsed from exhaustion and hunger.

He cleared his throat, hummed and aahhed and then said slowly, 'Culann, you be unlike any Druid I have ever seen or heard tell of. You stink, your clothes are filthy and you look like a savage from out of the Far Land. You be also the last living Druid of the Arverni. I know not why it is you sail to the Far Land, except it be you are a thread to be woven into a pattern of hope. *The People* are broken Culann, broken forever, so tell me now, what is it you seek in the Far Land that is so important the Chief of all Druids must bind me with geasa my life for yours?'

What could I say to him when its little enough I know myself, and so I said nothing. Silence built up between us heartbeat by heartbeat. He sighed, smiled ruefully and said, 'Aye, that's what I thought you'd say.'

'Some things are best left alone,' I told him. Then to break the seriousness of the moment, I suddenly grinned at him, slapped him playfully on the shoulder and said, 'It's little the Druid I've been these seasons past, what with the fighting and all.'

'Aye,' he said, 'so it is I heard, and I'm thinking I'll not be returning here, not in this house of flesh, Veneti though I be,' he spoke in a quiet sad voice.' I think he knew what was to come, what the fate of his people would be.

It is a terrible thing to leave your home, and know those you leave behind will kiss the sword or worse.

'Cumall laid geasa on me to sail as soon as you were aboard, else I'd stay,' he added, 'and die with my people. We cannot survive what Caesar and his legions will do to us. He wants everything with no Veneti living to dispute his claims. Now it seems I am to live whilst my people die. The pattern weaves as the *Maker* wills,' his voice broke with emotion.

'We are a fierce, proud people who see no shame in displaying our emotions. It is I believe, our way of draining out spiritual poison that otherwise would accumulate and fester like a winter boil.'

He said, 'There be some few ships still at sea. Where now will they go once the Romans close all ports to them. If'n they escape capture, maybe to Egypt,' he mused, 'or far Cathay (China). Well,' he suddenly cheered up, 'I'll think on it.' He turned, clapping me on the shoulder, 'now we sail lad, we sail, but first, it's a bath you'll be having, then a bite of food and drink, and then sleep my friend, sleep.'

Ψ

CELTIC SUNSET

Chapter Seven

In the absence of good
Evil ceases to exist.
In the absence of evil
Good ceases to exist.
What then remains?
Except it be
The constant Fidelity of Being.

Culann
from - the Hidden Scroll

A Fresh dawn wind filled the huge leather sail. Under Adwin's watchful eye, sailors slipped our moorings, the great ship gathered way, moving slowly out into the bay, heading towards the open sea. Timbers creaked and groaned, coming alive beneath my feet. Tired though I was, a sense of hope and excitement for what lay ahead, flooded through me. Unknown it might be, dangerous and long, even so, I welcome it right gladly. For the first time in years I felt free, free of Caesar's dark shadow, free of his constant ability to generate hate and fear, rage and death. Perhaps his dark master would seek me out, perhaps he would not.

I cared not either way.

Turning my face towards the rising sun, I sang the song of welcoming, *all hail and praise the light.*

The town slid by as we slowly gathered speed. Moorland grey-green and purple hazed with distance, stretched out behind it. Here and there standing stones caught the rays of the sun, shining like stars midst a sky of bracken and fern, peat bog and small yellow flowered scrub trees.

Armed men gathered in groups along the great road running through the centre of town. What hope had they against the legions? None at all, even so, they would fight and scream in rage, and die upon the stones *a free people,* and be destroyed forever. My heart bled for them, my sorrow cried out.

These are my people brash and loud, they be proud and strong. They stand now, with sword in hand, long hair unbound and flowing down their backs. My people, whose like the world will never see again. Perhaps that too was cause for their destruction. They be so different from any other nation, and gifted with inventive skills no other nation possessed. Even the humble cake of soap was a wonder to others. I understood then how Adwin must feel when he said, if not for bonds of geasa he would stay and die with his people, his tribe.

No doubt when the slaughter ends, Caesar will sit down midst a reek of torn and bloody flesh and write his usual pack of lies for the Senate of Rome. They accept and believe every word that Caesar writes. It salved their conscience no doubt and enabled them to sleep better at nights. They, like all Romans were slave owners, dedicated arena enthusiasts, child killers, what else could you expect of such men. We named them well, I'm thinking, when first we called them barbarous, Roman Cruels, Arrogants and Haunts.

And I.

I will never forget that before Druid I am a Celt, a free person of *The People* who some will call *the once and future people.*

Caesar wrote to the Senate of Rome. He did blind their eyes with his victories, and omitted to mention the staggering amount of wealth he looted from temples, warehouses and homes. Wagon after endless wagon would eventually arrive at his estate near Rome, delivering incredible weights of gold and silver. Ingots of iron, sacks of silver coins, torcs of gold, rare timbers, jars of oil, grain, bales of dyed cloth, works of art inlaid with gold and encrusted with precious stones. He flooded the markets of Rome with so much stolen wealth, gold and silver became almost worthless, traders went bankrupt, shop keepers could not sell their goods, and the slave population became so large the life of a slave was worth less than a single pound weight of bread. And always the curse of Druid followed him. In this one thing light gave birth to a leach like darkness that not even Gaunt Man, Crom Cruach, Bowed One of the Mound could turn aside or negate. Slow acting it was, but in time it would feed of his flesh and drink of his blood, Brutus was its name.

The ship slowly gathered way, over sparkling sunlit waters. Blue was the sea, blue was the sky, cool the salt breeze on my face.

Once clear of the bay I would sleep, I felt as though I could sleep for ever. As the bows of the ship began to lift to the roll of the open sea, I was suddenly reminded of something Cumall once said in answer to a casual remark of mine concerning the Greek theory of atoms. Feeling somewhat confused, I had said in exasperation, 'How can they know or even assume atoms exist if you can't see them?' I was young and had much to learn concerning the origins of knowledge and its many and varied sources. Cumall gave that quirky half smile of his and said, his eyes bright with tolerant amusement, 'Culann,' he said, 'now and again when you are faced with the seemingly impossible think upon this. There is no land upon all the earth where man has not walked. There is no sea, he has not sailed, no desert he has not crossed, no mountain he has not climbed. All that we know and all that we would know, once was known.'

Oceanicus Atlanticus, the great salt sea.

Fair blew the winds that tumbled the ocean. Raw sunlight filled all the sky until it shone bright like some vast blue enamelled dome. Thick, yellow light bounced the crests of tumbling waves and made of the salt sea a shifting pattern of blue and gold, green and foaming white.

Glowing was the air, the taste of it pure and clean in my throat. Warm sang the wind in my face.

Salt ran my tears, the scald of memory open like some brutal unhealed wound.

And the long days spiralled down into the quiet of evenings full of starlight and moonglow, that burnished the waves until they glimmered and gleamed like molten silver. Days piled upon days in an easy familiarity of constant rhythm. Each day the same as the one before, healing it was, spirit balm and soothing.

Now and again, rain squalls blew up out of nowhere, refreshing and cold. We would all dash about then, filling anything we could find with rain water. Sometimes a following wind gathered its strength, filling the giant leather sail with a booming crack and creak as the thin supple leather strained and stretched. Wild it was and exhilarating, riding the shaped wood as it heaved and surged and flew through the waves. I could be a sailor, I would think to myself, and sail on forever following the sun.

We caught and ate fish and then caught some more. I loved it. The crew came to know that I was Druid. They accepted me with ease whilst somehow managing to maintain a respectful distance, until they came to know me better that is, then it was, that we became brothers, kinship born of the sea.

Slowly.

Slowly I began to re-weave the pattern of my life and to riddle again the *Maker's* thread.

I devoted a part of each day to exercise and weapons practice. Honing skills, dancing the shadow steps of sword and hand. I shuffled and danced until sweat streamed down my body, revelling I was in my own strength and skill and the sheer brute power of my muscles. Sailor men, owing to cramped conditions on board, often be short and I like a giant amongst them.

I also set aside a time for thinking, of going over old lessons inside my head to extract more, if so I could. My old life was finished, it died with *The People*, and with the death of our ways. Somewhere ahead lay new ways, a new life and perhaps new gods. Or would they be the same gods with different names? Perhaps all gods are simply faces of the *One* god, the *Maker*. Who can say, who can truly tell? No one, no one at all upon all this earth. God is the fourth way, peculiar and sacred to each individual, personal and ineffable from now until the last of all days, or until he bends down his head so that we might smell the sweet fragrance of his hair. God does not ask that we kill in his name, why then do we profane his name and stain forever the sanctity of his house. If I were Cumall I would say, riddle you this. I am Druid. It is expected that I think such thoughts. Can I then expect others to think anything less.

There would be fighting in the Far Land, I had seen it visioned behind my eyes, and something else, something shadowy and vague like a night time dream that blows away upon the wind of dawn. It had to do with something I become, or is it something I must do? What it might be, I do not know, I cannot grasp the sense of it. The sending was mist bound, wispy like smoke. It is a peculiarity of sendings that they be often of places and events, concerning others, never of self, never clear that is. There is some governance here I'm thinking. Some small protection that I know not of. Like a shield, it is held before you by a friend of good intent.

How bright the day.

Winding down shining hours that hang like jewelled moments about the glowing medallion of the sun.

We sail the blue sunlit ocean in a ship of painted wood and fly before the wind.

The crew eye me a little warily now. I did not intend it to be so. It was one of those things that happen and though you might think nothing of it, others swear that god bent down and placed his hand on your head.

The day had been clear and fine with a good strong wind blowing. After sunset it was, when dark clouds began to gather and pile one on top of the other, until it seemed that they filled all the sky and put out the stars. Adwin remarked 'That we were in for a bit of a blow,' he grinned like a wolf and advised me to stand clear of the decks.

Celtic Sunset

The storm burst upon us without warning. Wind shrieked through the rigging, filling the leather sail, until it stretched as tight as the skin on the head of a drum. All the days and nights of sailing that had gone before, were as nothing compared to the wildness of this night. I had never known such fury of wind or wave. It awoke something old and savage inside me. My heart began to pound, blood coursed through me, filling me with an age old excitement, a sense of reckless abandon that sneers at danger and makes little of your normal good sense and judgement. Such madness had only ever come upon me in battle. Now, standing upon that heaving deck, it filled me with its unfettered soul.

Adwin yelled at me, the wind whipped his words away. The storm filled me, pounding inside my head. I felt my muscles bulge and writhe beneath my skin, as I opened my mouth in a soundless cry of joy.

I made my way forward toward the bows of the plunging, rearing ship, brushing aside sailors, who thinking me sense fled, sought to stop me. I reached the bows, a thick wooden guard rail hip high on either side of me. Planting my feet wide, I rode the ship like a wild unbroken stallion. The ship reared high upon wind torn crests of dark seething waves and then plunged down into lightless troughs. Shuddering, shaking itself like a dog, the ship clawed itself free and climbed up dark walls of ocean, creaking and groaning in every timber. Mad it was, and glorious. I threw my arms up towards the storm racked sky, opened my mouth and howled a song of welcome to the wind.

Ragged banks of cloud fled across the sky, obscuring the face of the moon. Shrieking winds tore them apart, allowing cold white light to pour down through the raggedy holes and lay upon the raging sea in pools and swirling patterns of dirty silver.

I howled until my throat was raw, my long unbound hair streaming out behind me. My feet immovable upon the bucking Oaken deck. I can dimly recall sailors tugging at me, begging me to return, and then they would see the warrior's light burning in my eyes, and let me be.

The ship bucked and heaved beneath my feet, alive it was and calling to my senses. Well named she was *Manannan* who is, as all men know, god of the sea. It was the god, I think, who called to me through the Oak of the ship and recognised the fire burning inside my head. True it is I should be dead, thrown overboard by the violent roll and plunge of the ship, and drowned. I was not. I stood there, in the bows the whole night through, and sang to the storm in recognition of its needs. Waves broke over me again and again, and moved me not at all.

The storm blew itself out, as a pale lemon coloured dawn lit the rim of ocean and sky. Within heartbeats a thin watery sun heaved itself out of the ocean and up into the sky.

The ship sailed through long rolling swells that gave no hint at all of raging, night time fury.

Mind blank, I turned and staggered back along the deck, to my small sleeping cubicle. I felt dazed and weary, drained of strength and voice. Sailors regarded me with awe, as I stumbled by. Reaching my cot I threw myself down, soaked as I was, and slept the whole of the day through.

Adwin told me later that the crew thought I had cast a Druid spell to calm the storm, so abruptly did it cease. We both knew better, but did not enlighten the crew otherwise. Now it is, they regard me as something strange — and lucky, with promise of fair sailing days to come, whilst ever I am aboard.

Celtic Sunset

According to Adwin we sailed in a northerly direction, along the inner edge of a huge imaginary curve, that would eventually begin to bend, or curve as he put it, in a southerly direction that would bring us in sight of the warmer reaches of the Far Land. He said the far northern coast of the land was bitterly cold, and that he thought himself lucky to have survived one winter there, and had no intentions of returning. Adwin possessed charts with sea routes clearly marked, though how he came by them he would not say, only that they were very old and had served to guide other sailor men long before he was born. He also showed me a land map that had a thin line branching off, it was, he said, a great river (Mississippi, Missouri Rivers) that would take me inland as far as I would go. 'All I had to do was follow it,' he grinned, 'or sail it if'n you can find a boat, mayhap I'll build you one,' he cackled in glee. For all his humour he was aware of the seriousness of my journey, and his own. He could never return, not whilst Caesar lived and continued to carry out the designs of Gaunt Man — Crom Cruach, Bowed One of the Mound.

Twice during our voyage, we came in sight of islands. Adwin, knowing what he was about dropped anchor in small shallowy coves open to the sea. White sandy beaches, there were, hemmed all about with a thick tangle of trees and long ropy vines. Strange trees they were, of a kind I had not seen before. Hot it was and growing warmer the further south we sailed.

Adwin and his crew knew these places. Where to replenish our water supply from clear running streams, pick wild fruit and berries, hunt pig meat and fowl. At the second, larger island, we were attacked by dark skins as we dragged the ships small boat up onto the beach. Four of us there were, armed with long sword and spear. How many of the dark skins attacked, I could not say. They came out of the trees, all in a yelling rush and disappeared just as quick when we cut seven of their number down within as many heartbeats. They had not, it seemed to me, faced long swords before. I wish our meeting had not been so bloody, but it was they who attacked without good reason, and we stood in sore need of fresh food and water. Their weapons were poor things, of fire hardened wood, tipped with bone. I cut three down with three slashing blows when suddenly a club came whistling through the air towards my head. Ducking under the dark skins wide swing, I gave a quick snap of my wrist and my blade flicked out like a serpent's tongue slicing neatly through the poor fellows throat. We had no wish to kill these strange people, but they gave us little choice in the matter. We saw no others whilst we gathered what we needed.

One of the crew brought back a handful of small thick skinned green fruits whose flesh had a tangy bitter taste about it. When Adwin saw them he was overjoyed and ordered us all back to gather more. When he judged we had gathered sufficient, he commandeered the cook's cauldron, filled it with water and set it to boiling.

He cut the fruits into pieces and dumped them, skin and all, into the cauldron. He boiled the fruit, drained off the liquid and added it to our drinking water. He claimed it would prevent us from becoming ill and stop our gums from bleeding. As none of us were ill or suffering from bleeding gums, I cannot say if it worked or not.

Adwin claimed the knowledge came to him from Egypt and that the Egyptians had it from the Phoenicians, who had it from the Minoans who some do call Cretans.

Celtic Sunset

However it may be, knowledge is where you find it, and what is known by one, no matter how esoteric it may be, is invariably known by another or others. I have often wondered why it is that a person, or group lays claim to being in possession of a certain kind of knowledge they assume no others have. Then it was that as I grew, I realised that it was rarely the teacher, or source of knowledge who made such claims. It was made by their students, or those who came after, in the vain assumption (of study) of what they claimed to be original thinking. Incorrectly assuming it conveyed status, or lent them an air of, being different or unique, among their fellows. Indeed, I have met those who claim their study of a certain kind of knowledge ranks them as being amongst the world's elite. Conversations with such people are often limited, having only some knowledge of a single discipline, that is all they are able or willing to converse about, but then, they are not Celts, not of *The People* who prize eloquence and knowledge, above the attainment of a seasoned warrior's skills. That is why Druids, Harpers and Bards out rank fighting men, and stand second in rank only to the king. Of course as a Celt, I am too polite and well mannered to point such things out to the superciliously ignorant.

Throughout all the long days of our sailing we had seen no other ships or long oared galleys. Indeed, what sails would there be to see, no ship of Rome would dare these far deep waters. At least I did not think so, and of course I was wrong.

Adwin tells me that the Egyptians no longer sail to the Far Land as once they did. He said that the Egyptians, like the Carthaginians, and the small yellow skins, have lost their taste for deep sea voyaging and have not sailed these waters since the days of his great grandfather's time. 'That's why trading voyages to the Far Land (America) are so profitable for Veneti ships, what's left of them,' he would mutter with a scowl.

We had settled into a routine Adwin and I. When he was not on watch or otherwise needed, we would sit outside my sleeping cubicle, watch the sun go down and talk. He was, I discovered, a very intelligent man, who, for reasons known only to himself, tried his best to hide it from others. He was also a collector of ancient writing. If he could not read what he bought, he hired scholars to read them for him.

Cumall had much, Adwin had little, but what he had was very selective, and so we talked. I like to think that we both gained much from those long, warm moonlit evenings, certainly I did, and I a Druid who already knew much and yet was aware of how little I really did know.

The sun slipped beneath the ocean, a ball of fire staining the blue water red and silver. Streaking its surface with gold and a curious shade of palest green.

We sailed a calm sea. Warm moist winds filled the great leather sail. Timbers creaked and groaned. Cordage hummed as it tightened and then slackened off as the wind fell away and then gathered again. Apart from the helmsman and a single lookout up in the bows, the crew relaxed. Voices murmured above the rattle and roll of dice bones. Now and again someone laughed, the sound of it floating easy upon the warm balm of gathering darkness.

The mast creaked and swung in a small lazy arc across the sky. Pinpoints of light winked on as stars became visible. The hard frosty glitter of them adding to the mystery of the night.

Celtic Sunset

I sat on the deck, my back resting against the thin wooden wall of my sleeping cubicle. Adwin sat beside me, a cup of watered wine in his hand. He waved his free hand towards the stars and sighed. A nearby lantern drenched us both in a pool of thin butter coloured light.

For awhile we sat in silence, allowing our senses time enough to drink in the night and its awesome beauty. By and by the moon slipped into the sky, taking its rightful place amongst the stars, outshining those nearest to it. Its drizzling silver light added to that of the lantern's and made of the night an almost bright as day thing. I am not given much to words, I have not the gift, even so, this one particular night moved me, deep inside where I indwell within my house of flesh. Magic is something I shy away from like an unbroken colt shies away from a stranger's outstretched hand, and yet, I can find no other word that so aptly fits this night.

'It be magic,' I breathed softly.

'Aye,' Adwin said, 'that's god's own truth you're speaking lad. Be you familiar with gods?' he asked.

'No more than anyone else,' I replied. 'We acknowledge the existence of gods, but unlike other nations, we do not worship them or offer sacrifice the way Romans do. They are here amongst us, and that's a truth. They possess powers we do not and yet, they never seem to know what to do with them. We often laugh at our gods, but never in a cruel way. Like us they love the wearing of fine and beautiful clothes and seem not to realise they have no need of wearing them at all, so beautiful are they in the shiningness of their attainment. We Celts have something, no other nation I know of, seems to possess. We have a spiritual loveliness in balance and harmony with our world and our house of flesh. I have sometimes wondered if it is this, our ideal spiritual existence and not just our wealth, that so drives the Romans to destroy us. They see us for what we are, and hate us for it I think. We have no demons or monsters, only Crom Cruach and, to balance his dark intent there is the *Maker* who is also *An Ruad Na Ro fhessa,* The Lord of Perfect Knowledge. Unlike Romans, we are not burdened with an over abundance of deities, we have the *Maker* and for *The People* it is enough. All other deities are no more than what we allow them to be. Those other higher beings, the *Opalescents*, the *Shining Ones*, we rarely see, or wish to. Even *Eochaid Na Ollathair*, Father of All, is simply another name for the *Maker*, he is three, *Ruad, Eochaid* and *Maker* and he is **One**. The **One** who is three, the three who are **One**. So it is that we have erected a spiritual felicity about our *Ways* and the *Spiral of Immortality*. We know where we are going (spiritually) and we know how to get there, to attain that which all beings seek, no matter denials of mouth. Other nations stumble along, or so it seems, misunderstanding the very concept of god and the weave of his pattern. Yes, oh yes,' I said to Adwin, 'they must indeed destroy us. Roman Cruels tremble with fear at the mere thought or mention of a slaveless world. A world of free people. We Celts have achieved the unthinkable, the almost but not quite impossible realisation, of an almost perfect balance and harmony with earth, flesh and spirit. Those who are not of *The People* cannot allow such harmony and balance to continue or survive. Our destruction ensures the world will always have its slave masters.'

'You speak candidly Druid,' Adwin said, 'why is that, do you no longer guard your secrets?'

'What secrets,' I laughed harshly? 'There be no Druids left to harbour such notions, except I, and I journey towards a strange Druidless land, wherein one day I may place a secret, until then, what care I for who knows or does not know of what I speak. There is a book of Druidical lore. One day it will be found, no matter wheresoever I may hide it. We can only hope that those who come after, are able to understand what they read. If'n they can read it at all,' I added.

Adwin said, 'Think you not we be the get of gods,' his eyes filled with mirth.

'Divinely descended, do you mean,' I countered.

'Aye,' Adwin said, 'something like that. Those ancient writings of mine set more riddles than any they might answer. What say you, Druid?'

'Have you heard of Polycrates,' I asked him?

'Yes,' he replied slowly, 'I've heard of him, but the stories surrounding him are many and at best unclear, to me that is.'

'Why, what is it you know,' I said? 'Do you know how he died?'

'Aye, he was stoned to death by his own students.'

'Yes, he was,' I replied, 'and just when his theories were starting to get interesting.'

Adwin's teeth gleamed in the moonlight, 'now that, I didn't know,' he said, 'tell me about it.'

I told him of Polycrates.

'As a young man he studied the works of Thales and Anaximander of Miletus, an ancient city long revered as a centre of learning. He read Pherecydes, Pytheas and Socrates, and came to accept and believe in a single almighty god, like his contemporaries, the Hebrews. It is said that his studies burnt a hole inside his head. He became restless, determined to travel and seek out wisdoms of his own. He rode the old glory road of invasion, the Alexandrian road, the conquerors road that runs between the Tigris and Euphrates rivers, towards Babylon.'

'Polycrates, like many other scholars of his time, was familiar with the Babylonian Scriptures and their recounting of man's creation from earth, and his life with woman within the Garden of Beginnings, known as the Garden of Edhen by the Greeks, and their eventual expulsion for daring to question the word of the god of their creation. Polycrates did not disbelieve the teachings of the temple, he simply felt that man's origins were more prosaic than those that claimed divine creation. He walked a thin scholastic line between acceptable theory and being found guilty of committing an offence against the gods. I tell you true Adwin.'

'For a supposedly intelligent man, Polycrates was at times particularly obtuse. He, like others of his time had already worked out that the world was round, but Polycrates went one step further, he assumed the unknown half of the world (Southern Hemisphere) contained a single land mass. It was of course unknown, he simply assumed its existence. He named it *Terra Australis Incognita,* Land of the South Wind, the hidden (or unclaimed) South Land. His theory was not well received by the temple priests. Polycrates remained oblivious, obstinate towards priestly displeasure. One day, whilst walking the streets of Babylon, he found himself amongst a small crowd gathered about a street entertainer, who was, to the delight of the crowd, coaxing a large hairy ape to perform a series of tricks. Polycrates had never seen a hairy ape before, and was astounded by the ape's manlike mannerisms and its ability to stand erect upon two legs.'

'He bought the ape and studied it for the whole of a single year. It was not enough, he needed to know more, to observe, if he could, an entire tribe of hairy apes in their natural habitat.'

'A wealthy man, Polycrates organised a vast well equipped expedition. Hiring black skins to guide him into remote, hitherto, unexplored regions of Africus, where the largest of all the hairy apes (Gorillas) could be found. It is to his credit that he did not kill the huge manlike apes. He simply studied them, as best he could, from a distance. An astounding theory began to take shape inside his head. he gave no thought to its implications, only to its conclusions that were, he now thought, obvious, and in hindsight somewhat elementary. he had however, overlooked something, the ability to differentiate between right and wrong. He made no distinction between man's supposedly, gradual evolution from hairy apes and the dawn of awareness of self as an independent spiritual tenant, dwelling within a house of flesh, whose presence alone determines how the flesh may act. It is, as all Celts know, the very foundation, the soul of all thought and reason. In the absence of spirit, a house of flesh is unthinking and unaware of the *Maker*. Its life is short, mean and ugly. Polycrates knew this, and yet he chose to ignore its implications within the framework of his theory. For all his wit, he was a fool.'

'Five years later, he returned to Miletus and opened a school for mature students. He wrote a book in which he outlined his theory in great detail. He called it *Evolutions*. It caused an uproar. Priests of the temple demanded his death. "Guilty," they said "of an offence against the gods." '

'Mobs rioted in the streets. His students were horrified, they would be found guilty by association, and driven into exile. They did the only thing they could do, to prove to the priests of the temple, that they were repelled by Polycrates theory and revered their gods.'

'They stood outside his house and called him forth. When he emerged they stoned him to death.'

Adwin remained lost in thought for a few moments and then said softly, 'There is something very odd about all that, my friend, I'm not sure what, but there's a feel to it and that's for sure.' His face took on a distant pensive look. 'I sometimes think it is only within the lands of *The People* that reason can be found. All else is chaos, and full of dark intent. What is it, I'm wondering, that man fears so much, he is driven to worship gods so terrible, so dark and bitter, they demand human sacrifice in return for life? If it be that gods created life, then why take it back in such a casual bloody handed manner?'

'Perhaps Polycrates had the way of it, and they be no more than creations of man's own dark dreaming.' Adwin smiled then and looked out across the ,moonlit sea. He spoke softly, his voice no more than a whisper. 'Praise be to the *Maker*. There is a place,' he continued, south of the Far Land, (Mexico) A City it is, built of stone deep within the forest. *El-Tajim* it is called, home to more than fifty thousand. They use concrete like the Romans. It's better, stronger, more durable. The centre of the city is dominated by a huge flat topped pyramid. It has 365 windows, one for each day of the year. Carvings cover its outer surface, hideous they are, depicting strange and terrible mutilations of men. And yet these same people chart the heavens, construct wondrous water ways and canals. Their engineers and architects rival those of Rome, and Egypt. Once each year the pyramid and the entire city is painted all one colour, one year green, then blue, then red.'

'They worship a god of the underworld and kill to honour him with the spirits of the slain who, for one year, dwell in the underworld as spokesmen for the people. The twelve monthly games are dreadful, the losers decapitated or strangled, or if they lost badly, buried alive.'

'The temple of the pyramid, towers above a long narrow court. They call it the Court of the Ball. Unlike our own game of kick ball the players are not allowed to use hands of feet. They can only use their hips, knees and chests. They use a huge solid ball of forty weights (40lbs) that is made from the sap of a tree (rubber). You would not think a ball of such weight would bounce. It does and it is dangerous. Think you Druid, of such a weight hurtling towards you and hitting your chest, it would crush your bones. The players wear chest armour and thick pads on their knees and hips. Even so, the ball can still crush and maim with its weight. They score, one team against the other by hitting or bouncing the ball high into the air and through a round opening above their heads, that is only slightly larger than the ball. There is no escape for the players, the court is walled and when the game starts its entrance is sealed. the losing team is decapitated on the spot, the winners hailed as heroes, though they be often crippled for life, those who survive that is. The city cares for them, they are regarded as being almost holy. Apart from the annual game, their priests claim blood sacrifice whenever they consider there is a need for additional spokesmen to claim divine intervention, from the god of the underworld. What I am trying to say Culann is, well, look you. We do not worship our gods. We accept them as equals amongst us. They wear fine clothes, are clean and neat, their long hair shining. And if we of *The People* should chance upon them, they are well mannered and polite. Pranksters they be, and sometimes tricky, but never cruel or demanding of blood. I have heard it said that gods often reflect the image and nature of those who worship them. If this be so, then riddle me this Druid. Why be men so cruel and bloody natured? Why do Romans kill our children?'

'It is the reptile within them,' I answered, 'we of *The People* have risen above its need, many have not. It crawls through their dreams and adds spite to their words, that are often more wounding than blades. We are closer to the *Maker*, more spiritual if you like. We know we are only tenants of our flesh and when its time is done, we leave and take up residence in a new born house. Memory is the key that opens the lock. We know what we are, what we have done and what we hope to do. We are aware of spiritual self. We follow the spiral and climb, we remember, we rise and seek knowledge, to aid our spiritual expansion. Many do not, they don't even read or attempt to follow any path. Knowledge is ignored, for many it simply does not exist and so they remain, rememberless, and slowly fall down the Spiral of Immortality. We Celts have known since the dawn of our time the true meaning of *Trinitas* (three). It alludes not to the mystery of a god, that is something entirely different, but to the mystery of self. Before you spiral up towards the light, towards the *Maker*, towards an expansion of spiritual awareness, you must at least know what the *Trinitas* is. Any child of *The People* can tell you that. It is the key that opens *The Three Fold Way*. It is the one law that must never be forgotten or put aside, else you deceive and make of yourself less than what you are. We are all *Trinitas*, body, mind and spirit. A *Trinitas* is, one who is three, three who are one. That is why so many nations regard three as a sacred number. It is the *Trinitas of life*, when you understand what is no longer a mystery, you awaken, you become spiritually aware and the world about you is never the same again.'

'Like a child full of wonder you ingest and grow, you climb the Spiral of Immortality, you change forever. So simple,' I said to Adwin, 'and yet, so wondrous, is it not?'

'Yes - well,' he grumped, 'you'd be knowing that now wouldn't you, what with you being Druid an' all. And if its so simple why, outside *The People* does it remain unknown?'

'It is known, it has always been known, its the understanding of it that people lack. The words are simple, its the understanding behind the words that is not, many prefer blood upon the sand, and the enslavement of their fellows, to understanding. To many, power, wealth and position is a more immediate and easily accessible commodity than re-recognition of a single spiritual law. One is forever, the others are not. The choice is yours. Besides,' I added, 'if you can see in others what you know of self, its not so easy to enslave them. There is a price to be paid by such men, never think there is not. Soon or late, this life or whenever, it will be paid.'

Adwin yawned and stretched. 'I be only a poor simple sailor man, yer lordship,' he grinned, 'who loves poking his nose in dusty corners, and you my friend can talk like a drunken Harper reciting genealogies, god strike me down if I'm wrong.' He glanced up toward the night sky. 'Well now and its the fine talk we've been having,' he yawned again, 'now its away to my bed and the sleep I'll be having. And you, Culann of the Arverni, would do well to think upon what awaits you yonder. We'll be there soon enough, I can smell the green smell of land on the wind,' he added with a wink.

After he had gone, I sat for awhile drinking in the beauty and calm of the night. What lay ahead, I couldn't say. Who it was awaiting my coming, I didn't know, nor how I was to find him. There would be fear and danger and the excitement of walking a new land, of grasping a whole new way of life. What would I be? What might I become? Would I be welcome, or must I fight?

I went to my sleep thinking it isn't that I know little of the Far Land, its simply that I know nothing at all, which is, in its way a beginning. To admit that you know nothing, is to take the first step towards knowing something.

I slept well that night.

Roy Edwards

How high the sky?
How deep the blue water beneath our keel?
Bright is the sun. Cool blows the wind.
We sailed the long days down into starlit evenings and moon drenched nights. To be a sailor man upon wide uncharted waters, sailing towards a distant unknown land, is to live a special kind of life only sailor men understand. For all that there is discipline aboard ship, there is also a kind of inner mental freedom I have not known before. Perhaps it comes from the contemplation of an immense and overwhelmingly empty sky, or the sight of ocean filling all the horizon and we no more than a piece of drift wood, small and irritating upon its skin. A blue desert, the weeping eye of god. Winds push and blow, and you wonder where it is they come from. Waves rise and fall, creating their own kind of music about the ship. What powers their ceaseless rhythm, if it be not Manannan's breath? What secrets have I yet to learn, what mysteries yet to plumb? There is a snarl inside my head, a knot I have yet to untangle, an unknown destiny I have yet to fully understand.

Cumall said I will come to it late and that is, he said, better than not at all. What did he mean? What is it I have missed? He did not, I'm thinking, tell me the whole of anything, and that worries me, it surely does.

I had need of information. I must not stand upon that distant lonely shore with no knowledge of its breathing inside my head. Adwin trades along its coast as did his father before him and his father's father. What ever it is he knows, I too must know. Perhaps he would consent to take part in a Druidical memory recall.

Adwin raised his eyebrows in mock consternation, grinned widely and agreed to my request. It was, after all, only a small thing, none the less I appreciated his trust in me, and his faith in the way of Druid. Some think the word Druid is only a name used by priests of *The People*, it is not. To *The People* the word is — *the way*. The word identifies a spiritual path that is only one amongst many. It is the one we have chosen to follow and call Druid, so that others might know we have chosen, we do not cavil. We follow right gladly and our choice was made as a free people.

We sat down, Adwin and I, in the red-gold light of a late afternoon sun.

We sat with our backs resting against the thin plank wall of my sleeping cubicle, facing forward toward the bows of the ship. The sea was calm and flat like a beaten copper sheet, now and again a small light wind ruffled its surface. The air was hot and moist. Timbers groaned and creaked in the way of all ships of wood. Our small world upon the sea was familiar and ordered, full of easy talk and drifting voices, the waters beneath our keel benign. I would be sorry to part company with these men of the sea.

Adwin turned, facing me, light from the sinking sun flared his face ruddy and shadowed. His blue, deep set eyes had a far away look about them, as though he could see things others could not.

We wet our throats with watered wine, sat in silence for the count of forty heartbeats and then I said softly, 'Tell me of the Far Land Adwin. Talk of anything you might think of, anything at all. What you have seen, what you have heard, what you know and what you think you know, or can guess at. What you surmise or have deduced from your dealings with those you call Indians. If something be not true, speak of it anyway and help me to taste the breath of the land and the way of its secret beating heart. If you know the tongue of the tribes, say so and you can teach me the way of its saying. Speak of anything, be it true or false. Speak my friend, grasp the image of your memory. If you cannot see it, then speak of what you feel or can sense and the image of it all will follow. Begin anywhere, give no thought to order or what should come first, middle of last. Just talk, and as you talk you will begin to remember more and more, your memories will become clearer, more concise, as little things, minor details and such, push forward.'

I coaxed him on until he met his memories in much the same way that Cumall had once led me, when first he sat me down to find out what I knew, or thought I knew.

I asked Adwin to tell me of stories he had heard, rumours, what he considered, or thought of the Far Land. 'It is,' I said to him, 'the only way you can help me to face what is to come, with at least a bit and piece of knowledge. I ask this of you as a friend, and though we part when we reach the Far Land, should you ever be in need, come you there, and I will find you.'

I swore then, the sacred oath of friendship, which is as all men know, binding unto death.

> *Your enemies are my enemies. My home is your*
> *home. I will never lie cheat, or desert you. Nor*
> *with intent, will I harm you. Let no shadow come*
> *between us, nor distance weaken our bond. This*
> *I swear beneath the eyes of the Maker. You are*
> *my friend until the last day of forever.*

It was the battlefield oath of friendship, Adwin recognised it as such. He nodded his acceptance and swore the oath in his turn.

We drank wine then, to seal our pact and he began to talk, slowly at first, and then with more assurance as his mouth caught up with his memories.

Celtic Sunset

'You understand Culann, we traders of the sea are a secretive lot. It is ever so if we are to keep our source of supply out of the hands of others. We never speak of our sea routes. In answer to any inquiry as to where we obtain our goods, we are vague at best, or we simply invent a place, that always lies west of the sun.' He smiled at that and then continued, 'what we of the sea have known for hundreds of years, others who are not of the sea are just learning, and they think what they learn is new. Druids have always known in which direction blood circulates through the body. Roman physicians have but recently come to understand this and consider the knowledge to be new. They scoff at the idea that it was already known by others. You know what I mean Culann, new knowledge to some, is ancient to others and so on. Well, its the same with the Far Land, we have known of it for centuries and you are just finding out.'

'Men of Tarshish (Southern Spain) sailed to the Far Land almost five hundred years ago, in search of tin, copper and other metal bearing ores. They searched for new areas to mine, and so it was, that they began to explore the land only to find out they were not the first. The land is vast, there was enough and more for everyone. They began to bring settlers to the land. Men skilled in mining and building settlements of stone. The settlers were Iberian (Spanish) Celts, who linked up by sea with other older settlements originally established as trading posts, with no interest at all in mining, or colonising farther inland. Many of those early trading settlements were founded by Egyptians, Phoenicians and there descendants, the Carthaginians.'

'Later from the north of Africus came the Libyans. They, like the Iberian (Spanish) Celts before them, began to establish small settlements along the coast. They traded with the tribes (Indians) and began to search for metals.

Travelling far to the north and south, some few of them married into tribes along the way and established a more or less permanent trading centre in the hot land (New Mexico).'

'So long have they been there, that now, the Shiwa and Hopi tribes of the area, speak more Libyan than they do Suni, there own language. It is so with most tribes who trade with us. We have all been coming here for so long, that the tribes we trade with began to pick up bits and pieces of our language, enough to be understood, that is. You will find much that is strange here, and much that is familiar. Some of the tribes have adopted many of our customs, some have not. Others have taken on the ways of the ones they trade and live with, though when it comes to fighting they are more Celtic in their ways than anything else. Their religion too is very reminiscent of ours and, their way of being in harmony with the land, that too, is very Celtic. Though in truth,' Adwin said, 'they lived in harmony with the land long before we came.'

'Now it is, that a tribe in one land (Ohio) build mounds and are known as the Mound Builders, and another tribe (The Hopewellians) who live along the great river (Mississippi), build huge, flat topped earthen pyramids. They be fine copper workers too, though the metal be soft, they fashion it into breastplates and cover all its surface in intricate designs and symbols of the Spiral of Immortality. Fine jewellery do they make of gold, set with fresh water pearls and bits and pieces of blue stone (Lapis lazuli) they trade from other tribes. They carve soft stone into birds and animals and pipes for the burning of a sweet smelling grass, and their pottery and weave of cloth be of the finest.

Most all the different trading centres have taught their own way of reading and writing to the tribes around them. They be quick to learn Culann and that is something you must remember. Many of their ways are not like ours, but never make the mistake of thinking them to be no more than a simple people copying the ways of others. They take only what they can use, and politely ignore anything they consider to be worthless to their way of life. They admire courage, wisdom, generosity, endurance, eloquence (oratory) good manners and fortitude of spirit. They consider them to be the seven virtues of a warrior. Which are, you must admit Culann, very similar to our own recognition of what it takes to be a warrior besides weapons skill.'

'You are not a sailor man Culann. You have no knowledge of these things. We of the sea have traded and lived here for hundreds of years. Some stay and marry into the tribes. Some wander the land and do not return, others return years later and speak of strange sights they have seen. Of Indians who, for all the years of our being here we know not of. They speak of huge walled cities surrounded by desert lands that once were fertile (The Anasazi cities of New Mexico and Colorado) and of ancient stone circles, known as *the ring of eagles* and *the ring of crows*, there is even one called *the ring of doves*. Places of ancient worship perhaps? No one knows who placed the stones or why. The Indians say they were there when they came into the land, and those who once used the circles disappeared and became shadows. One traveller who returned, said he had seen a circle full of swaying shadows, even though there was not a single cloud to be seen in the sky and the sun stood at midday. He said he was told by the Indians he was with, that if he walked into the ring when it was full of shadows he would not return. The shadows would take him to the other side. The rings sometimes act like openings. If you stay and listen, you will hear the sound of many voices singing and chanting, the sound of it faint and distant seeming. You can only hear them, he was told, when the shadows gather. And I tell you this Culann, there be not a sailor man amongst us who isn't believing the way of it all.

'It is a strange and haunted land into which you go my friend, be careful and above all be strong. Its people are many and varied. Some are warlike and savage, others are not, and yet they must know how to defend what they have, else they would have nothing. All will trade but only a few tribes plant crops, or vegetables and suchlike. Many hunt, and gather what the land provides in the way of fruit and root. There are permanent villages and towns of stone, wood and earth. Those who live inland (The Great Plains) live in lodges made of skin that can be taken down and carried, as they move over the land in tune with the seasons. They are a fierce, proud people who live close to the earth.'

'To such people every day is a holy day, everyday is worthy of praise for its gift of light and life. Like us, they bathe twice each day, and though I have never met any of the inland tribes, I am told they be not unlike us. Some have skin the colour of copper, whilst others are much darker, and here and there, light skinned tribes are to be found. Perhaps they be descendants of lost explorers. Who is there to say it is not true, when so much within the land is strange and yet has a semblance of familiar roots.'

'You say someone out there waits for you, that he stands on a plain of grass looking towards the west. Perhaps that is true, perhaps it is not. Yours is the sending — only you can know. You be Druid and therefore more than I. We call each other friend, therefore I know you do not lie, but what is true for you may not be true for another, so be careful my friend, be very, very careful.' Adwin's face creased into a thin half smile. The last rays of the setting sun staining his teeth hot ruby and his flesh glowing rock.

Celtic Sunset

'You go alone into a vast wild land,' he continued, 'you must have fortitude my friend,' emotion ringed his voice. 'You must be very strong, stronger than ever you were, when you faced Roman Cruels.' His voice changed, 'Indians have different values and yet in many ways they are similar to *The People*, but this you must come to know for yourself. They are a spiritual people in a way that I think only we Celts can appreciate. They know of the *Maker*, they call him *Wakantanka* and they know of *Skan taku Skanskan*, spiritual vitality, something in movement, it is the core of their being.'

'Some will try to kill you, some will avoid you, most will watch and wait to see what kind of man you are. There are mound builders, earthen pyramids, towns of stone built out in the desert and high amongst mountains. Houses there be, built inside massive caves, that are hidden within deep winding canyons. There are trails that seem to lead nowhere. Rings of stone built atop flat topped mesas. Here and there strange round houses have been found, roofless they are with dry stone walls. Standing alone and secret in odd, wild corners of the land. Each house has a small hole in the floor, it symbolises man's emergence from darkness. He came from the dark below, up through a hole into light. And no matter where you might wander Culann, sooner or later you will hear of the *Anasazi* (The Old Ones). They trade, and wander over vast areas they call the Four Lands (Utah, Colorado, Arizona and New Mexico).

A strange, mixed lot, tall with honey coloured skin, dark eyes and black hair. It is said that they be not much in the way of fighters, and why should they be, no one fights them because everyone trades with them. Some few of the Anasazi remain aloof and want little to do with anyone who is not of the Anasazi, they be priests and such like. The rest, well it all happened a long time ago. They mixed with and married Libyans and Celtic Iberians who had wandered inland. Libyan sea voyages are legendary amongst sailor men,' added Adwin. 'Of course, they be descendants of the Hamites, but well, its not their fault is it,' he grinned. 'After they had all sorted themselves out they started building a round city of stone. I've never been there, but I've heard it said that upwards of thirty thousand live in and around their two main cities. I don't think they will last too long Culann, I really don't, not beyond a few lifetimes anyway. There are too many of them in one place. They are out of balance and harmony with the land, I'm thinking.

They farm, trade and build and soon they will have cleared vast tracts of forest and scrub. I've heard it said that the desert has already begun to creep in. When there is nothing left and the soil is unable to replenish itself and the rains don't fall, they will leave. They will simply up and walk out of their cities and towns and a season or two later it will be as if the Anasazi had never lived at all. Cities are useless things without farms to sustain them. And from what I hear, the Anasazi bleed the earth dry, sucking out its life blood, season by season. You think I ramble Culann? Well maybe I do.'

I assured him I was content to sit and listen. Night had fallen, the air was cool and bright with starlight. It was a good night for listening.

Adwin continued. 'They are doomed my friend, but as yet they cannot see it. They have lost the *way*, if'n they ever had it at all. Their holy men will not speak of their mysteries to anyone who is not a full blooded Anasazi, and that too contributes to their inevitable demise. That and something else, something unclean and shivering.' Adwin's voice dropped to a whisper, 'They trade with those of dark aspect, whose priests demand the Ball Court Sacrifice. Their rulers and priests are guided by Gaunt Man — Crom Cruach, Bowed One of the Mound I'm thinking. He is of one aspect but his minions are legion, so Cumall once told me, when we spoke together of these things. He died hard Culann, very hard indeed.'

He cocked an eyebrow at me and said softly, 'Make sure you don't go the same way my friend, you are the last of all our Druids.' He said, 'the Anasazi are doubly doomed even as the Roman Caesar.'

Adwin fell into silence, he sipped his wine and stared into the night. I could hear the soft hiss of our hull sliding through water. The night was mild with a soft fur feel about it. He had told me much and had not yet finished. I waited for him to continue, I sensed the memory in his head had begun to wind down, but there was still a bit and piece he would have me know. I began to count the stars, waiting. It is a thing of friendship, that you both can sit in an easy, unstrained companionable silence, without feeling compelled to talk, or like I, knowing my friend had yet more he wanted to say, content to wait until he was ready to speak.

Eventually Adwin said, 'What it is you must do or become amongst the tribes I do not know, but first you must learn to survive. Druid you will be, in a Druidless land and always, beware of those dark ones of sacrifice. Have I left anything out now?'

'Only the Greeks,' I replied with a laugh, 'most everyone else seems already to know of the Far Land. There is one thing I'm curious about,' I said to him.

'And what might that be?'

'The Eagleman,' I said, 'what do you know of him?'

'Not much,' replied Adwin, 'not much at all, considering he sailed with me a time or two.'

327

Roy Edwards

'We were taking on cargo in a Gaulish port when he first came aboard, offered me gold to carry him to Egypt. As it happens Egypt was scheduled to be our last port of call after we'd finished trading around the Greek islands. Though how he could have known that I don't know, my crew didn't even know, I hadn't told them. Some destinations I don't reveal until we are at sea, there are too many sharp ears about and ships captained by lazy avaricious men.' Adwin grinned, 'well yes,' he said happily, 'I be one too.'

'So,' he said breezily, 'I carried the Eagleman to Egypt, and put him ashore in Thebes. He told me he wished to speak to the priests in the temple there. He never came back. I waited for a day or two and then set sail and gave no more thought to him at all. I meet lots of strangers,' Adwin said defensively, 'he was just one more, or so I thought. I should have known there was something different about him. It was there for me to see, but somehow I missed it. I didn't the second time though.'

'We had a good year. I allow the lads a little space below decks to carry trade goods and we had all done well.'

'We ended that voyage at Crete and he was waiting on the docks there as we tied up. As you know Culann, the Cretans are superb shipbuilders, almost as good as the Veneti,' he added with a grin, 'and I intended to lay over for awhile and refit for a voyage to Bri-tain. The seas can be rough in them parts and I wanted to make sure Manannan was sound from stem to stern so to speak. Again he had somehow riddled our destination. Said he would wait and turned up on the morning of the day we were ready to sail. How he does that, damned if I know. He sailed with us to Bri-tain where he disappeared for a day or two arriving back on board as we made ready to sail for Hibernia (Ireland). He went ashore there at a small trading port on the west coast, and said as he walked ashore, that he would not be rejoining the ship. He turned up again about three years later in Carthage. Only the *Maker* knows how he got there, but somehow he did. I tell you Culann, everything about that man is a mystery and he's more close mouthed than most about himself, and that's the truth.'

'Surely,' I asked, 'he must have said something, where he came from, for instance, or the reason for his journeys. He spent months aboard your ship. He cannot have remained silent for the whole of his time on board, surely. That,' I said pointedly, 'I cannot believe.'

Adwin ummed and aahd and then said reluctantly, 'Well you're sort of right.'

'What do you mean,' I queried?

Adwin said, 'Well, now I'm thinking on it, I suppose he did say quite a lot, in a roundabout, vague sort of way. Little things, that don't really mean or say much until you add them to other little things he's said. Yes,' mused Adwin with a faraway look in his eyes, 'I'm thinking he did speak often, I just hadn't realised it.'

'Talk to me Adwin,' I said softly, 'tell me what you know of this man, and what you can remember of his conversations with you, talk,' I urged him. 'It could be important for me to know of him. I sense I will meet him again, somewhere down the years. Talk my friend, speak of anything, anything at all that you can remember about the Eagleman. There is something here Cumall has not riddled and I'm wondering why, unless,' I paused, 'unless he knew, but for reasons of his own, kept it from me. It would not be the first time,' I added for Adwin's benefit.

Adwin said, 'I asked him once what it was he searched for? He said, for what is lost so that it might be found again and hidden. Now there's a riddle for you and no mistake,' grumped Adwin.

I said, 'He knew me, and he knew about me. How? Why? What is his purpose? To find something and then hide it. There is no sense in that — unless — thought burst like heated stone inside my head, — unless — in hiding what he finds, he seeks to protect it. Protect what? What could be so precious, so rare it be considered lost? Wealth perhaps. No, not wealth. Who would care for wealth when there is knowledge to be found. Knowledge, something written perhaps. Writings be easy to destroy, quickly lost, soon hidden, and when found, false copied, often deliberately so. Could that be it. Yes,' I looked at Adwin, my face alight with recognition of the Eagleman's purpose.

'He seeks out originals, that is what he does my friend. He seeks out the original of what has been copied down by others. He seeks the original writings of masters. He does not want copies of the originals. He wants the first rough drafts, the first clay tablet. The original manuscript of the Hebrew book. The Observations of Hanno, written by Hanno.' The enormity of it all staggered me. Such a mission would have to be huge in scope and involve others, a great many others.

'The Eagleman seeks out written knowledge and then hides it. Why? Why would he want to hide it? To preserve it. Yes, it had to be for that reason. He collects and preserves writings for the future, for those who come after, which means — somewhere — there is a huge library. A secret, hidden place known only to the Eagleman or others like him. The Brotherhood, the *Brotherhood of the Book*, that even we of Druid know nothing about beyond an odd rumour of its existence.'

'Adwin.' I spoke excitedly, 'That has to be it, I'm sure of it. Such a man would not be so base as to seek out hoards of hidden wealth for the sake of its acquisition, he knows there is no knowledge to be gained from wealth.'

'It can be bought,' Adwin said in a dry cynical voice.

'Aye, it can at that,' I agreed, 'wealth can be exchanged for anything, anything at all, from tomb to temple. It can even stay the hand of kings, destroy a nation, buy a man free of his crucifixion or subvert a temple. It cannot however, placate gods, no matter a bought priest's fervour of petition. No,' I said aloud, 'it must be knowledge, I can feel it in my bones. Oh but I would very much like to meet that man again, oh yes indeed. Perhaps he knew or had divined in some way, what it was that I carried about my person.'

Adwin spoke up then, dusting the warm darkness with his words. 'Perhaps what you say is true Culann, he seeks out original writings. I for one, cannot riddle him, I never could, though it wasn't for the want of trying,' he added wistfully. 'You know Culann, sometimes he would sit in the same position, unmoving, for almost the whole of a day. He would sit where you sit now, with his back resting against the wall of the cubicle, breathing easy, slow and light, his face calm and smooth, his eyes unblinking, unseeing they were, as though he be in some sort of self induced trance, I suppose he was, Druids can do it so why not others. Hours later, he would suddenly stand up, a sort of lithe flowing motion and ask for food and drink to be brought to him. Hungry he would be, and thirsty, like a man who has worked the fields beneath a hot summer sun. He had a way of looking at you, his face easy and open as though he had just risen from a deep refreshing sleep. Weird it was, though harmless enough, once the crew became accustomed to his ways. Now and again he practiced a strange form of physical discipline until sweat poured down his body. Whatever it was it had the grace of a dance about it and something else, something deadly, I'm thinking. I saw him fight once, if you can call it that. We'd gone ashore for a bite of food and cup or two of wine.' Adwin searched his memory. 'Aye, Thesbos it was, a small port, but busy like, with many a foreign sailor man about. We'd had a bite and were talking quietly amongst ourselves when a great bearded oaf came up and seemed to take exception to the eagle design on the back of the Eagleman's shirt. Our friend did not want to fight, his hair was bound and we had left our weapons aboard ship. The bearded man would not let him be. In the end it came to push and shove, you know how it is. The Eagleman would have none of that and stood up. As he stood the other man aimed a blow at his head. The Eagleman sort of swayed to one side and slashed him across the throat with the edge of his open hand. Fast he was, very fast indeed. The big man went down with a thump. He died from a crushed throat, couldn't breath you see. We sailed on the evening tide.' Adwin grinned, 'Whatever he is, he is also a fighting man, a warrior.'

Adwin said, 'Who he is, I don't know. Where he comes from, I don't know. He once told me that he came from the west, which is just a little bit vague, don't you think.'

'Oh yes, it's vague all right,' I added with a laugh.

Adwin said, 'He did say that long ago he had lived for awhile amongst the tribes of the Far Land.'

'Now that,' I said to Adwin, 'is well worth knowing.'

Adwin said, 'There was one day there, when I showed him my collection of writings and such like. He recognised most of them and seemed surprised at my interest in such things, wanted to know if I could read them. He looked very thoughtful when I said yes. We spoke for awhile of this and that, and he said, 'it was a pity that Babylon had taken the left hand path,' whatever that may mean, 'and that Egypt could not walk the middle path for much longer. They stagnate,' he said, 'they are no longer seekers and have forgotten much that they once knew. Ancients wisdoms are learned by rote,' he said, 'and there is no one living who knows what they mean. They don't understand the words any more, they have let their own wisdoms slip through their hands, eventually,' he said, 'Egypt will be gobbled up, its past glories forgotten, its knowledge destroyed or buried beneath the sands, it is inevitable, in much the same way that the fall of Babylon or Troy was inevitable. There seems to be an inimitable law in existence that governs such things. Or, is it as you Celts believe, all part of the pattern of the *Makers* weave.'

'Since then,' Adwin said, 'Rome has flexed its muscles and I doubt not that one day soon the legions will take Egypt like a ripe plum falling from a tree.' Adwin continued, 'The Eagleman always paid in gold for his passage. Red gold it was, the rare kind that is much sought after by goldsmiths and the like. Its colour has something to do with minerals found in the rocks from where it is mined. Or so it is I once was told.'

We talked far into the night as I pressed Adwin for anything he could remember, no matter how trivial or unimportant he might consider it to be. By the time the moon began to slip down the sky I think we neared an end of most all Adwin could tell me of the Eagleman.

I will meet him again I think. Somewhere down the years, he will stroll back into my life and be the cause of what, I really don't know.

Adwin said, 'He told me once, that he would return to the Far Land, to finish something he had started there a long time ago. What, I don't know, he wouldn't say and good manners forbid me the asking. He also said he could never return to Gaul (France) if ever it came under Roman domination, and that it would be a pity as he also had unfinished work there. He sometimes studied, he said, the rise and fall of nations. The cause of it all and the effect when they fall. The effects are like ripples spreading out from a stone cast into water. The larger the stone, the wider more far reaching are the ripples. He called it the ripple effect, and said that men of learning and wisdom had been aware of its far reaching, diverse effects for centuries. The saddest part of it all being the slow but inevitable decline into periods of darkness that often lasted for centuries, resulting in a total loss of reading and writing skills, arts and crafts, building, production of food crops, indeed most every discipline it is possible to imagine a once great and thriving nation to possess.'

'It is always the same,' the Eagleman said, 'when a nation seeks to destroy or dominate other nations and impose by force, if necessary, its own values. Thereby stifling and often completely wiping out any kind of alternate thinking, or individual create. Wisdoms are lost. Dominant religions are ridiculed into obscurity or changed beyond any recognition of former teachings. Whatever is gained is always less than what is lost. Nations like Rome are directly responsible for the darkness that follows in the wake of their demise. Before they came there was no darkness. They destroy the individuality of nations and pave the way towards their own slow decline and eventual fall, thereby creating shadowy pools, however distant they may be. By that time of course,' the Eagleman said, 'there is no one left who remembers what it was like before the Romans came. Suddenly free of a centuries long oppressive rule, rare are the people who can remember that their ancestors once lived a free people and led a contented, more productive life. I think future historians will come late, if at all, to such realisations or recognitions, might of Empire will blind them.'

Adwin paused and then said softly, 'I had not thought to remember so much my friend.'

I remained silent, staring out across the moon shot waters.

'That be all Culann, there is no more.'

I thanked him then and wondered what it was the Eagleman had warned me about. That it was a warning I didn't doubt, but about what. Certainly not Rome, they were a rising power not a descendant one. Now this be something else I must riddle.

After many days of fair weather sailing we came at last to the edge of the Far Land. We sailed south along the coastline, heading towards the mouth of a great river that would carry me inland toward mystery, danger and the eventual fulfilment of a vague destiny I had yet to riddle.

Somewhere in the vastness of this new land I would meet *the one who waits*.

There be many settlements here.

I will not sail the great river, I am determined to strike out on foot — alone. I will travel the land and learn of its ways and its people, until the breathing of it all is as familiar to me as the beating of my heart.

Well provisioned and armed. I wear my long hair unbound, let those who would, take it if they can.

I am Druid alone in a Druidless land, therefore I must strive to be more than Druid.

Ψ

Roy Edwards

I sense that *he who waits* is aware of my feet upon this land. Vast it is, and old, very, very old, my spirit doth reach out to its memory.

Even so, my weapons are ever close to my hands.

I no longer think of Beltain, Samhain or Lugnasadh.

Now it is, I think only of seasons and their passing. I travelled through spring and walked the long hot summer down into autumn. I travelled through winter and a mild one it was.

Avoiding settlements, I lived off the land, it teemed with wild game, nuts and berries. Sun and wind darkened my skin, my body grew lean and hard. Here and there I came upon ancient places, giving greetings to the air, so that the old ones who might yet remain, would know I held them in respect. I crossed mountains of bitter stone and wandered through wide shallow valleys. Forests there were, thick and deep.

The great river lay off to my right somewhere. A journey of many days. I had felt the need to turn away from its banks and head inland. Sometimes I dreamt of a vast plain, of mountains and ranges of small rolling hills and always — of *the one who waits*. He calls to me I think, spirit guiding me on. Certainly I had no fear of walking in the wrong direction.

I saw no one and yet I was aware that others walked the land around me. If eyes of Indians beheld me they did not reveal their presence or otherwise offer me harm. Perhaps they recognised me, perhaps they did not.

During my second year of wandering, Season of Green Leaf it was, I became aware of change within me. The land had already changed me in many ways, but I did not know I was wounded until I began to heal.

Spirit wounded I was, and unaware of the hurt I carried. Healed, a weight of burden fell away from my head and shoulders. My body felt lighter, my feet whisper soft upon the earth. Soul ruin I recognise in others, how difficult it is to recognise it in self.

My people have gone down in blood and tears and all but vanished from the face of the earth. My dearest friends died in agony. I won countless small battles but never a war. I put aside Druid and lived only for the sword in defence of my homeland and its people whom I love.

Ravaged and torn, I lay bleeding inside my own memories. Hot, copper-salt rage too often expressed, until I stood captive within a prison of darkness. How close Gaunt Man, Crom Cruach, Bowed One of the Mound, came to claiming me — I shudder to think upon it now.

That distant day upon the moors when I turned to face those who pursued me. I killed them with a lusting thirst to see their blood pooling bright upon the grass. To kill, to protect loved ones or a way of life is one thing. To enjoy killing, to kill for the shiver of pleasure it brings is a foulness. It degrades you spiritually and I had almost, willingly, entered its trap. That was my wound. That I, Druid, had come to enjoy the stench of my enemies blood. I had become an abomination.

I cleansed my spirit in the way of Druid. I walked the land and burnt my memories down. I threw them away and replaced them with a sanity of vision of all that had happened. I mourned anew for Bridgit, Cumall and Bardvar the king. I wept again for our murdered children and those sold into slavery and, I grieve forever the destruction of our nation and its unique way of life. I cleansed my spirit of its taint, and thereby gained recognition of *An Ceathair Na Bealach*, the Fourth Way of the Spirit.

It opened before me like a dreaming eye, I drew back, my thought coldly clear, not yet ready am I to weave its pattern or riddle its stones.

Whatever I am, or might become, it will be because that is what I wish to be. *An Ceathair Na Bealach* I choose not to tread.

I am Druid, my hair is long and unbound, challenge to anyone who thinks he can take it, and this I know, I will kill again, not in joy, not in shivering lust, but I will take life and that is my constant sorrow, my crux of wood. One day I will bind my hair and put aside my weapons. Until then I be Culann of the once Arverni, Druid and warrior and a sometimes haunt upon the land. I am exactly what I should be.

Spirit healed, I strode out with renewed vigour, travelling deep into a strange vast land of changing beauty.

I walked spring down into a breathless summer of shimmering heat. Dry was the grass, brown and gold was the land. Above me the sky was a vast, inverted bowl of deepest blue. I followed a dim winding trail that beckoned me on with its elusive suggestion of leading me somewhere. It would no doubt, like other trails I had followed, eventually peter out in the middle of nowhere.

Adwin had spoken of a desert city somewhere in the Four Lands, called the Red City. Carved out of red sandstone, he said, standing five times the height of a single house. It is also known as the Hidden City, some have found it whilst others have not. It was built by an unknown race called the Navateans who it is said, crossed over to the *otherside* leaving their city behind to mark their passing. There are many such tales, not only in this land, but also in others and who amongst us can say with certainty that all such tales be true or false.

I wondered then, if other lands also had their share of trails that seemed to lead nowhere and yet must lead somewhere, if only we can riddle the way of their walking.

Summer flowed into autumn like blood from an open wound. Days became cool and full of soft hazy sunlight. The nights were cold and grew steadily colder. Until, one morning I awoke to a crusting of frost and crackling ice about me.

I had by then reached the edge of a vast plain that stretched out before me, rolling on forever, or so it seemed. Cold the air was, and growing colder. A plains winter would not be easy, it would not be easy at all. I gave thought then, to what I must do to survive.

Ψ

Roy Edwards

Survive I did — and more.
I came to know the secret breathing of the land.
I lived in harmony with its breath.
My old life was over, it peeled away from me like dried up skin.
I embraced my new life, turned my face up towards the sun and sang a welcoming song of harmonious rebirth.
A soft green wind blew down my throat.

Ψ

PART TWO

INDIAN DAWN

Roy Edwards

To be Indian is to live in harmony
With the elements of life and earth
In the way the Great Spirit
Intended human beings to live.
To harmonise with seasons is to be Indian.
Wakantanka — the undiscovered law
Is the mystery of the way of Indian.
Skan Taku Skanskan — something in movement
Spiritual Vitality
Is the way of its achievement.
This is the law.
The first and last law of 'The Human Beings'
The Indians.
Only through knowledge of earth and spirit
Can the law that leads to the Fourth Way
Be known and understood.
The way of Indian is harmony
The harmony of earth and spirit.
It is the natural way of all human beings.

Culann-Touch the Clouds-Running
Circa AD 10

SEASONS

Moon of Drifting Snow	January
Moon of Bitter Cold	February
Moon of Windy Rain	March
Moon of New Grass	April - May

Strawberry Moon	
Moon of the Red Flowering Lilies	June- July
Moon of Ripe Berries	

Moon of Black Cherries	
Moon of Ripe Plums	July -August
Tall Grass Moon	

Moon of Making Sweet Fat	
Dry Grass Moon	September -October
Moon of Changing Season	

Yellow Leaf Moon	
Moon of Falling Leaves	October - November

Moon of Popping Trees
Cold Season Moon

December

Seasons of Cold Moons

Winter

Seasons of Warm Moons

Spring - Early Summer

Seasons of Ripe Moons

Early Summer -
Summer - Autumn

WINTER COUNT —
A yearly pictograph record of important events. (Calculated
from Spring through to Spring)

All Winter Count records were eventually destroyed by
invaders, who then claimed such records had never existed.

BELOVED WOMAN —
(Praise name - an honour bestowed) A Beloved Woman is a
woman who has done something special for the tribe and is,
upon her naming henceforth held in the same regard and
respect as a Chief and/or any other important dignitary. She
has - *Catkuta* - Honour.

Celtic Sunset

THE SEVEN DESIRED VIRTUES — of a Human Being, a Warrior

When all seven virtues are attained collectively, the Human Being is — of the spirit, and is not considered to be merely an earthly being of human kind.

Not listed in order of importance

        GENEROSITY
        COURAGE
        WISDOM
        FORTITUDE
        ENDURANCE
        GOOD MANNERS
        ELOQUENCE

CELTIC SUNSET

Chapter Eight

Solo

I Stood alone beneath a vast and empty sky
The cold wind whipping
I have listened to the sound of voices
Singing down the breathing air
I have stood alone and cried out
How small our strengths, how frail our faiths
I have followed in HIS footsteps
Uncounting of the years
And stood, silently weeping beneath the beauty of HIS face

Chorus

Have you heard the MAKER sing
Or looked upon the pattern of HIS weave
Have you walked through the green valley and sensed
The sweet fragrance of HIS hair
Or knelt in awe
Beneath the quietness of HIS eyes

Druid Song of Adoration
from the Hidden Scroll
Culann Circa AD 12

Celtic Sunset

Each day White Owl did the same thing.

In Summer camp or Winter, it made no difference, only the location changed.

Each day, somewhere around midafternoon, he walked out and away from the camp and stared long and hard towards the west. His sharp dark eyes quartering the plains. Resting briefly on patches of cloud shadow or low hummocks of grass. He noted every stone and bush, every gleam and glimmer of water, dismissing them all one by one. He sensed the hawk high above and heard the harsh cry of crows squabbling over some bit and piece of rotting carrion.

Slowly, he scanned the horizon, his gaze resting briefly upon a distant range of low, round hills, shimmering beneath the heat of a yellow white sun. He could see nothing that should not be there, no movement he could not account for. All was as it should be, he sighed and turned away, walking slowly back towards the camp.

Each day was the same.

He was a patient man, sure of his visions. One day the tall stranger he had seen inside his head would come. All he had to do was wait.

White Owl was a prophet of the Dakotah, the Sioux, he had faith in his own dreaming.

He had begun to look for the stranger four Winter Counts ago. He would continue to look and wait until the stranger came, and come he would. Today, tomorrow, this season or next, it made no difference. He would wait, and one day the stranger would come, striding out from the sun with long shadows falling all about him.

He would come from the west. A solitary remanent of a once proud nation. He would bring something with him, a small mystery wrapped in cloth.

What it might be, White Owl didn't know. He knew only that in some strange way he would become its guardian and his sons after him. That made him smile, as yet he had no sons. Maybe soon he thought.

He had, long ago, found a secret place where the mystery would be hidden and safe, for as long as the mystery might want to conceal itself.

It is, he once thought to himself, the way of all secrets, to remain hidden whilst ever there is no need of them, and to be found, discovered, when there is need. Before he faced the great spirit he would pass the location of the mystery and its guardianship on to another chosen, hopefully to his as yet unborn son. And so it would continue, down through the hundreds of years, until there was no more need for a guardian and the secret stood revealed.

The seasons had dealt kindly with White Owl.

He was tall for a Sioux, broad across the shoulders and deep of chest. His upper arms still thick with muscle despite the strands of white that streaked his long unbound black hair. His hair flowed across his shoulders and down his back. His copper skinned face was remarkably unlined for a man of his years. Hawklike it was, with a brooding intensity about the eyes. His tribe held him in high esteem, knowing few tribes could boast of a prophet living amongst them. Often, such holy men went away to commune with the spirits and were rarely, if ever, seen again.

White Owl was different.

He had always been different, even as a child. So it was that his tribe cared for him and thought themselves lucky to have him amongst them. He never lacked for food or water and when the time came to move the village to its summer or winter camp, there was always a group of giggling young girls willing and eager to take down his lodge and carry it.

Celtic Sunset

Of course White Owl had not always been a prophet, nor had he always owned his true name of White Owl. *The People* remembered this. It was recorded in the skin book of the Winter Count, how he received his name and what he had been before. It was an honour to be included in the book of events and thereby, to be remembered forever. Few there were to gain such an honour and none now living except for White Owl.

In the time before his true naming, White Owl was known as Ten Bears. The bear was sacred to the Sioux and therefore not to be harmed in any way. Of course this did not apply, if the bear attacked you and you were unable to run away or climb a slender tree that the bear could not. During the years of his warrior training, White Owl was known as Thinks-a-lot. Often when asked politely, if he would like to do this or that, he would answer equally politely and say, perhaps later, I am thinking. He never spoke of his thoughts, but the tribe recognised the distant look in his eyes and knew he was spirit walking ancient memories. The spirit, after all, has a long life and is not confined to the use and lifespan of a single body. Everyone knows this, but it is not something to be spoken of in a casual chattering manner. Each day is a wonder, unique in its own creation. Every ray of sunlight gives wealth. Every standing one (tree) is a breath of richness adding to the air.

It was during his warrior training that Thinks-a-lot was given his first name. Ten times without reason, during five Winter Counts, he was attacked by bears. He killed two with his hunting bow and one with a lance driven through its throat, the others he managed to run away from.

High Hawk, a *Wapiya*, a sacred man of the tribe, named him Ten Bears and said that the bears had been sent by the

349

great spirit to test the *Wanagi*, strength of spiritual self, of Thinks-a-lot. No one said it wasn't true, therefore it was.

During the seasons that followed his naming, Ten Bears became a famous, and later legendary warrior of all the Sioux Nation, *The Human Beings*.

He led a series of successful raids against the *Kange* - the Crows and the fierce *Sintehla Wicasa*, People of the Lance, the Comanche. Once, to the hilarity of an entire Sioux raiding party, Ten Bears led an infuriated band of Crow warriors who had tenaciously pursued them for two days, after the Sioux had raided their village, directly into the path of a *Malpiyato*, Arapaho hunting party. The Arapaho, being hereditary enemies of the Crow immediately attacked. In the ensuing confusion the Sioux escaped and returned to their village without losing a single warrior.

The incident became a much talked about thing throughout the plains tribes. The Crows, humiliated by Ten Bears trick, declared Ten Bears to be their mortal enemy forever, thereby unwittingly enhancing his fame and prestige as an already remarkable and courageous warrior.

During the seasons that followed, bands of Crow warriors roamed the plains and hills, hunting Ten Bears with fury in their hearts. When the end came, it was the Crow who cried enough, not Ten Bears.

Ten Bears had grown tall and strong, his strength evident in the hard swell of his muscles. Young girls sighed over him, mothers smiled and offered him food. Warriors copied his ways and hung upon his every word. Ten Bears, oblivious to the attention, would sit in some shady spot and contemplate his inner thoughts.

Once, whilst sitting alone by the side of the river, yet still remaining in sight of the village, he was attacked by six

Crow warriors who had lain in concealment hoping for a chance to catch him alone. Ten Bears heard them creeping towards him through the undergrowth moments before they attacked.

He stood, feeling distant from his body and yet incredibly aware of his surroundings. Waves of anger swept through him. 'You hunt me here,' he shouted at his attackers, 'here, in sight of my own village.'

They came at him then, in a silent rush, feet whispering over the ground, weapons raised and swinging, faces painted for war.

Unarmed, Ten Bears moved to meet them, fast and light on his feet. Ducking under a swinging war club, he hurled the warrior down wrenching the club free of his hand. Armed, he turned to meet the warriors, who had fanned out in an attempt to enclose him within a circle. Ten Bears didn't hesitate, he charged the warrior nearest to him and broke free of the circle. With his back to a tree, he faced them unafraid and waiting. They closed in, wary of his speed and strength. The fallen man groaned on the ground, nursing a broken arm.

Ten Bears filled his lungs with air, a wild feeling of battle joy coursing through his veins, his eyes alight and burning. His face creased in a fierce wolfish smile, his attackers paused, Ten Bears willingness to fight, unsettled their certainty of victory. And then they charged, whooping and shouting. Ten Bears screamed, his voice rising in a wailing savage cry of rage.

It was the war cry of a lone warrior, standing unafraid, and facing overwhelming odds. His cry echoed and rang, belling through the air, alerting the village to the danger of imminent attack.

Ten Bears lunged, swinging his war club. One blow crushed a skull, another blow smashed an arm raised in defence. Suddenly a lance came driving in towards his chest. He turned aside, the spearhead narrowly missing his heart, and with a single savage blow caved in one side of the spear wielder's skull. He felt something hot slice his left forearm. And then he was moving, dodging and weaving about his two remaining opponents. One slashed out wildly with a knife only to feel something terrible crash into his testicles. The pain cast him down into a deep well of darkness from which he would never return. The remaining warrior turned to flee. Ten Bears picked up the fallen lance and drove it through the fleeing man's back. Withdrawing the lance, he turned and pushed it slowly through the throat of the one whose testicles he had crushed. The warrior with the broken arm began to sing his death song. Ten Bears silenced him with a curt command to shut up, as he did not intend to kill him.

'Go back to your tribe,' he said. He smiled then, someone must carry word of your warrior's deaths. 'Go now,' Ten Bears said, 'go swiftly.'

The surviving Crow scrambled to his feet, turned and fled as swiftly as his broken body would allow.

By the time Sioux warriors arrived from the village, it was all over. Only the Crow dead remained to give mute testimony to Ten Bears' victory.

His legendary status as a warrior increased.

Ten Bears said little and wondered, not for the first time, what else there might be, beyond warrior, that is.

Counting Wolf was old, very old. He had lived through more than one hundred and thirty summers. He could remember when the Sioux fought the Kiowa and the Comanche, taking away their traditional lands, forcing the two tribes to travel west in search of new hunting grounds.

Celtic Sunset

He could remember when during the Moon of Black Cherries, tall, sunset haired strangers came, and the other smaller men who wore much metal. The Sioux, ever curious, welcomed both groups and sent them on their way carrying many presents of food and shirts of soft leather. Travellers, walking towards the sun, where, they said, they would meet with others of their kind.

'The land is filling up,' thought Counting Wolf.

His long years of wisdom were valuable to the tribe. So it was, that he came to sit in the honoured position of Chief Councillor of the Council of forty four Elders.

The Council advised the tribe of many things pertaining to their continuance upon the earth. They ensured that everyone upheld the law within the confines of the village. Appointing when necessary, a temporary man-of-the-law, to control rowdiness and to promote harmony within the camp.

It was to the Council, that the observers and advisers who accompanied every war band, or raiding party, reported to. Verifying individual warrior's boasts of courage, or not, as the case may be. They reported on how warriors conducted themselves, naming those who showed promise and those who were obviously unsuited to being or becoming warriors. There was no shame attached to anyone who was unwarrior like, it was simply suggested that they try something else. If they did not want to accept the suggestion, then of course they were free to follow the warrior's path. It was of course, then made clear that they were unlikely to survive for very long.

The Council advised, they did not compel anyone to follow their advice. It was given freely, as a gift. The one who received the gift was free to do with it whatsoever he wished. Generosity without restraint, is one of the seven virtues, a virtue regarded highly by warriors, so it is with gifting. A true gift is one you would like to keep, but do not. Such gifting is a measure of generosity without restraint. The one who receives the gift, is free to do whatsoever he wishes with it.

Observers also reported on how the war or raid leader planned his raid or attack. Did his plan work, what did his plan accomplish, and how. Excluding war, when raiding, if any of the raiding party were killed, then no matter how rich or plentiful their spoils might be the raid would be considered a failure, walking wounded were acceptable injuries. Raids were a means of testing young men, not killing them. There is no reward in death. And who knows what wonders the young dead might have contributed to the tribe if they had lived. Therefore it behoved older, more experienced warriors to advise and guide them, for the sake of the entire tribe.

Long ago when he was yet a young man, Counting Wolf had almost died. It happened during the Moon of Yellow Leaf when, whilst hunting, he had quite unexpectedly, come upon a small band of Pani, Pawnee, and they of course had attacked him immediately.

Counting Wolf fought bravely, but he was no Ten Bears. He killed two Pawnee with arrows, but the Pawnee were fierce like Comanche, and considered him easy prey. He fought with a small knife of metal he had gotten through trade with a wondering *Sinagleglega*, a Navaho, one of the striped blanket people. His blade made a difference but not much. Growing weak from small wounds, that bled a lot, he considered himself dead and would indeed have died, if not for the intervention of a Sioux hunting party. The Sioux killed all the Pawnee and carried the by now unconscious Counting Wolf back to the village, he recovered swiftly. If he had died, there would now be no one of his long years amongst the tribe to advise them, or to advise Ten Bears to seek out his own spirit trail.

'I am exactly where I should be,' Counting Wolf was sometimes heard to say.

Ten Bears enjoyed raiding and confounding the enemy, but it was no longer enough. He had now killed so many Crow warriors, that they no longer hunted him, for fear that he would single handedly reduce their fighting men down to a mere handful. Ten Bears had become, *Nagi Napeyapi,* a psychic shock, to the Crow, he literally, made their spirits flee. It wasn't enough, something of his *Wanagi,* spiritual self, was missing.

He began to listen with care and attention to the *Eyanpaha,* News Criers, heralds, who travelled in complete safety from tribe to tribe. It was death for anyone who harmed a News Crier, they were the communication lines of the whole of the land. *Eyanpaha* carried news and messages. They spoke of where they had been, of what they had seen and of what they knew, of things heard but not witnessed. They spoke of the mound builders and of the many villages built of stone. They spoke of tall, green and blue eyed men. Of small, dark coastal traders, whose emblem was a hooded snake (Cobra). They spoke of travellers, explorers who looked for rocks that melt in fire. And once they spoke of the *Dreadful* people who live behind the sun, beyond the western desert lands (Mexico - South America). They spoke of huge wooden houses that float across the blue waters that taste like salt. Of houses of stone built high in the mountains. Of broken walls found in the desert, whose surface was covered in strange pictures and symbols (Hieroglyphics), built of square stones so heavy it would take four strong men to lift one. News criers travelled everywhere, working in relays, constantly on the move, for the whole of their life.

Ten Bears listened eagerly to everything they had to say. And when they moved on he felt a vague, restless dissatisfaction with his life stir deep down inside his belly.

It was during the Moon of Red Lilies when he first began to feel that he had been chosen. He could not have explained why he felt that way. It was a feeling, vague and misty that came to him sometimes during the night, when restless, he tossed and turned in uneasy sleep. It would be with him when he awoke and then it would be gone, like smoke through a hole in an enclosed lodge. He did not feel he was chosen just to be a warrior, but to be, or become something else. Only he didn't know what it was, and it troubled him.

During the Moon of Ripe Plums, Counting Wolf spoke to him.

Ten Bears sat outside his lodge in the late afternoon sun. Its warmth felt good, its light lending the air a look of melting honey. The blue sky was hazed almost white, milky looking and hot. Small puff ball clouds hung unmoving above the horizon's rim. A rich smell of roasting meat and melting fat filled the sultry air. A murmur of voices could be heard, sounding distant and flat beneath the suns layering heat.

Ten Bears sat cleaning his weapons, his eyes lost in some inner contemplative dreaming.

Counting Wolf coughed politely, announcing his presence.

Ten Bears looked up with a start, and then to show his good manners, he lay his weapons aside and invited Counting Wolf to sit beside him. They sat together in silence for awhile and watched the flow of life about the village.

Celtic Sunset

'Look,' Counting Wolf said, 'see how the children play, unaware of tomorrow or the day after. They live only for the now moments.' He spoke in a soft voice, 'You cannot do that Ten Bears, it is not enough for you, your *Wanagi*, spiritual self, will not allow it. Once you were called Thinks-a-lot. I have noticed you have been doing a lot of that this season.'

Ten Bears remained silent.

'It is good to sit here in the sun beside a friend,' Counting Wolf said. 'Friends know how to talk to each other. Between friends there can be silence,' he added. 'I have never understood why some people feel they must fill a friendly silence with words. Is it because they are young and cannot fill silence with *Wanagi*, spiritual self, or is it because they are afraid of silence and the loudness of their own thoughts. It is a mystery I think, but only a small one.'

Counting Wolf glanced sideways at Ten Bears, then looked away towards the centre of the village.

He said, 'I will tell you a story. It is only a little story, one you may have already heard. I like it, it is a good story.' He paused for a moment then said, 'You may have forgotten it, he smiled slightly, a busy man like you who thinks a lot. I will tell you this story and when I am finished you can tell me if you remember it.'

Ten Bears looked at the old man to show that he was attentive and listening.

Counting Wolf hawked and spat in the dust.

He said, 'It begins like this.'

'Long ago when I was a young warrior, though not as famous as you, I fought the Pawnee and almost died. They are very fierce, the Pawnee. I did not die and when I recovered, I did not feel the same. Something had changed, and I no longer felt like Counting Wolf. I felt like someone else. This new person was a stranger to me, he did strange things that made me worry. The stranger did not want to be a warrior, he wanted to be something else. I did not know what it was the stranger wanted to be. It was a mystery to me and this also caused me worry. I became a very worried man, but I do not think the stranger worried, he was too busy doing strange things. I had never met anyone who worried as much as I did. The stranger ate and slept well, but I did not. I was too worried to sleep or eat. I came to look upon the stranger that lived with me inside my head, as *Hmunga*, a mystery to be dreaded. I decided to sweat him out, to make him go away. I stayed in the sweat house for one day and one night, but the stranger did not go. The only thing I lost was a lot of weight. I came out of the sweat house and swam in the river to cool my body. I was very weak, I was also very worried, so I went to the *Wapiya*, the sacred man who heals. As you know the *Wapiya* is also a seer, he recognised the stranger and told me what to do. I went up into the hills and stayed there alone for the count of seven days, when I came down I was alone. I was Counting Wolf again and this I have never forgotten. Since then I am always exactly where I should be. I cannot be anywhere else, wherever I am is the right place to be. *Wanagi*, spiritual self, must be centred and balanced, if it is not, you become a stranger to your familiar voice.' Counting Wolf smiled to himself and said, 'Sometimes the stranger does strange things, but I don't worry so much any more. That is the end of my story. It is a good one, I think.'

Before Ten Bears could reply, Counting Wolf rose to his feet and said, 'If you would know peace within your heart, peace inside your head, you must find your own spirit trail and follow it to its end. For some it is a vision-quest, for others a sacred duty, you alone can decide. You are a free person, listen to your familiar voice and answer only to your self. You must see yourself for what you are, not for what others say you are. Find your spirit trail, be exactly where you should be, then you can never be anywhere else. My familiar voice tells me it is so, therefore it is.'

Without a backward glance, Counting Wolf turned and walked slowly away. 'It is good to help a friend in need,' he thought, smiling to himself as he began to softly hum the secret summer song of bees making honey in the hive.

During the Moon of Making Sweet Fat.

Dawn touched the sky with a blush of pink and arcing spears of soft, dusty gold. Pastel shell colours crept across the land, casting shadows and pools of thin morning light.

The sleeping village awoke. Curls of smoke began to drift lazily up into the air. Somewhere a child cried, it's voice wailing and lonely. Warm arms gathered the child up, smothering the sobbing voice against breasts heavy with milk and love. The child suckled greedily, dark button eyes moist and shiny as morning sunlight fell across the child's contented face.

Warriors yawned and stretched, wandering out of the camp towards the piss trench, where they stood and scratched and urinated. Others squatted over the shit trench venting sighs of relief.

Before going down to the river to bathe, the warriors ambled through the camp in a loose silent group, heading towards the open plain and the solitary figure sitting cross legged on the dusty ground. They looked, agreed nothing had changed, and turned away strolling leisurely towards the river.

Now and again during the course of the day, groups of young boys and girls would gather and stare in round eyed wonder at the unmoving figure. Sometimes Counting Wolf would come and with a small smile on his face take note of his friend's rigid immovability.

The figure sat within the centre of a small square, marked with a smooth round stone at each corner, instead of within the traditional circle. The square was symbolic of the vision seeker's desire to break out, and seek one or more of the four paths, willingly forsaking the endless cycle symbolised by the circle. The four points of the square allowed the spirit to flow out in any direction, so long as the four points remained un-joined. Only warriors possessed of a courageous heart and great spiritual strength, dare attempt such an awakening. Some did not come back, only the shell of their bodies remained, in a mindless state like a new born child. Such empty bodies died quickly, unless the spirit returned to claim it. No one had dared attempt the *Ritual of the Four Paths* for over one hundred Winter Counts. Those who did were regarded with awe, and if they returned unharmed and sane, were known forever as *Cante Tinza*, a Brave Heart. A Brave Heart often became a prophet, but not always. Even so, a Brave Heart's status within the tribe was unique. He need never want for anything whilst he lived, and was completely free to do anything he chose to do.

He was, the tribe knew, exactly where he was supposed to be, he could never be anywhere else. He was perfectly balanced. In motion and harmony with earth and spirit.

Ten Bears sat cross legged on the prairie, his arms resting lightly across his thighs. He faced towards the west, the direction of his dreaming.

Rays of orange-gold sunlight, lay hot bars of flame across his naked shoulders and upper back. His flesh began to bead with sweat in the rising heat. Above him the sky stretched on forever, vast and aloof, a perfect curve of blue stone. The sun, a ball of glowing amber set within its smooth curving surface.

Ten Bears sat unmoving, it was his third day. He stared sightlessly out into the heat hazed distance, his gaze unfocused and vacant as though he had stepped out from behind his eyes. His muscular chest rose and fell in a slow rhythm of shallow breathing. He was aware and yet unaware. He was here and he was not. His *Wanagi*, spiritual self, occupied a different space and yet remained within the world of men. A day and a night went by, whilst he formed and contemplated a single thought. He was *Wanisugna*, creative force, within his own universe. He had been here before, in a long ago time, when the world he knew was younger — more innocent.

A second day and night went by. He thought he could return and claim his body, he wasn't sure. He would try, but not yet, he was uncertain if he really wanted to.

Two days merged into three.

To go outside your body is to exist as spirit outside of time. A debatable concept that is true only for those who have experienced it — and returned. Such people rarely, if ever, speak. The experience is ineffable, intensely personal, and is the door that opens to the *Fourth Way*.

On the eve of the third day, Ten Bears opened the door and looked — outside.

Somewhere an eagle screamed. The harsh sound of it, high and distant, as though it came from the outside of nowhere, that is always located somewhere, and for some, it is exactly the right place to be. Unlike Culann of the Arverni, Ten Bears chose to open the door and step through.

A cool breeze wandered across the plain, bending the tall grass around his body. Sun dry stalks rustled and rubbed, clicked and clackled against each other, creating a grass song that would ripple and bend, sigh and sing almost forever. Above his motionless body the sky throbbed, a deep clear blue song in perfect harmony with his every heartbeat.

Ten Bears found his spirit trail.

More correctly, his spirit trail found him.

He opened the door and stepped through, into an achingly beautiful sunset. For the first time he could see the *invisibles*, who are sometimes called the *Shining Ones*, the *Opalescents*. In time they will be known by other names. No matter what they are called, the essential nature of their being, remains unchanged.

It was then, as he opened the door, that Ten Bears understood the true meaning of *Wanagi Yuha*. He was *Wanagi Yuha*, spirit owner, he owned himself. It was not *Wahupa*, realisation of the ultimate enlightenment, it was a beginning, a step, a forward motion along the spirit trail, the Spiral of Immortality.

Vague memories stirred his spirit self. Had he walked this trail before? He didn't think so. The vision before him was unexpected, and yet, familiar. The memory of it faded, replaced by a feeling of, *now* is the only memory that shall be.

Before him a group if *Invisibles* sat on a bench inside a sunset that was stunning, in its intimation of what every sunset should be.

They wore fringed, doe skin breeches and thin shirts of soft white skins, painted with the sacred symbol of the cross within a circle and a flaring sun burst. Strips of hide, dyed deep red, were bound around their foreheads, holding in place four eagle feathers, symbolic of the Four Ways of Seeking and, The Four Attainments.

Celtic Sunset

They smiled and beckoned him forward, praising him with their eyes. Ten Bears felt welcome and recognised. Something, belled inside his head. He felt as real and solid in this wondrous hall, as he did in the other place, the world of his walking, the world of men, or so it seemed to his dreaming mind. Tranced he was, so it is some would say, in an attempt to deny the depth and certainty of visionary reality.

The day mankind understands and melds the two worlds (physical - spiritual) is the day he owns the earth and sky and all the spaces and worlds between.

He stood within the Sunset Hall of Invisibles, mute and alone. His spiritual self recognised its own silence, and understood there was no need to carry thoughts here, there was nowhere for them to go.

'Listen,' said the voice, 'the colour of Wakantanka is blue.'

'Listen,' said the voice, 'to the rhythm of your heart. It is the unheard rhythm of the universe, the eternal source of awareness, the rhythm of beginnings and the rhythm of endings.'

'Listen,' for the third time, the voice said, 'to the familiar secret of self, residing softly without a shell.'

'Listen,' for the fourth and final time, the voice intoned. 'From this single moment, until the last of all moments, the Black Hills shall be, and will remain sacred, to the Sioux. The whole of the Sioux nation shall have care of them.' The voice said, 'There is now a heart shaped path, a spiritual hoop encircling the Black Hills, and you Ten Bears, have chosen yourself to care for, and protect, what has yet to be hidden within its folds. The world will change,' continued the voice, 'but you, and those who spring from your seed must remain, until the sacred hoop is broken and consecrated anew in a time of turmoil and travail that has yet to come. Your trust is binding Indian Man and cannot be broken. You have chosen yourself Ten Bears.' The Invisibles smiled, the voice belled softly, 'You are now exactly where you should be. You can never be anywhere else. Wherever you go, it is the right place to be.' The voice continued, 'There is one who will come to you from out the west. He will be a stranger from a far away land. His people are no more, and only he retains the ancient wisdom of their holy ones. The Sioux will become his new people, and you, his wisdom will share. He is both priest and warrior, seer and philosopher, a walker of spirit trails. His, is an old spirit wisdom, different from yours. Both are different, yet similar in many ways. The two must become one, else neither will survive the long walk of years. Both wisdoms will lose something of themselves when they merge as one, even so, the one wisdom that will then remain from the melding of the two, will be greater than both. In this way they are balanced. To gain, first you must lose. To give, you must be willing to accept.'

'To seek knowledge is not enough, Indian Man. Nor is the climb towards spiritual awareness enough. First you must come to realise and accept without reservation, that you, and only you, are your own spirit owner — *Wanagi Yuha* — and that you have fallen. You must forgive yourself, and in self forgiveness find again that love and approval of self, that you have forgotten you own. THAT IS THE LAW - THE FIRST LAW THAT MUST BE UNDERSTOOD. In its absence all else fails. To seek spiritual awareness, unaware of its existence is to fail. Soon or late, all other laws, states of being, break down when the first law of the *way*, is ignored or incorrectly understood. No being is above the law, it is the very governance of being. To alter, ignore or otherwise step above the law, is to step out of the state of being. Know you this

Celtic Sunset

Indian Man,' the voice thundered, 'and beware, there is a final, unlooked for state, of no-being, no awareness, nothing. Though it may for a time, seem otherwise. Eventually all the wisdoms of spirit fail, in the absence of observation of the first law. They wither, growing dry and brittle like stems of long grass beneath the sun of summer's heat. Listen, and you will hear your familiar voice tell you so, therefore it is.' The voice continued, the faces of the Invisibles unsmiling, 'Only through a blending of the two wisdoms, can the one wisdom survive, to be used again and again, whenever people are spiritually low, hungry for truth. The wisdom will change itself to fit once and future times. No wisdom, no matter its source, can remain unchanging, else it be ignored and useless within a world of constant change. It was your choice to come here Indian Man. Now walk you the *way*, without fear, walk you the *way*.'

Ten Bears stood in the Hall of Sunset, a blank slate, upon which the Invisible wrote with a voice of bells.

Suddenly, he felt himself falling, in an easy floating down sort of way. The image of the hall and the Invisibles grew small, fading into an immensity of blue black sky, and a tangled weave of stars.

A tendril of something warm, whisper licked inside his head. 'Your new name is White Owl,' the voice chimed softly, 'bringer of wisdom. Beware,' the bell voice urged, beware the Dreadful People.'

Ten Bears flowed like a river, soaking down through the air, his thoughts alive with unanswered questions. His acceptance of all that he had seen and heard within his vision was, total. His memory of it clear, clean and sharp. He had travelled the spirit trail and returned where many before him had failed or returned as *Heyoka*, clowns and contraries. Ten Bears *Wanagi*, spiritual self, said it was so. Therefore it is.

Roy Edwards

Dawn of the fourth day of the Moon of Making Sweet Fat.

He remembered his name, it was White Owl. Once he had been known as Ten Bears and before that he was called Thinks-a-lot. Now he was White Owl, three who are one. Some people, he mused, spent their whole lives with just one name, how sad. Could they not recognise change. Some people do not *feel* like the name they are known by. Names are important, he thought, you must choose a name you feel comfortable with, a true name that fits the nature of your being. We name our children and know it will remain, only until the child chooses his own. To expect otherwise is to deny the child its freedom to choose, names are like colours, suited to some, unsuited to others.

His heartbeat increased. He breathed deep, filling his lungs with air and — awoke.

Dew lay heavy on stem and leaf of the tall grass. Drops of moisture sparking like eyes, all a glimmer with sunburst flames. His stirring body revelled in the cool, damp feel of it all. His nose inhaled its fragrance, heady it was, like the exotic perfume of white flowers that grow during the season of the Strawberry Moon.

Sunlight flared, a scattering fire of orange and gold and dusty pink. It reminded him of the way a shaft of falling sunlight burns, when it passes through a spider's web all ringed and spangled with shivering drops of dew. He filled his lungs with cool, sweet air, swelling his chest, easing muscles, stiff and achy from holding an unmoving position for so long.

Celtic Sunset

Slowly, tentatively, he craned his head round against protesting neck muscles, until he could see the Black Hills rearing up behind the village, outlined against the clear, pale blue sky of dawn. The sacred Black Hills of the Sioux. Satisfied, he faced forward and slowly, carefully pushed himself up onto his feet. He swayed giddily for a moment, and then, as his head began to clear, he raised his arms above his head. 'I embrace the sky,' he whispered in a dry, cracked voice, 'and the earth and all that lies in between.' He looked towards the west, 'One day you will come, until then, I am content to wait.' He lowered his arms, turned, and walked slowly towards the village with a firm sure tread.

Around the outer edge of the village a silent crowd had gathered. There was something of wonder about all their faces and a touch of awe behind their eyes.

Counting Wolf sat alone in his lodge feeling well pleased. 'He has returned,' he thought, 'and alone, bringing no stranger with him.' Counting Wolf chuckled quietly to himself and said aloud, 'I am no longer a worried man.'

White Owl, prophet he was, and warrior too.

The waiting Sioux applauded his return politely. White Owl smiled, there bright, beaming faces said everything, there was no need for words. It was enough.

Weak he was, from lack of food and water. Even so, he walked unaided, tall and proud through the admiring throng gathered about him. Laughing and smiling, the crowd followed him to his lodge. Before he entered, he turned and said in a loud carrying voice, 'I am White Owl, prophet, warrior and seer.' He gestured towards the Black Hills. 'These hills are sacred to us now, they are given into our care. One day,' he continued, 'a stranger will come amongst us, an old one of wisdom. His people are dead, only he remains. He will live with us and become one and part of the Sioux. He will be honoured amongst all the tribes, even those who are our enemies.'

The crowd gasped in amazement at this. The sound of their voices hoo hooing around the camp.

Inside his lodge, Counting Wolf heard the gasp of wonder and smiled. Everything was exactly as it should be.

White Owl said, 'All that I have told you,' he paused dramatically, allowing tension to build, 'The *Invisibles* told to me, therefore it is.'

The crowd fell silent, no one raised their voice in dissent. The whole tribe recognised that now White Owl was *Cante Tinza,* a Brave Heart, and *Wapiya,* a sacred man, seer and *Wakanhca,* a philosopher. That he had touched, or drawn close to *Wahupa,* realisation of the ultimate enlightenment, they didn't doubt. Awed by his attainments, the crowd began to silently drift away.

$$\Psi$$

CELTIC SUNSET

Chapter Nine

What is the colour of God?
I cannot say
I have not seen his face, therefore I do not know
Choose
God is all colours to all men, therefore I cannot choose
Choose
If so I must, then
The colour of God is blue
Blue is the colour of God
Choose
I have chosen
Then follow

Chant   *Praise the Maker*
Beneath a clear white light
all Praise the Maker

from the Choice of Thomas
Circa 7,000 BC

Roy Edwards

It was hot, very hot.

Wispy bits of fluffy white cloud drifted across the face of a brass and blue sky.

The sun, a pulsing disc of molten copper.

The air dusty and heavy with heat.

A shallow breath of wind touched my face, cooling it was, if only fleetingly.

Trees and water, grasslands, dim winding trails, vistas of a kind of rugged grandeur I had not seen before, beautiful. The soul of the land breathing, seeping deep within me. Where now the Arverni, where now my people? Will Caesar's dark infamy ever be known? Who is there left to speak of it? Rome certainly will not. And I, in this far land, what use now my passionate denial of Rome's tardy accomplishment. The healing of my spirit has not rid me of the thought of Rome's insensate, profligate waste of human life, as though it were of no account, and Romans be all that is bright and worthy of life within the firmament of the universe. Offal they be, and when they fall, then shall they rue their willing acceptance of Gaunt Man — Crom Cruach, Bowed One of the Mound, who is Baal, Prince of Flies, and Molekh, devourer of children. The one of dark aspect does not walk here, in this new land. Perhaps he never will, though I do not think so. Soon or late he walks every land.

I wandered the land.

Striding long and easy, lazily walking the yellow sun down.

I had been travelling in a rough south east direction before I turned inland, towards the west. I avoided most settlements, swinging wide around them, except for now and again when I stood in need of something.

370

Celtic Sunset

Passing through the land of the mound builders, I wandered into a large village and, traded for a bit of flour and a bite of something to eat that I hadn't cooked myself.

The mound builders, were a fine people. Well mannered and friendly. Tall they were, though slim of build. Their women handsome and regal, with a straight back way of walking about them.

I stayed in their village for a few days, resting and attempting to master their language, of which I already knew a few words, thanks to Adwin.

Mound builders they are, Hopewellians, and though I was too well mannered to say so, I thought they had copied many of our Celtic ways almost to perfection. Fine craftsmen they are, though they work only with soft metals. Not yet riddling the way of mixing tin with copper to produce bronze. Some few of the Elders could read and write Punic script, having picked it up from the coastal traders who visited their settlements three times in a single year. The Hopewellians would eventually be pushed out of their lands by invaders from the north, wandering, a broken people remembered only for the mounds they left behind.

The tribes of this broad land were not as ruthlessly savage as I had been led to believe. Indeed, though I avoided settlements, I knew my wonderings were observed by hidden eyes, whose owners bothered me not at all. I was told it would not be so, out upon the great plains.

I hunted, walked and slept. As the long days grew short and then long again, I slowly came to know and recognise the land and the way of its breathing. I soared within my house and blessed the *Maker's* wisdom and the scope of his vision.

It was good to be alone.

To walk the land in silence.

To think upon many things.

Of the mystery of the flute playing I sometimes heard drifting on the wind. This land is old I think, very old and guards its secrets well. And who or what were the Dreadful People? The ones the Hopewellians said came from the south, from behind the sun, and who were the mysterious people of the city that has fallen. All I could learn, was that the ruined city lay in a desert somewhere south west of the plains of grass.

One young Hopewellian had shown me a coin. It was a Roman coin of silver. Astounded and just a little uneasy, I asked him where he had found it. He said he had gotten it in trade at the settlements during the Moon of Windy Rain. The traders killed them all he said, the ones who brought these round silvers. The traders killed them and burnt their long ship so that no trace of them remained. 'And that,' I thought with a shiver, 'is one Roman expeditionary force the less. Like Hibernia, they will not come again.'

The same fate would befall a second expeditionary force of Romans along the coast of the Gulf of Mexico. Around AD180 Rome's greatness had begun to tarnish like old unpolished silver. It coincided with a dramatic decline in sea voyages by seafaring nations. Armies of City States had begun to move and growl, marching through north Africa, scooping up what Rome could no longer defend. Ships sailed from their home ports and did not return. Like the Veneti before them there was nothing to return to. Eventually, no more ships sailed to the Americas. Those who remained, Libyans, Men of Tarshish, Celtiberians, Egyptians, Carthaginians and others, gradually merged, married, or were adopted into various tribes. Some few of them, hardy adventurous explorers, trekked the length of America and deep into Canada, where they settled and lived out their lives amongst a tribe of Indians, whose language, to this day, contains Egyptian and Semitic words.

How swiftly we forget.

How swiftly we forget and lose what once was common to all. The ability to read and write winked out amongst the tribes like a snuffed out candle, along with imported building and farming techniques. Within the space of two centuries it was as though the long years of foreign settlement and trading had never been. Though it is true, many ruins and bits and pieces of inscribed stones and statues remain.

Looking back now, it is hard to describe my wonder of the New Land, and that strangest of strange days when I came across a ruined wall where no wall should be. The wall reminded me of something Adwin had said concerning the Norittes, who, he said, had sailed to the New Land after they had been driven out of their own. When they reached these shores, they destroyed their ships, and marched out into the desert lands. Where they travelled, or what they might have built, no one knows? Did they die of thirst and hunger, or did they in time become another tribe of Indians whose name is lost to us now?

Who are the Dreadful People? Why are they dreadful? Where did they come from? What kind of faces do they wear? In later years I came to learn the truth of the Dreadful People, but that is far away and yet to come. Though it is in my mind to speak now, at least of where it is the dreadfuls came from.

Much of what I know came from the mouth of a captive, who spoke freely in return for my promise of a quick death. That he would die was certain, it was the manner of his death that worried him. I would not, of course, allow any of these people to live, else they taint others with their soul sickness. In sadness did I think that Gaunt Man — Crom Cruach, Bowed One of the Mound had come all too soon to this distant land of broad horizons. True, his shadow as yet, stained only the hot, distant south land. But he was here, and I had thought to have left him far behind, at least for a space of years. Druid I was, I should have known better. Though it is true for me to say that I became less of a Druid with each passing day and more like a holy one of the Human Beings, the Sioux.

Sometimes I think the weight of one life carries on into the next. What then, I wondered, would become of the Dreadful People? What else was there, that could be less than what they already are? Spirit sold, chained and shivering against a wall of cruel deceit, born out of the mouth of darkness. The people of the ball court sacrifice be guilty of a minor corrupt evil in comparison.

Could I be wrong? Was I wrong? What is evil? What is good? I rely for my interpretation of it all on one concept, one basic Druidical law. That is, to maintain a true and constant fidelity of being, not to any one god, but to self. To sacrifice and kill, to appease, to honour another, to kill in his name. Whose name if it not be yours? To whom do you offer human sacrifice if not to self? Who deceives you, if not yourself? Who is there to blame other than self, when, upon the last day of forever, you stand naked, stripped of all pretension upon the judgement stone? We of Druid know of these things. There is a price to pay, there is always a price to be paid for your actions, and the judgement of it all is as inevitable as the rising of the sun.

To me, the Dreadful People are a terrible darkness, who can no longer be allowed to wander outside the confines of there own land. I tell you true, where so ever I find them, I will kill them upon that instant. Even though I am aware that

Celtic Sunset

I must pay a price for their deaths when I stand upon the judgement stone.

The Dreadful People, descendants of Babylonian sea explorers from the time of Nebuchadnezzar. Amulk it was, who led his party ashore, and with force of arms subjugated the areas primitive tribes.

Amulk declared himself king, supported by Naamuk, a minor Captain of guard.

Using slave labour, Amulk built a great city of stone, erecting a towering Ziggurat to mark its centre. He declared himself to be the mouthpiece of the gods and demanded that the natives kneel down and worship him. Taking 365 native women to wife he began to sire children. His first son was born during the second year of his reign. To celebrate the birth of his first born Amulk demanded human sacrifice.

It was he, who tore out the first heart from a living victim, seared the heart in flames and consumed it. The body was then hacked into joints. The pieces cooked and eaten by all who attended the birth feast, to refuse to eat a portion, was to die. No one refused.

The following year Amulk declared that the gods had spoken to him, demanding that human sacrifice be offered up to honour them, one victim for each day of the year. The great sacrifice to be held annually, upon the first day of the fifth month. The flesh of the victims to be cooked and consumed by all who lived within the city and thereby enjoyed the god's providence.

The victims of course were always primitives, never city dwellers. Eventually, the Dreadful People wiped out the surrounding tribes and had need to travel far in search of new victims.

Soldiers of the city began to raid deep into the Indian lands. It was at that point that I became so enraged, I hacked off the captives head and threw it in the shit pit, shouting *Avada Ke Davra*, may the thing be destroyed. White Owl nodded his approval.

Days poured down into a sieve of seasons.
The body of me lean and hard with the walking.
I gave no thought to Beltain or Samhain or any rites in between.
There was warmth and there was cold.
There was hunger and thirst and seasons of plenty.
It was enough.
I had reduced my needs down to the essential basics of clothing, food and shelter.
Balanced, I was, and humming inside my head.
My life had become a song.
And then, one day I stood on the edge of a great plain bathed in the gory light of a swollen blood red sun. I knew then, that soon my journey would end and a new journey would begin.
Any thought of destiny had long ago fled from my head.

The tall grass of the plain, rippled before the wind like waves on the ocean.
There was game and water and patterns of sunlight.
I lay awake long into the night, staring up at stars so thickly clustered, there scarce seemed room enough for the sky between them. Sometimes I listened to the howl of wolves, or the quiet beating of my heart.
One morning I awoke to find myself surrounded by warriors.

Six warriors sat on their haunches forming a circle around me. They seemed to regard me with a quiet, inner amusement.

So deep had I slept, I hadn't even sensed their approach, that annoyed me, though of course, I didn't let it show.

These were a different kind of Indian to any I had met before. Fierce eyed, lean and hard with a look of savage competence about them. Armed they were with bow and arrows, knife and club, each man also carried a long, deadly looking lance, adorned with feathers about the shank of the spear head.

Six pairs of dark eyes regarded me in silence.

Slowly, carefully, I rose to my feet and buckled my weapons about me, allowing my right hand to rest lightly on the hilt of my sword.

I think the height of me surprised them. With exaggerated care, I bent down and added sticks and bits of dry grass to my smouldering fire, blowing on the embers to ignite it.

Taking some strips of meat from my pack I skewered them on sticks and broiled them over the flames.

No one moved or spoke.

When the meat was done, I handed it to a warrior close by me. I cooked more and passed it round and then cooked some for my self. I offered them water from my skin. If they were going to attack, I reasoned, they would have done so by now. I had yet to learn how notional Indians can be.

Suddenly one warrior said, 'Sleeps well,'

Another said, 'It has something to do with his height, I think,'

They all chuckled softly.

I smiled, more from the fact that I could understand them, than from anything else. Again I stood, this time unsheathing my sword in one fluid motion.

They were on their feet instantly, lances levelled at my heart and throat.

'Easy,' I said softly, 'I simply show peaceful intent, and lay my sword down, near my feet.'

Six lances lowered. One who seemed to be the leader, said, 'You show courage. We could have killed you.'

I said, 'No, you only think you could have killed me.'

The leader eyed me in silence, and then, driving his lance into the earth, he stepped forward and said, 'we fight, bare hands, for sport, for fun.'

'He's testing me,' I thought, 'to find out if I'm windy words or something else.'

'No,' I answered, 'not you alone.' I gestured towards the others, 'All six of you, or none at all.'

His warriors gave whoops of delight and quickly lay their weapons down, and then, without warning all six swarmed over me.

Towering more than head and shoulders above the tallest, my arms and chest thick with muscle, I moved amongst them like a hungry cat, striking twice with empty hands. Two warriors fell, their breath whooshing out as they hit the ground. Turning, I picked one warrior up and hurled him aside, plucking another from my back as he tried for a strangle hold. Laughing, the remaining two hurled themselves at me. Shrugging them off with easy strength, I stood, hands on hips, grinning at them all.

'Do you want to try again,' I asked?

Their leader, whose name, was Red Cloud, shook his head. We sat down, gathering up our weapons.

'Who are you,' I asked.

'Comanche.'

'Ah,' I breathed out softly, the lance people.

'I have heard of you,' I said. 'You are warriors, everyone says so.'

They all beamed at that.

'And you,' Red Cloud said, 'who are you?'

'I come from a far away land,' I said, 'that lies beyond the great ocean.'

A subtle change came over the Comanche.

Red Cloud said, 'You come from the west.'

'Yes,' I replied.

They looked at one another uneasily, avoiding my eyes.

'You are the last of your kind?' asked Red Cloud.

Caesar had hunted all of Druid kind ruthlessly, I might very well be the last. Certainly I was the last of all the Druids of the Arverni.

'Yes,' I said.

'Hieee,' the Comanche chanted. They looked shocked, the way someone does when they unknowingly offend another. The Comanche rose to their feet and moved a few paces away from me. I stood up slowly, unsure of what had happened to suddenly change their mood.

Red Cloud said, a question in his voice, 'You are an old one?'

I thought carefully, unsure of his meaning. Feeling my way, I said, 'Once I was a holy man of my people, now it is that my people are no more. Our wisdom is old, it sits inside my head.'

No one spoke.

I took a deep breath and said, 'We fought those who came to kill us, but their numbers were uncountable, like the stars. My people fought and died, now it is that only I remain to honour their memory.'

Still no one spoke. I looked at them, each in turn and said, 'I come here in search of *one who waits*. Who he is, I do not know. Where he is, I do not know. I know only that he is aware of my presence, and that now and again he calls to me in my dreams, so that I might know in which direction to travel.'

The Comanche expelled their breath in a soft whoosh of surprise and wonder. Red Cloud stepped close towards me, his back straight, his face grave and unsmiling. He placed his right hand over his heart and said, 'We apologise old one, we did not know who you were. We should have known, the News Criers have spoken of your coming. You are the fulfilment of White Owl's prophecy.' He pointed west, 'Go old one, go in peace, and know always, that you are welcome in the lodge of Red Cloud and in the lodges of all the Comanche. The one you seek is White Owl, he is of the Sioux who are our enemies.' With that he turned and walked away, his warriors following him in a subdued group.

I watched until they were out of sight, then, gathering up my bits and pieces, I headed west.

I crossed the land of the Comanche and entered the lands of the Sioux.

Somewhere far to the south a small army of Dreadful People marched. Frustrated by their lack of success as tribes melted away at their approach.

Moloch was the name of the one who led the army. Of noble birth, as were all those who lived within the city, he knew his life would, none the less, be forfeit if he returned with less than the required annual quota of 365 sacrificial victims.

It was nearing the end of May, the Moon of Growing Grass. He had less than twelve months to return.

Celtic Sunset

The army of the Dreadful People travelled swiftly, covering up to forty five miles in a single day.

All they found was empty land and deserted villages.

In desperation Moloch turned West. Like all who lived within the city, he claimed divine descent from the god Amulk, who had according to sacred lore, founded the city and given birth to the Amulkittes. It never entered his head to carve out a new life for himself, or simply, to fail to return to the city. Nor did he view the eating of human flesh or the tearing out of living hearts, as anything other than the natural order of things. After all, primitives were beasts like any other beasts of the field. That is what they were there for, to be sacrificed and eaten. That was their sole function in life and like all beasts, you had to hunt them down.

Moloch had command of an army of 2,000 hand picked fighting men.

Evening sunlight slid down the cheeks of the darkening sky, like god's molten tears. The heart of me moved strangely from the grand sight of it all — and — from what stood before me bathed in slanted rays of light.

Ψ

Behind me the sun went down in a blaze of red and gold fire, long shadows crept over the land. In the distance, I could see a hazy hump of hills thrusting up against an indigo sky.

Directly in front of me stood a middle sized man with good shoulders and a broad scarred chest. His dark intense eyes radiated welcome, his long black hair was unbound. A small wind streamed it out behind him, like a ragged flag. There was something about him, an inner calm and strength, that separated him from other men. He reminded me of my old friend and mentor Cumall.

He was, I realised, both holy man and chief, what else he might be I had yet to learn.

White Owl stood in front of a huge silent crowd.

I didn't know it then, but the whole village had turned out to witness the arrival of the stranger, the old one. A roving scout had spotted me out on the long grass. The same scout had also witnessed my meeting with Red Cloud and his band. He had seen Red Cloud talking to me holding his hand over his heart, which means, I speak only truth, or, I am of peaceful intent.

Standing in front of White Owl I said, 'You are *He who waits.*'

'The Invisibles foretold your coming,' he smiled, 'now I am no longer *He who waits*. It is good,' he added, 'that you can speak our tongue.'

I smiled at that, and then, before I could reply, a young boy broke away from his mother, dodged around White Owl and wrapped his arms around my legs.'

Indians, I came to learn, love children and are very tolerant of their behaviour. Even so, a collective gasp of dismay went up from the crowd. They already thought of me as a *Wapiya*, a sacred man, seer and healer and therefore unless invited, untouchable.

Bending down, I picked the young boy up, and then on impulse, raised him above my head to the full extent of my arms. The young boy shrieked with delight. Stretching his short chubby arms up towards the sky, he began chanting, 'Touch the clouds, touch the clouds.'

I laughed and kissed his cheek, before setting him down.

The crowd were delighted by all this and clapped their approval.

'He names you well,' White Owl said.

I didn't know it then, but the height and breadth of me amazed them all.

'My name is Culann.'

White Owl savoured the sound of it and then with a grin said, 'Coollaan, Touch the Clouds.'

He turned, parting the crowd, and led me to his lodge.

From that day forth, the Sioux accepted me as one of their own. A Human Being, a Sioux. I had, they loved to inform me, always been a Sioux, and then for a little while, was something else. Now you are Sioux again. Now you are exactly where you should be, Culann, Touch the Clouds.

Before the Moon of Yellow Ripeness swallowed itself, I could not imagine myself anywhere else.

Ψ

During the Season of Cold Moons, White Owl began to share his knowledge with me, and I shared with him the way of Druid.

How similar they are and yet, in small ways, hauntingly strange and different. We gained much from each other, and would continue to do so, until our houses of flesh could breathe no more.

It was a known and accepted thing that as a returned old one, I could move freely about the tribes. From the Comanche to the Pawnee, to the Crow and the Cheyenne. I was a sacred man, a seer and healer.

I began to try my hand at making a crude form of papyrus. The idea in my head was that one day I would have need of it.

I began to teach White Owl Greek and Latin.

Now that I am familiar with the seven virtues and the way of the warrior, I sometimes wonder if the Sioux might not be descendants of some forgotten Celtic tribe, so closely related are their warrior ways to the way of the Celtic warrior.

During the Cold Moon of Popping Trees, I handed over to White Owl the Book of Druid Lore. He said, a secret place had already been prepared, and he its guardian, foretold by the Invisibles.

A sending, bitter and awful, came to me during the Moon of Drifting Snow. Beware the Dreadful People, and something else, something I could not quite define. It worried me.

Celtic Sunset

I honed my weapons and began to practice the sword dance.

During the Moon of Snow Melts, I began to run, increasing the distance a little more each day. I used heavy stones, lifting them above my head. Down and up, again and again, thereby increasing my already considerable strength.

Sendings come and go. Some are clear, most are vague, shadowy things, often, little more than a feeling. And the feeling I had, was that one day soon, I would have need of all my strength, my fighting skills and my ability to run over a long distance.

Ψ

I spoke of my feelings to White Owl, and my sense of the Dreadful's approach.

He was astonished to hear that they came this way, whilst admitting, that he too had once been warned of the Dreadful People. It was during a visit to the Hall of Sunset, he said.

White Owl has shown me a secret cave deep within the Black Hills. It is agreed that my house will lay there, when I am no longer a tenant of its flesh. The cave is well hidden and will remain so. I do not know where the Druid book has been placed, only that it is somewhere, safe within the Black Hills. It will be found, when it chooses to be found. There is no need to know more, the book is safe, and I am content that it should remain so. It crossed my mind to ask White Owl, if he knew anything concerning the Eagle Warrior, I will ask him soon, I think.

The Dreadful People draw close, I can feel them, sense them. The darkness of their spirit shivers me through, the breath of their rotting guts fouls the air. They are an abomination. I will kill them, no mercy, not ever. They be a foulness from out the arse end of Gaunt Man — Crom Cruach, Bowed One of the Mound. Like vomit they are, the out step of being.

Ψ

Celtic Sunset

Moloch brooded the cold winter down.

Bitter winds faltered, and then blew a warming breath.

Sunlight thickened, hazing the air with droplets of moisture sucked up from the Earth's cold outer skin.

Warm winds blew.

The Amulkittes marched.

Moloch of the Amulkittes had failed.

He brooded through the winter, failure gnawed his bones. He was doomed, his life forfeit. Death would be the chant when he returned. Sixty thousand voices chanting 'Death to Moloch the failure, death, death, death.'

He could hear it now. The thunder of it all deafening, unless, unless he could think of some way to appease Amulk, the god, and the fury of his priests. He thought upon it through long, cold sleepless nights.

It came to him upon the breath of spring. He rejoiced, in his heart and in his head. The solution to his dilemma was truly a gift from Amulk himself. Having failed to return in time for the annual sacrifice he now had about twelve months to redeem himself and return.

The only way he could do this was by offering up to Amulk, not one year's quota of sacrifices but three year's. The entire thousand and ninety five to be sacrificed in a single day.

His heart leapt at the thought of such a magnificent spectacle. There would be a feasting on human flesh, the like of which the city had never seen before. 'Magnificent,' he breathed, 'it would be magnificent. He, Moloch, would be remembered for ever, as the greatest procurer of sacrificial beasts in the entire history of the city.'

He almost wept for joy, at the thought of such a grand, awe inspiring spectacle of sacrifice, and only he, Moloch, could provide it. The simple beauty of it all, was that he knew where to find the sacrificial human beasts. He began to think that Amulk had planned this to happen all along. Enticing him away from the south lands so that he might better fulfil god's grand design.

The divine plan was beautiful, beautiful, and he, Moloch, had been chosen to carry it out.

'Truly, I am blest,' he thought within the core of his unquiet soul. 'I will give unto thee, living hearts, blood and a banquet of human flesh, enough to sate the most gargantuan appetites.

Moloch fell down upon his knees, and in a shaking voice full of love and devotion, he thanked his compassionate bountiful god, with the joyous flowing tears of the truly repentant. Oh, how he wept. Still weeping, he said to his soldiers, Amulk, our god, in his love, hath given us chance to redeem ourselves.'

Moloch, like many other field commanders of the city had heard of the Plains tribes, of their numbers and way of life, but the distance was great and no one had yet attempted to capture the beasts, and herd them back to the city.

Moloch would be the first to do so. His fame was assured, his place in the history of the city secured. Religious ecstasy filled him with orgiastic lust.

All he had to do, was succeed. How could he fail, god sanctioned his holy quest. In his name he would hunt the beasts down.

For an intelligent man, Moloch was at times incredibly stupid. Like others before and after his time, his intelligence was buried beneath a weight of religious fervour, a blinding light of dogmatic unreasoning zeal. His faith was his ecstasy. And are we not all blind in some unreasoning way, be it secular, theological, inspired by theomancy or otherwise, there is a blindness to us all that can ever reduce the most intelligent of men, to no more than articulate mental cripples.

Indoctrinated since birth, in the way of worship of the dreadful god Amulk, Moloch was a product of priestly teachings. Redemption, salvation, sainthood, all lay within reach of his charnel hands.

All he had to do was round up human beasts, herd them back to the city, kill, roast and eat their flesh, all in the name of his god, who once was a man. I love thee, he prayed, I worship and adore thee, blessed be thy name — Amulk — Adonai most high. I praise thee, I adore thee. I Give thanks unto thee and all those who wear thy sacred Robe of Blood. Blessed by thy name — AMULK — ADONAI — MOST HIGH.

Moloch led his army west, in a punishing race to overrun tribes before they could flee.

Here and there his pounding army ran down small primitive bands of nomadic hunter gatherers, who had not yet mastered the art of bow or lance making.

The Amulkittes killed and ate them, greedily roasting their flesh over small hastily prepared fires. Eating, sleeping for awhile and then on. Running towards a confrontation they could not even begin to guess at.

Human beasts don't fight, they run, they do not know how to fight. That is what the Amulkittes believed, what there scholars believed and taught in schools from the narrow, short sighted, arrogance of their not inconsiderable intellects.

They had mapped the stars, built a huge complex city of stone. They were masters of science and medicine, art and roads, and wrote upon thin sheets of wood that were made into books.

Roy Edwards

Of course they were right, Amulk had said so, when he came down from the stars, falling through heaven, to show them the way.

They were the Dreadful People. Purveyors of an ancient, wandering Darkness that chanced upon the earth in company with his brother Light.

Cool it was, and dim, within White Owl's lodge.

'They are close,' I said, soft voiced, 'very close.'

It was the Moon of Black Cherries. Long, hot lazy days and short cool nights. Winds blew across the plains, bending the long grass. Drenched in moonlight the singing grass became waves of rippling silver.

Waiting we were. Scouts searched the land, none had yet returned.

The People were aware that danger approached and moved about the camp in a quiet, alert manner. Every able bodied warrior carried a weapon. I told the village Elders that I had seen the Dreadfuls approach in a vision. It simply confirmed what they already claimed me to be, Wapiya, a sacred man, an old one returned. Of course, I did nothing to discourage such thinking. The Sioux were my people now, our fates irrevocably joined for good or ill, they were my Arverni. And like the Arverni, the Celts, they considered everyday to be a holy day. Not like some of the sun worshippers, I had met beyond the sea, who worshipped their god only one day out of seven, and called that day of worship, the Sun Day, or Day of the Sun.

The Sioux, as did all the tribes, bathed in the morning, so that they might greet the new day and the presence of the great spirit, clean in body as well as in mind. They recognised the sacredness of earth, and that we do not own it. We only borrow from it, taking only what is needed, anything more is avarice, a vice unbefitting a true man, a human being.

The earth sings to those who listen, and sometimes you can feel its heart beat beneath your feet. The perfect way of the Sioux is an equal balance of spirit, through mind, to body and earth. They are the Four Sacreds, and that is why Four is a sacred number. The three that are one, work and live in complete and utter harmony with the one (Earth) that is complete. The *One* sustains and provides the bodies needs, so that the spirit has somewhere to stay on its journey, along the spirit trail.

The tribes are aware of the close relationship of spirit working through mind, to reach the body and the earth beneath. When we dig for edible roots we only make a small wound, and fill it in carefully as we go, we never take everything. During the Moon of Ripe Berries we always leave something, we never take all the fish from the stream, or eggs from the nest. For us there will never be a last buffalo, we never kill or take the last of anything. We do not cut down trees to burn them, we burn only what the earth no longer has need of. The earth is a blessing given into our care by the great spirit, Wakantanka, the undiscovered law. We use and treat the earth with respect, lest it be taken from us, and given into the care of others who yet dwell beyond the earth, on the other side. If the earth were taken from us, we would have nowhere to go. No place to return to when flesh has died and a house is sought whilst we journey on, towards our purity and eventual un-need of houses of flesh.

White Owl spoke much of such things, and said he thought the Celts, of whom I spoke, must surely be related if only in spirit, to the Indian nations. How else, he said, to explain our two wisdoms, born so far apart, yet so familiar, one unto the other. It is a mystery tall friend, a great mystery. Whenever he spoke thus, I recognised the *Maker* Wakantanka.

Here in this vast, unspoiled land of contrasts we live close to his breath. His weave, and the pattern of it all so obviously evident, there be no need at all to be speaking of it. We are the *Wanisugna* a creative force, upon the land, I'm thinking.

White Owl spoke, his voice soft, insistent, the sound of it tugging me back from memory walking. I looked at him inquiringly. 'Something is wrong,' he said. His dark eyes mirrored his concern, 'I can feel it in my bones and my flesh. The scouts have not returned, they should have returned yesterday. They did not. They should have returned today. They are not here. They will not come tomorrow or the day after that.' His voice dropped to a whisper, 'They will not come at all. Something is wrong, Culann Touch the Clouds, something is very wrong. It worries me, and I have never been an overly worried man before.'

We looked at each other through the dim light permeating his lodge. He expected me to do something, and so I would. 'Prepare the sacred lodge,' I told him, 'this night, I spirit walk.'

The rituals of spirit walking do not invoke magic, they calm and cleanse the body, easing away burdens, so that nothing remains that might restrict sight or inhibit the spirit its leaving. Also, I enjoy performing the rituals, if only for the sake of their pleasantness.

The whole tribe gathered around the sacred lodge.

What I was about to do, was for *The People*, its outcome affecting everyone. Whilst I remained inside the sacred lodge, the whole of *The People* stood guard over my flesh.

Celtic Sunset

I danced my intricate own Druid's dance, around a small ceremonial fire of aromatic leaves, grasses, and sweet berry wood. I inhaled the smoke, wafting it into my face with an eagle's tail feather. I danced and sang a tumbling song of flowing streams. I had not the time to sweat myself. 'Let it be enough,' I whispered into the silent falling night. A small breeze whisper licked against my skin, its fingers dancing across my naked chest. I breathed deep of the night, and listened to its whispering song and the sigh of the long grass bending before its breath.

The dance carried me away, and away, and away. Beware when you dance the sacred dance, and sing the song of streams, lest you dance yourself away, knowing not the dance and song of returning. I spiralled beneath the surface of my flesh. Soon I would pour through and drift away, wheresoever I willed.

I entered the sacred lodge, fastening the flap behind me. Turning towards a thick pile of soft hides, I lay down and closed my eyes.

The plain stretched out beneath me, I was here and yet not here, its features both familiar and strange. A ripe yellow, falling down moon sat a hands breadth above the distant horizon's rim. I could see the tall grass bending before a night wind even though I could not feel its breath.

It was wonderful.

The ultimate freedom, only those who leave their bodies and return, can appreciate.

Even so, there is danger. There is always danger.

Some who go, do not want to return, and only a true caller can reach out, and persuade them otherwise. Some get lost. Some cannot see or hear or sense anything at all and spiral down into panic. Some are seduced away by the siren's song of the universe in hopes of finding the beginning, the source of all its singing. Some are overwhelmed by loneliness, and the lack of sight of others of like kind.

How small we are, how few, in all the vastness of the universe. Though it be true there is a beginning, it be equally true that as yet there is no end. Being Druid, I know of these things. Whilst I am tenant of a house of flesh, I keep my outbody journeys short.

I sensed it then. A dark awfulness, emanating from something foul and unclean. Thoughts are energies, pulsating, radiating out like ripples.

I flow without movement.

There. A cloud, dark dusty particles floating, drifting up and out, spreading like vomit across the land, tainting, turning, twisting, pervading.

Those who cannot see, do not believe, or want to believe, how easily the dark, bitter, twisted thoughts of a selfish few, can affect the clear thinking of many.

I can see it, therefore, I know. Sad it is so few do not. We of Druid have always known, you negate the power of prayer, of positive thought at your peril. Traps there be, waiting for such *unwaries*.

Above the stain. Counting, seeing, returning.

I awoke drenched in sweat, my limbs trembling, jerking in agonising spasms. That familiar, awful sensation, of falling from a great height, fading as I gulped air, deep breathing to calm my body's agitation.

Moments, heartbeats, light seeping in, around the edges of the entrance flap. Still, warm moist air filled the lodge. Outside, I could hear a soft murmur of voices. 'Calm, safe, free, I embrace life,' I thought lucidly, 'life and freedom. I am exactly where I should be. I can be nowhere else. Calm, safe, calm, safe,' I intoned. Suddenly my guts growled. Hungry I was, and thirsty too. The throat of me parched and dry rasping.

Rising, I opened the flap and stepped out into a morning full of sunshine and polite murmurs of welcome.

I sat opposite White Owl, outside his lodge, eating meat, drinking water. The tribe slowly gathered in silent ranks around us.

Whatever I had to say would be heard by all. The danger was too near for it to be otherwise. Hunger and thirst satisfied, I wiped my mouth and said to White Owl, 'They are a *darkness* upon the land.'

'Aiee,' intoned White Owl softly, 'they are the Dreadful People.'

I spoke calmly sure of my intent. 'We cannot allow them to live. Not one must escape, else he returns to his city and leads a great army against us.' I bent forward to emphasise my words. 'We must wipe them out so that no trace of them remains. Nothing they own must be taken. No bit of cloth, no weapons, no jewellery, nothing. Everything must vanish, every body and every single thing. And the earth beneath which they shall lie, will be a place of uneasy spirits — forever.'

I said, 'We cannot do it alone.' I looked round at the gathered crowd, my voice including them all in my address. 'Their numbers are too many.'

'How many is too many,' asked White Owl?

'About twenty counts of one hundred,' I replied.

White Owl looked appalled, 'So many,' he whispered.

The People groaned in dismay.

I held my hand up signalling quiet.

'Be calm,' I spoke loudly, so that all could hear. 'I know a way.'

White Owl jumped to his feet. 'Then speak,' he cried harshly.

I smiled grimly. 'There are many tribes of Sioux, but only one is here, beneath the shadow of the Black Hills. In this tribe there be four hundred warriors. It is not enough.' I paused, then said, 'The Comanche are your enemies.' Silence. 'The Pawnee are your enemies and the Crow are your enemies. You must surely be great warriors,' I added, 'to have so many enemies.'

The crowd chuckled at that and smiled at each other.

'I am Sioux,' I continued, 'everyone says so. You are my people.' Every eye was upon me now. 'I am the sacred man, the old one returned, for whom you waited. Only I, can walk in safety amongst all our enemies. Only I, can ask of them knowing they will not refuse. I am Culann Touch the Clouds, a free person of the Sioux.' My voice rang out deep and clear. 'All the tribes know of me. I am as sacred to them as I am to you. They have named me. I have stayed in their lodge, an honoured guest. I have sat and talked with their Chiefs. Red Cloud of the Comanche calls me brother, as does Black Hawk of the Pawnee, Dull knife of the Cheyenne, Stone Wolf of the Crow.'

'Listen then, the Comanche have not yet broken their Warm Moons camp.'

'I will go to the Comanche.'

No one spoke.

'They be your enemy, but in this one thing you shall fight together. When the fight has been won, then let them be your enemies again.'

A few faces smiled at that.

Celtic Sunset

'It is the only way, else we all perish, if we fight alone, we die alone, and next year the Dreadfuls will return. They will keep on coming until there are no more plains tribes left,' my voice thundered. 'I have spoken, therefore it is, unless there be one amongst you who claims it is not so.'

Before anyone could speak, White Owl turned to me and said, 'Tell us what you want us to do.'

'You,' I pointed at White Owl, 'must lead our warriors to *the hill that stands alone*.' It was a small squat hill a full days run, away to the north of the Black Hills. It was an oddity all the tribes were familiar with, rising up from the plain like a mound. Round with sloping sides. it stood alone with not another hill in sight. A few trees grew around its base in scattered ones and twos, fed by a small stream that flowed from a spring, bubbling up from the ground, within a jumble of boulders and broken rock.

'You must leave tomorrow, at dawn. Take my long blade with you. Today, I will go to the camp of the Comanche. In three days,' I said loudly, 'counting today, the Dreadful People will be at *the hill that stands alone* and we my people, will be waiting. The Comanche will come. They will aid us in this one thing. I have said it will be so, therefore it is.' I turned away then, motioning White Owl to follow me.

'I must prepare. Will you help, I asked him?'

The Sioux would do what I asked. If I could not bring the Comanche to *the hill that stands alone* we would all die.

Ψ

397

'It is a long run,' said White Owl.

'It is a thing to be done and I will do it.'

I sat in the lodge of White Owl painting my face for war.

White Owl's two young daughters, Hands On Hips and Laughs A Lot giggled as they tied four eagle feathers in my hair. They wanted me to let them braid it, but I insisted it be left unbound.

'Let our enemies take it if they can,' I told them. 'It is the way of my once people. A warrior wears his hair long and unbound, a challenge to his enemies.'

'It is more than one hundred miles,' said White Owl.

I looked at him and placed a hand on his shoulder. 'Do not worry my friend. It is a thing that must be done. I will do it. I have said so, therefore I will and there's an end to it. Now, carry my long blade to the hill, I run light, and I'll be needing it when I meet you,' I grinned at him and stepping out of his lodge, I jogged through the camp without a backward glance.

Grim, silent faces stared at me as I passed. Stripped to the waist, I wore only a breechclout and hard running moccasins on my feet, replacements tied around my neck.

The Sioux had placed their lives in my hands. The lives of wives and husbands and Elders, sons and daughters. 'I will not fail you,' I breathed, 'I will not fail or desert you *not now not ever* this I do promise.'

I ran.

Pounding the long grass down.

The prairie stretched out wide and empty.

The sky a hot blue shimmer above me.

I ran wide and easy. The long legs of me eating the ground up in a loping wolf run.

Celtic Sunset

Between dripping sweat and thudding heartbeats, I found my rhythm and the way of its breathing, knowing I could keep it up until the heart of me burst.

Like Philippides the Athenian, I thought, though I'd not be trying for his fate. He was an ordinary soldier of Athens. The whole bright host of them marching out to Marathon to fight the Persians. Miltades had command and it was he, who in a casual sort of way said to Philippides. I'd like you to run to Sparta and tell them we need their help to fight the Persians, and run he did. All 130 miles of it in a day and half of a day. the Spartans said yes of course they would come, but not yet. The moon was not yet ready and would not enter its battle phase for five days. They would march but not for five days.

Appalled, Philippides carried the news back to Miltades. He ran the return journey of 130 miles in a day. Fought in the battle of Marathon and then ran 26 miles to Athens. He entered Athens shouting, 'Rejoice, we conquer,' and fell down dead from a burst heart. He ran 260 miles, fought in a battle and then ran a further 26 miles. He is a hero I think. Though men remember only the feat and honour the man, not at all. It is a shame, I'm thinking.

I came in sight of the Comanche village as the Moon of Dusty Trails rose from its bed.

Dogs barked, voices yelled, armed warriors gathered to meet the shadow pounding towards them through a falling drizzle of moonlight.

I breathed easy and began to slow the rhythm of my legs. By the time I reached the gathered warriors, I was walking, deep breathing and trying to smile.

Paint mixed with sweat streaked my face and my chest. I asked for water, someone threw a water skin. I caught it deftly and drank deep, the coolness of it shivering me through.

Red Cloud stepped forward, offering me greeting and a place by his fire.

Grimly I told him of the approaching Dreadful People, the Sioux, and their willingness to stand even though they were vastly outnumbered. I knew that would touch the fighting pride of the Comanche. A sort of, why should the Sioux gain all the honour from fighting a mutual enemy.

'Is there not enough of the enemy to share with the Comanche,' Red Cloud said, a small smile creasing his face.

I said, 'The Dreadfuls number twenty times one hundred.'

The murmur of voices around us fell into silence. Red Cloud's face registered his shock, then he wiped it clean, and said calmly, 'That is a great many,' his was the only voice to be heard in all that gathered silence. I pushed, just a little.

'It is not enough,' I growled. Raising my voice I said it again, louder this time, 'It is not enough. Against the Comanche and the Sioux, IT IS NOT ENOUGH.'

Shouts and yip yip aiees of approval filled the air. Red Cloud said, 'Once,' he held up one finger, his voice rose above the noise, 'once only will we join with the Sioux. Now is that once only time.'

'How many,' I asked him, 'how many warriors can you gather?'

'Seven one hundreds.'

My heart quailed, we would be outnumbered two to one. Well, and had I not, once led two thousand against a legion. I smiled grimly and said, 'It is enough.'

'Now I must go, my people look to me to lead them in this.'

'Of course,' Red Cloud said politely, 'it is expected.' He pushed me gently, 'Go my friend, run like the wind.'

Celtic Sunset

'Follow,' I told him, 'we meet at *the hill that stands alone.* Be there by sunrise of the second day from now, or earlier if you can.' Waving farewell, I jogged out of the village, eating handfuls of boiled grain, a water skin slung across one shoulder.

'Be there,' I breathed silently, 'else we die.'

$$\Psi$$

Roy Edwards

Fine running the wind down, through hollows of moonlight.

A dust of starlight fading into that eerie false light that comes before true dawn.

The blood of me hot flowing through my body.

I had run the night down.

I felt like molten metal beading on the edge of a knife, fine balanced and keening.

The soul of me chuckling through my bones singing deep songs inside my head.

The eyes of me wide and seeing beyond, walking the Hall of Sunset.

I am no longer Druid or Shaman.

I be only *Touch the Clouds Running* and I am exactly where I should be.

Who is there upon all this land who can say he is anywhere else.

Running easy.

The grasslands flowing by beneath my feet.

Freedom.

Sweet red poppy juice in my blood.

Muscles slide and bunch one against the other.

Breathing.

Bellows pumping in out in out.

A weirding breeze of haunts against my face, cooling, gulping air.

Feet, whisper lick across the grass.

I am the wind and the air.

The earth beneath me.

Its beating heart in tune with mine.

Culann Touch the Clouds Running, forever, forever, forever.

Celtic Sunset

Reaching down inside, eyes focus.
A gaunt sky, pale with light, a hill rears up.
Its umber flanks deep scarred by wind and rain.
A scattering of trees.
Rush, swooping towards the hill.
Figures rising up out of the grass.
Voices, distant sounding, echoing inside my head.
Familiar faces, hands reaching out towards me.
Falling, drifting down into darkness.
Glitter sparking stars behind my eyes.
Water, cool, fresh, clean, splashing over my face.
Focus, sensation of falling inside my guts.
Words, words.
'I hear you,' I croaked, 'I hear you. The Comanche will come. Tomorrow, at sunrise.'

White Owl's voice, insistent, demanding my attention. 'The Dreadfuls, they are here, soon, midday, no more, Comanche come too late. Sleep, rest, drink.'

I slept through the morning and awoke feeling refreshed and hungry.

Through mouthfuls of food, I said to White Owl, 'We will hold them here, we must. We have no choice,' I added.

He looked doubtful.

'Do not look so, my friend. I tell you in truth, the Dreadfuls have never faced the like of a Sioux warrior before. All their victories have been against small, unwarlike people. They think us to be no more than beasts easily caught. We will kill them,' I said in a cold voice. 'We will kill them all.' I stared into his eyes, 'We will kill until there are no more to be killed, no captives, no quarter. They are like a deadly infectious disease, if we do not contain it, we die, and,' I added with a savage growl, 'if any surrender, we kill them anyway.'

'Of course,' replied White Owl calmly, 'it is understood.'

I prayed to the *Maker*, that the Comanche be not delayed. If they had started soon after I left their village, they should be here by the time the sun began to go down. I prayed it might be so.

We stood, four hundred strong, with our backs to the hill, facing two thousand armed and seemingly demented men.

They howled at us like beasts. Holding up lengths of rope, shaking them in the air. Surely they could not, I thought in disbelief, expect us to meekly step forward and allow ourselves to be bound and led away to be slaughtered.

That is exactly what Moloch expected us to do. Our warlike behaviour confused him.

Chuckling, I began to enjoy myself. Leaning on the hilt of my sword, I told White Owl to group our warriors together and, on my signal, to loose their arrows in a single volley.

The day was hot and still, the air heavy with heat. The hill glowed a dun colour in the afternoon sun. The hollows of its worn flanks, strewn and shadowy. Banks of white clouds hung above the horizon's rim. The white of them startling against the deep ocean blue of the sky.

I breathed deep, whirling my sword above my head, enjoying the play and feel of my muscles. I felt strong and sure of my skills, eager for the coming fight. We had not looked for it, they had brought it to us. Now let them pay. My heart beat faster. I do not seek out battles, and if I can I will walk away. If I cannot, if there is no other avenue open to me, if men come at me intending to maim and kill, then will I have at them right gladly. And who would not fight in defence of loved ones or to preserve a preferred way of life.

Celtic Sunset

When all the talking is done, there is no other way, else it will be taken from you. Those who beat their swords into ploughs die, or at best, live out their lives ruled by men with swords. Hungry wolves never herd sheep, they eat them.

I thought then of the Nemeds of my youth. Of Bridgit's Nemed and, how it was that from a nation of warriors, no more than a handful were ever accepted to learn the true nature of the sword dance and its pattern. And of those no more than two, perhaps three, mastered its steps. Vercingetorix was one, I the other, and the third, who knows, certainly I do not.

The Dreadful People began to move slowly towards us. The afternoon sun, highlighting their green and red feathered hats. They wore short battle kilts and stout leather sandals. Oddly, they carried no bows. What weapons they had, appeared to be crude, primitive things. Certainly not the product of an advanced civilisation, capable of building a huge complex city of stone. Perhaps those with knowledge died out and only shadow men remain, feeding on past glories. The truth of it was, they had become addicted to eating human flesh. The gathering of it gradually taking precedence over every aspect of their lives. Armed with crude stone hammers, clubs, stone tipped spears, swords of ironwood edged with sharp splinters of bone, obsidian knives and short swords that looked to be cast from impure bronze, they continued to advance. Compact, hard looking men, with sharp cruel features.

'Where,' I though desperately, 'are the Comanche?'

I let them advance well into bow range. Raising my sword above my head I swept it down. four hundred arrows hissed through the air in answer to my signal.

Howls and screams of outraged disbelief filled the air. I didn't know it then, but Moloch was stunned when our arrows ripped into his ranks, killing and maiming about seventy five of his men.

We fired a second volley and a third, and then each warrior fired at will until he ran out of arrows.

The Dreadfuls milled about in confusion never having fought under arrow fire before. 'And isn't it a pity,' I thought, 'that we didn't bring more arrows,' as it slowly dawned on the Dreadfuls that our arrows had ceased to fly.

I judged that we had dropped about three to four hundred of the Dreadfuls, some dead, others mostly wounded. Little enough considering the numbers still facing us. About now would be a good time for Red Cloud to show up, I thought grimly.

Screaming and shouting the Dreadfuls surged forward.

We stood alone in the shadow of the hill facing fearful odds. Pitying our meagre numbers against hundreds. Not one of the Sioux broke and ran. I did not think any would, though if they had, who would live to blame them, certainly not I.

It is a fine thing to talk of what you will or will not do. It is a brave thing to do it. To stand and face a screaming horde of armed fighters, ah, now there be a measure of your manhood. 'Come ye,' I screamed, 'come ye all.'

The Sioux do not talk of what they will do. They say quite simply that they will do a thing and then go out and do it. Letting the action of it all speak for them.

I flexed my muscles and cocked my blade over my right shoulder. These be not armed and armoured Romans, though deadly enough, it would be hack and hew I'm thinking, with little enough of skill about it. The ground trembled beneath the weight of their pounding feet, the air thick with hoarse screams of rage and frustrated fury.

Celtic Sunset

Oh, how we danced.

The Sioux. Poems of painted beauty, flowing through and about our enemies like water. Striking right and left, whirling to strike again and again. Never still, moving, always moving, swirling around me as I danced and spun, leapt and lunged, cutting down Dreadfuls with every stroke. I quickly realised they had never faced an iron long sword before. Laughing, I reeved a sheaf of heads whilst they gawked in wonder at the hard sharpness of fluting death.

I had left White Owl behind as an observer/adviser. Trusting to his battle knowledge, to order our withdrawal when he deemed the enemy had gotten over their shock at our willingness to carry the fight to them, and were beginning to offer a more organised resistance. They had the advantage of numbers and we but a small force amongst them.

I heard it then, White Owl's call.

Shouting to the Sioux around me, I began to fall back, blood spattered, panting and weary.

It was then, that the blood began to boil and surge through my head in heated waves of blind unreason. Battle madness, an ancient affliction of all my race, as even mighty Alexander, who men do call Great, found out to his cost.

'Back,' I screamed, as warriors milled around me. 'Back, all of you. Give me room,' I roared, 'give me room to use my blade.' Thy obeyed, leaving me to stand alone in a patch of bright sunlight. My long hair blowing free and unbound behind me.

I whirled my sword above my head. The long blade catching the sun, reflecting shards and splinters of light.

The Dreadfuls halted, silent now, unsure of my intent. Well, and wasn't it plain enough.

Roy Edwards

The Sioux stared at me. Something of awe in their eyes. They knew me as an *old one returned*, not as a sense fled warrior.

'Come,' I screamed at the Dreadfuls. 'My Hair is unbound,' I roared, my voice savage and snarling. TAKE IT IF YOU CAN.

I towered above them, my upper body slick with sweat, the muscles of me standing out in hard knots and ridges. My eyes wild, my lips curled back from my teeth in a snarl. Red and black paint streaked my face. I don't know what the Dreadfuls saw in me, standing there in front of them. Perhaps they thought me the living embodiment of all the horror that clung to their souls. Or did that ancient god tower above me as he had once before. I saw more than just a little fear reflected in the eyes of those who faced me.

I leered at them. Paint mingled with sweat, dripping down my face, staining my teeth red and black. I looked like a haunt come out alive from all their worst dreaming. No one moved. I growled deep down inside my throat, like some foaming rabid wolf. Eyes widened in horror. And then a wild eyed figure, brandishing a short sword came pushing through their ranks, breaking the spell, shouting, screaming at them to attack. The Dreadfuls had been trying to capture us all, alive, to take us back to their blood stained city and tear out our hearts before consuming our flesh.

The shouting man, Moloch it was, had lost all reason. 'Kill them,' he urged, 'kill them all as sacrifice to dread Amulk. NOW,' he roared, and leapt forward his warriors charging behind him.

I cut the head from his body with a single stroke.

And then I began to dance. I became a whirling, slashing arc of steel. No one could touch me, I was faster, stronger than I had ever been before. Bodies piled up around me. I stepped over and out of the ring and cut down more.

Celtic Sunset

White Owl told me later that by his count I killed more than forty three. But he is a friend and proud of me, I think he exaggerates.

I felt my speed slacken, my blows lose some of their force. I was beginning to tire. Slowly I began to edge backwards. My blade weaving a net of steel around me. I bled from a score of small wounds, their slow steady drip draining even my great strength. I felt my battle rage drain away. I fought a thinking fight now, calling up new patterns to confound the enemy. About then White Owl used his judgement and ordered the waiting Sioux forward. They swarmed around me, yelling savage war cries.

We fought then, side by side. The dance had gone, it was just savage smash and cut. The Dreadfuls began to press us back. Using their weight of numbers to crowd us together. Herding us they were, like cattle. Well, and I was having none of that. I dug deep, calling upon hidden reserves of strength locked away in my muscles, in the very fibre of my being, and when I used it up, I would die. Well, and isn't it a fine day to be dying. Facing enemies sword in hand, side by side with friends, and the bright sun shining down on our heads. Who is there who would ask for more.

Breathing deep, filling my lungs with air, I bellowed out in a voice loud enough to crack thunder, 'I BE CULANN TOUCH THE CLOUDS RUNNING.' The Dreadfuls faltered, stunned by the sheer volume of my voice. 'MY HAIR IS UNBOUND — TAKE IT IF YOU CAN.' I screamed out the last words and crashed forward, using my height, and weight to smash through their front ranks. I began to hew my way through. It was like trying to wade through thick, sticky river mud.

Even so, my charge had opened the way for the surviving Sioux. They smashed through the encircling press of bodies and fanned out. Dodging, weaving, working their way deep into the tight packed ranks. Fighting in small groups of three or four. Moving, always moving, never allowing the enemy to pin them down.

And then I was through, and about to turn back into the wheeling, yelling mass, when movement snagged the corner of my vision. I glanced sideways, my blood spattered face creasing into a grin.

A solid wall of Comanche warriors led by Red Cloud, burst into view. Stripped for infighting, wielding lances, knives and hand axes, they fell upon the Dreadfuls like the wrath of god.

A few Pawnee fought alongside the Comanche and here and there I could see tall Cheyenne warriors towering above the Dreadfuls as they smashed them down with contemptuous ease.

In all, Red Cloud had brought almost a thousand warriors with him, picking up the Pawnee and Cheyenne hunting parties along the way.

Together, we swept the remaining Dreadfuls away. Sweeping the earth clean, with the terrible, sharp toothed rage and breath of elder gods strengthening our arms.

Within heartbeats, the still, sultry air was overlaid with the cloying sweetish smell of blood and the sound of small screams. The mouth of me had a bitter dust and ashes taste about it.

The battle was over, and though I liked not the wanton slaughter of its end, I deemed it necessary. And yet I was troubled, the spirit of me uneasy in its house, as though somehow it divined horrors yet to come.

To my regret, I shrugged the feeling aside, and somehow during the days that followed, it slipped away, only to return when I least expected it.

Celtic Sunset

I kept one Dreadful alive for questioning, the rest were killed. When I had finished with my prisoner, I killed him and threw his headless body in to a shit trench. No one escaped. No one at all.

We cleared the area of dead, our own, to carry back and honour.

The Dreadfuls were dumped in a nearby ravine, and the sides caved in to cover the bodies.

We agreed. Henceforth the area was a place of bad spirits. From that day forth the plains Indians avoided the place, of *the hill that stands alone.*

To the wonder of us all, the Sioux, had fifty or so walking wounded and twenty five dead.

The Dreadfuls never came again and in time were lost from memory. Mention of them to be found only in an old book of Winter Counts.

What happened to their city I cannot say. No doubt it lived on beyond my time, eventually falling to some new invaders (Aztecs). It does not concern me, and yet they, being an awful people will probably be remembered long after I am forgotten.

During the years that followed the defeat of the Dreadful People. The Comanche and the Sioux ceased to be enemies. It is a good thing. Though my familiar voice tells me that when Red Cloud, White Owl and myself are no more, they will begin to fight each other again. I love them. The thought of their *might soon be enemies again* saddens me. Even so, I have yet a way to walk, and though there is much I will not commit to these scrolls, there is still a bit and piece to be done.

Ψ

CELTIC SUNSET

Chapter Ten

Here I am
I am exactly where I should be
I can be nowhere else

Culann Touch the Clouds Running

I came to the cave in the winter of my life.

I planted a peach tree in its shadow. It will survive whilst I live, and when I am gone it will wither and die. This is not a good place to plant a peach tree, but I know of no better place close by.

A small band of striped robe people (Navaho) had journeyed far from their homeland to bring me this present. There is nothing more precious to the striped robe people than their peach trees. Of all the tribes only the striped robes know the secret of their care. Peaches are a vast treasure to them, almost priceless in trade. They have orchards that number over five thousand trees. The first tree came to them by way of trade with a coastal settlement. The fruits are called tears of the sun. The striped robes honour me greatly with such a gift. I can do no less than ensure it thrives for awhile. Who knows, perhaps it will continue to grow even when I am gone, perhaps it will not. Winter, here in the Black Hills, can be a cold and bittersome thing.

I have given much thought of late, to the writing of a scroll other than this one. A separate scroll, of sacred lore and knowledge, a combination of the two wisdoms, of Druid and Indian. It would be something to be hidden. To be found and read by those who come after. Something that would be found when the world stands in need of its knowledge. A thing of power, of spirit and the way of walking the upward path of the *Spiral of Immortality*. In its writing I would have need to use words of power, the ancient words of Druid that Cumall once said few now remember. And of those that do, even fewer understand what it is they think they know.

Words to hide the scroll and words to find it.

My familiar voice tells me that if I do not write it down all the knowledge I possess of the wisdoms will be lost, and only a faint shadow of it all will remain to be remembered. And that it will in a future time be grossly misunderstood, and all but denied. Even by those who profess to study its nature and lay claim of knowledge and an understanding of its intent. Of course, such ones be not Indian or Celtic in the nature of their spirit. Bringing nothing of *Skan Taku Skanskan*, spiritual vitality, something in movement, to their study. In its absence such people can not even begin to understand, even though they would have you think otherwise.

I have seen this, though the sending of it was small, and below the Invisibles. Who can say what the future might or might not be. The Opalescents, those who shine from within, perhaps they might know. I do not.

413

I will write the scroll that must be hidden.

During the night, a sending came to me, the like of which I hope never to receive again whilst ever I tenant this house of flesh.

I can speak of it to no one.

During the twelve of months that followed the defeat of the Dreadful People, White Owl's wife, Eyes Shining, who is a Beloved Woman of the Human Beings, the Sioux, gave birth to a fine, strong son, during the Moon of Making Sweet Fat. They named him Yells a Lot.

During his youth he roamed the hills and ancient trails.

People began to call him Walks the Hills. The name remained with him until his initiation into the Hawk Lodge. Thereafter he was called Swooping Hawk.

It is in my mind to take a wife, though as yet I have not done so. It is a desire to sire tall sons that kills me I'm thinking. Sons of strength to walk my footsteps and learn perhaps, a bit and piece of knowledge along the way. It is needful, my inner voice advises, if *The People* are to survive that is. Such feelings worry me and bode ill for the future of all the tribes. I will do what I can, though in truth only those *who are yet to come* will know the final worth of it all. The Celts are gone, I pray to the *Maker* that my new people suffer not the same fate.

Swooping Hawk, son of White Owl visits me often. He listens, whilst I talk quietly with Red Cloud, Dull knife of the Pawnee, or Black Bull of the Cheyenne. Black Bull visits rarely, but is always welcome. He knows much that others do not. He is a sacred man amongst his people and much revered amongst the tribes. I enjoy his visits.

Swooping Hawk accords me much honour.

He is a man, that one, and will cast a long shadow. He asks if he might carry my name, Touch the Clouds Running, when I am gone. It is a thing to be thought upon for there is this about it. To carry my name is to ask if his line might bear it on down through the long swell of years, when all is white bone and dust, whilst ever one lives, the name will remain, the son will inherit from the father and so on. And with the name will go the secret.

White Owl approves.

Swooping Hawk says the Eagle Warrior has come amongst the Sioux. His appearance here confounds me. How is it he walks the plains unseen? Where does he come from? Where does he go? What is his purpose? What does he seek and why? Even so, I welcome his presence amongst us. Did he not say in the shadow of the Veneti ship that one day we would meet again. 'Look for me in the Far Land,' he said. Now he is here. Welcome I say, right welcome indeed.

We sat together, in my home amongst the Black Hills and spoke of many things.

He said that he journeyed towards the east in search of the mysterious People of the Bell. He spoke of the city of AD of the Ubarittes that lies far to the south. The Ubarittes, he said, trade in frankincense, perfumed amber, that is much sought after by the coastal traders. We spoke of the Weeping Prophet and his Cup of Tears (Holy Grail) that is said to possess the power to heal and to bestow upon its owner insights that lay beyond the veil. He stayed with me for three days, our talks lasting long into the night. I, eventually seeking my bed with my head all a whirl with what he told me.

He was, he said, a member of a secret lodge. A brotherhood of men bound together by common cause. The Brotherhood is over 12,000 years old, he said quietly. We are few in number and can be found in many lands. He told me their secrets and the story of his life. He spoke of that strange and terrible prophecy concerning the Indians, saying that the first part of it had already come to pass. He asked me to join the Brotherhood and to swear the oath. I did so. After which he revealed more secrets and a mystery 12,000 years old.

Of course, there is much I have not written down. Looking back down the years as I have done of late, stirs old memories. It is easy to see what I should have done, but did not. What I should write but as yet have not done so. There is much concerning the Indians that I have not spoken of. Nor have I told you of the Ancient Ones, the ones who came before, those of the six fingered hands.

Last of all the Ancients called me friend. We walked the hills together and spoke much of the old ways and of wisdoms we shared in kind. He told me from where his people came — and why, he was the last of all his race and had been long upon the Earth. It was he who helped me to understand *An Ruad Ro Fhessa*, the way of the Lord of Perfect Knowledge, and why it is necessary for many of humankind to believe that *An Eochaid Na Ollathair*, the Father of All, has in his care, the destiny of all of humankind. He knew of the Weeping Prophet and his Cup of Tears. He has walked the shores of the Isle of Magicians, a fabled isle, I had though not to exist outside of rumour and legend told over a winter's fire with many a jar of foaming ale to aid the telling. And of course I have spoken not at all of the book of Druid Lore and what it contains in the way of secrets. No doubt it will be found sometime down the long run of years.

Perhaps I will write of all these things, perhaps I will not. Should I choose to do so, then, like the Hidden Scroll, it will be placed elsewhere. There will be a guardian, though not one of the *Brotherhood of the Book*. True, I have sworn the oath but none the less, I do not trust them and there is that about their envoy, the Eagle Warrior, that my inner voice bids me beware, he is not all he claims to be. True or false, I cannot say, though I am not inclined to ignore my inner voice of caution. There is something he held back, some higher purpose to which he and the Brotherhood work. What it might be I cannot claim to know. I cannot be sure that it exists at all and yet — there is something, I can sense it, it worries me.

And to you who hold the scrolls, you give me cause to wonder. Who are you? What are you? Can you count the stars? Can you see the windy places in between? Have you reached the Hall of Sunset, have you passed beyond *An Ceathair Bealach Na Spiorad*, the Fourth Way of the Spirit, surely you have, or have you not? Are you Druidlike, in your care of the Earth and your house of flesh, are you able, as its tenant, to enter and leave when you wish? No — I don't think you can. Else why the need to carry beyond the sea and hide in a new, Druidless land, the only surviving book of Druid Lore. Who are you then? What are you? What have you become if not masters of *An Bealach, The Way*?

What have you done, these thousands of years?

Is *An Bealach, The Way*, lost to you now? How terrible that must be, how ineffably sad. Is that why I carried the book here, is that what you must seek? Oh! What have you become, what darkness clouds your mind? Is it Gaunt Man, Crom Cruach, Bowed One of the Mound, who rules you now? In the name of the *Maker* I pray that it be not so. Say only that you have lost your way and now seek to regain the path, else you be something — something I cannot begin to imagine you to be.

TRUST YOU THEN IN THE CONSTANT FIDELITY
OF BEING.

Culann Touch the Clouds Running

Celtic Sunset

AFTERMATH JUNE - AUGUST 1996

Long ago, this time of year was known as the Moon of Red Lilies, or the Moon of Black Cherries. Now it is simply July or August. The romance of it all has gone.

The day was sun bright and warm. A solitary middle aged man walks the Black Hills. A small man with good shoulders and a look of wiry strength about him. Grey penetrating eyes enhance a sensitive, scholars face, framed by thinning overlong grey hair.

His restless eyes flick from trail to hill, from crevice to shadowed rock. He investigates everything, every hole, every shadow, every trail. He has wandered over and through the Black Hills for almost a year. He will continue to wander and search and investigate mounds and hollows, nooks and crannies until he finds what he seeks.

He is a patient, painstaking man who has never yet failed to find what is lost or thought, safe hidden. He had heard of words of power but has yet to find evidence that such exist. He is something of an iconoclast in his thinking. For all his vaunted intelligence, he has not yet realised that words of power look much the same as any other words currently extant, perhaps he never will. After all, it is what the words say that bind them together and give them power, not their shape or look.

He is diligent and tenacious. Indeed, any college or university would literally gasp with orgastic pleasure should he ever offer his services. He is a learned and respected man, whose name and reputation borders upon the legendary within scholastic circles the world over.

He is also a member of the world's oldest secret society, the *Brotherhood of the Book*, who can trace their roots back

419

to around 12,000 BC. When you add on to that figure the years AD, it makes the Brotherhood about 14,000 years old.

He was seeking four things. The whereabouts of the tomb of Culann, the Hidden Scroll, the Book of Druid Lore and a missing scroll that may or may not have been written. They are in the Black Hills somewhere. That much is known. Perhaps they are together, perhaps they are not. Find the tomb, he was advised, and you will find the rest, or at least some clue as to their whereabouts. Clouds covered the sun, he shivered even though the day was warm. An eerie feeling of unseen eyes watching his every move washed over him. He smiled to himself in satisfaction. I am close he thought, I am very, very close.

He did not know that behind him a tall, copper skinned man followed his trail, his questing eyes, hard and shiny like twin pieces of polished black stone. His face grim and shadowed in the slanting rays of the late afternoon sun. Around him the silent hills shimmered in thick enveloping heat. The tall, copper skinned man walked with a curious fluid like motion, that was utterly silent and left so faint an imprint in the dust of the trail, that his tracks were all but invisible to the untrained eye.

He was the *Keeper of the Secret*. A direct descendant of White Owl, the one whose name is written in an ancient book of Winter Counts, beside that of his brother, Touch the Clouds Running, who, the book records, was an old one returned.

Ψ

Celtic Sunset

MAY 1996 - Moon of Growing Berries

A murmur of small talk filled the room. Those present were a mixed bunch, made up of academics, archaeologists, anthropologists and a worried looking, minor government official, responsible for the coordination of local Indian Affairs.

Surprisingly, there was no actual tribal official present. The speaker, who had not yet arrived, was unknown to all that august gathering, at least by name. What little they did know was shrouded in mystery, based upon a rumour that refused to go away. Rumour of the existence of a line of Indians who acted as guardians of some ancient secret. Today's speaker was supposed to be such a one. True or false, that was what they were here to find out.

They gathered not as friends, nor even as academic equals, but as bitter rivals in an area that has probably given birth to more intellectual imbeciles than any other. Each one striving to improve his or her reputation - position, over the prostrate carcass of contemporaries. Even to the point of violence or worse, should one publish findings that disagreed with the already published findings and/or datings of another. Intellectual buffoons, so bound up in the curvature of their own, dogmatic inability to accept anything, anything at all if it doesn't fit into a set pattern of what they claim, or say events, artefacts of the past should or should not be, that they tread the road towards extinction and/or eventual replacement, by a new breed of thinking explorers of the past versed in not one, but several disciplines. This new breed striving more for enlightenment than for reputation or pride of office or academic position.

421

Roy Edwards

A door creaked open, heads turned, silence fell as a tall, copper skinned man with long unbound hair walked into the room.

'My name is Touch the Clouds Running,' he grinned like a wolf and began to speak.

The assembled group, about twenty of them, sat in shocked silence. Touch the Clouds Running, played them like fish on the end of a line. The assembled group wanted to believe what he told them. Some few knew they dare not, else their careers fall down in ruin about them. At the back of the room unnoticed and forgotten, a recording engineer sat hunched over his console, faithfully recording the speaker's every word.

$$\Psi$$

Celtic Sunset

MAY 1996 - Moon of Growing Berries

During the first week in May 1996 an unusual interview had taken place in a busy midwestern city.

The interview (if so it can be called) was recorded on tape by a local radio station. The station ran a midweekly half hour early morning program that dealt with Western History, Plains Indians and any local points of interest with regards to the city's founding fathers. The program enjoyed modest ratings and was considered to be one of those bread and butter programs, without which, few localised radio stations could survive. It attracted listeners, which was all the more surprising in view of its early morning time slot.

The presenters of the program had, some few days earlier, advertised a forthcoming program of events and made mention of their hopes to obtain an interview with a high ranking official of the Sioux Nation.

The program went to air as usual. No mention was made of the advertised interview. Disappointed, a few listeners rang the station to inquire if the interview with the Sioux official was to be included in a forthcoming program.

A spokesman for the radio station denied having any knowledge of such an interview having taken place. And that was that. Only it wasn't.

The radio station had indeed recorded the interview and then somehow the master tape had gotten lost. No one was to blame, the tape had simply disappeared.

However, before the master tape mysteriously and conveniently disappeared, a technician ran off, as was usual, a high speed copy of the master. The master tape was then, as usual, routed through to the station's library and the copy marked for the attention of the appropriate programmer, presenter.

The master copy disappeared enroute to the library.

The second copy never went on air.

But it was replayed, where, is now academic, and by whom, no one knows. Certainly, personnel working inside the radio station were suspect. After all, a typed copy of the transcript was made within hours, if not minutes of the second tape being marked for the attention of the host of the early morning program.

It was assumed that the station's in house computer, word processor had been used. By whom, no one knows or at least none of the station's personnel will admit to knowing. The computer was clean, no record of the tapes remained. Memory of the tapes being introduced into its system had been erased.

As far as the station's manager was concerned the incident didn't rate an internal investigation. Tapes get lost, it happens, its regrettable, but what the hell, who cares about an interview with an Indian?

Someone cared, someone cared very much indeed. They cared so much, they stole the tapes to ensure no one heard them. But someone did. In all probability it was the same someone who typed up the transcript.

Why? Why bother to type something that you are going to steal anyway? What would be the point? And what had taken place during the interview that was so important, or damning that it needed to be suppressed?

Did it perhaps, in a vague sort of roundabout way have something to do with *The Culann Scrolls*? Was it in some way connected to the search being carried out by the *Brotherhood of the Book*? If so, what did they hope to achieve, what did they hope to find? Had they already found

Celtic Sunset

it? What could be so important as to tempt, if only briefly, a secret Brotherhood out into the light of day? How could they know the interview had taken place?

Ψ

Roy Edwards

Montana USA - October 1911
(Moon of Falling Leaves)

Touch the Clouds Running, a Sioux Indian and Sacred Man of the Standing Rock Reservation, North Dakota. In an address to a group of visiting politicians and congressmen at the Little Bighorn Council Grounds in Montana, gave a memorable, impassioned speech that was suppressed up until about 1985.

Touch the Clouds Running began his reply to the portentous, patronising speech of Congressman Horatio (Rupert) Morgan with various quotes and stories followed by a disturbing speech of condemnation. He accused the assembled dignitaries of being avaricious, opinionated weaklings who were only interested in maintaining or aspiring to high office at the expense of the few surviving remnants of the Indian Nations. He spoke scathingly of their intentions, saying:

'There is nothing upon this earth more worthy of scorn, than avaricious invaders who consider their ideology and way of life to be superior to other races, and who, in pursuit of their invasion, do so in the name of god. IT IS THE SUPREME JUSTIFICATION, that has allowed invaders from the dawn of time to prosecute their invasion and slaughter with a clear, guilt free conscience. Even though they use their supposedly superior ideology to exterminate and visit horrendous acts of savagery upon those who inhabit the lands they invade. Who then,' he goes on to say, 'is more civilised, the victim or his killer?'

426

Celtic Sunset

At the conclusion of his speech Touch the Clouds Running turned his back upon the gathered assembly and walked away from the Little Bighorn Council Grounds.

He was never seen again by anyone other than his own people, the Human Beings, the Sioux.

Ψ

Roy Edwards

The following quotes and stories were delivered by Touch the Clouds Running, prior to his address to visiting dignitaries at the Little Bighorn Council Grounds, Montana 1911.

We are not slaves
Slaves have value
We do not
We should have died when you came into our lands
You should have killed us all
It is better to die
Had we known the way you would make us live
We would have killed ourselves
Now we die slowly
Just a little bit more every sunrise.

Yellow Hand
Sub Chief of the Pawnee 1862

You came to us a broken people.
We cared for you.
We nurtured your spirit so that it might grow straight and tall like a young tree in the forest.
You went away, and then came back to kill us.
Why?

Stands Tall
A visionary of the Blackfoot 1863

Celtic Sunset

When we dance and sing and praise the Great Spirit
Your priests come uninvited into our camp
Disrupting our sacred ceremonies with angry voices
Sometimes your priests
Bring men with guns to kill us when we dance
Why do the mouths of your priests say one thing
And their actions another?
Do they kill us because we are happy?
Does their Chief Jesus tell them to do this?
We shall dance and sing no more.

Counting Horse
Sacred Man of the Crow
from an address to Samuel Brighton
visiting Deputy Head of Indian Affairs 1875

You have killed our young men and taken our daughters.
Our children will not return.
They will never return.
There is nothing for us here any more.
Let us dance the old dance.
Maybe we can dance our spirits into a new world.

Black Fox (of the Beautiful People)
The Cheyenne 1878
(Black Fox died along the now infamous Trail of Tears)

429

Roy Edwards

We were 297 people.
Ten thousand soldiers with guns were sent against us.
Why?
What have we done?
Except to live in the way of our fathers
Upon the lands that now the pale skins want.

Hawk Broken Wing (of The Beautiful People)
The Cheyenne 1879

You have killed us.
You have killed us all.

Counting Wolf - Sioux Indian - 1896

Celtic Sunset

Listens to Trees - Cherokee Indian said

We lived in four great towns 30,000 strong, generation
after generation, in harmony with the earth and its
Beautifulness.
Taking only what was needful, always leaving something.
We fished the streams and great rivers.
We planted seeds in the earth.
Our sons and daughters grew straight and tall
In harmony with the great spirit and the land.
Our life was good.
Our old ones lived 130-140 winters.
We were never cold or hungry.
Our way of life was — a song — as old as the earth.
We never asked for more.
We did not want more.
Our way of life was perfectly balanced.
When the white man came, we welcomed him.
We never made war against the white man.
Why should we, there was enough for all.
We did not know he wanted everything.
We are no more than — a broken song.
You killed us, you killed us all.
In less than one generation our way of life has gone
Forever.
Only a few of us still live.
WHY? WHY DID YOU KILL US ALL?

Listens to Trees
Sacred man and seer of the Cherokee
31 July, 1884

431

Roy Edwards

Wind in the Trees - Seneca Indian said:

'Sometimes when our bellies are full, we sit around the fire and tell stories. Everybody likes a good story. Good stories are best. You can tell a good story many times, nobody tires of hearing a good story. A good story makes everyone feel good. That is why a good story is best. A good story reminds us that our way of life and our oneness with spirit and earth is a good way. It reminds us that because our way is good our sons and daughters grow tall and strong with clear eyes. Our bellies are always full. Our crops always flourish and are abundant. The fish always swallow our hooks. The animals of the forest never evade our arrows. Nobody is hungry. Nobody is alone. We love our children. We take care of our old ones. Many times those who have much, display ownership of the seven virtues, and share something of what they have with those who have little. During the cold moons we are never cold. Our lodges are always warm. Sometimes we tell a bad story. No one likes a bad story. A bad story takes something away from the light and makes the spirit uneasy. Sometimes a bad story is necessary to remind us of how fortunate we are to be Indian, when their are bad things on the earth as well as good things. One bad story is very old. It is as old as sixteen counts of one hundred (1600 years).

It is a story of a strange people who wandered far from their own lands. They came into our land and tried to take us away. Of course *The People* would not go and so they began to kill us. They killed many of our people. They cut out their hearts and ate their flesh. It was horrible. We did not know there lived men who did such things. Why do they do this, we asked, for what reason? We had never met them before, so of course they could not be our enemies. Enemies always know each other, that is why they are enemies. Enemies always want something you don't want to give. They are unwilling to share and so they try to take everything. We sat in Council for a long time. It is a terrible thing to realise someone you have not met is your enemy. We asked them politely to stop killing us. They laughed at us and would not stop. The smell of roasting human flesh was very offensive to us. The Council agreed that they were our enemies forever. *The People* agreed with the Council. We filled our hands with weapons and we killed them. We killed them all. We named them the Dreadful People.

We have asked the pale skin strangers who live in Jamestown to stop killing us and to return all our sons and daughters they have taken away. They will not listen to us. I think we must go away before they kill us all. I think the Dreadful People have come back. I think the Dreadfuls have come back into our land to stay forever. They will never go away.'

Wind in the Trees - Seneca Indian and Sacred Man
of the Five Nations (Iroquois Confederacy)
AD 1634

Roy Edwards

Our prophesies are written in stone, they are sacred to us. The sacred writings were given into our care a long time ago.

The sacred stone tablets speak of our land as being the spiritual centre of the Sioux Nation, the Sacred Hoop, the heart shaped path and what will happen should the sacred heart be desecrated.

You came into our land uninvited.

You have taken it away.

You tore open the sacred heart until all our land lay bleeding.

Since then many of the prophecies have come to pass.

We must all return to the spiritual path of nature, peace and harmony, or perish.

Touch the Clouds
Sioux traditional religious leader
August 1995

The age of the stone tablets, remains unknown, however they are thought to be around 2,000 years old. The appearance of the inscribed stone tablets coinciding with the legend of — an old one returned — bearing ancient wisdoms and sacred knowledge to *The People* who lived on and about the Great Plains.

R. Edwards 1996

Celtic Sunset

Counting Wolf - Sioux Wiseman said

Sometimes I watch grass grow.
When grass grows tall
Someone always comes along and cuts it down.
Some people are like that I think.
When they see someone grow in spirit
A little bit more each day, like the grass
They come along uninvited to cut it down.
I have never wanted to be cut down.
I think that is why the grass gave me its secret.
It is better to be like a rock
And grow in silence
Knowing
You must always give something of yourself in return,
Even if it is only the sound of your voice.
I thanked the grass for gifting me its secret.
It was a good present
The kind you can always use.
Watching rocks grow
I came to understand my nature
The balanced harmony of earth and spirit
Residing softly within.
The rocks taught me how to approve of myself
And to recognise who, and what I am.
Watching rocks grow
I came to learn that, like the rock
I am exactly where I should be
I can be nowhere else.
Wherever I am is the right place to be
It is movement without movement,
Spiritual vitality
That comes from maintaining a constant fidelity of Being.

Roy Edwards

I came to know this
From watching rocks grow.
Sometimes an old comfortable way is best.
It is like a familiar song
The kind that comes and sings
Without words inside your head
And refreshes the spirit.
Nobody sings new songs
Only old songs in different ways.
I came to know this
From watching rocks grow.

Counting Wolf
Sioux Wiseman and Seer
from The Book of Insights

Celtic Sunset

Touch the Clouds Running - October 1911
Little Bighorn Council Grounds.

You think you know who we are.
You do not.
You think you know from where we came.
You do not.
You think you know all we achieved.
You do not.
You think you know the way of Indian.
You will never know what it is to be Indian. You will never understand the completeness of our way of life that existed before you invaded our lands. You cannot even begin to conceive our spiritual link with the earth.

For us every day is a sacred day. Every day is holy, not just one day out of seven. What we are, only the truly civilised can recognise. I understand that you are new come to civilisation and have yet much to learn. Therefore I excuse your ignorance. Civilisation is a thing of the spirit, it is not merely one of worldly achievement. Nor is it one of material gain, or the building of monuments, or cities wherein spirit is trapped and squeezed into forgetfulness, midst canyons of stone that breed chaos, and allow only a brief flickering glimpse of what life should really be, before it drowns, submerged beneath the unseen collective will of the I wants of your people. Before you killed us, our old people lived 120 sometimes 130 years.

I have heard you speak of the mystery of Roanoke. What mystery? There is no mystery. There has never been a mystery where Roanoke is concerned. The only mystery is your own unwillingness to face truth. The only mystery is inside your head where you are afraid to look. You want the mystery more than you want the answer. Spirit children, you have yet to grow.

When the first of your people came to Roanoke North Carolina, we saw your need and welcomed you. Our faces were smiling, our hearts were open. We gave you food when your bellies were empty. We gave you clothes when your own rotting cloth fell from your backs. We gave you seeds to plant. We built log huts so that you would have a dry warm place to sleep. We taught you how to plant and hunt and fish the waters. We welcomed you into our land of plenty. We could see you were weary travellers who had journeyed long upon the open sea. Our land is wide and broad. There is enough for all, we said. Stay, be our brothers. You are welcome here. With our help you soon had command over all the things we taught you. We rejoiced, you were no longer helpless children in need of care.

And then you began to kill us. You stole our women and used them for your pleasure. Some you killed, some you did not. You stole our children, and used them as slaves to serve you and work your land. Soon there was not enough land for everyone. You became greedy, wanting more and more. What is it with you people, that you must always want more. To you ownership is power. It is a fool's power even your own Jesus said so.

You did not ask for more land. Why? Did your mouths no longer work. You killed those who lived upon the land you coveted and claimed it for your own. It is our right in the eyes of god, you said. What god? Whose god? What is god, except he be a name you use to purify your actions.

We spoke against you and you killed us. We knew you were only children. It was our mistake to try to reason with you. You killed us. You would not stop. You were Dreadfuls. We killed you to save ourselves. That is the mystery of what happened to the colonists of Roanoke. There is no mystery. You are fools to think otherwise. You ask, where did those first settlers go, how could they vanish without a trace. There is no mystery here. There has never been a mystery, only killing and your promise of more until there are no more Indians left.

You want the mystery, never the answer. You are afraid to face what you have done. You will always be afraid to face what you and your armies have done. How dare you then call yourselves civilised.

The Spanish came and killed us. The French came and killed us. The English came and killed us. We have knowledge, (even though you disavow our knowledge, it none the less remains true), of others who came here many hundreds of years before you. They did not kill. We lived in harmony, we dealt in trade with many different races who came from across the sea.

Who are you to say what is, or is not true? Who are you to deny our memories simply because they say you are not the first? We know our history, you do not. We do not speak of it to you. Why should we, when you do not listen. You do not want to listen. Our history takes something away from you, therefore you erase it. You only want what you can shape in your own image.

Do you truly think there is any part of this world where men have not walked? You cannot be so lacking in wit, as to maintain that you are the first. There are no discoveries, there are only re-discoveries. Your own arrogance has made you blind.

Why bother to come here today?

Why do you bother to listen to anything I have to say?

I do not know you.

I will never know you.

Roy Edwards

You are nothing to me.

That is why you hate us, why you kill us.

Because no matter your accomplishments, we do not consider you to be above us. You are not superior to us, you are not our masters. We live a broken people beneath your rule and still it gnaws at your guts.

The unspoken thought you see in our eyes, our pride, our knowledge that whatever you are, you are less than what we consider ourselves to be. We are far advanced upon the spirit road, that is our secret knowledge you can never take away. You have chosen a different road to travel, the material road. We chose the spirit road. It is this you envy when ever you look at us. The unspoken need inside you will never be satisfied. What use your material gains whilst your spirit yearns for something else. You deny your own longing. You lock it away. You are something I know nothing about. How can I know you when you deny your own *Wanagi*, spiritual self. How can I see you when you deny the existence of *Wahupa*, the realisation of the ultimate enlightenment. You think you know everything, when you only know a part of something. Perhaps one day you will discover *Wakantanka*, the undiscovered law, perhaps you will not. You destroy us for what we know, not for what we are.

What are you then?

I have heard your historians speak of the Pilgrim Fathers and of Jamestown. You look with pride upon any who claim descent from those early invaders of our land.

I did not know it was a thing of pride amongst you to claim descent from slave traders and brutal killers. Was it not Grenville of Elizabeth's England who came here and cut off the heads of Indians with a knife whilst others held them. Was it not these early settlers of whom you are so proud who cut off the breasts of our women to make tobacco pouches,

440

and cut out their San (vagina) and tied them to sticks. And through the bitter years that followed, you slit open the bellies of Indian women heavy with child and killed them both. You sold Indians to ship owners who carried them to your islands in the West Indies where they were sold as slaves to plantation owners. You invited Chieftains to feasts and killed them whilst they ate. You cut off the heads of Chieftains and impaled them on sticks.

Roanoke, Jamestown and a thousand other places. No wonder you hate those of us who still live. You fear what we might say. Whilst ever we live we remind you that your hands drip with blood and that your spirits are small and mean.

I will tell you this.

The Indians of that time did not want to believe that all the terrible things they heard concerning the pale skin invaders were true. They could not conceive of how it was possible for a people who, though small in spirit and ignorant of the way of the spirit, could be so terrible, so unbelievably dreadful. They did not believe what they had heard.

Unlike you, Indians do not prejudge on hearsay, they accept you for what your actions show you to be and for what your words say you are.

So it was that they did not fight you when you came seeking new lands. We did not know then, that you wanted to own all the land.

You were welcomed and fed and clothed. In return you killed Indians, used and sold them as slaves. Grenville, the Butcher of Ireland, taught your settler, invader pilgrims well. Indeed, so polite were the Indians they did not tell you how much you stank. The Indians, accustomed to bathing twice each day were appalled when they realised you rarely washed your bodies, and thought of washing your clothes not at all. You had lice in your hair and you carried disease with you. Spreading it about wheresoever you did go. Who then, is there amongst you, who would claim prideful descent from such Dreadfuls.

In all the years that followed, you killed us. You have never stopped killing us. Once we were many (about six to ten million), now we are few (about 500,000). Where now are the Comanche, the Iroquois, Osibwa, Osage? Where are the Arapaho, the Crow, where are the Indians? Of the six - seven hundred tribes, who now is left, how many? Maybe two - three hundred tribes, and of those few tribes some are made up of less than one hundred people, when once they counted their numbers in thousands.

What are you then?

I do not know what you are.

You are something I know nothing about.

I do not want to know you.

You are nothing to me.

We were put here by the great spirit to care for this land. Now you have taken it. You do not care for it. One day that will be your ruin.

There is a secret prophecy known only to a few sacred men. It is something we speak of amongst ourselves only now and again, when we meet, and sit in the sacred place amongst the mountains (Rocky Mountains).

It is a secret thing that is passed down from sacred man who dies to the one chosen to take his place. I will tell you a little and that is all. The prophecy is from a long ago time of an old one who returned. He was not the same when he returned to the Sioux, but we recognised him. He became a great warrior, a healer and a sacred man and something else I will not speak of. His prophecy is written though not in words you might recognise. Much of what he prophesied has yet to be, much has already come to pass. He foretold your coming and how you would destroy us, and of how one day the land will return to those who will heal its wounds. He has written of ancient races and long forgotten times. He taught an old wisdom and mixed it with ours, so that we came not to fear death. Unlike you, we know we will return. For you, in your ignorance of the spirit road, it is not so certain.

Your eyes say so.

Your mouth says so.

Your thoughts say so.

Because of this we will always be different from you. You have destroyed our heritage, the richness and warmth of our past, and replaced it with misleading histories of your own. You have tried to destroy our philosophy, our oneness of spirit with earth. In that one thing you have failed.

You deny the few of us who survive, the right to live as human beings, in the way that we choose to live. We are a broken people, striving to survive, midst a shameless people who barely acknowledge that we live at all. You, who cannot recognise the way of the spirit or live in harmony with the beating heart of the land. You strive to deny us the right to find and rejoin the broken pieces of our fragmented hearts so that we might heal our spirit wounds.

Do you fear the truth of our voice?

Is that why you are here? To ensure our silence.

There is that which is hidden that one day will be revealed and not all your machinations can prevent it. In the years to come you will find that the way of the spirit has a way of revealing itself.

The prophecy says so, therefore it is.

Before you came.

Roy Edwards

Our way of life was perfect. Our span of years long.
The great spirit placed us exactly where we should be.
We could be nowhere else.
Can you say as much.?
I am Touch the Clouds Running.
I know who I am.
I am exactly where I should be.
I can be nowhere else.
My familiar voice tells me so.
Therefore I am
Something - in - movement
Residing softly within.
I embrace

THE CONSTANT FIDELITY OF BEING.

After this address, Touch the Clouds Running was never
seen or heard of again. He lived and died within the sacred
hoop, the heart shaped path that encircles the Black Hills,
and only his people, The Sioux know where his bones might
be found.

And like hidden scrolls and secrets, there is much that has
yet to be told.

Celtic Sunset

Postscript

Archaeologists, Anthropologists and scholars have argued for years, for and against the existence of the inscribed stone tablets of the Sioux. If they exist, let us examine them, is the usual cry.

What they fail to realise or even remotely understand, is that proving the stones existence remains a matter of supreme indifference to the Sioux, who, unlike westerners, are not driven by any compulsive need to prove to anyone at all what they know to be true.

The ancient city of Troy did not exist until it was found. the pyramids of South America were mere exaggerations until viewed. The Great Wall of china, a traveller's myth. The Book of Druidic Lore was never written.

A Celtic Druid's tomb was never found. The Sphinx, thousands of years older than any Egyptologist would care to have us believe, the list is endless. The west has a tendency towards disbelief of most things outside the influence and control of western thought, which is primarily derived from what the ancient Greeks and Romans bequeathed, and therefore, limiting.

Differing viewpoints are not the sole prerogatives of a favoured few, and/or supposedly learned few, though some of us I'm sure could be forgiven for thinking otherwise.

R Edwards 1996

FORTHCOMING

Celtic Sunset
A Trace of Blue
Brotherhood of the Book
Johnny! I'm Running Too
A Memory of Blue
Old Bones And Candlelight
The Book of Insights
The Culann Scrolls Volume II
(Indian Dawn)

About the Author

Roy Edwards was born and educated in England. Wandering the globe for many years, he finally settled in Australia, currently residing in Perth, Western Australia with his wife and four children. His interests are varied, chief amongst them music and books, physics, archaeology, ancient religions/wisdoms, philosophies, Native Americans, Celts, gardening, cookery and motor bikes.

Dedicated to the well being of his family and somewhat reclusive by nature, he rarely agrees to interviews.

His first published work was released during the early seventies. Since then he has never stopped writing.

Richard Coyne.